Minor League Heckler

A Novel Baseball Story

Craig Faanes

PublishAmerica
Baltimore

Softcover 9781627091374
PUBLISHED BY PUBLISHAMERICA, LLLP
www.publishamerica.com
Baltimore

Printed in the United States of America

Dedication

For Joe Aryault and the 2009 Sarasota Reds

You were all winners despite the final scores

"I didn't mean to hit the umpire with the dirt,
but I did mean to hit that bastard in the stands"
—Babe Ruth

1

Miguel Rodriquez strode to the batter's box and could not avoid the annoying taunts from the Heckler. That loud mouth had been following him and the Tigers around the state all season. For some reason the Heckler had chosen the Tigers as his team to badger, and no matter where they played, he was there to taunt them. The Sarasota Reds, the Heckler's home team, needed all the help it could get because they had the worst record in the Paradise League. Even with the Heckler pestering the other teams their record stank.

Heckler had scored some impressive distractions during his travels around the state supporting the Reds. On several occasions he distracted the opposing batter so they would swing at pitches that were obviously outside the strike zone and he convinced others to watch as a perfect strike cut through the center of the zone. On more than one occasion the Heckler could convince an opposing catcher chasing a passed ball to throw to a base where there was no play by yelling at the catcher that the play was at a different base.

Taking the plate and digging in for the first pitch, Miguel heard Heckler start his taunts. Miguel swung the bat several times and focused on the pitcher. With luck he could get an idea of what type of pitch was next by seeing how the pitcher held the ball in his glove. Miguel was ready for any of them.

What he wasn't ready for was the barrage of invective coming from the Heckler sitting in his usual seat behind home plate. Tonight, the Heckler was more aggravating than most nights. "You guys suck like the real Tigers," he yelled in a reference to the major league Detroit Tigers team who had the worst record in the major leagues. Miguel could almost agree with Heckler on that call.

The pitcher wound up and was ready to throw the pitch. Miguel was ready for a slow speed ball to come his way and he developed thoughts of seeing it sail into the palm trees just over the left field fence. With twenty-two home runs to his credit already this season, Miguel knew that any more would certainly grab the attention of people in the front office who would take notice of his exceptional season and maybe even bring him up to the majors for a couple games before the end of the season. All it would take would be to send this incoming changeup on an outbound blast to those palm trees in left-center field.

The pitcher let loose a tremendous fast ball. "Strike one" the umpire bellowed as Miguel finished his swing. At the same instant that the ball hit the catcher's mitt, and before the umpire could make his call, Heckler was on his feet and yelling. "Did you learn to swing like that in kindergarten?"

The pitcher took his time preparing for the next pitch. He then looked in for the sign and this time saw two fingers presented like someone from the University of Texas would present them if they were supporting the Longhorns. Had it been the index finger and middle finger he would have known that the catcher wanted a curve ball, but this sign was for a change up. Looking over the bases, the pitcher settled into his normal routine. He wound up and as he did he held the ball like most pitchers do when they are going to throw a fast ball. However this time just like the last time he sent a different pitch. This one came in slow and easy and maybe wobbled a bit before it crossed the plate. Miguel, expecting a fast ball, was again fooled and this time swung forcefully even before the ball reached the catcher's mitt.

"Strike two" the umpire bellowed as Miguel kicked the dirt and waited for the next pitch.

Michelle Coburn was in the stands watching this game. Her entire life, now that both children were off to college, was devoted to baseball. She took great pleasure in Miguel because he was her discovery. She sat in the stands this evening watching her protégé. As Miguel prepared for the next pitch it occurred to her that if he succeeded and made it to the show his success could be the route to her own success.

With the count 0 balls and 2 strikes, Miguel dug in and waited. That pain in the ass in the stands behind him was not going to ruin his time at bat. At least he told himself that. As the pitcher let go of the ball it looked like it was coming straight at Miguel's head. Curve balls do that at times and this was one of those times. A batter has just a split second to decide what kind of pitch has been thrown at him and how he wants to respond to it. Miguel's initial thought was that the ball was coming directly for his head. Instinctively he jumped back from the plate and just as he did the ball defied both physics and logic and broke heavily away from him and toward the plate.

From Heckler's vantage point behind home plate the pitch appeared to be more than perfect and he was sure it was a strike. The umpire watched it sail toward him and noticed in the millisecond before the ball crossed the plate that it had curved a bit too much as just missed the corner.

"Ball one," the umpire yelled as the ball smacked into the catcher's mitt. Miguel was relieved but Heckler was livid.

"Ball one? If that was a ball then you're a Rhodes Scholar and we know that didn't happen, ump!" The umpire heard the screed and wasn't impressed.

Looking in for the sign the pitcher agreed with what the catcher wanted. He threw a fastball that was high and inside just missing Miguel's head. Tiger staff in the seats behind home plate were holding a radar gun and recording information on each pitch that pitchers from both teams were throwing. After this pitch, the radar gun held by Wellington Jones, a rich kid from Denver with a wicked sinking slider, read 98 miles per hour.

"Ball two," the umpire said.

"The next one is in your ear" he heard the Heckler scream.

With the count two balls and two strikes the pitcher looked in for the sign. Miguel watched as the ball seemed to focus on his head. Instinctively Miguel lay backward and thrust himself onto the dirt around home plate. As he hit the ground he heard the loud "thwack" of the pitch hitting Jose's glove. The speed indicator on the scoreboard showed the pitch at 97 miles per hour.

"Wow, what a pussy" he heard the Heckler screaming from behind him. "I hear the Rookie League calling for you."

Having just missed a collision between his head and a ball pitched at 97 miles per hour, Miguel didn't really appreciate being called a pussy and the last thing he wanted was to hear the words "Rookie League" mentioned near him.

Miguel dusted himself off and waited for the next pitch.

"Full count, 3 balls and 2 strikes" the umpire said.

The pitcher wanted to throw a fastball. Catcher David Morgan had different plans and instead called for a slider over the outside of the plate. The pitcher nodded in agreement then began his wind up. Miguel started his swing just as the ball began to move away from the center of the plate. His bat connected with the ball but sent it off toward the stands.

The pitcher was pleased with how his slider worked and liked the fact that Miguel swung at it and fouled it off. He would have preferred a strike but a foul ball is better than walking a batter.

He looked in for the sign and was glad to see that David was thinking like him and calling for another slider. Certainly this one was going to breeze by Miguel and he would have a strike out.

Reality doesn't always fall in line with fantasy and Miguel fouled off the next seven pitches. Each of them went into the stands behind first base and each foul ball was greeted with more invective from Heckler. There was always something new in what he yelled. It didn't matter what or when, Heckler seemed to always have something different to say. Miguel was beginning to wonder if it would ever stop because now with the count full and him having just fouled off eight pitches in a row, Miguel needed a break. He just wanted to get on base and get away from the constant harassment behind him.

Throwing so many pitches was beginning to take its toll on the Reds. It was Florida in late August so naturally the heat was oppressive and the humidity more so. Sweat was rolling off the shortstop and much of it was dripping in his eyes. The first baseman kept taking his cap off and rubbing sweat from his head. Because of all the sweating the second baseman was starting to feel a bit weak, almost as if he was going to faint if he couldn't get off the field soon.

Ricky Sanchez, the third baseman had taken precautions for the heat and drank a huge glass of water before taking the field at the beginning of the inning. Now Ricky was paying the price for being prepared because he had to piss so bad his ear drums pulsed. The entire team, it seemed, was going through its own quiet drama as they waited and waited for Miguel to strike out.

Miguel wanted it over also, but for him he wanted something that would motivate the team, and more importantly something that would help his already substantial batting average. As of this afternoon, Miguel had the fourth best batting average in the Paradise League, a more than respectable .328. Still, there is always room for improvement.

Having thrown 13 pitches at Miguel, the pitcher was running out of options. Plus his arm was starting to feel like rubber. The anabolic steroids he was swallowing at irregular intervals were supposed to help him to build muscle and not feel pain. He needed to talk to that doctor in Venice who gave them to him.

Even the Heckler was getting tired of waiting. It's tough duty trying to come up with witty comments that piss off batters all the time and he was about out of his usual repertoire. To save face, if nothing else, Heckler was wishing that the next pitch was strike three so he could take a break.

Tracy Goodwin sat in the box seats eight rows behind Heckler. A baseball groupie since high school, she was married to a guy who still delivered pizza for a living. With her Bachelor's degree from the Michigan State and a Masters from South Florida, Tracy was head and shoulders above her pizza boy husband when it came to intelligence. Because of her

Detroit ancestry she was naturally a fan of any team that came out of the city. It didn't matter if it was Tigers, Pistons, or Red Wings, if they had Detroit in front of their name Tracy was a fan and she followed each team religiously. She even liked the Lions!

She moved to Florida because she needed to spread her wings without being confined by her family. Devout Catholics, her brothers and sisters considered her a heathen if she missed one church service. And if she woke up one morning with a severe hangover, then they might as well call a chariot to haul her sullied carcass away. Having heard one too many lectures about how her life was going to hell in a hand basket, one day Tracy wished her family a hearty adios and moved to Florida. There she met the pizza boy one evening while hanging out at a bar. He told her "I love Italian girls with big tits and blue eyes" and for Tracy the rest was history. She and pizza boy were married six weeks later.

Pizza boy was from Tarpon Springs and hardly ever raised his voice to anyone. Tracy learned this not long after they married when some high school kids decided to do figure 8's in their lawn with their cars. Pizza boy, afraid of a confrontation, sheepishly asked them to "please stop this foolishness before you hurt my pansy garden."

"What is wrong with you," Tracy asked him. "Those little creeps are ripping up our lawn and you stand there and take it!" Pizza boy had no response. As time went on and other incidents occurred pizza boy continued to show the spine of a jelly fish and Tracy quickly lost interest. "What I need is a real man" Tracy told herself. "I need someone who isn't afraid to open his mouth and make waves and let people know where he stands."

The pitcher looked in and shook off the first sign.   From behind the plate the pitcher saw the catcher give him an index finger signal. "Good," he thought, "I'll just give this guy the heater, strike him out, and go sit down and take a break."

With the start of the pitcher's wind up, Miguel decided that there were few options for him. As the pitch was leaving the pitchers fingers Heckler turned on his mouth. Miguel saw the ball coming and knew instantly it was going to be a fast ball. Heckler didn't care what it was as long as Miguel missed it. The ball was moving so fast it was in the catcher's mitt before Miguel began his swing.

At the start of Miguel's swing, Heckler spewed out a new line. One he hadn't thought of until that instant. Something that he knew was bound to upset any Dominican male and especially one standing in the batter's box. All Miguel was aware of from that point on was Heckler bellowing out "Tiene le pene del nino, mericone!"

That was the final straw. The camel's back was broken. Miguel could put up with many things but to hear this jerk tell him in his native tongue "You have the penis of a small boy" was just too much to bear. And then to add "faggot" at the end took him over the edge. There was no excuse for this.

As Miguel finished his swing he rather accidently on purpose let go of the bat as it passed over his back. Let loose and with the laws of physics on Miguel's side the bat rocketed away from him and directly at the open mouth of the Heckler who, for an instant, was shocked as he watched the bat racing toward him. Protected by a large mesh screen that best resembled a gill net used by fishermen, Heckler was almost certain that the bat was not going to hit him. Still he wasn't sure. Stranger things have happened and how was he so sure the mesh was going to hold.

He ducked just as the bat hit the mesh. Because of its mass and the speed it was traveling, contact with the mesh slowed down the bat but didn't stop it. The fibers of the mesh were strained as the bat kept its course toward the Heckler.

What unfolded in front of Heckler reminded him of the penultimate scene in the classic baseball movie "*Fear Strikes Out*" where Anthony Perkins playing the part of internally tortured Jimmy Pearsall flips out and starts climbing the backstop behind home plate. For Perkins' character the scaling of the backstop was just the latest in a long history of fighting off demons that had haunted him since childhood. For Miguel, the climb up the backstop was to shove his fist in the mouth of that guy who had pestered him and made him swing at bad pitches all summer.

Security guards in the stadium quickly recognized what was happening and as the Tigers players circled around Miguel trying to pull him down from the fence, the guards entered the scene trying to keep Miguel from killing the Heckler if he somehow got through the fence.

As the scene unfolded in front of her, Michelle Coburn sat in her seat with her head in her hands. The best prospect she had ever seen let alone signed to a contract just committed baseball's version of suicide and did so in front of hundreds of fans. "I'll get that mouthy bastard if it's the last thing I ever do," she resolved herself to believing.

Tracy watched as the guards spirited Heckler to safety and thought, "Damn, I want that man."

2

J. Christopher Ramsey, a native of Jamestown, North
Dakota, was upset. He sat in Jim Sheppard's office waiting for
the inevitable. Sheppard, the manager of the Lakeland Tigers,
explained to Chris that top management of the Detroit Tigers
had determined it was time for a change and part of the change
was who played for their farm teams. First on their list of
needed changes was the Class A minor league teams. "Chris,"
the manager began, "we've decided to make some changes
and move on. Unfortunately those changes don't include you
and we are releasing you from your contract with the Tigers."

With a substantial bonus, Chris had signed with the Tigers
not long before finishing college where he had a brilliant
career as a catcher and as a biology student. Well, his biology
grades weren't that good but Chris was still a very good
catcher. He had to be good. His father once was invited to try
out for the Chicago Cubs. Good enough to try out but just not
good enough.

From the time he could walk, Chris was playing catch with
his dad. Out in their backyard one evening Chris announced
that he was going to be a major league baseball player someday.
His fantasy was the same as tens of thousands of other boys
that age. Unfortunately his dad, who lacked common sense
and parenting skills, told Chris "you're not good enough to
make it as a ball player." With considerable resentment Chris
vowed to one day prove his dad wrong.

Through Little League and Babe Ruth League and later
in American Legion League, Chris was always the starting

catcher. It didn't matter if he felt ill or had a twisted ankle or if his arm hurt from throwing the ball too hard in practice. Chris was on the field dressed in his catcher's gear he lovingly referred to as the "tools of ignorance."

Baseball coaches from the time of Little League encouraged Chris to get on the backs of opposing hitters. "Do whatever it takes to piss them off," his Babe Ruth League coach Mike Sorenson told him. Then his high school coach told him, "I don't care what you say to that batter, I want you to make an ass out of him." For Chris this was all the guidance he needed.

In a game against the Benson County Bulldogs, Chris singled out one player and heckled him mercilessly from behind the plate. All the Bulldogs had to listen to him but for some reason their shortstop, Harold Anderson, received most of Chris' attention. The leadoff hitter for the Bulldogs, Anderson stepped into the batter's box and immediately started getting harassed. "Is it true someone caught you with a sheep last week?" Anderson looked back at Chris but told himself to shrug it off. Just as the pitcher was releasing his fastball, Chris started bleating like a sheep. Anderson swung and missed, then slammed his bat to the dirt. Chris knew he was getting to him. Through the next two pitches Anderson heard other references to him and sheep. Each time he did he swung at pitches and missed. He was the first strike out of the day.

In the fourth inning, in his next at bat, Anderson heard all about the next pitch that was going to hit him in the head. Chris sent a call to his pitcher for a curve ball and before it was delivered yelled "Stick it in his ear, Terry" hoping to distract Anderson Even though it was unintentional the curve ball forgot to curve and hit Anderson in his left ear.

Picking himself up from the dirt, Chris made a comment about Anderson's sister. Apparently Anderson had a sister because he yelled "Don't talk about my sister you pig." This turned out to be the wrong piece of information to pass along.

By the seventh inning, the entire Bulldog team was fed up with Chris and his mouth and among them Anderson was upset more so than most. As he took his position in the batter's box the tension between him and Chris could have been cut with a knife. Anderson, a right handed hitter took three practice swings and then settled in to wait for the pitch. From behind him he heard "so is your sister as good as the sheep you've been shagging?" Strike one.

As the fast ball left the pitchers hand headed toward Anderson, Chris asked "is your sister really as ugly as you are?" Strike two. Visibly upset now, Anderson took two more practice swings as the pitcher looked in for a sign. As Chris thought about what pitch to call next, he casually said to Anderson, "If your sister wasn't ugly I'd fuck her just to prove to her that I'm male."

Standing at the plate a right handed batter holds his left hand at the base of the bat and wraps his right hand around the bat just above the left hand. That was the way Anderson held the bat when he came to the plate. Now, after the final insult to his sister, he switched his hands around, held the bat as a left-handed batter would hold it, and calmly but forcefully swung and hit Chris squarely in the middle of his catcher's mask sending him rolling backward away from the plate.

Anderson's team mates were likewise fed up and as they watched Chris roll away from the plate they each emptied the bench and ran toward him. Chris' team, the Jamestown

Jewels, cleared their bench and a huge fight between the teams followed. Eventually the game had to be suspended because of the pandemonium on the field.

Sitting in the stands watching this melee was a scout from a small private college in Florida who had heard reports about the mouthy catcher from Jamestown, North Dakota. Now in mid-May when the snow had finally melted the scout flew to North Dakota to watch Chris play. Although not a Babe Ruth by any stretch of the imagination, Chris was a decent hitter and the scout figured with the properly warm environment of Florida where you can play baseball every day of the year, Chris' hitting would improve.

The scout already knew about Chris' impressive defensive statistics, including no passed balls in 61 games from his first game as a freshman three years earlier. Then there was Chris' ability to throw out runners trying to steal second base, and his accuracy in throwing out runners who had strayed just a bit too far away from first base. Of course there was also Chris' reputation for distracting opposing batters. That and his fielding skills and the potential for making him into a passable hitter convinced the scout that it was time to offer Chris a baseball scholarship to play in the Sunshine State for the next four years.

In Florida, Chris met and married Michelle Adamson, a petite brunette who was about as avid a baseball fan as Chris. His college record was not gold plated but it was good enough to land him a contract to play in the Detroit Tigers organization. His marriage to Michelle, tempestuous at best, ended the day Chris signed his contract with the Tigers. His professional baseball career like his marriage lasted two years. It was time to make some major changes in his life.

3

Leaving Florida and Michelle behind him, Chris moved to Michigan where he earned a Master's degree and his PhD at Michigan Tech University in the frozen northernmost tip of Michigan. There he met a redhead from Marquette named Renee whom he married. Completing his degrees and landing a job with the US Fish and Wildlife Service, Chris spent the next 31 years traveling around the country trying to protect a little bit of what still remained. A somewhat typical male, Chris' priorities became turned around and focused on his career more than his family. Eventually after nine years with Renee, and after having two daughters with her, that relationship ended and Chris was once again alone.

Naturally his thoughts of Michelle had become less frequent as time went on and eventually he stopped thinking about her at all. Likewise he hadn't spent much energy heckling baseball players. Much of Chris' career was spent staying out of the way of tornadoes that seemed to like to focus on his new home town along the Platte River in Nebraska. After contributing 31 years of his life to working, Chris retired and moved to Florida. There he wanted to live like Jimmy Buffett as much as humanly possible.

His plan all along had been to live somewhere south of Interstate 4. It had long been a known fact that the further north you go in Florida the further south you get. Chris had spent three years of his career in Georgia and that experience cured him of ever wanting to live in the south again. Florida south of Interstate 4 was another story.

Having found a condo in Sarasota, Chris was unpacking his belongings when he picked up the *Sarasota Herald-Tribune*, and saw that tomorrow was opening day of spring training for the Memphis Mockingbirds, a major league team of less than World Series prowess that had just relocated to Sarasota from Miami. Even baseball players couldn't take the craziness of Miami and the Mockingbirds moved north.

Chris had followed baseball throughout his career and attended games in Kansas City while he lived in Nebraska. He saw the Washington Nationals on more than a few occasions when he lived in Washington DC. Maybe it was the effect of 31 years of having to kiss the ass of the person higher in rank than you but for whatever reason Chris had lost his ability to heckle. It had been such a part of him but now it seemed to be gone. Putting away his collection of Tim Dorsey first editions, Chris decided it was time to check out the local baseball stadium.

A crazed Italian named Marco was sitting in the ticket booth selling tickets when Chris walked up. Looking at the seating chart, Chris asked if the first seat in the first row in section 14 was still available. Checking the computer Marco found that it was and when he looked at the seat he remembered a few minutes ago selling seat 2 in that row to a woman.

"Here's your ticket," Marco began. "I just sold a ticket for the seat next to you to a brunette with an ass to die for. I watched her walk away from my ticket window and wanted to close the ticket booth and follow her into the stadium."

It had been a long time since Chris had spent much time thinking about women. The last one in his life was Denise, a woman whose hair color changed like the leaves on trees in Vermont in autumn. After living with Denise for five years Chris discovered that she had been spreading the wealth around. It was eerily similar to how he found out about Michelle's indiscretions many years before. Denise had followed Michelle's plan to the letter, even letting Chris discover that someone else had been in their bed with her while he was on a birding trip in Chile. The irony, Chris thought, was just too much.

Following the tradition of baseball everywhere, Chris sought out the concession stand where he purchased a huge bratwurst that was smothered in sauerkraut. With it he grabbed a 32 ounce glass of Landshark Lager beer and found the condiments where he lathered on the mustard. There was to Chris almost nothing in baseball more sacred than a brat and a beer.

Entering the stadium through one of its several breezeways, Chris asked an usher for help finding his seat. Walking past all of the fans lined up in the standing-room-only section he saw his seat in the desired place directly behind home plate. To a catcher there is nothing like being there. That place. As close to home plate as humanly possible without actually being squatted down behind the plate. You might no longer be a player, but by sitting in that seat you can feel like you are. Sitting directly behind home plate puts you in the driver's seat. You can see every move on the field. You can see every pitch as it hops and dives and zips around on its 60 foot journey from the mound to the plate. It's here behind the plate where you can heckle the batters and question the umpire and just generally enjoy the game like nobody else. It's the best seat in the house.

Finding his seat Chris greeted the woman Marco had told him about at the ticket booth. "Hi. Are these Mockingbirds any good," he asked. She looked up at him preparing to give a smart assed reply. This had to be, in her long career of being an attractive woman, the weakest line she had ever heard.

"I'm sure they are better than you ever were," Michelle said.

She wore a sleeveless top trying to get as much sun as possible. The body full of freckles he remembered from long ago was just as freckly now as it was then. Instantly he remembered all the times they lay in bed playing connect the dots with his tongue and her freckles. A lot of water had trundled over the dam since that day. Relationships had started and ended. Next marriages had started and ended. Baby daughters had been born and moved on to college. Old friends had died and new friends had been made. The cycle of life continued but in that instant when they looked at each other in the ball park, it seemed like 35 years of time had never passed. It was like yesterday was yesterday not 35 years ago.

"So, what are you doing here in Sarasota," Chris asked.

"I'm here working as a baseball scout," she said.

"You're a scout? Are you with the Mockingbirds or what?" She was far from being with the Mockingbirds.

"I would rather eat dirt than watch a Mockingbirds game,"" she said with a huge smile. "They suck and anyone who knows baseball better damned well agree. I'm with the Tigers."

"What got you into being a scout?"

"I've always been a baseball fan, even when I was in love with you. That's part of the reason that I fell for you. If we hadn't had baseball I don't know what we would have had." Women, it seems, always have the upper hand on saying the most hurtful things possible. Michelle just proved that point once again. They sat together during the game and Michelle was diligent in her recording of data on players for both the Memphis Mockingbirds and the Detroit Tigers. If nothing else, she was determined to ensure that her home team was cheered for no matter who was sitting in the seat next to her.

A curve ball thrown by the Tigers pitcher in the fourth inning appeared to have a life of its own as it flew wide of the plate until the last second and then vaulted over the edge of the strike zone and into the catcher's mitt. "Ball three," the umpire bellowed.

Chris was beside himself with the call. He was sitting directly behind the plate in a seat giving him an unobstructed view of every pitch. A blind person, as he would say, could see that this pitch should have been strike three not ball three. "Hey, ump. Why don't you use your good eye for the rest of the game," Chris asked.

Then, tearing off his glasses and holding them in his hand, Chris yelled "here, ump, use my glasses. You obviously need all the help you can get." Until now she had been reacting rather coldly to Chris and his comments. Yet when she heard him start to heckle the umpire some of the long-dormant feelings she had for him started to gush back to her.

"My god," she thought, "do I still like him?"

4

Osvaldo Castro peered out the window of his office at the corner of Duval Street and Caroline in downtown Key West. From one window of his corner office Osvaldo could look down Duval and watch all the crazy tourists who were convinced that Key West survived on an endless supply of alcohol. Looking out the other corner he saw the gaudy edifice known as the La Concha Hotel and beyond, near the Truman Annex he saw Fort Zachary Taylor State Park. It was from Fort Zach that Osvaldo first saw the United States. He had ridden in a boat that sailed from Havana during the Mariel boat lift in the 1980s. All the other boats that departed in that armada found their way to Marathon and the Upper Keys. For whatever reason, Osvaldo's boat was the only one that arrived exactly where it was supposed to arrive.

When Osvaldo's boat came ashore an irreverent park ranger from the Florida Park Service raced up to the Cubans and demanded that they pay the park entrance fee before stepping from the boat. "You must each pay the $3.00 entrance fee or I can't allow you in the park," he said.

Among all of the twenty or so occupants of the boat they would have been lucky to have three cents let alone three dollars. Pedro Gomez, the leader of the group and captain of the boat, tried to explain in broken English that the people on his boat were all escaping Cuba and each just wanted to come ashore and start a new life.

Greg Lipscomb, the Florida Park Service ranger, a little man with visions of grandeur, wasn't going to let a bunch of

Cubans get in the way of his perceived meteoric rise. With the ineptness of Barney Fife, Lipscomb grabbed his radio and called his office asking for backup saying "I have a whole boat filled with Mexicans that just washed ashore. I need help."

Immigration and Customs was called along with the Monroe County Sheriff's Department and the Key West Police Department. The scene at the entrance to Fort Zach soon resembled a coffee break at Dunkin' Donuts. There were easily 60 officers present to handle the 20 Cubans on the boat. Along with the donut-eating police force was the media. It seemed like all of the Keys media was there. It was November after all, and the peak of sweeps season. A story about Cubans coming ashore could only make for better ratings. Better ratings meant higher advertising revenues and that could translate into higher salaries.

A breathless reporter from WEYW television in Key West said in a live broadcast that a group of Cuban revolutionaries had come ashore. She was convinced they were an advanced armada of Cubans sent to Florida by Fidel Castro to eliminate the Cuban resistance movement in South Florida. She approached Osvaldo and asked him for an interview. "Is it true your boat was filled with Castro supporters who want to eliminate the resistance movement in South Florida?"

"What are you talking about lady? We just wanted to get the hell out of Cuba." Osvaldo said.

He then added, "What I really want to do is play baseball in the United States. I played ball with the Havana Daydreamers but there is nowhere to go with baseball in Cuba."

Dejected by his non-political response the reporter simply walked away from Osvaldo. Twice in fifteen minutes in his new country Osvaldo was disrespected. It was starting to annoy him.

After interrogating and processing the Cubans and allowing them to view themselves on WEYW and CNN, the authorities took Osvaldo and his countrymen to the detention facility on Krome Boulevard in Miami.

Their departure from Cuba had been less than spectacular. After all, Fidel (who was no relation to Osvaldo – but you can never be sure) wanted to get rid of as many criminals in Cuba as possible. He thought sending them north to the United States would be fitting after what the Americans did at the Bay of Pigs in the 1960s. Bobbing along in a thirty foot boat with twenty passengers plus crew left little room for privacy let alone finding a place to sleep. Although it was only ninety miles from Havana to Key West, if the currents are not right or if you leave Havana on a rising tide, it can take forever and a day to cross the Straits to the Keys.

As they made their way across the ocean Osvaldo couldn't stop thinking about why he wanted to risk the ride to America. Baseball was what he had dreamed about since he was a little boy. It was what motivated him to keep going every day. Baseball was the only reason he could think of to stay focused when all around him was falling apart in Cuba. Baseball, as the character portrayed by James Earl Jones in the movie *"Field of Dreams"* would say, "… is the one constant thorough all of time."

Now, just a few miles to the north of whatever position his boat was occupying was the land of endless baseball. Even though it was forbidden by Fidel's regime, Osvaldo's family regularly listened to Radio Free Cuba, a propaganda station created by the Reagan administration to tell Cubans what they were missing by remaining in Cuba. It was almost like an official invitation from the United States government to any Cuban listening to defect.

Many times on summer nights Radio Free Cuba would broadcast baseball games. Osvaldo heard games from all over the United States. One night it was the Seattle Mariners and the Minnesota Twins. Another night it was the Cincinnati Reds and the Atlanta Braves. The next night it might be the Toronto Blue Jays and the Boston Red Sox. However the one team that always caught his attention was the Detroit Tigers. It seemed like no matter what they did or where they played the Tigers could do no wrong in Osvaldo's mind.

Laying in his bed listening to games, Osvaldo began fantasizing about the day he would wear a Tigers uniform and step to the plate in Tiger Stadium and face down major league pitchers. He was going to be the next Al Kaline or Willie Horton or Norm Cash. It didn't matter. Osvaldo was going to be one of them and that day couldn't come soon enough. The only problem was being in Cuba. He had to find a way off the island and into the United States. Once across the border his rise to stardom would accelerate like a rocket. His chance came with the Mariel boat lift.

After the ordeal with the boat crossing to Key West, Osvaldo decided that Miami was not the place for him. As funny as it seemed at the time there were just too many Cubans in Miami. He left the country to get away from Cubans; the last thing he wanted to do now was be surrounded by them. And from what everyone said there are probably more Cubans in Miami now than there are in Cuba.

He decided that he would prefer living under a highway bridge anywhere before he would stay in Miami. Catching a Trailways bus he headed back south along the Keys highway and stayed on it until Mile 0 near the Key West courthouse. He was back where he started.

Baseball is what brought Osvaldo to America and it was time he started to play again. On his arrival back on Cayo Hueso the only active baseball was at Key West High School. At 14 years old Osvaldo entered school as a ninth grader and immediately showed up for baseball practice.

"Who the hell are you," Pedro Gonzalez, coach of the Key West Conchs, barked at Osvaldo when he showed up in mid-week for his first day with the team.

"I come from Cuba to play American baseball. I want to be in the major leagues someday like Cepeda and Clemente. I want to be the best like they were."

"Standing there with your finger in your ear isn't a good way to show me what you have kid. Grab your glove and get out there."

What he had was an excellent arm. With it came an eagle eye at the plate, and he wasn't bad at running the bases. He quickly was made the starting right fielder and throughout his first year helped the Key West Conchs win their first conference championship in eleven years. Much of their success could be explained by Osvaldo. It looked like his career in American baseball might be taking off. Osvaldo was selected to the Florida All-State team during his second, third and fourth years of high school. He was the best right fielder in the state and nobody could deny that. His arm improved, his hitting got better and by the end of his fourth year he held the state record for most stolen bases in a four year career.

Karl Greenfield, an alcoholic scout for the Cincinnati Reds, was trying to sit upright at the end of the bar at the Hog's Breath Saloon when the sportscaster for WEYW flashed up a story about Osvaldo Castro being selected for the third straight season as an all-state right fielder. Karl was in town on vacation and like almost all the people who find themselves at the end of the Keys Highway, Karl was smashed. It didn't matter if it was nine in the morning or four in the afternoon, most of the occupants of Key West bars were smashed. Karl was no exception. It was nine in the morning.

Watching the story about Osvaldo caused a few functioning synapses in Karl's brain to fire. If this kid was as good as the reporter said he is, maybe Karl could sign him while he was on vacation in the Keys. If he did then maybe upper management wouldn't look so poorly on his performance in recent months. Not many baseball scouts would take time from a hard earned vacation to work and doing so might do his career some good.

The Conchs were playing the Key Largo Reefers that afternoon. Perhaps if he stopped drinking in an hour or two, had a few cups of coffee and a cold shower he might be in some condition to watch the game and make an assessment. If nothing else, he could file a report about his scouting activities while on vacation. Hopefully someone in Riverfront Stadium would care.

The Conch's took the field at three that afternoon, just three hours after Karl had chugged his last Red Stripe of the morning. Showered and shaved, Karl was almost presentable and would likely not cause a great embarrassment to Reds management if anyone knew who he was and what he did. In the top of the first inning, Karl watched Osvaldo make a diving catch on the warning track to rob a Reefer of at least a double. In the bottom of the first Karl watched Osvaldo wallop a pitch that looked like it was going to clear the fence for a center field home run. It was headed that way until a cattle egret flew into the ball's path and absorbed the impact. The egret died and the umpires called it a home run. And that was just the first inning.

Throughout the game it was obvious why Osvaldo was an All-State team member. He was simply the best person on the field. He really could hit and throw and his stolen bases in the fourth and seventh innings were just icing on his cake. The final score was Conchs 7 and Reefers 0. The win clinched the conference championship for the Conchs again this year and it caused a half-sober scout in the audience to take notice of who he had just watched.

Over the next couple of days, Karl checked Osvaldo's statistics and looked into his background. Everything seemed to fit and he seemed like a good prospect. He had no plans for college in the fall with the exception of maybe Florida Keys Community College. Karl decided to make him an offer. Osvaldo accepted the offer. The day after he graduated from high school Osvaldo showed up in Sarasota and put on a Sarasota Reds uniform. He was officially a professional baseball player. Now he could make the impression on American baseball he had dreamed about since he was little.

5

The Sarasota Reds, the Class A team in the farm system of the Cincinnati Reds had some promising players. In a story that would repeat itself throughout the season, the Reds had been beaten soundly by the Lakeland Tigers in their first three games of the season. At home now, the Reds hoped for better luck against the Brevard County Manatees.

Alonso Soto, an expatriated Cuban from Havana was the top pick of everyone watching the Sarasota Reds. If you had to bet on who was going to make it to the Show the easy money was on Alonso. He was going there – it was just a matter of when. The only thing Alonso missed about Havana was sneaking into La Floridita and drinking mojitos and reciting stories just like his hero Ernest Hemingway used to do.

David Morgan, a raccoon-hunting southern boy from Valdosta Georgia had the catcher's spot sewed up for the season. "Just call me Captain," Morgan told his team mates. He was the second best choice on the team to make it to the majors. His only problem was his selection of music. His most favorite song was about a coon hound.

Nefthali Rodriquez was solid at third base with an arm that was the envy of many in the league. Few batters made it to first base on a hard hit line grounder to third base. Tali's glove was like the hookers in his native Puerto Rico; it sucked up everything that came near it. With solid hitting statistics and the highest home run total for any of the Reds, Tali was quite likely going to make it to the majors, maybe after this year.

Dennis Philomena was one of the many stars to come from San Pedro de Macoris in the Dominican Republic. Many people were betting on Dennis to make it to the majors. When he hit the ball it was usually out of the stadium. But the operative word was "when" because it didn't happen often. Then there was his tendency to think that any baseball hit to right field was supposed to come to him not the other way around. Charging a baseball that didn't make it to him was simply out of the question. Dennis had to work on that.

Dave Apfel was the best hitter on the team. His average was .318 the year before and many in the Reds organization looked at him as maybe the next Pete Rose. It just involved Dave learning to hit for percentage rather than hitting for home runs. This was despite the fact that one night in the Clearwater Sharks stadium he hit the first ball pitched at him. The sound of the bat against wood told anyone in the stands that the ball was not long for the planet. A few seconds later it crashed through the roof of the tiki bar in left center field.

These five players, all with a real potential to make it to the show, were the core of the Reds offense and defense. Add to them pitchers like Enerio de los Santos, Derrick Costner (no relation to actor Kevin Costner of baseball movie fame, but Derrick liked to claim he was when he was hitting on girls), and Whitney Eno whose knuckleball was the best in professional baseball, and the stage was set for a potential Paradise League championship.

Sarasota's opponent for this opening day game was the Brevard County Manatees. As a farm team for the Milwaukee Brewers, the players were each required to wear a miniature Cheesehead hat with the outline of a West Indian manatee etched on the side. The Brewers were quite proud of their

Wisconsin cheese heritage and wanted everyone who played a Brewers farm team to be reminded about Wisconsin's place in the world of cheese making. It didn't make any difference that the players looked completely ridiculous with a wedge of cheese on their heads. However, Brewers management made the proclamation so the Cheesehead hats were part of the uniform.

Chris showed up at the ball park half an hour before the game was scheduled to begin. There he bought a ticket for the same seat behind home plate where he sat for the Memphis Mockingbirds game the day he re-connected with Michelle. He had not seen her or heard from her since that day. The fact that he was so flustered that he'd forgotten to give her his cell phone number may have contributed. Still when he bought his ticket from Marco the crazed Italian he was hoping he'd hear that the cute brunette with the great ass came back for another game.

"Nope, sorry, that woman must have been a one-day wonder because I haven't seen her since that day. I would have remembered her too. She has the best ass I've ever seen and I spend a lot of time looking at them as they walk away from the ticket booth."

Chris bought his ticket for Section 14, Row 1, Seat 1, and hoped she would show up later in the game. With a beer and bratwurst occupying his hands, Chris walked through the breezeway and into the cathedral that is any baseball stadium. Most of the seats in Ed Smith Stadium were not occupied. In fact maybe no more than 500 seats were. A group of fish crows, tired after chasing an osprey from a nearby light pole, sat like stodgy old men on the backs of several other seats so maybe the attendance was 520.

Ed Smith Stadium had seen its better days. The seats, all 5,500 or so of them had spent way too much time in the broiling Florida sun and now were covered with quickly fading blue paint. The seats were narrow which would have been sufficient for most Americans thirty years ago when the stadium was built but now the width of the average American ass was three inches wider than it was thirty years ago so a tight fit was usually experienced by everyone.

The distance down the first base and third base lines was 330 feet to the fence. Straight away dead center field was 400 feet from the plate. Unlike baseball fields in the majors, the grass in Ed Smith Stadium was the real thing. Any Class A outfielder would have to quickly adjust to fake grass once they left the minor leagues.

The outfield fence was cluttered with advertising signs for all sorts of businesses including one for a local gynecologist. His sign on the fence and those that hung inside the door of each of the women's rest rooms in the stadium read carried a picture of the doctor's smiling face along with his name and phone number. The signs said "I'm a Gynecologist. Let me take a look. Call Dr. C Harry Beaver, Gynecologist (941) 555-4957."

Ten minutes before the game began the umpires strode out to the home plate area after having emerged like woodchucks from their burrow on Groundhog Day. Working the bases today was Dennis Hastert, Jr., the son of the former inept Speaker of the US House of Representatives. Just like dad, Junior had a bit of a beer gut that he had to work off. Paradise League management decided before the season began that Hastert would work the bases until the beer gut was gone.

They reasoned that all the running he would have to do would be good for him.

Behind the plate tonight was Justin Reed, a recent graduate of Florida International University who always wanted to be a baseball player but he was just never good enough. Instead he followed the old adage of university professors that goes "If you can't do it, teach it, and if you can't teach it, teach how to teach it." In Justin's mind he was going to teach all the other umpires he worked with how to umpire.

Exceptionally good looking in his 6'3" frame, Justin had amassed a huge debt in college. His parents encouraged him to go to college, but there were eight children in his family and Justin's father was a bus driver while his mother stayed home and herded children. They simply did not have the money to pay for Justin's education so he worked his way through college and took out tens of thousands of dollars in loans. Working as an umpire for the Paradise League wasn't the most lucrative way to pay off his debt but for Justin at this stage in his life it was just what he needed. He could be a part of baseball games almost every day of the week and he would get paid to do what he loved. As far as the college debts were concerned Justin was convinced that something would turn up eventually to make it easier.

At five minutes to seven, Harry Dodge, the announcer for the Sarasota Reds bellowed into the microphone that all should rise because the National Anthem was about to be played. Selected to sing the song this evening was Tonya Schultz, a seventeen year old blonde with serious bimbo potential who attended the Sisters of Perpetual Guilt Catholic High School in Sarasota. She had an exceptionally pretty face, and a body that boys in her school will talk about for years to come. What she lacked was a singing voice. In fact it was totally absent but Tonya was convinced that she was a singer and when she flashed her left boob at one of the Reds management team he immediately agreed that she could make her singing debut in Ed Smith Stadium. She walked out to home plate and all eyes in the stadium were on her.

The music began and she put the microphone to her mouth. What came out of her mouth could best be described as the screams of a cat being strangled by a giant Rottweiler.

"Oh say can you seeeeeeeeeeeeeeeeeeeeeeeeeeeeeeeeeeeeee, by the ddddddddddawns early lighttttttt." It became progressively worse as the song went into the second stanza when Tonya, flustered by her horrible performance, forgot the words and had to pull a piece of paper from her pocket and read from it. "O'er the rambooooooooooooooooooooooooos we watched were so gallantly steamingggggggggggggggggggggggggggggggggg ggggg."

By the time Tonya got to the last line and sang "and the hooooooooooooooooome of the braveeeeeeeeeeeeeeeeeeeeeeeeee eeeee" most of those in the audience realized that long ago when Francis Scott Key penned the words to this song, his mention of the "brave" was a reference to anyone who sat in a stadium in Sarasota and listened to Tonya Schultz butcher his song.

When she finished and people could unplug their ears, Tonya turned to the crowd and gave everyone a huge Florida sunshine smile. From in the stands behind third base someone yelled "Throw her a fish." After Reds management explained to her that the fan's comment was about her sounding like a sea lion in the circus, Tonya broke into tears and ran from the stadium. Thankfully she never sang again in public.

First up for the Manatees was third baseman Jack Musgrove. He had a respectable .280 batting average last year with 16 home runs and 44 runs batted in. His on base percentage was one of the highest in Paradise League history. He likely wasn't going to make it to the show but it wouldn't be for lack of trying.

Digging in for the first pitch, Jack stared down Reds starting pitcher Jason Webb and just for the hell of it blew him a kiss. Webb, a staunch Baptist who said a prayer for his team and all the sinners on it before each game, was incensed. A homophobe from the word go, Jason wasn't about to let some smart assed pretty boy throw kisses at him.

Despite the catcher calling for a curve ball, Jason wound up and threw a fast ball directly at Jack's head. Musgrove fell backward onto the dirt as the ball whizzed by where his head used to be at a staggering 99 miles per hour. Stepping back into the batter's box Jack took three practice swings as Webb looked in for the sign. This time the catcher called for a change up and Jason executed one perfectly.

The ball's trajectory looked at first like it would be a ball but then it slid slightly to the left and was aimed at the inside corner of the plate. Jack started his swing, broke his wrists but then held back. The umpire called it a ball and the Reds catcher immediately asked for an opinion of Umpire Hastert on first base. Hastert agreed with Reed that Jack had not broken his wrists.

Jeremy Benjamin, manager of the Reds, was a 47 year old former minor leaguer who had a lot of promise to be a major league manager. A bit hot headed at times Jeremy was learning how to chill out but this obvious strike called a ball was not a good way to begin. "That was a bullshit call ump, and you know it," Benjamin yelled from the Reds dugout.

Justin Reed, never one to go for any kind of language he would consider vulgar walked over to the Reds dugout and warned Benjamin that one more outburst and he was out of the game. Jeremy thought this was a bit strange. He had sworn at umpires before but "bullshit" was more a state of mind than actually a swear word. He wondered if the umpire had not gotten much sleep last night.

Stepping to the plate again, Musgrove took his requisite three practice swings and waited. Jason Webb wound up and threw an arching curve ball that was clocked at 89 miles per hour. The ball crossed the outside corner of the plate and was called a ball. The same thing happened with the next pitch. Jason Webb had walked the first batter of the season on four pitches. He had never had that poor a start to a season in his life whether it was high school, college, or in the minor leagues.

Craig Haney was up next for the Manatees. Their first baseman, Haney was a solid hitter with a .276 average last year, 13 home runs and 38 runs batted in. Haney had a tendency to crowd the plate and that earned him the distinction of leading the Paradise League in the most times a batter was hit in the head by a pitched ball. Haney took eight in the head the year before. It was a league record that all other batters in the League never entertained a thought of surpassing. Haney took the first pitch high and inside for an obvious ball. The second pitch was almost in the same place as was the third one. The count was now 3-0 with nobody out. Jason had thrown seven straight balls. A little rattled when he threw the next pitch, it too was a ball.

Benjamin sent Charlie Guzman his pitching coach out to the mound for a chat with Jason. "What's going on Jason? Where is your control" Guzman asked.

"Damned if I know coach. I got rattled by the calls on that first son of a bitch and I can't shake it off. With the second batter I thought I would put it past me but each time I thought of that bullshit call when he broke his wrists I got pissed and couldn't control the ball." Guzman told him to take deep breaths, think of nothing but the next pitch and strike the next batter out.

Paul Sievert, the Manatees left fielder was up next. A solid hitter Sievert was better known for his remarkable arm than his bat. Last season in a game against the Palm Beach Cardinals, Sievert caught a fly ball on the warning track. The runner on second base tagged up and was almost to third base by the time Sievert let go of the ball. His throw had perfect trajectory as the Cardinals runner streaked down the third base line. To observers in the stands it looked like the ball was going to hit the runner in the back.

The ball flew past the runner and into the catcher's glove as it sat just two inches above and in front of the plate. The runner slid into home and was out. That was the kind of arm that Sievert had. All through his career starting with Little League, Paul's father had coached him to never under any circumstances swing at the first pitch. His father didn't explain why he shouldn't go for it but Paul never did. In today's game with the Reds he followed what his dad had instructed him to do. He watched as Webb threw a 96 mile per hour fast ball that was cutting home plate in half just at Sievert's belt buckle. "Ball one," the umpire called.

Benjamin was ready to climb out of his skin but didn't want to get ejected so soon in the season. There would be many more opportunities for that to happen later. He kept his mouth shut. According to everyone's count Jason had now thrown nine straight balls even though at least three were obvious strikes. "What is up with that umpire," Jason wondered to himself.

The next pitch was wide of the plate and so was the one after it. The count is now 3-0 and Jason has thrown eleven straight called balls. Then the twelfth one was thrown. The bases were loaded and nobody was out. Not the most auspicious beginning to a new season.

Batting fourth and clean-up for the Manatees was Bobby Minkel, a slender blonde kid from northern Wisconsin who wore his hair in a buzz cut. Bobby was a terror for pitchers to face. Last year his batting average with runners in scoring position was .388, almost unheard of anywhere in professional baseball. He was one of the best in these situations.

Normally if there was one or even two runners on base when Minkel came to the plate wise managers would call for an intentional walk to keep him from getting hold of the ball and scoring too many runs. Yet today with the bases full Benjamin had no alternative. He had to let Jason pitch to Minkel.

Following his recent trend, Jason's first pitch was low and outside. "Ball one," the umpire called. The second pitch was a fat one. Jason was getting a little reckless because other obvious strikes had been called balls and he let this change up get a little too fat.

Jack Musgrove, the runner at third took a large lead away from the base. It was probably too large but his coach told him to do so. Musgrove had never stolen home so the Reds weren't too worried about him making an attempt now. He just stood out there nine feet from the base, poised and ready to run if Minkel could get a piece of the ball.

The change up came in fat and juicy and Minkel got good wood on it. His swing was down and when the bat connected with the ball, the ball first touched the earth half way down the third base line. It bounced twice and Reds third baseman Tali Rodriquez charged the ball as Musgrove was streaking for the plate. Rodriquez transferred the ball from his glove to his hand and threw with laser perfection to home where David Morgan was standing one foot in front of the plate. Morgan caught the ball, then braced for the collision of 220 pounds of Musgrove streaking for him. Morgan wasn't too worried because he was solid also and covered with protective equipment, the most important being his nut cup. Musgrove decided not to slide but instead to try running David over and knock the ball from his hand. That's exactly what he did.

Chris Ramsey, sitting in Section 14, Row 1, and Seat 1 saw the play perfectly. Catching the ball, David tucked his head and held the glove against his chest. He held onto the ball when contact was made, touching Musgrove in the chest and making the out.

Only Umpire Reed didn't see it that way, "SAFE" he yelled. The Manatees scored their first run of the game.

Jeremy Benjamin, himself a former catcher, saw red when the umpire called the Manatee runner safe. Benjamin left the dugout like he was on fire, his blood pressure building with each step as he ran to the plate. "What kind of a call was that Reed? Huh? What kind of a bullshit call was that?"

"He was safe. Your boy didn't touch him with the ball. He was safe"

"You blind bastard Reed, I have a six year old who could make better calls than you do."

"Your ass is out of here! One more word out of your filthy mouth and I'm reporting you to the Paradise League."

"Report me all you want to you blind bastard. Your days umpiring are all over. You'll be selling GPS units at Best Buy a week from today."

"Benjamin, I told you to shut up. You are now getting reported."

"Report me you miserable bastard. Go right ahead and report me." For added measure Jeremy kicked dirt in the umpire's face. In baseball only calling someone a cocksucker is a greater sin than kicking dirt in someone's face. Jeremy spent the rest of the game in the Reds bullpen where he composed an email on his Blackberry and reported Reed for his flagrantly obvious missed call. He wanted his complaint registered with the league before Reed could send his. This was the first time in his career he had ever been thrown out of a game in the first inning. He had a feeling this was going to be a long year.

Charlie Guzman, the pitching coach took over managing responsibilities but his luck was only slightly better. Umpire

Justin Reed kept making bad calls in favor of the Manatees and against the Reds. Through four pitching changes the game finally and mercifully ended with the final score Manatees 12 and Sarasota 1.

6

The White Horse Pub was the unofficial official hang out of the Sarasota Reds when they were in town. To encourage the Reds, the owners gave 75 percent off on all drinks and food served to any Reds player, coach, or manager. Given the lousy salary that Class A ball players make, any discounts were greatly appreciated. Understandably the Reds flocked to the pub.

This marketing ploy worked throughout the previous season. Most of the Reds' fans knew the players hung out at the pub and many of them showed up there just to talk baseball. Every fan who played baseball as a kid, relived their own "glory days" as Bruce Springsteen once sang. Great debates broke out among fans who were Monday morning quarterbacking every game. And the more they debated the more the pint beer glasses had to be refilled.

The real windfall was the number of twenty-something women who started to hang out in the pub hoping to score with a potential million dollar baseball player. It didn't matter that they now made nothing it was the potential for the future that drew them to the Reds players. That and gallons of estrogen coursing through their veins creating a persistent itch that could only be scratched one way. Reds players were more than willing to do the scratching. If one of the women hooked up with a player and he didn't make it to the majors she could always divorce him. It was the American way. Chris went directly to the Pub after the game. It was the only way he could rationalize what just happened on the field.

The following night Chris purchased his ticket for his favorite seat directly behind home plate. Marco had no reports of the brunette with the great ass he'd seen before. Chris could only hope.

It was dollar night at Ed Smith Stadium. Admission was one dollar. Hot dogs were one dollar. Popcorn and cracker jacks one dollar each. Even bratwursts were one dollar. The only thing that wasn't for sale for a dollar was beer. Ed Smith Stadium during the summer minor league season offered only Budweiser and Budweiser Light so it was highly debatable if it was actually beer. Having spent so much time traveling in the tropics Chris had learned what real beer was all about. Budweiser, in his mind, wasn't beer. Still it was better than drinking water.

Taking his seat Chris looked around the stadium getting his bearings and more precisely looking to see if Michelle had sneaked in to watch the game. Looking down the first base side of the stadium, in a box seat almost directly behind the Reds dugout, he saw an attractive brunette with hair about her length and a chest that certainly could have been Michelle's Her face didn't resemble Michelle's but that could have been because of the third pint of Stella this afternoon or maybe a hallucination because of the supposed beer he was drinking now. He would have to keep an eye down that side of the stadium to tell if it really was her.

Michelle wasn't at the ball game tonight but Tracy Goodwin, the busty Italian girl with blue eyes married to the pizza delivery boy was there. She was sitting in a box seat just a few rows behind the Reds dugout. She wasn't there because of the Reds. She was there to check up on Chris.

Angel Guerrero had excellent control tonight. So much so that the few balls that got past the batters were so obviously strikes that Umpire Reed had no choice but to call them strikes. The Manatee leadoff batter hit the first pitch thrown to him, an 88 mile per hour slider that went deep into left field where Dave Apfel easily hauled it in. The second batter took a called strike for the first pitch and then drilled the second pitch directly back at Guerrero who easily caught the ball for the out. The third batter looked at two strikes before hitting the third pitch weakly toward second base. A simple 4 to 3 put out and the inning was over. Guerrero had three outs on six pitches. This was already better than last night's performance.

Dave Apfel walked to the plate to lead off the bottom of the first inning for the Reds. He kicked dirt around the batter's box, readjusted his nut cup, took a few practice swings and began staring down the pitcher. From behind him he heard Chris start cheering him on.

The first pitch was wide and outside. The umpire called it a strike. Livid, Chris yelled "Hey ump, the batter's box is not the strike zone." The next pitch was in almost the same place and was again called a strike. From behind home plate the umpire heard Chris bellow "Hey ump, I thought only horses could sleep standing up." The third pitch was almost identical except that it was an inch closer to the plate yet still wide of the strike zone. "Strike three!"

Chris yelled "Hey ump, you blind bastard. Flip over the plate and read the directions before the next batter."

By the bottom of the fifth inning the Manatees had a comfortable 10-1 lead over the Reds. One of the Reds' supporters who had an advertisement hanging on the left field fence had been offering a free pizza to any ticket holder if the Reds scored seven or more runs in a single game. This was now the third season they ran this promotion. So far they never needed to pay up. By the looks of tonight's score they weren't going to have to this evening either.

As the Reds batter came to the plate, Umpire Reed bent over to clean dirt off the plate. For most of the game the dimensions of the plate and its placement on the surface of the earth had seemingly nothing to do with the way strikes or balls were being called. Chris found it curious that the umpire actually cared about a clean plate. As the umpire bent over to do this task Chris couldn't help himself as he yelled "Hey ump. You're going to make someone a fine wife one day."

Standing upright the umpire walked back to the fence and stood in front of Chris saying "You are one smart assed comment away from being kicked out of this stadium tonight."

Chris thought it over a second and said, "You know Justin, you are right. I am one comment away and this is the comment. Diarrhea has more consistency than your strike zone."

Reed bellowed "You're out of here!" He then called for stadium security who escorted Chris from the stands.

Seeing him being removed only heightened Tracy's desire to have him. After all it was only a few short weeks earlier when she watched Chris at the Memphis Mockingbird's game that she decided she wanted him and she made that decision because as she saw it, Chris was a man's man. She'd never have to worry about him delivering pizza.

Tracy, the frustrated 35 year old wife of a pizza delivery man was wearing white shorts, a pink top and nothing under it to hold up her world class set of 34Ds. Someone once described the sensation of watching her chest as she walked as being like "watching two bobcats wrestling in a paper bag." The low cut of her pink pull over made it certain the bobcats were easily observed.

"Hey wild man," she yelled at Chris. "That was some show you put on back there. Do you like getting kicked out of baseball games?"

"It was like getting an award being thrown out by that blind bastard Reed," Chris started. "I'm not sure what his story is but he's the worst damned umpire I've ever seen. And calling him an umpire is being kind."

"So," Tracy started, "what are you going to do with the rest of your night now that you've been kicked out of this lousy game?"

"There's a British pub up the street that I usually hang out at. Most of the Reds players come there after the game. I'm headed there now."

"I'm coming with you."

The White Horse is a small tightly packed replica of a real British pub somewhere in the English Midlands. Walk in the front door and you can go to the restaurant on the right or left to the pub with its 16 different kinds of nectar on tap ranging from the standard Guinness to Monty Python's Holy Grail ale. Signs for several English and Irish ales and beers hang prominently from the walls. Several television sets are constantly on, usually tuned to a soccer match or maybe a rugby match. That is to satisfy the Brits. For the rest of the patrons there is nonstop baseball.

Mark Bennett, a sports fanatic of the highest order was behind the bar pouring pints. Newcastle was on the tube beating the hell out of some team from Slovenia and the Brits in attendance were inhaling beer as fast as Mark could pour it. Chris and Tracy took their seats at the bar near the beer cooler. Not only did the pub have sixteen beers on draught but it also had an extensive collection of bottled beers including Landshark Lager, Chris' favorite. Sitting at the bar was Disheveled Dave, an expatriated Brit who may or may not be living out of his car. Nobody was quite sure. Seated next to him was Brent, a graphic designer who recently graduated from a fine arts college and who now drinks lots of Guinness while designing websites. Next to Brent was Canada Jim, a curious expatriated Canuck who only drank Pabst Blue Ribbon. Norm, a local businessman who maintained a second office in Manhattan, was seated next to Jim. Norm was famous for his quadruple-layered pepperoni pizza that was made especially for him. "Just ask the cook to make the 'Quadruple Bypass'" he once told a bar patron.

Scattered around the bar were the requisite soccer fans watching the match and sprinkled among them was a healthy crop of twenty-something blondes waiting for the Reds players to show up after the game. Chris with his Landshark and Tracy with her bottle of "Beaver is Better" a microbrew from Maine with an alcohol content of 8.5 percent soaked in the characters in the bar. Tracy asked him first why he loved heckling baseball players.

"Heckling is the essence of baseball. It is what makes baseball unique from any other sport."

"But some people see it as harassment."

"I see it as an art form."

"I need another Beaver."

Midway through her second Beaver, Tracy told Chris very directly what she was interested in and why. "Ok. I'll stop messing around. I am so sexually attracted to you it makes my head spin. Maybe it's the daddy thing. I don't know. What I do know is that when I watch you in action I've thought about that loser husband of mine and wondered why I ever married him."

Chris asked her why she married him if the guy was such a loser. "I don't know. I was horny and he likes big tits. I slept with him a few times and thought at least this guy is consistent. Soon he was so crazy about me it was hard to understand. I guess I married him because he was safe. Now I'm tired of being safe." She then added, "All I know now is that I would give my left ovary for the chance to screw your eye lids off. I don't care where it is or when. I just have to have you."

7

Osvaldo Castro had a remarkable first year with the Sarasota Reds. He led the Paradise League in doubles and runs scored. Some also considered giving him an award for the most transformed physique in a year. For whatever reason his upper body strength increased exponentially throughout the year with his chest size increasing from 42 inches to 48 inches. Along with the increase in chest size was an increase in the thickness of his biceps. Almost everyone who watched Paradise League baseball games saw his improvements. Most people wanted to know what kind of weight lifting regime Osvaldo was following.

Sarasota was in Tampa to play the Tampa Yankees during an early June road trip. Just like the regular Yankees, the Tampa branch had the best record in their league with a win percentage of .713. The Yankees buy the best win record no matter what level of baseball is played

Osvaldo went one for four tonight getting a weak single in the sixth inning. Surprising everyone and mainly himself he stole second base, out running and out sliding the throw from the catcher by at least two feet. Now in scoring position, Osvaldo led off second base and waited for the pitch. The Reds' center fielder connected sending the ball to deep right field. Osvaldo rounded third and raced for home crossing the plate even before the right fielder could glove the ball and return it toward the infield. This run was the only one the Reds scored that night but it was enough to defeat the Yankees. Life was good.

Following their victory, several of the Sarasota Reds retreated to the *Rigid Nipple*, a strip joint in Ybor City reputed to have the most seductive strippers in Hillsborough County and maybe the entirety of Florida's west coast. One stripper in particular, a buxom 26 year old blonde named Kari Bastrop, was the focus of desire of almost any patron of the Nipple.

Osvaldo made it a point to stop in at the Nipple every time he was in Tampa and he was soon considered a regular there. He spent a lot of time and much of his hard-earned salary chumming it up with the strippers at the Nipple. However through it all he was focused on Kari. Maybe it was better to say he was obsessed with her.

Entering the Nipple about 11:00, the Reds players found the bar packed with people suspended in an ocean of cigarette smoke. There was even a whiff of something that smelled like burning leaves. The center of the bar was dominated by a long table reminiscent of where contestants walk during the Miss America pageant. In the center of the table was a long brass pole that extended from the floor to the ceiling. Surrounding the table was a continuous row of bar stools.

The table's main attraction was the nightly arrival of Kari Bastrop whose strip show was legendary. In incredibly good shape, Kari was able to dance to almost any song and at the same time make her breasts heave in unison independent of the music. Only precision muscle control could explain her ability. Kari's other talent was her ability to drive men (and some women) to distraction when she slid around on the brass pole, which she usually did when she was down to just a crotch less thong. After twirling herself around on the pole six or seven times, she would breathlessly step away from the pole and ask in a rather seductive voice, "Does anyone want a sniff?" It was usually at that point when Kari's tips for the night increased tenfold.

For the next hour, until Kari took the stage, the bar patrons would have to satisfy themselves with the Kari wanna be dancers who were more than willing to work for a tip. Women like Brandy Glass. The last time Osvaldo was at the Nipple he watched as Brandy danced up and down the stage wearing only a bra that covered her nipples and a thong best described as a piece of string with some elastic in it. As Brandy made her way across the bar she stopped in front of Osvaldo who was drinking a long neck bottle of Budweiser. As Brandy twisted her hips and teased Osvaldo with her almost non-existent thong, she then squatted over his long neck beer bottle and inserted it in her. She stood and danced in front of him nearly hitting Osvaldo on the top of the head with the bottle.

Completing her dance she strolled back to Osvaldo, squatted again, and spit out the bottle. Amazed by Brandy and what he had just seen, Osvaldo turned to the man seated next to him and asked "Do you think she's still a virgin?"

Sitting at the edge of Kari's table directly in front of the brass pole, Osvaldo inhaled several shots of tequila and waited for her show to begin. She emerged from behind a stage wearing a blouse over a tee shirt that covered her bra. Below her waist was a seductive skirt that over laid a bikini bottom and all of her clothing was overshadowed by a huge Florida sunshine smile. She was ready.

Kari strutted across the table, bowing and tipping to show off the maximum amount of cleavage. This was always a great act for getting her audience ready to shell out more five dollar tips. As had become normal by now Osvaldo took notice as he inhaled his fifth shot of tequila of the evening. Or was it the sixth? He couldn't remember. All he knew is that Kari was on stage. To him the world just stopped spinning.

Kari continued her act sliding seductively down the table, cupping her breasts in her hands and yelling "I need a hand, guys." As she did, Osvaldo told himself that tonight was the night he was going to have that girl. It didn't matter what was involved or if he had to go to jail. He was too overwhelmed by Kari to let this go on any longer.

With at least six shots of tequila in him Osvaldo felt like he could be a dancer on stage just like Kari. In fact, he just might become one tonight. She had completed three dances and collected more than $200 in tips when the disc jockey played Olivia Newton John's current smash hit *Let's Get Physical.* Kari knew Osvaldo quite well after seeing him in the Nipple many times in recent weeks. She even remembered him sliding in a five dollar tip one night. At least she thought it was him.

When the song began Kari started making motions with her hands toward Osvaldo who, in his tequila induced euphoria, was convinced that Kari was singing the words to him. She had removed most of her clothes by now, leaving only a florescent orange bra and a matching thong covering her. For all Osvaldo knew she could have been coming on to him right there on the table. A music video about the song showed Olivia Newton John working out in a gym but Osvaldo was convinced that was just a cover for what she really wanted to do physically.

Kari's gyrations added to the words of the song became simply too much for him. It could have been the tequila or maybe that pill he took after the game, or it could have been that white stuff the scruffy old fireworks freak gave him to put in his nose, but whatever it was Osvaldo was ready for action. Taking the words of the song literally Osvaldo leaped up on the stage and started pawing at Kari. Security staff saw this serious breach of Nipple policy and rushed the stage but Kari winked at them letting them know it was cool. At least for now it was cool.

Osvaldo started dancing with Kari, while pulling off his shirt and unbuckling his belt. This made some of the male patrons uncomfortable and jealous. After all how can this guy get up there and dance with Kari while everyone else couldn't? To spread the love around Kari started to pay more attention to the squeaky wheels in the audience but this did not sit well with Osvaldo who demanded all of her attention.

Security was now rushing back toward the stage as Osvaldo reached down to grab her thong. Two security staff tackled him but in a fit of rage Osvaldo struck back, slamming one of the guards head first into the bronze pole she slid down minutes before. Regaining his balance Osvaldo grabbed the other guard and put him in a head lock. More guards rushed the stage and several of the more sober patrons of the bar offered to help.

Osvaldo was a man on a mission and his considerable physique and especially those bulging biceps were more than adequate for keeping people at bay. During the melee that broke out, Osvaldo kept screaming at the top of his lungs, yelling more slurs about the buxom Kari and threatening to kill the guards. Bar patrons could now hear sirens in the distance as the Hillsborough County Sheriff's Department and the Ybor City Police descended on the bar. It took four beefy deputies and at least eight hits with a night stick to get Osvaldo subdued enough to put hand cuffs on him.

Damage to the bar was considerable and the brass pole Kari slid down was broken. As the police led Osvaldo toward the front door, Fernando Pena, owner and manager of the Nipple told Osvaldo he was going to have to pay for all the damage and lost business and that Osvaldo was permanently banned from ever returning to the Nipple. Osvaldo replied "I've been thrown out of better bars than this dump."

Fernando said "And now you're out of this one."

Taken to the Hillsborough County jail, Osvaldo was booked on charges of public indecency, disturbing the peace, public drunkenness, assault, resisting arrest, and with a new local law, "fondling a stripper aggressively." Apparently the Hillsborough County commission had no problem with fondling a stripper. They just didn't want it done aggressively. After booking Osvaldo into the jail, Pena showed up and gave his statement. He brought Kari with him now that she had some clothes on and she also gave her side of what happened.

"I was just dancing" she started, "and this crazy bastard from the audience leaped on stage, grabbed my boobs, sucked on my left nipple, reached for my crotch, and told me to dance like I do when I'm having sex with him. I'm not a virgin but I sure as hell haven't had sex with this idiot. After this incident tonight there is no way in hell that I ever will."

Tossed in his cell at 2:30 in the morning Osvaldo's blood alcohol content was .17, or more than twice the legal limit to be considered drunk in Florida. Unfortunately for Osvaldo the police laboratory that drew the blood sample kept it refrigerated. Nobody was certain why the sample was saved.

Reading the arrest report the next morning, Chloe Larson the assistant state attorney for Hillsborough County who was assigned the case looked at the booking pictures of Osvaldo and found it curious that a man with such an otherwise sleek physique should have such a muscular upper body and especially the biceps that were close to Arnold Schwarzenegger in size. Chloe suspected something and called the police lab hoping they kept the blood sample. "Run a complete test for every possible chemical substance that should not be in a normal person's blood stream," she ordered.

Later that day the tests were returned indicating that Osvaldo had some cocaine in his system which, this being Florida, was to be expected. He also had at least three illegal anabolic steroids, two with names so difficult to pronounce that even biochemists had trouble saying them. There were also traces of mydixafloppin, an experimental drug that would later be known as Viagra. Why a man in his early 20s needed this sort of boost was a curious discovery.

Now, in addition to the physical assault and other charges, Osvaldo was charged with using illegal growth hormones which explained his phenomenal upper body strength. For added measure he was charged with possession of cocaine because it was in his system. Larson wasn't sure what statute the use of mydixafloppin would come under but she had a paralegal that would spend the rest of the day researching it.

After sleeping off his massive hangover, and waking up in a jail cell with six other drunks, one of whom had his hand on Osvaldo's right thigh, he was offered the opportunity to call an attorney. It was obvious Osvaldo would be spending some time as a guest of the Hillsborough County Sheriff. Checking a phone book, Osvaldo found the office of a law firm made up entirely of Hispanic attorneys who specialized in violent crime defense. He called the office and was put in touch with Raul Sotomayor, a Puerto Rican with an attitude and a particular disdain for Anglos.

Seated in a small conference room in the Hillsborough County Jail, Sotomayor explained to Osvaldo the charges against him and their seriousness. "First of all," he began, "you grabbed a woman's tits in public. Granted this was a strip joint and people get carried away, but the law doesn't smile on people who do that. Then you resisted arrest, you were obviously drunk because of your blood alcohol content, you were taking illegal steroids to build up your body, and to top off all of that, you have a drug called mydixafloppin in you and nobody understands why. Everything but the mydixafloppin is illegal and it might be also. What do you have to say about these charges?"

"God I love that woman Kari. She has the hottest body on earth. I saw her dancing to that Olivia Newton John song saying *Let's Get Physical* and I thought she was talking to me. What is a guy supposed to do? I'm 22 years old and constantly horny. These drugs I've been taking are making me crazy and I wasn't thinking straight."

"I'm sorry, Osvaldo, but 'I wasn't thinking straight' is not a really healthy defense."

"OK. I admit I screwed up. Now it's your job to get me off. Remember, when I'm in the majors. I'll be making lots of money and will be able to more than pay you back for helping me now."

"About going to the major leagues, Osvaldo, that is another issue."

News of the middle of the night raid on a stripper's chest in Ybor City had already filtered back to Reds management in Cincinnati. To say they were upset was an understatement. The Reds had contributed heavily to the Republic Party for many years because of the pro-family values façade. Adding hilarity to this façade was the chairman of the pro-family effort, Dale Edwards, a future congressman from Florida who had a thing for little boys.

Still, the Reds had a public face they needed to maintain and a lot of patrons who also contributed heavily to the Republicans. By 9:00 that morning the public relations network in the Reds front office released a statement to the press. It read:

"The Cincinnati Reds family was dismayed to find out this morning that one of our brightest prospects for the future of the Reds, Osvaldo Castro with the minor league Sarasota Reds in Florida, was involved in an unfortunate incident last evening. Although not all the details are available at this time, we are certain that when the facts are known Reds management will be able to move forward to protect the game and its fans from any undue and unwarranted attention."

The statement made it clear that Reds management was putting as much distance between it and Osvaldo as possible. What was most important was keeping up the public image of a family business and a family venue for good Christian families to visit in Cincinnati.

Press coverage in the hometown *Sarasota Herald-Tribune* was a bit more specific.

"Police were called to a bar in Ybor City last night to break up an incident involving Sarasota Reds outfielder Osvaldo

Castro and a scantily-clad woman whose role in the bar is not known at press time. Authorities cited Castro with at least six different misdemeanors and felonies the worst of which was possession of cocaine and possession of illegal steroid growth hormones. Reached for comment, Reds General Manager Ken Murray said about the incident and Castro in particular, 'Osvaldo is (expletive deleted). That's all I have to say about that."

8

The Reds home stand against the Manatees was nothing to write home about. In fact, Ned Bruenmeuller, a sports writer for the *Sarasota Herald-Tribune* summed up the first seven games of the Reds season in two words, "they stink." Nothing was clearer than Ned's description.

At the completion of the first seven games the Reds record was 0 wins and 7 losses. Through 63 innings played, the Reds scored 7 runs on 15 hits. Only one Red got on base with a walk and there was one hit batsman. The most telling number however was the strike outs. In 63 innings played there were 189 outs. Among those outs, 101 were strike outs. Slightly more than half of all the outs were by strike outs. According to Paradise League archival records no team in the League's history had ever performed so poorly.

After the disastrous home opener against the Brevard Manatees, the Reds went on the road playing first in Jackie Robinson Ball Park in Daytona Beach. Although much better known for spring break parties and as the town where Jimmy Buffett got the idea for his smash hit "Fins," Daytona Beach has a long and distinguished baseball history. Daytona is where Jackie Robinson long ago broke the color barrier in major league baseball.

Dave Apfel led off for the Reds and the count quickly went to 0 balls and 2 strikes. Sitting behind home plate, Chris had to agree with both pitches. There was nothing suspicious about these calls.

A pair of osprey had been circling the field throughout most of the team warm up and batting practice. Foolishly they built their nest on the top of one of the poles in left field, directly above the Cubs bullpen, and the nest now held two eggs.

Apfel dug in for the next pitch. Usually with the count 0 and 2 the pitcher will throw a pitch that isn't as accurate as a fastball. Maybe he would throw something off speed like a change up or a hanging curve ball or maybe a slider. Apfel anticipated this and stared down the pitcher waiting.

Although the first two pitches were nearly perfect there are always opportunities to heckle as there was today when Chris yelled at the pitcher, "Hey pitcher, you have as much control as two rabbits on their third date." Even some of the Cubs fans laughed at him.

Halfway into his wind up Apfel caught a glimpse of how the ball was held and then waited for a curve ball. When the ball was released it at first appeared like it would be inside to a right handed batter. Laws of physics took over maybe 40 feet from the plate and the ball began its quickly arching curve toward the center of the plate. Apfel was ready when the pitch was in flight and unleashed a tremendous swing and connected solidly with the ball.

Having just returned from a fishing expedition on the bay near the ball park, the male osprey of the pair nesting on the light pole was bringing home dinner for his mate who was incubating eggs. In his talons was a rather hefty snook whose weight was enough to slow down the forward motion of the bird. As the ball moved in an ever increasing arc, the osprey continued to lumber toward the nest. With the ball at the apex of its trajectory, it was obvious it would clear the warning track, the fence and maybe part of the tennis courts outside the ball park. That was until the osprey flared in his flight to gain a little altitude as it approached its nest. When it did, the solidly hit baseball and the osprey carrying the large snook became one.

On impact there was a loud resounding thud followed by the scattering of feathers. Luckily for the bird the ball collided with it near its tail and just above the feet. Any further forward and there could have been serious consequences. As feathers were peeling off its body, the bird let go of the fish it had been carrying in its talons and the fish did tumbling somersaults on its journey toward the ground. Had the fish not already been dead it certainly was when it hit the ground. Brent Allerson, a Cubs relief pitcher from Baltimore was in a warm up pitch directly beneath the fish as it plummeted toward him. With his arm in full extension getting ready to bring the pitch to the plate, the fish hit Allerson's hand knocking the ball free.

With the fish on a collision course with the relief pitcher, the recently assaulted and battered osprey began its plummet to the earth. As it did the osprey instinctively spread its wings but this only caused him to pirouette to the ground where it, also, hit Allerson who was recovering from the collision with the falling fish. Brian Anderson, another Cubs relief pitcher, saw the fish hit Allerson and then watched the osprey follow the snook. The bird was still breathing when it hit the ground. Anderson picked it up in his hands and yelled "is there an ornithologist in the house?"

Pitching Coach Bruce Bell called the press box and asked that the announcer ask the same question that Allerson just asked. The bird appeared to be alive but these guys know about baseballs not birds. Long time Cubs announcer Earl Smith was a good old boy Florida cracker who didn't know about people with "ologist" in their titles. In fact the only ologist Earl knew was a proctologist he saw on a regular basis because of persistent hemorrhoids. Earl drawled out what he had been told to say "Ladies and gentlemen, is there a hornythologist in the crowd? I'm not sure what a hornythologist does but I think I'd like that job."

After some laughter from the audience, Earl came back on the microphone and corrected himself in his Cracker twang. "Ah, excuse me ladies and gentlemen. That was for an or-nee-thol-o-gist. Is there an or-nee-thol-o-gist here? Seems that the ball nearly knocked the stuffin' out of this here osprey and it needs help." Earl then added, "If the osprey dies does anyone have a recipe for 'em?"

Chris heard the announcement and jumped up offering to help. He hadn't been in the stands long enough to annoy any players or umpires so he raced to the Cubs dugout and said he was an ornithologist. Why they wanted one was beyond Chris because a veterinarian would be much more appropriate. Still there was an injured bird in the bullpen and with his PhD, Chris certainly knew more about how to keep it alive than did a relief pitcher from Baltimore.

After identifying himself as an ornithologist, Chris raced across the field to Cubs bullpen. Eddie Peterson, a reserve catcher for the Cubs met Chris at the entrance to the pen. He said, "This is some crazy stuff man. Did you see that fish land on that pitcher in the bullpen? I blew cola out my nose when I saw it. It was so funny."

Chris quickly examined the osprey and couldn't feel any broken bones. There was considerable swelling where the ball hit the bird and he was concerned about internal bleeding. Then there was the issue of the bird's breath. For a very long time ornithologists had called the osprey the "fish hawk" because of its propensity for eating fish. In fact about 99 percent of its diet was made up of fish. None of these were cooked, broiled, blackened or beer battered. Ospreys eat it raw and their breath and most of their body have the distinctive odor of raw fish.

Getting himself past the halitosis issue, Chris cradled the osprey in his arms checking its eyes and the rest of the bird and concluded that it was in shock from the collision and probably from a loss of blood. Opening a can of cola he poured some in the bird's mouth and gave the rest to the pitching coach. Rather than simply throwing the bird into the air and letting it fly with a possible injury Chris decided to stay with it in the bullpen and watch its progress in regaining itself.

Time in the bullpen was an added treat. It was the first time since his removal from baseball that he had walked on a professional baseball field and it had been even longer since he last sat in the bullpen and watched a game from that angle. It made heckling a moot point but sitting out here with the players made him feel even more like a kid again than he did when he was sitting behind the plate heckling from the grandstand.

Apfel's osprey collision ball was ruled a home run because the home plate umpire, who once took a class in physics, was convinced that there was no way the ball would have not gone out of the park had the osprey not been in the way. The Reds had their first lead of the year and it lasted for most of the game.

In the seventh inning the Cubs scored two runs on a double, a single, and another single. It looked like Reds pitching was quickly going south again. The Reds came back with two runs in the top of the eighth inning regaining the lead.

Between the seventh and eighth inning Chris overheard two Cubs pitchers talking about the game. "I thought someone was buying off the umpires but after the way the Reds played tonight I'm not so sure that they are," Peter Stargell, a lanky relief pitcher from South Carolina said.

"I know. I've heard something about that too" said Kendrick Lahrem, a starting pitcher from Cumming, Georgia.

Chris tried to be inconspicuous with his listening but it was obvious he was more interested in what these two Cubs were saying than he was in the osprey in his arms or the action on the field. Finally he approached Stargell and asked "So, what are these things you've been hearing?"

Peter was surprised at first but then told Chris, "I don't want to talk about it here. Meet me at the Ocean Deck after the game and I'll tell you what I know."

9

Michelle Coburn sat in the American Airlines Admiral's Club on Concourse D at Miami International Airport waiting for her delayed flight to Caracas, Venezuela. It seemed like no matter where she flew any more the flight was delayed. For some reason it was even more regular in Miami than anywhere else in American's system.

She had worked her way up the ladder of scouting new talent for the Detroit Tigers. Her first job was to scour the countryside in Tennessee, Kentucky, Mississippi and Alabama looking for potential prospects to join the Tigers team. Born in Paducah, Kentucky it was rather like moving back home when she was assigned to this part of the country.

Following several interviews with Tigers scouting management, Michelle was hired for her first job and moved to Nashville. There she excelled in her profession, making shrewd decisions on which players to pursue and which to pass. Her efforts the first few years led to the Tigers signing Billy Bob Baker, a left-handed relief pitcher from Bowling Green, Kentucky who was now with the Triple A Toledo Mud Hens and destined for the majors next season. She had signed Travis James from Tupelo, Mississippi who was now the starting shortstop for the Tigers. Michelle had also signed several other players who were making their way through Class A and Class AA leagues and who would probably be moving up.

Her choices proved to Tigers management that she could recognize talent and recognize what was best for the Tigers.

A promotion to more responsibility was inevitable. The first one came at the beginning of her third year with the Tigers and it sent her back to sunny Florida. Soon she was moving into her new office in Joker Marchant Stadium in Lakeland, the spring training home of the Tigers. Although a small town, Lakeland had many advantages not the least of which was access in one hour to the airports at Orlando and Tampa where the Caribbean, Central America and South America, her new territory, were sometimes only a nonstop flight away.

Michelle made her first trip to the Dominican Republic where she found and signed Miguel Rodriquez her hottest prospect until the unfortunate incident late last year when Miguel flipped out at Chris' heckling and had to be carried from the ball park and eventually sedated. Tiger management will put up with a lot to help a prospect advance but the media circus following Miguel's behavior that day was too much. Miguel was likely back chopping sugar cane and maybe playing Dominican League baseball. He would never become a Detroit Tiger. Today's trip to Caracas was to check out Roberto Martinez, reputed to be a distant cousin of Boston Red Sox catcher and former All-Star Victor Martinez. Like his supposed cousin, Roberto was also a catcher. It was a position the Tigers needed to develop talent for and to do it soon.

While sipping on her second glass of merlot, Michelle was busily scanning her lap top for the latest news of baseball around the nation and especially in Latin America. A Trinidadian player named Robert Greenridge who was also a world-class steel drum player was now playing in the Venezuelan League. A left fielder with a reputation for towering fly balls that seemed to rocket out of stadiums, he was someone Michelle wanted to learn more about.

Robert had taken a break from baseball and was back in Port-of-Spain for the International Pan Festival. Michelle had never been to Trinidad and thought this would be a good excuse to not only talk with Robert but to soak up some Trinidadian sun and steel drum music. If nothing else this would be a hard-earned break that she desperately needed. She made a note to contact her administrative assistant about setting up a flight to Port-of-Spain once she was done in Caracas.

Maybe it was the second glass of merlot but something made her think about Chris. She hadn't seen him for maybe 35 years. Why had he come back onto the stage? She knew virtually nothing about him and it was starting to bother her that she was so poorly informed. A quick Google search for "J. Christopher Ramsey" revealed nearly 9,000 hits. From the search she discovered that Chris spent a lot of his career doing research on birds. His list of publications from his time at a research center in his home state of North Dakota was quite impressive. There were references to meetings he attended, conferences where he presented research results, and a list of awards and accomplishments compiled during his long career.

There were also many links to several blogs where Chris had posted comments. One of them with the strange name "Skewering the Chimp" drew her attention and she went to it. The introduction to the blog read: *"This blog is a repository for some of the better emails and other communication I've had with the "president" since it was appointed by Tony Scalia and the Supremes. I also include some of my other rants against the Republic Party and the conservative biased media."*

She continued scanning the files and there was no mention anywhere of a wife although there was mention in several of his posts on another blog about his children. "So," she wondered, "he has children but no mention of a wife. Come to think of it I didn't notice a wedding ring when I talked to him the other day. At least he's still a screaming liberal."

Suddenly she wondered why she was having these thoughts. It wasn't like they had anything in common any more other than their obvious interest in baseball. It also wasn't like she was having any trouble attracting men. At 5"2" with brown hair, deep brown eyes, and a toned body that had obviously spent considerable amounts of time in a gym, Michelle looked 35 years old despite her passport showing that she was 55 years old. She had experienced only three affairs since her marriage to Tim Coburn, an executive with an international investment firm in Detroit.

Pondering these facts she was snapped back to reality when the front desk of the Admiral's Club announced that their delayed flight to Caracas was now ready for passenger boarding. Putting away her lap top and collecting her carryon bag Michelle walked to gate D-28 to board her flight.

Having amassed more than two million frequent flier miles on American and having attained the status of "Chairman's Executive" in their program, she was virtually guaranteed free upgrades anywhere she flew on American Airlines domestically or in the Caribbean. For trips to South America that the Tigers were not willing to purchase a Business Class ticket, she used her miles for upgrades. She had done so for this evening's flight.

Seated at the port bulkhead window of the Boeing 767, she had room to work if she chose. However those two glasses of merlot in the Admiral's Club made her feel less than enthusiastic about working. Then her seat mate arrived and she lost all interest in anything to do with work.

At 6 feet 2 inches and 220 pounds with a deep south Florida tan, Ben Cooper epitomized the phrase "tall, dark, and handsome." Dressed in a three-piece pin stripe suit that covered his yellow shirt and red tie, Ben sent out an aura of success and professionalism. At 50 years old his hair was just beginning to gray at the sides. The president of an international electronics company in Tampa he was going to Caracas for a business meeting. If the meeting was successful, and they usually were when Ben was involved, his company would own its first electronics distributor in Venezuela. The money-making potential was enormous.

Melting when she saw him, Michelle thought, "I have him all to myself for the next four hours." She hit the flight attendant call button and asked for a glass of merlot before the flight.

American flight 1460 departed Miami only an hour late, rumbling down the south runway adjacent to Florida State Highway 836. Leaping into the air near the end of the runway the giant plane climbed rapidly through the heavy air that envelops south Florida and made its way east to the coast. Almost at the Rickenbacker Causeway the 767 began a gentle turn to the right passing over Virginia Key and then Key Biscayne. In the late afternoon sun the water below her surrounding the keys looked like the perfect shade of margarita green. On her first trip to the Caribbean long ago Tim had told her on their approach to St. Maarten that when you see green water you know you're in the tropics. She thought he was teasing until she saw the abundance of green water near the end of the St. Maarten runway. Each time since that first trip, the sight of green water reminded her of the tropics.

The sun was setting far off to the west as the climb out of Miami continued. The GPS map on the wall showed their projected path as a simple one. From Miami they would fly direct to Santo Domingo in the Dominican Republic. She had many fond memories of the Dominican Republic and the baseball players there. From Santo Domingo they would turn slightly southeast and proceed to Trinidad and then back to Caracas on the north coast of Venezuela. The inflight clock on the map said she was 3 hours and 44 minutes away from touchdown.

Following dinner of lobster bisque and French sole, and a glass of pinot grigio, Michelle was wasted. Since Ben had been essentially quiet since lift off she thought she would make the first move herself. Four glasses of wine helped make the task easier.

"So how can a man as delicious as you travel without a body guard?"

"What do you mean a body guard," Ben asked.

"Well," she slurred," I can't believe most of the women in Florida haven't showed up on your front steps to let you know how easy it would be to get to know them. I mean if I lived in your home town I'd sure as hell do it." Ben looked at her, then checked out her nearly perfect cleavage, then looked at the GPS map. They had only 100 minutes to go before landing in Caracas. He had to work fast.

He began telling a bit about himself. He was 50 years old, divorced for five years, three children, lived in Tampa and was president of a company that dealt in electronics. He was a graduate of the Harvard Business School where he earned a MBA and had lived in Florida for nearly 20 years. He was a sports fan and loved baseball. "You like baseball? I'm a scout for the Detroit Tigers. I'm going to Venezuela to check out a player."

"You're a scout for the Tigers? They have been my most favorite team since I was a kid," Ben lied. "I'm from the Detroit area originally, Canton, Michigan to be exact." He could care less about baseball and he grew up in Philadelphia. His only contact with Michigan was a meeting he once attended there. Luckily he remembered the name of the town.

He asked more about her job and what was involved with being a scout. Deep down the only thing Ben was interested in was that magnificent cleavage and what lurked beneath her blouse and dress pants. Hell, he'd be a fan of ancient Egyptian art if that's what it took. As the flight began its final approach to Caracas International Airport he asked Michelle where she was staying. "The Caracas Hilton of course. Whenever I travel if I can't stay in a Hilton then I don't go to that city. It's as simple as that."

"I'm staying at the Hilton also. Would you like to share taxi there after we get through customs?"

Still enjoying her wine buzz and the dampness between her thighs, Michelle happily accepted. It had been two weeks since she last slept with someone other than Tim. Since then she had sex only with her husband and that was getting old.

10

Taking a taxi into Caracas is the only sane way for a newcomer to venture into the city and especially at night. Travel in most South American capitals is simple but for some reason Caracas drivers are absolutely nuts. There is no other way to describe it. Road signs are nearly absent and almost everyone knows where they are going and they are going there at 90 miles per hour. It's best to leave the driving to someone who has a chance of surviving.

Checking into the hotel together they each found their room keys then decided to meet for a night cap in the lobby bar. The last thing Michelle needed was another glass of wine. They were both hammered by midnight. One night cap turned into two and they were both giggling and laughing and having a great time telling each other more things about themselves. After returning from the ladies room where she convinced herself it was time to make her own move, she came up to Ben saying "Well, it's time this girl went to bed. Are you coming along?"

They started kissing in the elevator and had a few stitches of clothing removed by the time they arrived at her hotel room. Once inside the remaining clothes flew off each of them with most of it on the floor. Ben laid his sports coat across the foot of the bed and Michelle found it curious.

Ben was ripped and obviously spent considerable amounts of time in the gym. His muscles seemed to have muscles. As Ben explored Michelle he was pleasantly surprised to see how nubile she was. Despite her having had two children, her stomach was flat and firm. Her breasts were full and he could now see why her cleavage had driven him to distraction on that four hour flight. He preferred his women unshaved and was a bit disappointed to find that Michelle had gotten carried away with her razor. Still, to Ben, this was just a one night stand so why complain about hairless bottom he would likely never see again.

After foreplay that seemed to last an hour they were both ready for what would logically come next and just as Ben entered her, the cell phone in his sports coat that was draped over the end of the bed went off. It wasn't a typical ring but a ring tone. Michelle commented on the ring tone and asked about it. "That's the ring tone for calls from my wife."

"You're what?"

"Didn't I tell you I was married? I thought that I did."

"No you forgot to tell me that. Now that I know you're married let's forget about the phone call for a minute. Just take me right now." When they had finished and Michelle was still naked on the bed Ben retired to the restroom. As the door closed his phone rang again. Michelle answered on the third ring and heard a female voice. "Hi honey. I'm glad you made it to Caracas."

"This isn't honey, this is Michelle Coburn. I am here in a hotel room in Caracas fucking your husband Ben. He told me on the plane down here that he was not married. I believed him and went to bed with him."

"Ben did what?"

"Ben and I have been screwing like a couple of virgin rabbits for the last hour. I thought you should know. Apparently this isn't the first time it has happened. I got the impression there have been many women in his life while he was married to you."

"Who did you say you are?"

"My name is Michelle Coburn. I live at 385 Grosvenor Place in Lakeland, Florida."

"And how did you get in bed with my husband?"

"I sat with him on the flight from Miami to Caracas this evening. He led me to believe he was divorced and I wound up in bed with him. We had fantastic sex until you called twice and disturbed us." She then added, "and you know what you're missing don't you Mrs. Cooper?"

Enjoying what she had done and the chaos it would no doubt cause, she kept the phone call live while still lying on the bed and waited for Ben to leave the restroom. "I think this call is for you, Ben"

Michelle could hear Ben's wife screaming at him as she opened the hotel room door. Then in a voice loud enough for Ben's wife to hear, Michelle added, "Call me in the morning Ben. Let's do it again before breakfast."

Elated with what just happened Michelle laughed herself to sleep. If Ben Cooper wasn't dead by morning she would sleep with him again. Putting on her standard large tee shirt which was the only thing she ever slept in, Michelle took out her lap top and pulled up Google again. She put in the words "J Christopher Ramsey, wife" and received no hits. This was a good sign. Next she entered "J Christopher Ramsey, telephone number" and received no hits. Finally she tried "J

Christopher Ramsey, email address" and she got one hit for baseballfan@email.com

She wrote him an email before going to bed. It was short and simple. It read:

Hey Chris –

This is Michelle. Remember me? It was a pleasant surprise to see you at the ball game in Sarasota. You're looking good for being such an old guy LOL. I was wondering if you live in Sarasota now and if so, would you be interested in lunch some time? Maybe we can catch a Tampa Bay Rays game? I think I would enjoy the time getting caught up with you and your life. I'm right now in Caracas checking on a player and then going to Trinidad to do the same. I should be back in Tampa on Friday.

Hope to hear from you soon.   M.

11

Chris arrived at the Ocean Deck a few minutes after eleven. Despite his rabid interest in Jimmy Buffett including having seen Buffett in concert 97 times, this was the first time he'd entered the Ocean Deck. Its importance to Buffett fans is that it was in this bar that Buffett saw a woman enter and immediately get hit on my a group of guys he later called "Land Sharks." Witnessing it, he came up with the idea for his smash hit song "Fins" one of his best party songs. To top it off, Buffett later named his own beer "Landshark Lager" which was Chris' favorite brew.

The upstairs was packed. Every table was full and every bar stool occupied. Chris walked downstairs and found it even crazier than the upstairs. The clientele was made up primarily of twenty-something women soaked with estrogen and twenty-something men hoping to reduce their stress. It reminded Chris of "the old days" in college long ago. Little, it seemed, had changed over all those years in the dance for companionship.

Peter Stargell and Kendrick Lahrem walked into the downstairs of the Ocean Deck. They had showered after the game, listened to their coach's usual post-game analysis of what went right and what went wrong, then smoked a joint and headed for the beach. Stargell entered first and surveyed the room. In a far corner near the window he spotted Debbie Mauer, a 24 year old blonde from Philadelphia who had escaped the cold of Philly when she graduated from high school and never looked back. Completing a degree at Embry-Riddle she was certified to fly small jets like the EMB-145. With the market for pilots flooded and few opportunities available, Debbie was working as a front desk clerk at the nearby Hilton. Peter had slept with her a few times and enjoyed her enthusiasm but her politics bothered him. Peter once told a friend after a night with Debbie, "You know she'd be a great woman to live with but she listens to Rush Limbaugh and only watches Fox News. Any woman with that little integrity is not for me."

That didn't stop Peter from bedding her on an as-needed basis. Recently she wasn't as needed because Marissa Newton, the lead downstairs bartender at the Ocean Deck, was filling that role.

Peter walked up to Marissa as she stood behind the bar, gave her a peck on the cheek and confirmed that they were on again for tomorrow night as soon as she could lock the front door and leave. Given how many people were in the bar and how loosely most bars interpret Florida laws about closing they would likely not be together until 3 a.m. at the earliest.

Chris saw Peter and Kendrick parade across the room and eventually walked toward them. Sixty years old and in marginally good shape, Chris was always looking at the twenty-something women in Florida and dreaming of the old days. Now that every one of these women was younger than his youngest daughter a slight damper was put on the excitement. Finally walking up to Peter and Kendrick, Chris greeted them and asked if they wanted a beer.

"Landshark for me," Peter said.

"I'll have a Red Stripe," Kendrick said.

After exchanging pleasantries they retired to the deck overlooking the ocean. The noise level was somewhat reduced and the pulsing of the bass in the juke box was much lower. They talked first about the game that the Reds had managed to win. "What is it with the Reds this year? Have you guys ever seen such bad luck for a Class A team," Chris asked.

"They are a good bunch of guys," Peter started. "The Reds have lots of solid hitters and some good infielders. The relief pitchers are among the best in the league. Still they keep losing games."

"I was watching a game last summer, it must have been in late August," Kendrick said. "The Reds had a two or three run lead and suddenly they folded. What looked like strikes became balls and balls became strikes. The batters didn't know what to do."

"Most of them," he continued, "simply stood there expecting random chance to be on their side. It never was. Instead the side was struck out three innings in a row and they were struck out on some pretty obvious calls."

"So," Chris asked, "what is going on with the team?"

"It's not the team," Kendrick said. "I'm convinced something is going on with the umpires. I'm not sure what but something isn't right. Of course everyone who plays them enjoys it because it's easy to get a win. Still something is just not right."

Peter said," We noticed it after that game Kendrick mentioned. For the rest of the season the Reds could do nothing right. They wound up with a .285 win percentage, the worst in minor league baseball." A .285 batting average is enough to make almost everyone take notice of the hitter accomplishing that feat. The same as a winning percentage suggests that something is unquestionably wrong somewhere. Even the Miami Marlins aren't that bad.

"Back at the ball park you mentioned something about some rumors you were hearing," Chris asked. "What is that all about?"

"Don't quote me on this or I might get in a lot of trouble, especially if it's true," Kendrick said. "Some people have been saying that money is being exchanged so a couple Paradise League umpires will throw games."

"Who are these 'some people' you mention hearing this from," Chris asked.

"Let's just say that I've heard other players commenting last year that something was wrong.' The three of them left the outside deck and returned to the craziness of the bar where they found a table near the entrance door. David Peterson, an extremely inebriated fan of the Daytona Cubs saw Peter and Kendrick sitting with some older man and came over to talk. David rarely missed a ball game and enjoyed Monday morning quarterbacking even if it was still the night before.

"You guys kicked some serious ass out there tonight, Peter, some serious ass," David said.

"What do you mean we kicked serious ass David, we were beaten by the worst team in the league."

"Well I still think you kicked some ass," he slurred.

As he said that one of the many mid-twenties women in the bar walked by their table and David asked the tree men at his table, "So you guys think she's still a virgin?"

Kendrick said he wasn't sure and thought David should ask her. By now she was seated alone at a table near them. David, fortified by a gut full of beer, decided to make his move and stumbled over to her. Approaching her table in full drunken swerve, he smiled at the pretty redhead and asked matter of factly, "Can I smell your pussy?"

The redhead, visibly unimpressed with his opening line, yelled "no" at the top of her lungs.

David quickly replied, "Well, it must be somebody else's then. Have a nice night."

Returning to the table he told the story of his being turned down but then decided there was another alternative. All week long David had been getting turned down by women in bars in Daytona Beach. If he was using the same line he used on the redhead it was little wonder.

Instead of trying further, David took out his cell phone and punched in the number 911.

David's side of the conversation was all anyone could hear.

"What's my emergency? My emergency is I can't get laid and I wondered if there was anyone in your office who would like to could come have sex with me."

"Repeat that? Ok. I said my emergency is I can't get laid and I wondered if someone in the fire department could come have sex with me."

"What a pompous bitch. She hung up!" David redialed 911.

"Yes, my emergency is that I can't get laid and I wonder if someone in the fire department would come have sex with me. I just called your office a minute ago but someone hung up on me"

"What's with you people there tonight. I said my emergency is that I can't get laid and I wondered if someone at the fire department would come have sex with me."

"Where am I? I'm at the Ocean Deck."

"What's my name? My name is David Peterson."

"I'm sitting downstairs with three buddies of mine. They can't get laid either."

"Oh, you'll send someone over? How about you send three more girls for my buddies here?"

"Ok. We'll wait."

Ending the call, Kendrick, Peter or Chris could not believe that Peterson was stupid enough to call 911 and ask for sex. Yet a few minutes later three Daytona Beach police officers entered the bar. They walked among the tables and settled on a table with four men seated together.

One particularly beefy officer walked to their table and asked," Are any of you guys David Peterson?" David, too drunk to keep his mouth shut said that he was. The officer asked for identification and David gave it to him. The officer then asked if he had a cell phone. David opened his cell phone and handed it to the officer who looked through the call log and saw that the last two calls were to 911 and they were made just a matter of minutes earlier. The beefy officer then read David his Miranda rights while one of the other officers handcuffed him and informed him he was under arrest for disorderly conduct and for making a false 911 call.

"What do you mean disorderly conduct? I'm not being disorderly," David pleaded. "I'm just really horny that's all."

Smiling at him, one of the other officers said "we'll just take you to the jail. I'm sure there are a lot of people there who will be glad to take care of your horniness." They then led him out of the bar.

Following David's early departure from the bar, Chris bought another round of beer and they kept talking about baseball. Well, baseball and the crop of twenty-something women strutting their stuff across the bar floor. He accepted the very real fact that he was too old for any of the women in the bar but it didn't stop him from dreaming and wondering. It was one of the down sides of aging.

"So," Chris asked. "How do you two think someone got to the umpires, if that's what is really happening?"

Neither of the players had a clue. It had seemed strange to them that the Reds were having such bad luck and so many bad calls were being made not only on strikes and balls but also when runners were trying to score or steal a base.

"It baffles the hell out of me," Peter said. "Something is just not right."

12

After a game in Sarasota, umpires Justin Reed and Dennis Hastert Jr. checked into the room they shared at the Days Inn on North Tamiami Trail and then went out for dinner. They might be professional baseball umpires but this was the Paradise League where players earned maybe $1,500 a month and the umpires a little less. This was the Paradise League where players traveled to games in chartered buses. The only jet planes a Sarasota Reds player ever saw was the nightly 7:00 p.m. arrival of the Delta flight from Atlanta as it flew over their stadium while it was on final approach to Sarasota International Airport. This was the Paradise League where money was so tight that staying in a hotel better than a Days Inn was a luxury like staying at a Westin Resort. Justin and Dennis were just damned lucky to have a roof over their head. They couldn't complain too loudly.

When they weren't umpiring baseball games Justin lived in Key West, and Dennis in Fernandina Beach. In the off season Justin poured drinks and doubled as a bouncer at Green Parrot on Whitehead Street in Key West. Just off the beaten path of all the rabidly drunk tourists on Duval Street, the Green Parrot still retained a bit of its original Key West charm. Although he was a solid baseball player in high school, Justin did not make the cut when he tried out for the Gators his first year in Gainesville. Instead of realizing his vision of being a baseball star, Justin majored in physical education and set his sights on being an umpire. Umpiring would keep him active in baseball even if he couldn't play.

Dennis was born in the suburbs of Chicago. Tired of cold winter weather he bought a one way ticket to Jacksonville on his eighteenth birthday and never looked back. Attending Florida State College at Jacksonville, Dennis majored in business administration and minored in cocaine importing. His father often wondered why Junior never asked for money while he was in college. A rabid Chicago White Sox fan while he was growing up, Dennis was a mediocre player at best in high school and never tried to play in college. They had a zero tolerance policy on drug use for Florida State College athletes and Dennis was certain he would fail every test. There was also the issue of him needing to be available to inventory and distribute his regular shipments of white gold.

After graduation Dennis sat in Lynch's Irish Pub in Jacksonville Beach nursing a pint of Caffrey's Irish Ale and waiting to hear from his contact. That day's edition of the *Florida Times-Union* sat on the bar. Out of curiosity, Dennis turned to the want ads and scanned them. Near the bottom of one column he saw an advertisement by the Paradise League seeking candidates for the position of umpire. League headquarters are in Daytona Beach, the center of a Congressional district that had never been represented by anyone other than a Republican since the district was formed. Curt Foley, the current Congressman, was someone his dad considered a friend, and whose district office was two blocks from Paradise League headquarters.

"I know my dad has all kinds of dirt on Curt Foley," he thought. Dennis considered it a little more and remembered a party at his home when he was in high school when Curt Foley became uproariously drunk. As he got drunker Foley started telling stories to the other Republican Congressmen at the party and one of the stories involving Foley bragging about hitting on one of the underage interns in his office.

Umpiring baseball games would be a great excuse to travel around the state making more connections for Dennis' thriving cocaine importation business. And he could do all the travel at someone else's expense. Opening his cell phone Junior called Senior and told him about his desire to be an umpire for the Paradise League. Junior asked Senior to contact his old friend Curt Foley for some assistance and if Curt was reluctant, Junior reminded Senior about the drunken confession at their party in DC that night.

Four hours later Junior's cell phone lit up like a Christmas tree. It was Ed Albertson, chief umpire for the Paradise League. "Dennis, we heard that you wanted to be an umpire for the Paradise League and wondered if you are still interested in the job?"

"Certainly, Mr. Albertson, I would like nothing better than to be an umpire."

"Well, Dennis, you have some very powerful friends and because of that we've decided just to hire you without an application or an interview. Can you come down to Daytona to fill out the paperwork? We could put you to work by the end of the week."

Dennis smiled knowing that politics had worked for him again. "Sure, Ed, I'll be there tomorrow afternoon about 1:00 p.m."

That was four years ago. In the meantime Dennis' importing business had grown as had his list of contacts. He chose to live in Fernandina Beach not far from the Georgia border because all of the big time importers were on the Gold Coast from Miami to West Palm Beach and over in Tampa. Living in a fishing village populated with rednecks was a perfect cover.

Following that night's game Dennis decided to treat Justin to dinner at the Ritz-Carlton on the bay front in Sarasota. The Paradise League gave umpires only twenty dollars a day for food. Dennis knew that his daily allotment combined with Justin's would barely cover the tip at the Ritz. However he was feeling benevolent so he took his colleague out for dinner.

Seated in the Ca' Zan Lounge they surveyed the menu. None of the entrees had a price by it. In fact nothing on the menu had a price by it. Each of them carnivores, they both had the gaucho style bone-in rib eye steak. Dennis had his medium rare. Justin's was medium well. This was after having a dozen mussels each for an appetizer.

"Where do you get the money to pay for all this stuff," Justin asked.

Dennis lied and said, "I inherited a lot of money when my grandmother died."

During the dessert course where each of them had key lime pie, Dennis asked Justin what was up with his umpiring. "Justin," he began, "I have been umpiring in the Paradise League for four years now. I've seen a lot of games and looked at a lot of pitches. I've called a lot of runners out at the plate and I've had more than my share of dirt kicked in my face. Despite all of that I have never seen anyone so obviously trying to throw a game as I have while watching you behind the plate these last few games. What is going on and why are you being so obvious?"

"What do you mean throwing a game? I've never thrown a game in my entire life."

"That's bullshit Justin. A blind pitcher stands a better chance of getting a called strike from you than any Sarasota Reds pitcher who comes in front of you."

"Do you really think I'm throwing games," Justin asked.

"Yes, and I think it's becoming more and more obvious to everyone each time you stand behind the plate."

Justin pondered this for a bit and then rather sheepishly asked, "So, can I trust you on this?"

"Trust me? I'm the son of a former Congressman. Of course you can trust me."

"Well," Justin began, "I've been a little short on cash and late last season this Mexican guy, maybe he was Cuban. Who knows; they all look alike. Anyway this Hispanic guy approached me after I called a game in West Palm Beach and asked to chat with me."

"What did he say?"

"He said he represented some people who had a deep interest in the future of the Paradise League. They were concerned with the direction the league was taking and wanted to change that direction."

"What does that have to do with buying you off to throw games?"

"I'm not really sure what it has to do with anything. All I know is that I was asked to do what I could to 'enhance' the scores of some of the games."

"Did they tell you how to enhance the scores?"

"No, they left that up to me. All they said was that I would receive a text message before each game they wanted enhanced. If the final score was what they wanted I would receive $900."

"They are paying you nine hundred dollars to throw a game their way?

"Yes they are paying me one hundred dollars an inning. How totally awesome is that?"

"Do they have any particular teams that they want to make sure are more enhanced than others?"

"The only two I have had any contact with are the Lakeland Tigers and the Sarasota Reds. My instructions are to make sure games I call involving these teams are usually won by whomever they are playing. They want the loss percentage about 80 percent for both teams. Don't ask me why."

"And you don't have a clue who or what group is doing this?"

"Not a clue. All I know is that each time a game goes the way they want it enhanced, an extra nine hundred dollars shows up the next morning in my Bank of America account."

"This sounds like one hell of a racket. Is there any way I can get in on it? I have a few connections that might be useful."

"I'm not sure. Let me ask my contact the next time I talk with him."

"There is one thing you need to do, though, Justin."

"What's that?"

"You need to be a little bit more circumspect when you are making some calls."

"What does circumspect mean?"

"You need to stop being so damned obvious with the way you call some pitches. If anyone got the idea that games are being thrown there are several ways people could figure it out."

"Figure it out? How in hell could anyone figure it out?

"I have a little side business," Dennis said. "In my business I have learned how to be a little less than obvious in the things that I do. Maybe it's time I taught you a little bit about how to be the son of a Congressman."

They asked for their check and weren't the least bit shocked when they saw it was $300. The bill was just three innings of work.

13

One advantage Chris enjoyed about being retired was that he had no itinerary he had to follow any longer. There was no set pattern to where he had to be at certain times. He had no asses to kiss. His manana attitude was now a pervasive part of his life and Chris pretty much did what he wanted to do when he wanted to do it. That included right now as he was driving out of Daytona Beach headed southbound on I-95 for West Palm Beach. One of the many things Chris enjoyed about living in Florida was that so many towns had the word "beach" in their name. He made a vow to one day visit every one of those towns.

Now that he was back among baseball teams and baseball players and he had his own hometown minor league team to watch and nurture, Chris decided that one thing he wanted to accomplish was to see a minor league game in each stadium used by the Paradise League teams. There were twelve teams in the league and they played ball in eleven stadiums. For a reason that nobody could explain, both the Palm Beach Cardinals and the Jupiter Hammerheads played in Roger Dean Stadium in Palm Beach County.

It seemed almost surreal that two teams that both called one stadium "home" would have to decide which team was the home team and who was the "visitor" in their home stadium. The confusion alone was worth a trip there to see a game. With games already seen in Sarasota, Lakeland, and Daytona Beach, Chris had eight stadiums to visit and he would have visited them all. A game in Roger Dean Stadium would make it only seven.

As he raced down I-95, Chris listened to WXEL-FM, a more or less news station from West Palm Beach. Today's headline was a story about John LaRoe, a member of the Palm Beach County Commissioners who had been arrested overnight in a sex sting in nearby Martin County. La Roe had been caught masturbating in a bathroom stall in the Treasure Coast Square Mall. The news reporter couldn't contain himself when he read his script saying the commissioner had been caught "red handed." Bursting into laughter he wondered aloud if that should have been "white handed" instead.

On being nabbed by the police, La Roe, a devout Christian and deacon in the local Baptist Church, claimed it was a case of mistaken identity. When confronted by the police officer who arrested him, La Roe said it wasn't him masturbating. He told the police "I just went in the stall to take a dump and found semen all over the toilet seat. I was just cleaning it off and the police busted in and arrested me. When my attorney gets done with you I'm suing the Martin County Sheriff for false arrest."

Still snickering over the story, the newscaster, himself a devout Baptist, reported that this was the sixth arrest in seven weeks in this same bathroom stall. Treasure Coast Square Mall officials had installed a special camera to watch over the stall, and local law enforcement was called each time someone entered the stall and didn't act like they were there for the purpose one would usually expect for a bathroom stall.

Ending the story, the reporter said "And for La Roe, this was his second arrest for public indecency in the last year. Last

October he was found doing the same thing at the Melbourne Dog Track in Brevard County." Chuckling at the news story, Chris could only say to himself, "I have no doubt now that I'm back in south Florida."

Chris checked into the Hilton Garden Inn on Kyoto Gardens Drive not far from the ball park. He always stayed at Hilton hotels while he was working and decided there was no point in changing that plan now that he was retired. Because of his Platinum status with Hilton, Chris was offered a free upgrade to a suite on the executive floor. His room overlooked the hotel garden and swimming pool. This being April the only people in the pool were tourists who thought 80 degrees was warm. Taking his lap top out of its carrying case, Chris logged on to check his email and noticed a message Michelle had sent last night. He opened the message and read it.

Hey Chris –

This is Michelle. Remember me? It was a pleasant surprise to see you at the ball game in Sarasota. You're looking good for being such an old guy LOL. I was wondering if you live in Sarasota now and if so, would you be interested in lunch some time? Maybe a Tampa Bay Rays game? I think I would enjoy the time getting caught up with you and your life. I'm right now in Caracas checking on a player and then going to Trinidad to do the same. I should be back in Tampa this Friday.

Hope to hear from you soon. M.

The email baffled Chris. He had received no correspondence from her in nearly 35 years. To him it was like he no longer existed in her mind.   There were no Christmas cards, no birthday cards, not even a threat of taking him back to court for some reason. There was no contact and now in a matter of weeks he sat next to her at a Mockingbirds game. Their conversation was cordial then but nothing that suggested any interest on her part.

It was like these two baseball fans sat together at a game and then walked away never to see each other again. In the case of Michelle and Chris there was a lot of history to deal with. There was no way either of them could just walk away and not think about the other. They had been each other's best friend and each other's confidant. They learned about love making from each other and cared for each other when they were ill.

He read her email carefully.

"It was pleasant to see you at the game in Sarasota." It was? She was almost like ice sitting there. I offered to get her a beer and a bratwurst and she acted like I was an axe murderer. Maybe she was shocked that I was next to her and she didn't know what to say to me?

"You're looking good for being such an old guy." Old guy? I'm 60 years old and she's 55. Who is calling who old here?

"I was wondering if you live in Sarasota now and if so, would you be interested in lunch some time?" Why does she want to know where I live? And how in hell did she get my email address anyway? If she was so interested in my living arrangements couldn't she find that from the Internet? What is she up to?

"Maybe a Tampa Bay Rays game?" Why the Rays? They had one season in the sun and they have sucked ever since. He checked his baseball schedule and saw that Detroit wouldn't be playing the Rays at home until early July almost three months away. Why is she asking about this?

"I think I would enjoy getting caught up on you and your life." Really? You haven't given a damn about me or my life for 35 years so why the sudden interest now?

"I'm right now in Caracas checking on a player and then going to Trinidad to do the same." It's interesting that she's going to Trinidad. There are no baseball players from Trinidad just cricket players and they sure as hell can't play baseball. What is up with Trinidad?

"I should be back in Tampa this Friday." For some reason he checked the American Airlines schedule from Port-of-Spain to Tampa this coming Friday. The plane left Port-of-Spain at 9:00 a.m. Trinidad time, arriving Miami at 12:00 noon. The most logical connection, leaving time to go through the menagerie that is the customs area at Miami International Airport is at 3:30 arriving in Tampa at 4:30. The Tampa Yankees are hosting the Sarasota Reds on Friday night. He still had not been to George Steinbrenner Stadium.

"Hope to hear from you soon." After more than a third of a century of no contact, you hope to hear from me soon? I think I'll make you wait a while longer.

14

Tonight's game between the Hammerheads and the Cardinals was sold out. This seemed a bit incongruous given that it was minor league baseball. However there were 5,185 fans in the 5,185 seats of Roger Dean Stadium. The stadium wasn't full because of fans dedicated to either of the teams playing tonight. It was full because of the latest promotion dreamed up by Cardinals management.

Several years earlier the San Antonio Missions had a "Used Car Night" promotion in which six fans were picked at random and each won a used luxury vehicle. Tonight the Hammerheads and Cardinals teamed up with several local dealerships who among them had donated ten used cars to be given away to ten lucky fans.

These weren't your typical Chrysler or Toyota clunkers either. They included one Bentley, one Rolls-Royce, two Mercedes, three Lexus' and three BMWs. The latter no longer really were considered a luxury car because even minor league baseball players could afford a BMW. They were thrown in because the dealership was way overstocked and needed a tax write-off. In fact all ten vehicles were donated not out of a sense of good will for the community but because the dealerships needed to find some easy tax deductions.

One car would be given away in the middle of each inning. The first three winners would receive BMWs. Winners in innings four, five and six would receive the three Lexus'. The two Mercedes would be given away during the seventh inning stretch and the middle of the eighth inning. The Rolls would be given away in the middle of the ninth inning and the grand prize, a 2007 Bentley with just 2,000 miles would be given away after the last out of the game.

Rules for the promotion were explicit. Immediately after the Hammerheads finished batting at the top of each inning, a number would be drawn at random from the bin holding copies of each admission ticket. When each winning number was called, the holder of the number had until the bottom of that inning to reach the guest service's desk behind home plate. Any later than the bottom of the same inning and your number was invalid and another number would be called. These rules guaranteed that nobody would leave until after the Bentley was given away.

Five minutes before the first pitch, Chris noticed that the umpires were walking to home plate from inside the Hammerheads dugout. They looked familiar to him because they were. It was Justin Reed calling balls and strikes behind home plate, and Dennis Hastert Jr. working the bases.

The leadoff batter for the Hammerheads went down swinging on three pitches. From Chris' vantage point all three pitches looked like legitimate strikes. The second batter grounded out shortstop to first on a 2-2 pitch. Nothing about his at bat seemed suspicious. The third Hammerhead reached second base on a double to right-center field. Jason Malden, the Hammerhead's cleanup hitter took the count to three balls and two strikes before hitting a slider over the pitchers head and straight up the middle scoring the runner on second and giving the Hammerheads an early 1-0 lead. Jeremiah Marvin, a Jewish kid from the Bronx was the fifth batter. He swung at a fast ball and lined it to the second baseman who threw him out at first base ending the inning.

Between teams at bat the owner of the Palm Beach Cardinals put his hand in the bin and pulled out the winning number for the first BMW of the night. Palm Beach Cardinals announcer Rick Stevens, a 31 year veteran of announcing Cardinals games read the number into the public address system. "The first winning number for tonight is 196969. The holder of this ticket has until the end of the first inning to claim your prize, a maroon 2005 BMW."

From behind the third base dugout a tall slender blonde man about 60 years old leaped out of his seat and yelled "I won!! I won!!" It was Paul Greissen, an out of work executive with a company that supplied ammunition to rebels in the now-ending civil war in Colombia.

By the bottom of the ninth inning the Hammerheads had amassed an impressive 6-2 lead over the Cardinals. There had been one play at home where the catcher tagged a runner. The ball arrived safely before the runner did and the put out was obvious. The same was true for two attempted stolen bases and one instance where a runner on first base took off after a solid hit to right field and tried to stretch his run into third base. A laser perfect throw from the first baseman arrived before the runner did and Hastert called him out. The Cardinals protested but Reed concurred with Hastert and the runner was out. There was nothing fishy about any of these plays.

When the game ended all 5,185 paid fans remained glued to their seats in anticipation of the grand prize of the night – the 2007 Bentley. Gold with a black roof, the Bentley simply exuded pretentiousness. It was the perfect car for the filthy rich to flaunt in front of the have not's. And despite all the money there was in Palm Beach there was no shortage of have not's. Announcer Rick Stevens cleared his throat into the microphone and said "Ladies and gentlemen. Thank you for remaining throughout the game and it was one hell of a game wasn't it?" There was hardly any applause as the fans could care less about the game. They wanted to know if they won the Bentley. Embarrassed when hardly anyone applauded, Stevens quickly changed his tone and went right to picking the winner.

"Ladies and gentlemen I have with me tonight Carrie Prescott, the reigning Miss Florida who will pick the number for the Bentley. Carrie, it's all up to you now."

"Thanks Rick. You sure look nice for an old man."

"Carrie, will you pick the number?"

From the audience people were getting upset and someone yelled "shut up and call the number will you." Carrie reached her hand into the bin and pulled out the lucky number. "The winning ticket number is 495387. That's 4 9 5 3 8 7. Whoever is the holder of this lucky number please report to the entrance to the playing field by the Cardinals dugout on the first base line in the next five minutes or we'll pick another number. The Bentley will be awarded by A. Charles Huntington, owner of the Palm Beach Cardinals. The countdown clock starts now!"

From the stands down the first base line fans could hear and then see a fifty something man leap from his seat and yell, "I have it!! I have it! I have the winning number!" Soon a bald man about 6'0 wearing running shorts and flip flops and a t-shirt raced to the edge of the first base dugout and handed someone his ticket. It contained the winning number and Larry Hooper, manager of a homeless shelter in Palm Beach County, and vice-chair of the Palm Beach County Democratic Party presented himself as the winner of the Bentley. A large but reluctant round of applause slowly built among the crowd as Larry walked to the microphone behind home plate where A. Charles Huntington and Carrie Prescott were waiting for him. Huntington was dressed in a three-piece pin stripe suit with kangaroo skin shoes covering his feet. Carrie was dressed in hot pants and a top that made it certain she could get a job at any Hooters restaurant after her reign as Miss Florida ended.

As Larry walked to them, Huntington reached out his hand and shook his then said into the microphone. "On behalf of the Palm Beach Cardinals, the Jupiter Hammerheads, and Braman Motorcars – Palm Beach, donor of this magnificent car, we want to present you with the keys to your own 2007 Bentley. Now Larry, do you have anything you want to say to the audience?"

Larry took the microphone, thanked Huntington for the introduction, looked at Carrie and wished he was 30 years younger and still had some hair, and then spoke into the audience. "Thank you," was all he said.

Driving back to the Hilton Garden Inn after watching the post-game festivities, Chris was thinking about what he witnessed during the game. He decided that he was still going to watch at least one game in each of the 11 stadiums but after tonight's game he was going to make sure that Reed and Hastert were calling the games in as many stadiums as often as possible. The irony of their calls tonight compared to what they had done to the Reds was not something that random chance could explain away. These umpires are up to something and Chris wanted to find out what it was.

15

Roberto Martinez, the Venezuelan catcher who was the reason for Michelle's trip to Caracas turned out to be a better prospect than she had hoped. His record the previous year was impressive. His batting average was .342 during 310 at bats including 31 home runs, 66 runs batted in and he had only two errors in 101 games. Anyone who has ever played catcher knows it is nearly impossible to have an error rate that low. At 20 years old Roberto possessed great potential for his future and for the future of the Detroit Tigers.

Before leaving Caracas, Michelle contacted Kyle Gomes a sports psychologist in the Tigers organization who was going to travel to Venezuela to evaluate Roberto. Kyle was going to be in the Dominican Republic and Puerto Rico doing the same thing for a couple other prospects so it would be easy for him to come to Caracas and evaluate Roberto. He would provide her with his observations in a few weeks. If the reports were positive, she would return to Venezuela and offer him a contract to play with the Detroit Tigers.

Sitting in the departure lounge for Aeropostal Airlines flight 123 from Caracas to Port-of-Spain, Trinidad, Michelle opened her lap top and logged on to check her email. Internet connections in Venezuela leave much to be desired but at least the Caracas airport was trying to provide free wireless in most parts of the international departures area. She had 48 messages. Most of them other messages were from Detroit Tigers management including one from her office manager in Lakeland reminding Michelle to make sure she brought in her hotel receipts from this trip on time so she could get her reimbursement paperwork in the mill and avoid the long delays she had been experiencing in getting checks like she had earlier in the year.

Scrolling down through the list of messages she was excited with anticipation that one of them would be from Chris. After the first sixteen however there was nothing with his name on it. The 17th message in the queue was from electronicsman@ email.com. It was from Ben Cooper whom she bedded in Caracas.

As Michelle read the message she wondered out loud how Cooper got her email address. She certainly didn't give it to him. Or had she? Damn, that's right. On the plane from Miami to Caracas when they were first starting to get to know each other, Michelle gave him her email address when she handed him her business card. At the time she wanted to impress him with the fact that she was a professional baseball scout.

The email from Ben read:

Dear Michelle -

I enjoyed our time together in Caracas. It was funny as hell when you talked to my wife. She's now filing for divorce which is something I have wanted for years. Now that I'm going to be free of her I'd like to see you regularly. With you in Lakeland and me in Tampa we should be able to work something out. Let's do it again soon. Ben.

She hit reply and sent him a short message:

Ben

How incredibly dumb are you? Didn't you get the hint that I wanted a one-night stand and nothing more? Good luck.

Michelle Coburn

Happy with what she had just done she scrolled on through the rest of her messages. None were from Chris.

Departure from the Caracas airport was to the east and Michelle was in a starboard window in First Class which offered her an excellent view of the chaos that is Caracas. The flight followed a southeasterly course away from the coast and eventually crossing an extensive area of grassland that stretched to the horizon. Soon the grasslands transitioned into an extensive forest along a huge river that reminded her of the Mississippi. This was the Orinoco River and they followed its course to where it emptied into the Atlantic. From there the plane turned northeast and soon the flight attendants were telling everyone to stow their gear because arrival in the Port-of-Spain airport was imminent.

All the passengers standing in the customs line were treated to a demonstration of steel drum music offered by a local band from near Piarco Airport. This was just a teaser for those who are attending the international pan festival would be hearing. Retrieving her luggage, Michelle stopped by the Royal Bank of Trinidad to exchange money into Trinidad and Tobago dollars. She had some Bolivars left over from Caracas and also converted them to local money. Taking a taxi from the airport for the 20 minute ride to the Hilton in downtown Port-of-Spain, she paid the driver his extortionate fare of nearly $80 US and then checked in.

It still bothered her that she had not received an email from Chris and she wondered if he had not received it. Maybe in her drunkenness and stressed state of mind she forgot to hit the send button. Ducking into the Business Center near the front desk she opened her email account and looked in her sent file. Yes, it was there. She had sent it after all. Maybe he's just too busy to contact me? Then again, he's retired so just how busy can he get?

She decided to re-send the message just in case and on top of the original message she said *"Just wanted to make sure you got this message. I'm staying tonight and tomorrow at the Hilton in Port-of-Spain. You would enjoy it here. M"* She hit "send" and hoped that Chris would at least acknowledge her messages.

It was about 3:30 in the afternoon and the hot humid air that envelops Trinidad every day of the year hung heavily over the city. Her plans were to meet Robert Greenridge at 6:00 p.m. this evening to discuss his interest in playing for the Detroit Tigers. Tomorrow was Thursday and at 8:00 a.m. she had a Tobago Express flight to Tobago where she was going to spend the day in the sun thinking about nothing other than the glass of merlot she would be holding in her hands.

She contemplated dressing more business-like for her meeting with Robert but the humid air outside and the fact that steel drum music was everywhere in the air made her decide that a more casual approach was necessary. Instead of a business suit she opted for white shorts and a salmon top. Underneath the top she wore a frilly bra and under her white shorts was a flesh colored thong. She might be 55 years old but she had the body of a 30 year old and besides, wearing a thong always made her feel sexier.

Robert Greenridge was only 22 years old, 6'4" tall, maybe 220 pounds, as lean as a greyhound and probably didn't have an ounce of body fat. He met Michelle in the lobby of the Hilton precisely at 6:00 p.m. as they had planned.

"Ms. Coburn, it is a pleasure to meet you," Robert said.

"The pleasure is mine, Robert."

At the recommendation of the concierge, for dinner they chose "Zanzibar" on Aubrey Jeffers Highway near downtown. It's in one of the safer parts of the city and many of the locals say it's a great place to hang out. A fifteen minute taxi ride away they found acceptable seats, ordered a merlot for Michelle and a Carib beer for Robert and then decided on seared tuna for an appetizer.

She asked Robert about his interest in the Tigers. He said he had always wanted to play professional baseball and he couldn't think of a better team than the Tigers. Robert's statistics from the Venezuelan league were impressive but she wondered how he would perform with some very advanced professional players in the American League. "There are probably fifty Venezuelans who have played in the major leagues in the United States. Every one of them started in the Venezuelan league." She realized he had a good point and switched the topic.

"So, if you were to come to the United States to play for the Tigers what sort of starting salary would you need?"

This was always a sticky question. Most players, even those that are less than star potential, will say they are worth millions and will usually ask for millions. They might be worth millions in the future but when they are coming up from the minor leagues, and especially from Class A ball in Florida, they will be hard pressed to make enough money to survive during their first year. Still the answer to this question can tell a scout a lot about the player and his potential.

"Actually, Miss Coburn, I don't have a price in mind. If you would be willing to take a chance on signing me I will accept whatever you think is fair."

Surprised by the answer Michelle told Robert, "That is a very honest answer. If you are signed by the Tigers or anyone else, however, you'll need to get an agent who will negotiate with the team for you so you can get the most money possible. Remember that management wants to get by as cheaply as possible so if you say you'll work for basically nothing they will gladly offer you nothing."

Michelle finished her merlot and ordered another one before their appetizer arrived. These were on top of the glass of merlot she was served on the flight from Caracas. They talked further and during the appetizer Michelle decided that she wanted to forego dinner and instead take in some of the steel drum music. The seared tuna would be more than enough for her.

Her visit to Trinidad was during the second week of the five week steel drum competition. The music was wonderful, the crowds gargantuan, and as they noticed when they entered the competition area, the smell of freshly burned ganja hung heavily in the air. By 11:00 p.m. Michelle had consumed two more glasses of wine and at least twice taken a toke on a joint being passed around the crowd. Not knowing the people around her it was likely quite risky to be smoking other people's joints but the wine had caused a lot of inhibition to melt away.

Eight the next morning came more quickly than she had hoped but at the appointed hour she was sitting on a Tobago Express prop plane ready to hop over to Tobago for the day. Just a twenty minute flight from Port-of-Spain, the island of Tobago is the Caribbean part of the country. Long and sinuous with sugar-like sand covering all of its beaches, Tobago is one of the best kept secrets in the Caribbean.

Her plane lifted off into the crystal blue Trinidadian skies and was quickly climbing over the Northern Range, a series of low hills that are the easternmost extension of the Andes Mountains of mainland South America. Today they are enshrouded in thick tropical rain forest that is home to hundreds of birds. As the prop plane sped northeast it passed over the northeastern point of the island and was then out over the Caribbean Sea. A few minutes later she saw the green water that ringed the island and again thought about that first time she saw green water. Her only wish now was that it had been with someone other than Tim.

Landing at Crown Point International Airport on the southwestern corner of the island, Michelle realized that she had no plans for the day. She didn't know where to go or what to see and had information on where she was. Long ago she developed a sense of wanderlust that had never left her. She wanted to exercise some of that for how ever short a time period it might be while she was here on Tobago. All she knew was that everyone who had been to Trinidad said to go to Tobago so she went.

A small tourist information office tucked away in a corner of the airport provided minimal amounts of information. After all, this was the Caribbean, just how much help could she expect from people hired to help people? She learned that the Tropikist Beach Hotel was just a five minute walk from the airport and for a minimal fee they would allow non-guests to use their facilities for the day. There was a day spa that provided massages, manicures, pedicures, and everything else that goes with being pampered while on vacation, even if it was just a one-day vacation. This sounded perfect because she had only her day pack with her. In it was a rather revealing bikini, a beach towel, a bottle of water and a trashy romance novel. Her plan for the day was to chill on a beach, get a slight buzz, walk back to the airport for her 6:00 p.m. return to Port-of-Spain, and just forget about everything around her and especially married men on airplanes.

Rather than walking, Michelle took a taxi to the Tropikist where she made arrangements as a day-user and was assigned a locker to secure her belongings. Checking into the locker she overheard a story on MSNBC News that was disturbing to her. Late last night a corporate jet leased by the Detroit Tigers baseball team crashed on departure from Detroit's Metro Airport. The flight was bound for Tampa. On board were two front office executives of the baseball team and Stuart Masterson, the Regional manager for Tigers scouts in the southeastern United States. Her boss was on the flight.

Taking her cell phone from its case she called Tigers management in Detroit and asked for the low down on what had happened and what was next. It was too soon after the crash for a definitive answer but the preliminary results pointed to icing. At the time of departure the air temperature was only 35 degrees in Detroit. This was late April but this was also Detroit. A steady mist was falling and the manager of the aircraft leasing company insisted that the plane be de-iced before it left the hangar and also before it took the runway. De-icing occurred at the hangar but at the end of the runway the pilot said that he didn't need to be delayed any further and chose to take the runway

On departure from Detroit the plane was immediately engulfed in thick clouds where the temperature was likely below freezing. Air traffic control lost contact with the plane just four minutes after departure when it was almost to the Monroe County line. A more thorough investigation had just begun now that the National Transportation Safety Board was at the crash scene. The only thing that was certain at this point was that nobody on board survived.

16

Osvaldo Castro stepped over several drunken tourists from Pennsylvania as he walked into the doorway leading up to his office. It was early May, not even the peak of tourist season, but the number of drunks on the streets of Key West was at February levels.

"Christ," he thought, "this is going to be a long summer."

A loud, obnoxious, bray came from the helm of the cruise ship Imagination as it slid into Key West harbour. Enroute from Cancun back to Miami this ship provided cruisers with their first island experience in the "American Caribbean." It didn't matter that most of them were Miami residents who could have driven to Key West faster than they arrived on a ship. The cruise line pimped the idea of Key West as a real "American Caribbean island adventure" and the cruisers ate it up like key lime pie.

Osvaldo could hear the phone ringing as he stumbled up the stairs to his office. He made a mental note to contact the building supervisor and have them try harder to keep the drunks out of his doorway. He had an image to maintain and drunks from Pennsylvania didn't enhance his image.

Camilla Bustamante, Osvaldo's receptionist, was back at her desk after spending six months in the Moore Haven Correctional Facility where she was a guest of the state after having been caught driving with a suspended license. The fact that there was a packet of some white substance in a plastic bag on the driver's seat may have also contributed. Camilla was a devout scientologist and in her mind she would never touch cocaine. She told the judge that but he didn't buy it. Now she was back in her home town with a commitment to stay out of trouble.

Camilla answered the phone when she saw Osvaldo coming to the door. "Square Grouper Imports, this is Camilla. May I help you?"

"Is that miserable cousin of mine in there yet," Arturo Kirkconnel barked into the phone.

"He's coming through the front door right now."

"Put his miserable ass on the phone immediately."

Turning to Osvaldo, she said, "Its Arturo again for you. He doesn't sound really happy this morning." Osvaldo darted into his office and picked up the phone.

"Art, my man; what's happening bro?"

"My name is Arturo you douche bag. Stop with this Art stuff. Do I look like my last name is Linkletter?" Osvaldo's day was not starting off well.

"Ozzie, the amount of profit you are bringing to the organization is the second worst of any of the associates. The owners are starting to worry that you don't have the desire to work for the organization that you used to have."

"No desire? I spend almost every minute of my life working. I'm traveling constantly. I have no home life and barely get the chance to watch a baseball game any longer. What do you mean I have no desire?"

"That is exactly what I just said, Ozzie. You go through the motions of looking busy and trying to make us think you're busy but your balance sheet shows that you are slacking off."

"That is pure mierda, Arturo, and you know it."

Square Grouper Imports once ranked in the top three offices in terms of volume of money brought into the organization. Their business was built on the transshipment from Cuba and Cancun, into south Florida, of authentic Cuban cigars. Its second most lucrative venture was the importation of Huatey beer from Cuba. An occasional ton or two of marijuana enhanced the bottom line and led to the name of the company. Only in Key West could a company be this obvious about its corporate name and not have to worry about anyone asking questions.

Since its inception, the cruise ship Imagination had been a perfect diversion for bringing contraband into the United States. Through some financial arrangements between the organization and the captains of the Imagination, the cruise ship would take on its larder of cigars, beer and marijuana in Cancun. Sailing at sunset for Key West the ship would stop at a predetermined point just west of Dry Tortugas National Park where it would be met by shrimp boats. The shrimpers would off load the contraband on to their boats for their inconspicuous return to Garrison Bight in Key West. In case any cruiser was up at the time of night when the transfer was being made, the crew of the Imagination was instructed to tell people that the ship's water pumps had been damaged and some local fishermen were bringing out fresh water for use until the boat could return to Key West and be fixed.

Once the cigars were unloaded in Key West, local Cubans who long ago worked in the cigar industry would repackage them and put on a label that read "Cohiba Cubana – Almost the Real Thing." The cigars were then marketed as a high end product, almost as good as real Cuban cigars.

Barrels of Huatey beer were transferred to the local Conch Republic microbrew on Stock Island where the beer was transferred to vats and then repackaged as "Cerveza Tropical." It was then marketed as an "authentic Cuban beer made from a pre-Castro recipe to satisfy your tropical thirst." The marijuana was sold to whoever would buy it. There was no need to repackage high grade Mexican herb.

Arturo demanded that Osvaldo pay more attention to detail. "It's this damned economic downturn Art. We keep getting screwed by the economy and the tourists aren't coming to Florida like they used to. Revenues are down and the Cubans in Miami are all expecting Fidel to die and for Raul to be taken out in a coup. They are just biding their time."

"God damn it Osvaldo, I told you to never call me Art. Are you deaf or what?

"I'm sorry my cousin." He hoped Arturo would just forget about it.

For almost seven months Osvaldo had been skimming a small percentage off the profits he was receiving from the activities of Square Grouper Imports. He thought he was being discreet enough that nobody would catch on. Apparently he needed to take some lessons in discretion.

Osvaldo finished his phone call with Arturo and sketched out a plan on his note pad. Until now he had been brutally honest with his cousins and the owners about the volume of contraband that was coming into Key West on the cruise ship. It was brutal honesty that landed him in trouble. As he pondered his options he decided that cooking the books was what he would have to do. Beginning with the next shipment from Cancun arriving on Saturday he was going to report that the volume of product taken in was six percent less than what it had been. He'd make up some excuse for why there was less. Last year the National Hurricane Center in Miami used the excuse of it being an El Nino year to explain why there weren't as many hurricanes as normal. He would have to come up with his own El Nino scenario to blow smoke past the owners.

Osvaldo contemplated the excuse and developed a headache. To counter act it he decided to walk over to Louie's Backyard on Waddell Avenue near the beach. The walk would take him twenty minutes but at least the temperature and humidity weren't yet at July levels. Once at the Backyard he knew that a large drink was just what he needed to quench his headache.

Seated in a corner outside the restaurant, Osvaldo scanned the home page for the Paradise League. The current standings made him forget about his headache already. With 15 games played so far the Sarasota Reds were at the bottom of the league with a record of 3 wins and 12 losses. Next to them on the bottom was the Lakeland Tigers with a record of 4 wins and 11 losses. All the other teams in the Paradise League were doing much better than either the Reds or Tigers. Still there was room for improvement.

Osvaldo took out his iPhone and scrolled through his address book. Finding the contact he needed he sent a cryptic text message that read,

"J – We need to talk soon. You decide if it's your hood or mine. O."

After he hit the send button it dawned on him that there were ways for people to retrieve text messages if there was ever a need.

17

With another baseball game and another baseball stadium under his belt Chris left West Palm Beach and was headed to Fort Myers. There the Sarasota Reds were scheduled to play the Fort Myers Miracle in Hammond Field, the spring training home of the Minnesota Twins. Because he's a native of North Dakota and because his ex-wife Renee moved to Minnesota, Chris had little patience or admiration for Minnesota. Still it was a baseball stadium that he had never visited so he held his nose and left. One game there can't be that bad.

Not far out of Clewiston, as he drove west on Florida highway 70, Chris had given up on ever finding any news on FM radio and switched to AM. There he found WOKC an AM station, and probably the only station, in Glades County. It billed itself as a country music radio station which was reason enough not to listen. Having grown up with that stuff in North Dakota and having heard country western singer croon Chris was less than enthusiastic about hearing any more. As he surfed through the station he heard a news teaser that made him decide to endure the potential for country music just a little while longer.

The night before on massive Lake Okeechobee, Brenda and Bob Brighton, two residents of Hendry County, had been hunting for alligators. This husband and wife team had a permit to take one gator each. Somewhere around 11:00 p.m. they captured and killed one twelve foot gator. Attaching a rope to its nose and another to its tail the couple worked diligently to haul the behemoth into their boat. Eventually successful they took the ropes off only to discover that the dead alligator was very much alive.

Their first mistake was shooting it with a .22 caliber rifle not something larger with more powerful. The second mistake was thinking that shooting it anywhere in its head would be sufficient. The third mistake was thinking it was dead without checking to make sure that it was. All of these thoughts ran through the couples head as the twelve foot long alligator sprang to life and started searching for a way out of the boat.

At first Bob tried to distract the supposedly dead gator by kicking it in the tail. This was after he had tied the gator's tail to the steering wheel of their boat. Instinctively the now-very-much-alive gator lunged at Bob's foot. He jumped over the gator causing the boat to start rocking and grabbed his wife Brenda who stood traumatized by the entire affair. Seeing four legs where there used to be only two the gator's reptilian brain realized there were twice as many targets as before and lunged again. When he lunged at them the boat began to list and Bob and Brenda lost their balance. Brenda yelled at Bob, "shoot the son of a bitch again Bob." The only problem was that the gun was in the stern and by now Bob and Brenda had migrated to the bow. There was little hope of shooting the gator.

Brenda reached in the pocket of her shorts and pulled out the cell phone she forgot had been in there. Opening it she called 911 and told the officer answering that she and her husband were being attacked by an alligator they thought was dead and would someone send help.

"Ma'am, please repeat what you just told me."

"I said my husband and I are being attacked by an alligator we killed and we need your help."

"How can the alligator be attacking you if it's dead?"

"Don't ask stupid questions. We need someone out here to help us now. Oh, God, the damned thing just lunged at Bob again. Bob! Bob! Are you ok honey?"

"Ma'am, there is no need to talk to me like that. Now where are you and I will send some help."

"We are in the middle of Lake Okeechobee."

"Where are you on Okeechobee? It's a very big lake. Where did you put in your boat?"

"We put in at Dave's Boat Landing near Moore Haven. Then we went east along the shore. We're probably three miles from Dave's now."

"Ok, ma'am, I am calling FWC to get their officers out there now. This is a wildlife issue and we only handle human issues."

"That's just fine. I don't care what acronym you call. We just need to get away from this gator. Oh my God he's after us again."

The last thing the 911 operator heard before the phone went dead was the sound of two very large splashes and then there was nothing. Brenda and Bob were now in Lake Okeechobee thinking it was safer there than in the boat. They failed to realize that the lake is full of alligators, many of them larger than the one tethered to their steering wheel in the boat that is now several feet away from them.

"So what do we do now Bob?"

"I say we swim for shore. It's only about a football field away from us."

"Swim to shore? Do you realize there are gators all over this lake? And it is dark out and we can't see a god damned thing? Did you think of that Bob?"

Bob obviously hadn't thought of much of anything. All he remembered was the gator lunging for what Bob was convinced was his crotch. Seeing that mouth full of teeth aimed at the family ancestry he grabbed Brenda and shoved them both overboard.

The alligator, now without any humans to restrict where it goes in the boat, could sense water and started to climb over the gunwale and eventually into the safety of the water. He had a bit of a headache from where the .22 shell had creased his skull but other than that he was none the worse for wear. Once in the water the gator instinctively dove and when it did he began to drag the boat behind him.

Bob and Brenda were trying to get their bearings when suddenly Bob saw the line from his boat moving by him and behind it was the boat. It was being dragged slowly and sideways through the water. "What the hell is our boat doing moving, Bob?"

"Damned if I know Brenda. Seeing that line makes me think the gator is toting it back to shore."

Bob knew he had lashed the fifty feet of line to the gator's tail. The steering wheel was about three feet from the gunwale and he could see about 30 feet of line being tugged in front of him. So, simple math said he was about 17 feet or so from the gator who now thought of himself as a submarine. Brenda, who had always been petrified of alligators, started swimming for the boat and away from the gator. Bob followed her and they both held on to the gunwale as the gator towed them toward shore.

From the west, off near Dave's Boat Landing, they could see the flashing lights of a police boat as it moved quickly toward them. Two large search lights were scanning the water hoping to find Bob and Brenda. Two minutes later the search lights found their boat and one of the duck cops onboard could see Bob and Brenda holding on to the rail.

As the Fish and Wildlife Commission boat pulled alongside Bob and Brenda's gator-powered fishing vessel, wildlife officer Tom Cordorman was in the bow, As a fifth generation south Florida cracker, Tom was as close as you can get to being a Florida native without actually being a Calusa.

"So what happened to you folks?"

Bob yelled, "Our boat is being pulled by a gator. Get us out of here and I'll tell you the story!"

The FWC officer lashed his boat to Bob and Brenda's and then pulled both of them from the murky water. Now that there were two boats lashed together it became almost impossible for the gator to make any forward movement and he surfaced to get some air.

Once they were safely onboard the FWC boat, Bob saw what he thought was the gator surface and turn toward them. Still having a hunting knife in a scabbard on his belt Bob waited for the gator to swim near them then grabbed the line and cut it as close to the gator's tail as he thought was safe.

Free of the gator at last, Bob put his knife back in its scabbard and Cordorman asked him, "So how in hell did you get in the water with a gator toting your boat?"

It was one of those stories that can only happen in south Florida.

18

Chris checked into the Hilton Garden Inn on University Drive in Fort Myers and then left for the game. It was dollar night at Hammond Field and all bratwurst and pretzels and beer were on sale for one dollar. Even admission to the stadium was one dollar. This ensured that the stadium was packed as it usually was every time the price of anything dropped to one dollar.

Chris entered the stadium and sought out his standard seat behind home plate. His arrival was in time to watch some of the Fort Myers team completing their batting practice. One of the players for the Miracle, their shortstop, was Mitchell Spinks. At 6'11" Mitch was the tallest player in professional baseball. Spinks had an impressive history with several records set during college in Louisville. To top it off he was a fifth round draft pick by the Minnesota Twins. Despite his disgust for the Twins, Chris figured that Spinks must be awfully good.

The umpires took the field five minutes before the game was to begin. Once again it was Justin Reed behind the plate but joining him tonight was M.J. Huffington, a 22 year old sports fanatic who had majored in medical technology at the University of South Florida but who secretly wanted to be a professional hockey player someday. It didn't matter that Huffington had never put on a pair of hockey skates. He still had visions of being the next Wayne Gretsky.

Dave Apfel led off for the Reds and reached first base on an error by the Miracle third baseman. Dennis Philomena, now batting second in the lineup, let the count go to two balls and no strikes on two pitches in the dirt that even a crooked umpire would find difficult to call a strike. The third pitch was right down the center of the plate and Dennis, not known for his ability to come through in the clutch, connected with the ball sending it speeding toward the left field fence. Fans jumped to their feet as the ball cleared the fence and the Reds took a 2-0 lead.

Next up was Nefthali Rodriquez the Reds shortstop. After taking a ball on the first pitch, he hit the second pitch solidly to right center field. Rounding first base he was given the go ahead by his first base coach to run for second. As the right fielder picked up the ball Tali already was half way to the base. The right fielder let fly with the ball just as Rodriquez began his slide into second base.

Base umpire M.J. Huffington was standing between second and third base as the throw arrived. From his angle he had a perfect view of the base and any potential throw outs. What Huffington saw was Rodriquez sliding into the base ahead of the throw. He was clearly safe.

"Safe" Huffington bellowed.

Mick Dean, the Miracle manager vaulted out of the dugout like he was shot from a cannon and focused on second base. Sprinting across the infield he was already screaming at Huffington by the time he reached the pitcher's mound.

"What kind of a call was that you idiot?"

"Dean, you need to keep your mouth closed or you will be out of this game before I can throw you out."

"That runner was out and you know it, god damn it."

"He was clearly safe or I wouldn't have made the call."

"That's bullshit and you know it, kid."

"Dean you're walking on thin ice here. One more derogatory comment and your ass is mine and when it is, your ass is out of this stadium."

"I want the home umpire's opinion."

Huffington walked toward home plate and motioned for Justin Reed to come toward second base. Reed saw the play from home plate but from his angle there was no way he could actually see the call because Miracle shortstop Mitch Spinks was blocking his view.

Reed walked to the second base area where Mick Dean was frothing at the mouth and Huffington was holding his own. Dean started, "This runner was out and he called him safe. I saw it clearly and so did the entire audience."

Reed kicked dirt as he listened to the diatribe and finally made a pronouncement. As the home plate umpire he was the arbitrator of final decisions on any matter regarding an active play or a player on the field. The home plate umpire was, in effect, the Supreme Court of baseball.

"From what I saw," Reed began, "That runner was out."

For emphasis Reed jerked his right hand with his thumb extended into the air. Despite photographic evidence taken by a fan on the third base line, the Reds runner was declared out. As Reed returned to his place behind home plate a livid Chris Ramsey bellowed out to him "Hey ump, you blind bastard, you need to go to confession after that call."

In the top of the sixth inning with the score Fort Myers 8 and Sarasota 1, Chris left his seat and migrated out to the concourse to get his last beer of the night. As he stood up he noticed a small group of Reds pitchers sitting directly behind him. One of them had a radar gun while the three others each held a clip board. The clip boards held paper on which there were diagrams of the baseball diamond. By each diamond there were ten boxes for recording the number of strikes and balls each pitcher threw at each batter. There was also a location for the speed of each pitch and the kind of pitch whether it was a fast ball, a curve, a slider or whatever was thrown.

Chris stopped and asked a Reds staffer who was keeping track of these data for every pitch thrown by every pitcher for every batter in every game what he was collecting and why. "Well, sir," he began, "baseball is nothing more than statistics in a uniform. No matter what a player or a coach or a manager does it is recorded and analyzed. Analysis of the data I'm collecting will be used by Reds management to determine the progress of our pitchers and also how efficient our batters are."

"Are you collecting this information just for tonight's game?"

"No, sir, we collect it for each game that the Reds play. Every team in the Paradise League has people in the stands collecting the same data."

"When you collect the data do you keep track also of who the umpires are behind the plate."

"No sir, we have no need for that. But the Paradise League keeps track of every umpire who calls every game in the League. They keep that information in their office in Daytona Beach."

"And what do the Reds do with these data?"

"At the end of every game we enter all the data in a computer and the data are sent to Cincinnati where someone makes sure everything is recorded."

"What happens after that? Who does the analysis?"

"The Reds have a bunch of statisticians who really get into all of these numbers. The stat guys do the analysis, and send daily reports to the shirts in the front office."

"Who would get copies of the reports back here in Sarasota?"

"Tim Blanchard is the assistant general manager for operations of the Sarasota Reds. Everything would come to him."

"And if I wanted to get my hands on the raw data to make my own analyses, who would I speak to?"

"I'd start with Tim. He's a righteous dude. Just feed him some beer and he'll do almost anything for you."

The revelation about the data collection, where and how it's stored and the analysis that the Reds make of it caused a few light bulbs to begin burning brightly in Chris' head. Being a Sarasota Reds fan he thought he had an in to get their data from each game. He wasn't sure how to get the data archived by the Paradise League but he was sure there was a way. This was Florida after all, where anything and everything can be had for a price.

After the game Chris retired to "The Real McCoy" a pub billed as the only "authentic" Irish pub in Fort Myers. The entertainment section of the *Fort Myers News-Press* had written a story on Irish pubs just a couple months ago about the time of St. Patrick's Day. At that time they determined that no fewer than eleven Irish pubs in Fort Myers claimed to be the "only authentic Irish Pub" in Lee County.

Seated at the bar, Amanda Cunningham asked Chris what he wanted for a drink. Normally he would have a Landshark but this being an Irish Pub and an authentic one to boot, he asked for a pint of Caffrey's Irish Ale.

After his third pint of Caffrey's, Chris took out his iPhone to check for emails. There were four new ones and one that had arrived a couple days earlier. He opened Michelle's message and read it again. Wondering aloud what she was up to he decided that it was time to answer her. He debated what to say but eventually settled on keeping it professional. After composing the email to Michelle he edited it before sending the message.

Hi Michelle–

I hope you're having a good time in Trinidad. That island is one of my most favorite islands in the Caribbean. I was wondering if you have been keeping an eye on minor league baseball games this year. There seems to be some sort of incongruity involving the Sarasota Reds and the way their games are being called by the umpiring crews. I would appreciate any insight you might have into this issue. Perhaps we could discuss it at some time in the future should we run onto each other at another Reds game. I look forward to talking with you about it. Again I hope you are having a good time in Trinidad. Chris.

19

Chris had plenty of time to think during his drive north from Fort Myers to Tampa. There seemed to be no doubt that at least Justin Reed was throwing baseball games to make the Sarasota Reds lose games that they might likely win. Still it made no sense at all. What advantage did he get for himself by doing this?

Maybe someone was paying someone to pay Justin to throw games? If that was true then why were they doing that? Who was the money behind this operation and what was there agenda? Was this revenge against the Reds for some reason? Chris didn't think that was possible given their abysmal record over the last couple of years. Then again, maybe there was a player in the Reds background who was cut. Someone who had a Postal Service mentality about things and was determined to return and get back at someone for doing something everyone else had forgotten. Could that be what was driving this?

And what about those data the teams collect for each game? Is there something in them that holds clues? If the data can be analyzed and some patterns shown who would believe them? Would the Paradise League want to admit to having an umpire on the take? If he found substantial evidence and the League blew him off who could he get to rectify this situation? Is this something the Federal Bureau of Investigation should know about? How about the Commissioner of baseball himself?

What about the media? His only hopes were the *Tampa Bay Times* or the *Miami Herald*, the only liberal leaning newspapers left in Florida and the only ones still mesmerized by facts and the truth, not advertising dollars. Then again, if there was a Cuban involved there was no way in hell the *Miami Herald* would touch the story.

As he crossed the Howard Franklin Bridge, Chris checked on Tampa flight arrivals. It appeared that American Airlines 358 from Miami was scheduled to touch down on the tarmac at 4:38 p.m. just a few minutes late. The trip advisor suggested that passengers could be met in the main terminal as early as 4:50 p.m. Chris checked the clock on his iPhone and saw that it was 4:15 p.m. giving him more than enough time to drop his car in the economy lot, catch the shuttle to the main terminal, and be there when Michelle stepped off the train from the E concourse.

What Chris hadn't factored into his arrival equation was the massive demonstration at the airport by a group of pseudo-environmentalists called the "Baby Seal Alliance." The Alliance was demonstrating the eighty eighth annual meeting of the American Association of Fur Buyers and Sellers being held that week at the Embassy Suites Hotel on South Florida Avenue in downtown Tampa. Demonstration organizers knew they had a sure bet to make fools of themselves in front of the news cameras while they were planted outside the convention center. What they decided at the last moment was to give conventioneers an early taste of what lay ahead at the hotel by heckling them at the airport as they got off their planes.

News crews from all the major news gathering organizations had satellite trucks in front of the terminal. Reporters from the *Tampa Tribune*, the *Tampa Bay Times* and even the *Ocala News-Banner* were crowded around the main entrance interviewing passengers and protesters. Airport police officials would later estimate that the thirty protesters had drawn more than one thousand people, 95 of them with the media, to the entrance of the terminal. Anyone wanting to enter or leave the building had a difficult time.

After finally squeezing in the front door, Chris walked by one protester who was dressed like a baby harp seal. The protester sat on his haunches on a large plant pot as he slapped his arms together making noises like you would see in a circus animal. Chris walked by this person and couldn't help but point out the obvious.

"Excuse me," Chris began. "Are you trying to imitate the animals in a circus act?"

"Yup, sure am buddy. I'm a harp seal"

"In that case did you know that the animals in a circus act are California sea lions not seals? The only thing they have in common with a harp seal is that they both smell like dead fish."

"Is that correct?"

"Yes it is and you don't help your cause by being so uninformed."

"Damn I didn't know that." He then promptly went back to making noise like a sea lion.

Another protester ran through the arrivals area and splashed red paint, meant to be seal blood, on the fur coats worn by the wives of two fur company executives. Anthony Leibowitz, CEO and President of the We Skin 'Em You Wear 'Em Fur Company in New York City yelled "You disgusting idiots. What are you doing?"

"We're upset with your wife here for wearing a seal fur coat."

"My wife Ginny is wearing a muskrat fur coat you idiot."

"She is?"

"Yes. Maybe you moron's would be more effective if you knew what you were talking about."

Most environmental groups lose credibility when they deal in emotions instead of facts. The Baby Seal Alliance was one of those groups.

A large clock hung from the wall at the top of the escalator announcing the time as 4:55 p.m. If the American Airlines arrival information was correct Michelle should have landed seventeen minutes ago. And if his calculation was correct she should be about ready to get off the train in the main terminal.

Because of the ruckus caused by the fur protesters, people had been slow to get on the escalator until now when everyone was rushing to get up to the departure level. The escalator was packed solid as Chris made his way to the first steps and saw there was no way he could make it past people to get to the top any more quickly.

As the escalator was about to reach the top of its run, Chris looked to his left and saw Michelle standing next to some man as they both rode the escalator down to the baggage level. Luckily for them they wouldn't have to put up with the nitwits from the Baby Seal Alliance just below them.

Michelle was talking and laughing with a man standing on her right when Chris saw her. At least he thought he saw her.

She was wearing the same white slacks and pink top he saw her in at the ball game in Sarasota. That looked familiar.

The down escalator was packed and Chris didn't want to make it too obvious that he might actually be at the airport to meet her so instead of taking the steps to try to keep up with her he simply walked toward the trains carrying passengers to their departure gates. He looked down the escalator at her wondering about the guy who was making her laugh so much. He wasn't certain, but he thought he saw Michelle looking up the escalator toward him as she descended.

What Chris didn't know at the time was that the man standing with Michelle on the escalator was Gary Lightner, a fellow employee of the Detroit Tigers who is gay.

20

The Yankees game had just begun when Chris pulled into the parking lot of George Steinbrenner stadium. He walked by the official team store and stopped in to purchase a Tampa Yankees baseball cap. This was another objective of the summer of baseball in Florida. Not only was Chris planning to watch all twelve Paradise League teams play in their eleven stadiums, he was also going to purchase a baseball cap for each team. A woman he once went out with told him that any woman worth her salt wanted a man with a great collection of baseball caps. Chris put this on his priority list.

Behind the counter in the team store was a snotty woman who probably failed every customer service class she ever took. Chris said, "I would like to get a baseball cap that is exactly like the ones that the players wear."

"If you want Yankees caps they're all over there, " she said as she pointed to her left.

"No. I would like to get an official Tampa Yankees hat. One that looks exactly like the one's that the players will wear on the field tonight."

"Well the Tampa Yankees stuff is over there you putz "she said pointing behind Chris. "If you wanted minor league stuff why didn't you say so?"

There was a large selection of Tampa Yankees caps to choose from. Some were solid blue and others were white with pinstripes like the real Yankees have on their uniforms. Others had multiple colors that reminded Chris of a trip he took on LSD once as an undergraduate. Still others were in camouflage to cater to the redneck fringe that occasionally comes to a Yankees game.

Tonight's game was between the Tampa Yankees and the Lakeland Tigers. Calling balls and strikes was Roger Schultz, a ten year veteran of the Paradise League. Working the bases with Roger was Douglas Clements. Originally from a little college town in Wisconsin, Doug was 57 years old and had migrated to Florida to get away from the harsh winters at a more northerly latitude. Doug had invested heavily in some dot com startup companies in the early 1990s and had enough sense and the right financial advisor to sell his stock just before the dot com crash of the late 1990s. Doug made millions off his investment and once the money was safely locked away in several offshore accounts in the Cayman Islands, he moved to Florida where he was intent on becoming a beach bum.

Chris was able to get a seat in the first row behind home plate. It wasn't his preferred location but what could he do with his late arrival? After six and a half hard fought innings the Yankees were beating the Tigers 9-4. Chris noticed that Schultz seemed to have a penchant for calling some obvious balls strikes against the Tigers and for calling obvious strikes as balls against the Yankees. He wondered if the same thing was happening to the Tigers.

During the traditional seventh inning stretch, Chris stood up and looked around the stadium. Perhaps 1,000 fans were in attendance tonight including a large vocal contingent from Lakeland just one hour away. As he looked back toward the press box that sits behind home plate he saw several Yankees staff and Tigers staff sitting near each other recording data on the number and kinds of pitches thrown by each pitcher, their speed, and also the box score for the game.

Chris walked up several rows of steps to the Lakeland Tigers data recorders. One kid, Elliott Weiser whom everyone just called "Bud" sat near the aisle recording information on a data sheet and then between innings transferring the data to his lap top. The data sat in the Tigers management office in Lakeland just microseconds after Bud entered it in his lap top.

"Are you collecting data on balls and strikes," Chris asked.

"Yes, sir, I am. Who wants to know?"

"My name is Chris Ramsey. I am retired and live in Sarasota and I'm just spending the season driving around the state watching minor league games."

"Must be nice being retired, huh?"

"It has its advantages. Now what's your name?"

"I'm Bud Weiser."

"Sure you are and I'm Prince Charles. Now what's your name?"

"My name is Elliott Weiser but all my friends call me Bud. I have no idea why they do that," he said as his eyes rolled in his head.

"Well, Bud, maybe you can help me. I'm doing some research on the frequency of certain pitches and their speeds that are thrown by minor league baseball players. I'm also doing research on how often certain umpires call certain pitches against the various teams in the Paradise League. I wonder if it would be possible to get the data that you guys collect so I can use it in my research."

"I doubt that, sir. This is proprietary information. If I gave you the data who is to say you wouldn't sell it to the Yankees?"

"Bud, did you happen to notice those Yankees pitchers sitting over there collecting the same information on your batters and pitchers that you're collecting on theirs?"

Bud, never a really bright bulb on the Christmas tree, realized he was wrong. "Well, sir, I can't give you the data. Only Stuart Masterson our regional manager can give you that information.   Unfortunately Mr. Masterson died in a plane crash in Detroit a couple days ago."

Chris remembered reading about Masterson's death in the online version of the *New York Times*. He then asked Bud who would be the next person in line to ask for the data.

"I'm not really sure. There's this fox named Michelle Coburn who is the chief scout for the Tigers. Her office is at our stadium in Lakeland. You can stop by there and talk to her."

Now he at least knew her last name.

"Thanks, Bud, but I don't have any plans to head over to Lakeland any time soon. I live in Sarasota. Any chance you have this Coburn woman's phone number?

Bud checked the address book in his computer and found the listing for Michelle Coburn. He then gave Chris her office number.   "Her office number is 863-555-2868." Give her a call and ask her."

"Thanks Bud. I owe you one."

"At least you didn't say 'this one's for you' like half the damned country does."

The game ended with the Yankees trouncing the Tigers 15-4. They scored six runs in the bottom of the eighth inning even after their coach had pulled most of the regular players and let the second string players have a chance for an inning. The thorough drubbing handed to the Tigers by the Yankees was another example of how efficient the Yankees are at winning games.

Reflecting on the game it seemed to Chris that it was likely thrown also. Were the Yankees behind this? They had enough money to buy almost anyone including the umpires but this seemed to be not about the Yankees so much as about the Tigers. And why the Tigers?

Chris checked into the Hilton Garden Inn by the Tampa airport. Once in his room he turned on his lap top and pulled up his email. Two emails were from an old colleague Mike Czarnecki from Michigan. He met Mike long ago in northern Michigan when Chris was a graduate student and needed a permit to collect common loons for a research project he was completing. Two more of the emails were from friends in Sarasota wondering when he was going to be returning to town and one was from his oldest daughter now living in Alaska. She sent pictures of her holding the first salmon she'd ever caught. Another picture was of a grizzly bear she found snooping around her tent one morning when she was camped in the Chugach Mountains near Anchorage.

There was nothing from Michelle.

21

Osvaldo's contact in the Paradise League kept him informed on which umpire was calling which game. On any given day Osvaldo knew where Reed, Hastert and Schultz were, what team they were umpiring, and what hotels they stayed in. It was always a benefit to have sources.

Knowing that Justin Reed was going to be in Fort Myers for a couple days Osvaldo decided that an impromptu visit was in order. The tongue lashing he received from his cousin Arturo was more of a wakeup call than anything else. He knew he needed to chat with the boy, get him settled down and focused and most importantly get him to stop being so god-damned obvious.

Conch Republic International Airport in Key West was packed when Osvaldo arrived. He never ceased to be amazed by the city fathers of Key West calling their airport international when there were no international flights arriving there. The line for Air Conch Republic was only half as long as American Airlines and Delta. Delta had just begun nonstop service from Atlanta using a larger commuter plane than the other airlines were using so more people were waiting for the already packed Delta flights.

This morning's flight to Fort Myers was on a nineteen passenger Beechcraft 1900 propeller jet. It was relatively roomy and you could certainly stand up in it, as long as you were less than six feet tall. At six foot one Osvaldo had to squat a little to keep his head from creasing the ceiling.

As he sat in the departure area waiting for the gate agent to call him to his flight, Osvaldo opened today's issue of the *Key West Citizen* one of three or four newspapers that each try to make some sense out of the insanity of the Keys. Time in Key West had taught Osvaldo that the most entertaining portion of the newspaper was the crime report where it seemed every wacko in Key West and some who weren't so wacko eventually winds up. Like today's edition where one news blurb was titled, simply, *"Shots Fired."*

Written by reporter Gretchen Dueholm, the story recounted a report from last night. The Key West Police Department received a phone call about 8:00 p.m. and officers were dispatched to a domestic disturbance. On their arrival at a Thomas Street address, not far from the Blue Haven restaurant, officers were confronted by Brian Benoit who was visibly upset because his wife Carolyn Benoit had opened fire on his belt.

Confused by what they had been told, the officers discovered that Brian had recently lost considerable weight and his clothing no longer fit him well. No matter which pair of pants he put on they were too large and he had to cinch up his belt. The only problem was that he needed more holes in his belt than were currently there. Carolyn, not known for being very logical, took out the couple's .22 caliber pistol and began shooting holes in the belt to make it more usable.

Reached for comment by the *Key West Citizen*, Mr. Benoit told the reporter, "That crazy bitch opened fire on my belt for Christ's sake. She was going to shoot holes in it with me wearing the belt but I convinced her to stop."

When asked by the reporter why his wife didn't use a knife or a screw driver to make the holes, Benoit's only response was "You need to ask her. I don't have a clue what was going through her head." Key West Police Department spokesperson Melinda Anderson told the *Citizen* that detectives were still investigating and as of press time there had been no charges filed.

Osvaldo finished reading the story and couldn't stop chuckling. It was just another in a daily barrage of stories that seem to only happen in south Florida. As he folded the newspaper, Air Conch Republic announced that their flight number 9583 to Fort Myers was ready to board.

Maybe fifteen minutes after departure the plane entered the boundaries of the Ten Thousand Islands National Wildlife Refuge near Marco Island. At first they passed over Cape Romano with its wicked currents and excellent fishing. Beyond it were the back country channels of Kice Island and Dickman's Island and Curry's Island. The land below them looked like a wilderness just like they had left behind near Key West. Yet as soon as the wilderness looked endless they passed over Marco Island and its pretentious, endless, gaudy and disgusting development. If ever there was a place in Florida in desperate need of a massive destructive hurricane it was Marco Island.

Beyond Marco they passed over Naples and then began their approach to Fort Myers. Had he driven to Fort Myers it would have taken Osvaldo at least five hours and probably two speeding tickets. Flying it took him 28 minutes.

Justin Reed would be staying at the Econo Lodge, Fort Myers Airport just a few miles from the terminal. There he would be sharing a room with Dennis Hastert Jr. Osvaldo picked up his rental car from Avis, declined the prepaid gas option, and followed the Daniels Parkway under I-75 and turned left into the parking lot for the Econo Lodge. Neither Reed or Hastert were expecting Osvaldo this morning. His arrival about 10:00 a.m. was probably going to be met with an unanswered door. If these two were like most of the other umpires in the Paradise League they had found a bar near the baseball stadium after last night's game and then proceeded to drink it dry of adult beverages.

If they had consumed vast quantities of alcohol like Osvaldo suspected then both Reed and Hastert were likely both in the nearby Denny's right now eating eggs and drinking coffee and trying to look a bit sober before they dressed for tonight's game. It was always a gamble with those two.

Osvaldo checked at the front desk and asked for the room shared by Reed and Hastert.

"Sir, I can't give you that information," the transplanted East Indian said in his Hindu-English lilt.

"Can't give me the information? Why can't you give me the information? Those boys work for me and I need to get in touch with them."

"Sir, I can call them for you to see if they are in their room but I cannot give you their room number. It's for security purposes."

"I thought they only used that excuse at the airport to scare people."

"No, sir, we use that at the hotel also. I mean. No sir, we are only concerned about the security of our clients."

"I'm concerned about them also. That's why I came here to talk with them. Now, will you call them for me and tell them that their boss is here in the lobby and wants to talk with them."

"Certainly sir, it will be my utmost pleasure to do so, sir."

The desk clerk punched in their room number and after four rings someone finally answered.

"Good morning sir. Your boss is here at the front desk and wants to speak to you. Would you please present yourself at the front desk, please?"

"Yes sir, he said he is your boss."

Looking at Osvaldo he asked, "Your name sir?"

"Tell either of them that it's Ozzie, that we need to talk, and we need to talk now."

"Sir, your boss said his name is Ozzie and he needs to talk with you precisely. Ah, thank you sir."

Looking at Osvaldo, "Sir, they will be here precisely."

"Thank you for your efforts."

Twenty minutes later two very bedraggled men showed up at the front desk both of them looking like they had fought with a Mack truck and lost the battle. Reed spoke first. "Ozzie, how the hell are you? What are you doing up here and so early in the morning?"

"Listen you morons we need to talk and we need to do it now. I didn't want to email you or text message you because I didn't want there to be any records of what was said." Osvaldo added, "So have you idiots had breakfast yet?"

"No, we just got out of bed," Justin said.

"Well grab your stuff and meet me down the road at Denny's. You need some food in you to sober up and I need some answers. I have a 1:00 p.m. flight back to Key West so I don't have time to waste."

Fifteen minutes later they sat at a large circular table in the far corner of the Denny's on Six Mile Cypress Avenue near the ball park. Osvaldo paid the hostess to keep other patrons away from where they were sitting.

"First of all," Osvaldo began, "you two are doing a good job. There is just one problem. You're doing your job too good."

"What do you mean we're doing it too good," Justin asked.

"I mean just that. You are making the Reds lose and you are helping the Tigers be next to the bottom but you're way too obvious."

"Obvious? How are we being obvious?

"The fact that you have to ask tells me this is going to be a long conversation."

Osvaldo continued, "to begin, even a blind person can see when you are calling pitches in the middle of the batter's box a strike. It doesn't take a rocket scientist for Christ's sake. Then there are the plays at the plate. Someone slides into home a couple seconds before the catcher even catches the god damned ball and you're calling them out if they are with the Reds and safe if they are with someone else. How god damned stupid do you think people are?"

Reed responded saying, "Look, Ozzie, I was approached by those people from Miami and asked to do what I could to throw games so the Reds and the Tigers lose. We have been paid $900 a game by those crazy bastards to do just that. If they want us throwing games and want to pay us that sort of money, then we sure as hell are going to throw games."

"Well," Osvaldo said, "the people in Miami called me yesterday and they are mad as hell because you two are being so god damned obvious. I told them I would have a talk with you and fix this. That's why I'm here in lovely Fort Myers this morning looking at all this god damned construction all over the place instead of down on Duval Street watching tourists puke in the intersections."

"Just so you know," Osvaldo continued, "the people in Miami are willing to take the money away from you and give it to someone else if you don't want to follow orders."

22

Michelle gave Gary a ride to Lakeland and then returned to her house near Joker Marchant Stadium. On their way from the Tampa airport Michelle tried to rationalize the meaning of Stu Masterson's death and more importantly what it meant to her future as a scout. Gary said the rumor mill was filled with possibilities but the foregone conclusion was that Dennis Jensen the regional manager in Charlotte was going to get the job.

"If that creep gets the job then I'm quitting," Michelle said. "I don't care how much I love baseball I will not work for a man whose eyes remind me of a lizard."

Dennis Jensen was a tall, skinny, redheaded man who reminded many of his acquaintances of Ichabod Crane. At least his acquaintances who read literature that is. At 6'3" and 160 pounds Jensen was anything but attractive. His face was splotched with freckles and his lips thin were usually chapped even in the heat and humidity of Charlotte, North Carolina. The clothes he wore were usually unkempt and he seemed to imitate the Europeans because of an apparent disdain for showers and to top it off Jensen still wore white socks with his suits. He clearly had some social issues he needed to address.

Tiger management kept him in his position in Charlotte because of his managerial skills. When it came to budgeting or to personnel issues there simply was nobody better than Jensen. Upper management could put up with reptilian eyes and body odor if that meant keeping the troops in line and office expenses under control. Michelle gave it more thought and again said to Gary, "If he gets it then I'm gone. I hear that it's cheap to live in Nicaragua."

Arriving home Michelle unpacked her suitcases, put away her many pairs of shoes, and sat down with her mail. With the explosion of electronic everything she received almost all of her bills electronically. She sometimes wondered why the country even maintained a Postal Service any more. Still there was a stack of fliers from Dillard's and Macy's and even one from J.C. Penny, each of them announcing the latest sale where everything was for Michelle percent off. She often pondered the abundance of sales and wondered about their legitimacy. Wouldn't it be possible for some company to just say they were putting everything on sale for X percent off? How could you know unless you were there and saw them changing the price on every item that the price tag you saw on sale day was really X percent less than it had been the day before?

Completing her mail, she opened a bottle of malbec that had been sitting in her wine holder for several months. Once the wine was properly aired she poured herself a glass. She then opened her lap top to check for email.

It never ceased to amaze her how quickly email accumulates. She last checked her account at about 3:00 that afternoon just before boarding the flight to Tampa from Miami. Concluding her flight and then driving home ate up another three hours and now here she was at 9:00 p.m. with thirty more emails. Where do these things come from? She had them arranged by when they arrived with the most recent arrivals first. They were then stacked in chronological order with the first email received was at the bottom of the queue.

Her first seven emails were Tigers-related issues including another one from her administrative assistant reminding her to turn in her travel expenses. "Christ," she thought, "Kristi is getting as bad as my mother was at watching over every move I make."

These were followed by two emails announcing upcoming concerts at the arena in Orlando, and the next one was another offer for an elixir to increase her penis size. It was relegated to the spam file like all the others had been. Next was an online statement from American Airlines' frequent flier program detailing her most recent activity and giving her an update on the number of miles in her account. She scanned the flights and saw that her Tampa to Miami and her Miami to Caracas segments had been credited. So too was her segment this morning from Port-of-Spain to Miami but the Miami to Tampa segment was too recent to be posted. With her Chairman's Executive mileage bonus on these segments her balance was slightly more than two million miles.

"I need to stop working so damned hard and start burning up these miles," she said to herself.

Checking the American Airlines partner awards chart she learned that with one million miles she could make six round trips in First Class to the South Pacific. She needed to start traveling for fun. Then she thought that those six roundtrips could also be used for three roundtrips in First Class if she took someone with her. She had never joined the Mile High Club and First Class on a 767 would be the perfect place to try.

Scrolling through the rest of the emails she came to the last one. In the column that read "From" all she saw was

"Heckler." She wondered who that was and more importantly why her spam filter hadn't caught the message. It read:

Hi Michelle–

I hope you're having a good time in Trinidad. That island is one of my most favorite islands in the Caribbean. I was wondering if you have been keeping an eye on minor league baseball games this year. There seems to be some sort of incongruity involving the Sarasota Reds and the way their games are being called by the umpiring crews. I would appreciate any insight you might have into this issue. Perhaps we could discuss it at some time in the future should we run onto each other at another Reds game. I look forward to talking with you about it. Again I hope you are having a good time in Trinidad. Chris.

She wondered why it took until now for the message to arrive. He had sent it more than 36 hours ago so why was it showing up now? And why was he so damned formal? Maybe he was just being cautious? Regardless she read his message carefully.

Thinking about the subject of his message she recalled hearing some comments somewhere in baseball about some lousy umpiring in the Paradise League. She blew it off as just the complaints of upset batters because it is a tradition in baseball to complain about the umpires. What would be the fun of baseball if there wasn't someone to complain about?

She hit reply and sent Chris a message.

Hey Chris.

It was good to hear from you. My time in Trinidad wasn't so great because of the death of a colleague but I had a blast on my one day on Tobago.

As I thought about the request in your email I remembered a couple of things from last season affecting the Lakeland Tigers that might fit what you are trying to figure out. I'm not sure if it's useful to you or not. Ever the researcher I'm sure you'll get to the bottom of it somehow. LOL.

So, how about having that lunch I suggested? We could talk about this issue you've raised and maybe get caught up on each other's lives a bit. That or how about a Tampa Bay Rays against the Boston Red Sox game on Tuesday night in Tampa? I will get the tickets if you buy my wine.

My phone number is 863-555-3865.

Looking forward to hearing from you. M

A few seconds later a Jimmy Buffett ring tone chimed out on Chris' iPhone announcing that he had a new email. He read Michelle's response and filed it away thinking, "maybe I'll call her Monday night."

23

Eduardo Sanchez was a buscone. He made his living by scouring Latin America looking for exceptional talent that he could sign for major league baseball in the United States. Most of his time was spent in the Dominican Republic where there was no shortage of good baseball talent. He had also occasionally traveled to Puerto Rico but that was out of necessity and now that the FBI was on his case he never went there even to switch planes.

His newest adventure involved Cuban baseball players. Since the Cuban missile crisis in 1962 Americans had been severely restricted from traveling to or in Cuba and conversely Cubans had been restricted from travel to the United States. It was one of the biggest most destructive cat and mouse games in the world. And the only people harmed by this idiocy were the people the policies were alleged to protect.

Reviewing the easing of restrictions as they were spelled out in an article in the *Miami Herald*, Eduardo realized that it was now likely going to be even simpler for him to sign Cuban baseball players, and get them visas from their government that would allow them to travel to the Dominican Republic for baseball games. There he would allow a select few Cubans, only those with the greatest potential to make it to the major leagues, to be processed by contacts in Santo Domingo who would provide the Cubans with Dominican passports. They would appear at the United States embassy claiming Dominican citizenship, they would go through the interview process and eventually they would be granted a visa that would allow them to travel to the United States to play baseball.

Eduardo's plan, although somewhat grandiose, was well grounded. As a business man he knew the risks involved. Most of the risks however involved the Cuban players because it was their neck on the line not his. Eduardo always figured that if the heat became too great he could slip out on any flight to Venezuela or Colombia and he would simply disappear into the masses. Through some shrewd investments and an earlier, lucrative, career in certain imports, Eduardo had a sizeable sum of money stashed in offshore accounts in the Bahamas Islands and in the Cayman Islands. If push came to shove he just needed to start drawing down from those accounts and he could live comfortably. Right now, however, he didn't need to worry. Right now he was on the verge of making some substantial money off the players he was preparing for the major leagues in the United States.

The word "buscone" means "searcher" in Spanish. A buscone was more than a scout but less than an agent. It was the job of the buscone to find talent, sign the talent to play with a major league team in the United States, collect his commission on the signing bonus, forget about the player and move on to the next one. Eduardo's success so far had been quite good. He would arrange the signing of good players who qualified for $75,000 to $100,000 signing bonuses. To take them into his trust, Eduardo would tell the players that his fee was just ten percent of the bonus. Most Cuban players had no concept of how much $75,000 to $100,000 was. For many it was ten times the amount of money they would make in a life time.

What Eduardo failed to mention to the players was that despite him saying his fee was ten percent, if they had thought to read the fine print of the contracts he had drawn up many times he was receiving ninety percent of the signing bonus. Suddenly what should have been a $7,500 to $10,000 payment to Eduardo became $60,000 to $90,000.

Once the players were burned by Eduardo's shady dealings they were less than excited about creating waves over being cheated. After all they were out of Cuba and living in a place where there was an abundance of food in the grocery stores, where there was a feeling of freedom, where they could watch anything they wanted on television or listen to anything they wanted on the radio. To the Cubans it was worth it just to get out of that mess they left behind back home. The Cuban players were more than willing to bite the bullet just to not have to go back. Yonder Martinez, a first base sensation from the Isla de Juventud said that once he found out how badly Eduardo had screwed him over, he would rather eat grits from a garbage bin in south Miami than grits from a garbage bin in Havana because at least in Miami there were some grits to eat.

When Eduardo wasn't bilking players out of a percentage of their hard earned signing bonuses he was turning them on to performance enhancing drugs. Obtaining them in Cuba was quite difficult as was any drug that could be considered illegal elsewhere. However once he got a player into the Dominican Republic it was much easier to get drugs to them that would convert a 6'2" 190 pound kid into a 240 pound mass of muscle in just a matter of months. And each time a kid put on a few more pounds of beef on his chest or his biceps the likelihood of them making it to the major leagues increased.

Eduardo had other, bigger, fish in the skillet that he also wanted to fry. Principal among them was working on players to sign him as their agent once so he had access to a percentage of their annual salary once they were in the majors. If he could get someone signed for $3,000,000 a year and take even a twenty percent cut of that action, he could clear $600,000 for his efforts. Make that happen for several Cuban or Dominican kids and soon Eduardo would be retiring to the Costa del Sol in Spain where nobody would ever think to look for him.

At least that had been Eduardo's plan until the nosey owner of the Cincinnati Reds discovered his scam and threatened to expose him to the entire major league baseball organization. Apparently one night at a get together with the management of the Reds one of the Dominican players, with one or two too many vodka tonics in his system, blurted out something about his buscone ripping him off for nearly fifty percent of his signing bonus. The buscone had told the Dominican that he would take ten percent but wound up with fifty percent. Checking with an attorney he learned that taking fifty percent of his bonus was legal and justified according to the terms of his contract he had signed.

"He screwed me and I didn't even get to smile. What else can I say," the Dominican player said to the Reds owner. Looking into the matter further, Reds management asked for the FBI to become involved. Because the reach of the FBI extends to Puerto Rico, the buscone had to curtail his activities there. Yet the Dominican market was still lucrative. One Dominican pitcher had recently signed with a $4.25 million bonus. They weren't talking chump change.

Because of the involvement of the FBI Eduardo didn't dare step back in the United States any time soon. And it was all because of that loudmouthed owner of the Reds. Maybe if he had paid her off a little she would have kept her nose out of it. Now, however, it was too late because the toothpaste was out of the tube. Eduardo seethed with anger because of what the Reds had done to him.

Although the market for Dominican players was huge and a good buscone could make buckets of money with little effort, the potential now for Cuban players was even greater and probably more lucrative. The Cuban baseball program was one of the best in the world outside of the United States and Japan. With silver medals at the 2000 and 2008 Olympics and gold medals in 1992, 1996 and 2004, it was clear that Cuba was a force to be reckoned with.

Some of the more pragmatic observers of baseball had argued for years that the only way for an American baseball team to really call themselves the "World Champions" at the end of the World Series is for it to actually be a world series including at a minimum teams from Colombia, Cuba, Japan, Mexico, Nicaragua, Venezuela, and the Dominican Republic. Those same people were probably concerned that with the quality of players out there they wouldn't be able to buy enough talent to beat the Cubans. Then what a political fiasco it would be for the Guantanamo Baywatchers or the Havana Daydreamers to carry the banner of World Champion.

The fact that Cubans were so good and had no easy avenue to follow to secure a place in American baseball was just the angle that Eduardo needed. And if he made it lucrative enough, and paid off the right people not only would he be a rich man but he could screw the Cincinnati Reds organization in the process. The thought of that caused a huge smile to cross Eduardo's face. All he needed was some people in the

United States who could handle a few details for him. There seemed to be no shortage of pissed off Cubans in Miami who might want to help.

Once his plan was underway, Cincinnati Reds management would be wishing they had never called the FBI.

24

The Sarasota Reds left Fort Myers and returned home for a seven game series. The first three games were against the Tampa Yankees who, naturally, were the best team in the league. As in the majors and in both Class AAA and Class AA ball, the Yankees were always the best. It was a testament to what buying talent can provide.

Justin Reed and Dennis Hastert Jr. had been selected to umpire the first games against Tampa and as usual Reed was behind home plate. Despite the Reds abysmal season record so far they were able to beat the Yankees by 10-1, 10-3 and 10-0. The Reds supporter who had offered to provide free pizza to any holder of a Reds ticket after a game in which they scored a minimum of seven runs immediately withdrew its offer. The vendor, Slippery Dick's Halfway Inn Pizza had nothing to worry about for the first six years of the promotion because the Reds never once scored seven runs in a game. The promotion gave Slippery Dick a lot of advertising but he never had to pay up.

Now with three consecutive 10 run games at home Slippery Dick found himself giving away more than 400 pizzas a night. It was severely eating into his profit margin. He called Reds management after the third game and asked to be removed from the promotions. "I never had any clue that those lousy bastards could score three runs in a game let alone seven runs. Now they did it three nights in a row and I lost more than $11,000 giving away all those god damned pizzas. I'm through." Slippery Dick was not a happy man.

Chris sat behind home plate and watched every pitch of the Monday night game. Other than the Reds actually scoring runs he saw nothing out of the ordinary. Reed seemed to be calling balls and strikes fairly. Nobody was called out at home when they were obviously safe. Runners caught stealing bases were called out and those obviously safe were called safe. It was like an entirely new team that was wearing red and white on the field.

During the seventh inning stretch with the score Reds 10 and Yankees 0, Chris took out his iPhone and contemplated calling Michelle. As he thought about it he felt like he was a teenager again calling a girl for their first date. Fortified by a couple of glasses of what was passed off as beer brewed by Anhauser-Busch, Chris hit the call button for her number and waited. After four rings her voice mail picked up.

Hi. This is Michelle Coburn. I can't come to phone right now so please leave me a message and your phone number and I'll call you back as soon as possible. Thanks and have a nice day.

After the beep Chris left her this message.

Hi. This is Chris. It's about 9:15 on Monday night. I'm watching the Sarasota Reds beat the Tampa Yankees. I never thought it would happen. The score right now is Sarasota 10 and Tampa 0 and we're in the seventh inning stretch.

You mentioned in your email going to a Tampa Bay Rays game tomorrow night. I would enjoy doing that if the offer still stands. If you would still like to do that give me a call and we can make arrangements about where to meet and when. You have my number. I'll wait for your call. Hope to hear from you.

He ended the call and wondered if he had done the right thing. Then he let reality sink in. For all he knew she has six guys she is going out with regularly and finding time to squeeze Chris in might be a huge challenge for her. Still, Michelle is the one who initiated contact after 35 years. Chris was the one who should be taking the upper hand not groveling around like a seventh grader asking some girl to send a note to Peggy Sue to find out if she likes him.

After nine innings the Reds had beaten the Yankees 14-1. The Yankees scored a run in the top of the ninth inning but that was the closest they came to a threat. It seemed like it was over before it began and the Reds had only their fourth win of the season. Several people in the stands had overheard Reds players saying they were going to the White Horse Pub to celebrate their victory over the Yankees if only they could hold on to the lead. Now that they not only held on to it but prevailed, it seemed that the pub on was going to be inundated with thirsty fans.

Although it was nearly 10:30 p.m. when the crowd started to shuffle in, Chris had still not had dinner. Sliding into his normal seat at the end of the bar, he ordered a spinach and pecan salad. He ate a spinach salad to show his health consciousness and washed it down with two pints of Landshark Lager to counteract his health consciousness.

Working behind the bar tonight was Shay Watson, a pretty half Filipina with big brown eyes. Unfortunately for all the males in the bar Shay was a lesbian. Most of the men there, including Chris on a couple of drunken occasions, had tried to convince Shay that they, too, were lesbian. Chris distinctly remembered telling her that after watching a porn movie he was convinced he was lesbian because "there was nothing those two women did to each other that I wouldn't do to them either." Shay never bought the argument and unfortunately never would.

His cell phone rang just as the salad arrived. Chris looked at the screen and saw that the call was from area code 863. That's a Lakeland number. Assuming who was on the other end he quickly picked up the phone.

"Hello, this is Chris."

"Chris. It's Michelle."

Long pause.

"How are you?"

"Great, Chris. And you?"

"I'd be twins if I was any better." Laughter.

"So Michelle where are you now?"

"Right now I'm sequestered in my office in Joker Marchant Stadium in beautiful downtown Lakeland. What about you?"

"I'm sitting in the White Horse in Sarasota eating a spinach salad and washing it down with a beer."

"You're only having one beer?"

"Well at the moment, yes." She was being playful. That's interesting.

"Chris, I'm sorry that we couldn't talk more when I saw you at the game. It was kind of a shock to see you there and sit next to you after 35 years with no contact."

"I know. It sort of blew me away too."

"What's this thing about the umpires, Chris?"

"I've been noticing some strange stuff going on at Reds games."

"I've heard a few things about the Lakeland Tigers also. What's up with that?"

"I'm not sure but this evening the Reds beat the hell out of the Yankees and I didn't see one call or one pitch that looked wrong."

"What are you going to do about this? If there are people throwing games then it could jeopardize all of the Paradise League and all its players, not just the Reds or maybe the Tigers."

"I have some friends in the Reds who are supplying me with their data on strikes and balls called against the Reds."

"What do you do with the data?

"I have an old colleague from when I was at the Northern Prairie Wildlife Research Center back home in North Dakota. Doug is probably the finest statistician in the Federal government and certainly the best one I worked with in my career. I'm going to talk with Doug about doing some statistical analysis of the data. If there is anything that is out of the ordinary, Doug Stauffer will be able to figure it out."

"That sounds way too scientific to me, Chris."

"It's statistical, not scientific."

"You've always been so damned anal, Chris!"

"Anal? I'm just being thorough. You know a few years ago my oldest daughter gave me a shirt for Christmas that had written on it 'Does anal retentive have a hyphen?'

"How old is your oldest daughter? How many children do you have?"

"Rather than talk about this on the phone let's talk at the game tomorrow night. I'll meet you at the gate 6 entrance at 6:00 p.m."

"OK. I'll have the tickets and I'll see you there."

When Tracy Goodwin arrived in Sarasota earlier that evening she took the University Parkway exit west toward the airport and checked into the Hyatt. She then followed Desoto Road to Tuttle Avenue and turned south to 12th street and Ed Smith Stadium. She purchased a ticket from Marco the crazed Italian and took her seat on the first base side near the Reds dugout. She saw Chris in his usual seat behind home plate but chose not to talk with him there. Instead she planned to follow him from the stadium and hopefully find him in a bar.

Sarasota Reds fans in the stadium began talking about going to the White Horse Pub after the game because they knew that the players would be there. The owners of the pub didn't realize it at the time but by making their bar the "official" bar of the team and giving the players substantial discounts on food and beer, they were making more money than they ever thought they would lose. The old adage about having to spend money to make money was proving true.

The bar was packed with fans and players and Chris had just finished his salad and second pint of Landshark Lager when Tracy walked in the door and while pointing at Chris said "I'll have a bottle of whatever that old guy is drinking." She said it loud enough for Chris to hear. She then walked over to where he was seated.

"Who in hell are you calling an old guy?"

"You are the old guy."

"So what are you doing in Sarasota? And where is your husband?"

"I'm in Sarasota because you're in Sarasota. I told the pizza delivery boy that I had a meeting but didn't tell him where. He knows my cell phone number but doesn't know what hotel I'm staying in."

Tracy packed away several bottles of beer during the game and was beginning to feel little pain. That and the line of nose candy she snorted before the game and she was essentially toast. She talked with Chris and tried to be coherent but every beer she had made it more difficult. Finally she took a bottle of Landshark and slipped it between her rather substantial breasts. Then, bending backward she chugged the beer and didn't miss a drop.

When the applause from most of the men in the bar ended, a fight broke out near the tables at the center of the bar. Sally Thompson and Mark Nelson, two bar regulars, seemed to have had a bit too much Bass Ale for the evening and they started to feel like they were invincible. That was especially true when Sally caught Mark drooling as Tracy chugged her bottle of Landshark.

"What are you looking at you jerk," Sally screamed.

"I'm not looking at anything."

"Like hell you aren't. If you want to see tits just take a look at these." Sally then ripped open her blouse exposing a set of 36C's that were once probably award winners, but now they weren't anything to be showing off and especially in a bar full of drunken baseball fans. Mark reached over to cover up Sally's chest only Sally didn't see it that way. Instead she thought Mark was hitting her and she hit him first. Her first punch landed squarely on Mark's nose and it erupted in a ribbon of red. Her second punch hit him on the other side of his nose and the blood flowed even more intensely.

"You crazy bitch I was trying to cover up your tits."

"Like hell you were. You tried to hit me and I had to defend myself. There's a whole bar full of witnesses."

When the second punch was thrown Shay called 911 and asked for officers to help break up a bar brawl. She didn't say that is was a husband and wife who were fighting. Mark bled profusely as Sally realized what she had done. Then the police walked in the door. All they saw was her standing over him and Mark bleeding like he'd been shot. The police asked what happened and Sally and a couple witnesses told their story.

The police arrested Sally for assault and when they handcuffed her, Mark leaped up and yelled "you're not arresting my wife." He lunged at the shorter of the two officers. Caught in mid lunge with blood streaming from his nose, Mark was easily subdued, especially after he landed on his nose on the floor. Once handcuffed, Mark's outlook changed dramatically and he tried to convince the officers that it was just a little family misunderstanding.

"Nothing really happened here officers. My wife and I had a little disagreement."

Tom Schneider, the older of the two officers said, "Disagreement? You call blood all over hell a little disagreement? I think a few hours in jail will change your outlook." The drunken couple was led from the bar in handcuffs. A large crowd had gathered outside. The owners wondered if all the excitement would be good for business.

After a long evening of drinking, Tracy Goodwin was in no shape to drive. Chris was the only person she knew in the bar and he knew she was out of it for the evening. He offered to take Tracy back to her hotel room.

25

Chris left Sarasota in late afternoon planning to meet Michelle in St. Petersburg. Arriving at Tropicana Field Chris quickly found a parking spot and walked up to the gate 6 entrance and found her waiting for him. Using her connections, Michelle obtained two seats that were only three rows back from home plate in a section of the stadium where seats usually cost $250 to $300 per person. At least for that price there are servers who bring food and drink throughout the game.

Although they were close to home plate there was something missing about being there. It seemed that heckling wasn't as provocative in Tropicana Field. Maybe it was because there were so many fans and there was so much noise and almost everything you said was drowned out by thousands of others yelling their cat calls. Then there are those annoying cowbells. Whoever dreamed up that idea should be punished by being forced to watch re-runs of Wayne Newton performances for the rest of their life. At the conclusion of the second inning Chris confessed to Michelle, "The minor leagues are where you can do some serious heckling."

They had a cordial chat in which Michelle asked questions about Chris' family and his children. She was sad when she heard that both of Chris' parents had passed away. She never really knew them well but still felt a connection to them. She asked about his daughters and what happened to his ex-wife. Chris told the story of putting his career ahead of his family and it costing him a family. It was something that despite the many years he still hadn't allowed himself to accept.

He told her about his third wife, Emily Carrington. "I met her on a bird watching trip off the coast of South Carolina. She had a body that simply would not quit and I let my little head do the thinking for the rest of me. I married her a few years later and instantly found out what hell that was. A couple months after Emily married me she told me that she needed to sleep with other men to find out if I was the right one."

"You're making this up aren't you, Chris?"

"No, I swear. That's exactly what she said."

"Wasn't waiting until after you were married to have that revelation just a tad inconvenient?"

"She was so bi-polar I think she was tri-polar. And the drugs in her background didn't help either. At least she had a nice ass."

"What is it with men and a woman's ass? There's more to us than our asses."

Michelle's cell phone rang during the sixth inning just as Tampa Rays star Evan Longoria stepped to the plate. Answering it she heard Dennis Jensen's reptilian voice on the other end.

"Good evening. I hope I'm not calling at a bad time."

"Hi Dennis. No, there's no problem. I'm watching Tampa Bay and the Red Sox at Tropicana Field."

"Always looking for more talent aren't you."

"I wouldn't say that Dennis, but what's up?

"A decision has been made on the new southeast regional manager to replace Stu."

"Already? Who was picked?" She was nervous now fearing that Jensen would say it was him.

"We aren't saying anything publically yet and very few in the organization know either. We want you to come up to Detroit tomorrow morning for a 1:00 p.m. meeting to discuss the new manager who will be there for you to meet."

"For Christ's sake Dennis, this person will be my new boss. Don't I rate at least a hint at who it will be"?

"Yes you do, but we are waiting until tomorrow to introduce you."

"Is it at least someone I know, Dennis?"

"Yes, you know this person very well."

"We want to discuss this with you in private so you know why the decision was made the way it was."

"Why can't you tell me now?"

"I'm just repeating what I was told from higher up the food chain."

"We have booked you on the 9:30 Delta nonstop from Tampa to Detroit tomorrow morning. You should get in at noon and with no traffic you'll be at the office in time for the one o'clock meeting"

"Why did you put me on Delta, Dennis? Don't you know that their motto is 'We'll get you there when we get you there'?"

"We'll see you at one tomorrow afternoon." Her cell phone went dead.

She turned to Chris and said "You are not going to believe this but those bastards have selected someone to be my boss and I had no input into the selection."

Chris chuckled and said, "Welcome to the way the Federal government works."

Distressed by what she was expecting to hear tomorrow, Michelle couldn't relax and enjoy the rest of the game despite the home town Rays beating the Red Sox 3-2.

"Chris, I need to leave early. I have to get back to Lakeland and pack. Then I need to get to bed so I can be back in here by 8:00 for my 9:30 departure. I'm sorry but I have to call it a night."

"Have you thought of just crashing at the Hilton Garden Inn at the airport and saving yourself all of the hassle with driving?"

"I could but I need clean clothes. This is a business meeting and I'm dressed in shorts and a halter top."

"Good point. Since the day I retired I have forgotten about clothing."

"It shows."

"Do you have any plans for this weekend?"

"Let me see. I have to go to Detroit tomorrow and I'll be home Thursday afternoon. Whenever I go up there I try to sneak in some time with my friend Lola Nelson so maybe I'll stay with her Wednesday night. If I'm back here by Thursday afternoon I should be able to do something this weekend. What did you have in mind?"

"I was thinking we could go bird watching and camping at Myakka River State Park."

"No camping. You forget that I'm afraid of snakes."

"So what time should I pick you up on Friday?"

"Meet me at my place in Sarasota at 6:00 p.m. Friday and we'll take it from there."

"It's a date."

26

Eduardo Sanchez held elite status in the Caribbean Airways frequent flier program. Although he was Cuban by birth he currently lived in Montego Bay. He was there because it was easy to remain inconspicuous in Jamaica. With Caribbean Airways route system he could hop over to Havana when he needed to work with Cuban ball players. It was just a forty-five minute nonstop from Mo Bay to Havana. When he needed to deal with his bank accounts he could catch a different Caribbean Airways flight over to Grand Cayman just thirty minutes away. Flights to the Dominican Republic were only an hour away and if he ever had to totally disappear he could be in Bogota, Colombia in two hours. It was the perfect set up.

Eduardo's only real concern in life was the remote possibility that he would be on a flight somewhere that had to be diverted to Miami or Fort Lauderdale or San Juan because of bad weather. Once on American soil he was subject to arrest and confinement because of the FBI's interest in him. Given that remote possibility Eduardo chose only to fly when there were no storm systems that could cause him problems.

Arturo Kirkconnell caught the 10:30 a.m. Cayman Airways flight from Miami to Grand Cayman. It deposited him on the island at 11:50 a.m. where, as he was clearing Immigration, he raised some eyebrows when he said he was taking the 4:30 p.m. flight that same day back to Miami. Most visitors to Grand Cayman stay a couple days and those who can afford it stay a week. Nobody in this Immigration officer's experience came to the islands for just four hours. This man had to be up to no good. He just didn't know what it was.

Arturo was carrying only a briefcase which required that the Immigration officers spend only a small amount of time searching his belongings. On inspection of the briefcase the officers found four pens, a stick of gum, two tablets of writing paper, and a cell phone with an international calling plan, his passport, and a John Grisham novel. There was nothing else.

"What is your purpose in the country, sir," the Cayman Immigration officer asked.

"I'm here to have lunch with a friend."

"Where is this lunch taking place?"

"We're meeting in fifteen minutes at the Margaritaville Café in the Anchorage Centre by the cruise ship dock."

"You have no other purpose in the country than lunch?"

"No sir, it's a business lunch and then I go back to Miami."

"And what business are you in, sir?"

Arturo handed him a business card identifying him as the President of "Island Importers." He then said "We import beer and liquor from the Caribbean and Latin America into the United States. I'm here to discuss the opportunity to import your new Cayman beer, Caybrew, into South Florida."

"You like Caybrew do you?"

"I am not sure. It's a new beer that I just learned about. I've never tried it but that doesn't mean I wouldn't like to import it. My meeting is to determine if that is what I want to do."

Having heard more excuses by travelers than probably any other customs office in the world, the Cayman officer sensed that Arturo wasn't being honest with him but there was nothing in his story to make him deny entry. "You're free to go. Enjoy your time on the island, mon."

Outside the arrivals hall Arturo hailed a taxi and asked that he be taken just a mile or two away to the Margaritaville Café in the old Anchorage Centre. There he met Eduardo who was already seated at a table away from the hordes of tourists who filed in constantly.

Eduardo stood up to greet him. "Arturo my friend, what's up?"

"I'm fine Eduardo. How was the trip down?"

"It was just a plane ride like all other plane rides. Customs got bent out of shape when I told them I was here for just a few hours. They bought the line about importing Caybrew though. That was a good idea Art."

Over a lunch consisting of a coconut shrimp and two glasses of Red Stripe beer they discussed the current action in the Paradise League. "I had a little chat with Osvaldo who talked with his umpires and they have agreed to make it less obvious," Arturo said.

"And how are they making it less obvious? From the stories I read in the Sarasota paper even a blind person could see what was up."

"Reed and Hastert have instructions to call the balls and strikes fairly and only make sure the Reds lose a game if it looks like the score will be close."

"And what about when the Lakeland Tigers are playing. Has that issue been resolved as well?"

"Yes they have been consulted."

"You seem very sure of yourself Arturo. What guarantee can you give me that this is over? I can't afford to have the damned FBI snooping around figuring out that I have something to do with this. "

"Eduardo, don't worry. We have it taken care of."

"Arturo, do you know what makes me really nervous? The first girl I ever had sex with told me the same thing. There was nothing to worry about because she was on birth control. Nine months later my first child was born."

"Eduardo, I'm serious. I don't have a clue how anyone can figure out now what is going on."

Their lunch finished, they walked outside into the brilliant Caribbean sunlight where they hailed a taxi and rode together back to the airport. Checking in for their flights and clearing departure immigration, they sat in the cramped quarters of the departure area waiting for their flights.

The Caribbean Airways flight was departing fifteen minutes early which, for a Caribbean airline, is unheard of. Arturo would be leaving for Miami on time at 4:30. He would be back in the United States by 5:45 and in heavy rush hour traffic on Florida State Road 836 by 7:00 p.m.

Eduardo would be back in the land of Rastafarians and ganja even before Arturo lifted off from Grand Cayman. When Caribbean Airways called the flight they stood up and shook each other's hand. Arturo gave Eduardo another confirmation that everyone and everything was ok and under control. "It damned well better be, Arturo, or someone's nuts are going to be hanging from a palm tree and they won't be mine."

"It's under control, Eduardo. Nobody will find out. Nobody can find out."

It was unfortunate that Eduardo and Arturo weren't aware that absolutely everything in baseball is written down and recorded somewhere.

27

Chris said goodbye to Michelle at Tropicana Field as she left for to Lakeland to pack for her early morning flight. He then returned drove back to Sarasota. It was his plan to check his email, read the latest nonsense to come out of the mouths of politicians, and then go to bed.

Opening a bottle of Landshark he sat down at his computer and logged on to his email account. The first message which was the last one he had received was from a friend in the Paradise League office in Daytona. Attached to the message was a massive zip file of data from the last two seasons of the Paradise League. In the file was a complete record of every pitch thrown the previous year, and the first half of the current season. Every ball, every strike, the speed of each ball thrown, the order in which balls were thrown, the teams playing each game, the date of each game and most importantly the names of the pitchers throwing the games and the umpires calling them. In a separate file there was another set of data on what players attempted to steal which base and whether or not they were called out or safe. Again the dataset included the name of the umpire covering the bases and making the calls. Finally there was another dataset that dealt solely with calls at home plate whether they were runners trying to score on base hits, on passed balls, or attempts to steal home plate. It was all there. Now all Chris had to do was figure out how to analyze the data and what all those numbers meant.

His friend and former colleague Douglas Stauffer was the premier statistician in the US government. Nobody was better than Doug when it came to analyzing data and making sense out of numbers. If there was a technique out there Doug had probably used it at least once and if he hadn't then he at least knew about it. He held the key to figuring this out if only he was interested in helping. Chris called Jamestown North Dakota information and asked for Doug's number. It was only 10:15 p.m. in eastern North Dakota. Doug was likely still up. He answered the call on the third ring.

"Doug, this is Chris Ramsey. How the hell are you man?"

"I'm fine Chris. We are just watching the news on Channel 4 from Fargo. You remember that don't you?"

"Is old Charlie still the news anchor there?"

"He certainly is. I think that guy will die on the set of that station some time. You should see him now with his hair as white as snow."

"Speaking of snow its mid-May now. Has all the snow melted yet?"

"Finally, yes finally. The avocets are back and Baird's sparrows are singing on the prairie by the Center. You should come up and see it some time. Breathing prairie air would be good for you."

"Actually, that is why I am calling. I have this statistical issue that I need some serious help on. I can't think of another statistician anywhere who can handle this so I am calling you."

"What is it, some bird observations from some place in the South Pacific again?"

"It's a data set but it has nothing to do with birds. I have reason to believe someone somewhere is rigging minor league baseball games here in Florida. I think what they are doing is making obvious calls against one or two teams for whatever reason."

"What makes you say that?"

"Watching these games from behind home plate I know what a thrown strike looks like and a thrown ball looks like. It's not been that many years since I was a catcher. But when obvious strikes are called balls against one team and obvious balls are called strikes against the other team it piques your curiosity."

"Who do you think is behind this, if it's happening?"

"There are at least two umpires who are making obviously bad calls against the Sarasota Reds and the Lakeland Tigers. Why they are doing it is anyone's guess. If I had to guess I would say someone got to them and is lining their pockets because umpires make such an abysmal salary here."

"There are many variables that could be involved here, Chris. Are you sure you have enough data to look into it?"

"Doug, I have with me the entire database for the last two seasons through yesterday. I have information on each pitch thrown against each batter, what kind of pitch it was, if it was a ball or a strike, how fast it was thrown and what happened to the pitch after it was thrown. I also know the name of the pitcher who threw the pitches and the umpire calling the balls and strikes. And I have all of this for each of the 12 teams in the Paradise League."

"You have all of that?"

"Yes, and I also have data on every attempted steal of a base and how it was called and the umpire who called it."

"In that case you might have enough data to do a couple analyses. How are your computing skills? Any better than they were when you were still here at the Center?"

"Let's not talk about that and let's just assume that my computing skills have not improved over the years."

"So, what do you propose we do?"

"I could email you the data but I would prefer to bring it up to you so we could look at the numbers and figure out what analyses to perform. If you are in the office tomorrow I'd like to fly up for the day and see if we can work this out."

"Chris, you know that we'd be using a government computer system for non-government work."

"Not really. If what I suspect is going on is actually going on, there are several Federal laws that have been broken and continue to be broken. Granted this is not about birds but it involves Federal law. My hunch is that the FBI and Justice Department will be thanking us for doing this if it turns out as I suspect it will."

"In that case come on up. Like I said earlier it will do you good to breathe prairie air again."

"Doug, I'll check schedules and text you my arrival time. Would you call that cranky bastard from Avis at the airport, the one who listens to Rush Limbaugh all the time, and set aside a rental car for me?"

"I'm acting Center Director right now. Why don't I just leave a government vehicle for you at the airport, and leave the keys at the Delta counter. We'll call you a volunteer if anyone asks why a non-Service employee is using a Service vehicle. That will save you some money."

"And it will save me from having to talk to that moron who listens to Limbaugh."

"See you tomorrow Chris."

"Good night, Doug. I'll probably be there in early afternoon."

Delta had only two flights a day from Minneapolis to Jamestown. One left at noon and the other at 10:00 at night. To catch the noon departure, Chris had to leave Tampa on the 9:00 a.m. nonstop that would deposit him in the Minneapolis airport at 11:15 that morning. He quickly purchased a seat for tomorrow returning on Thursday. He would worry about a place to sleep when he got to Jamestown. Finishing his travel arrangements Chris looked at the clock. It was 12:15 a.m. and he still needed to pack. It was going to be a very short night.

His alarm went off at six and Chris was on the road to the airport by 6:45. With little traffic he could make it from Sarasota to the economy parking lot at Tampa International in fifty minutes. This being rush hour it would probably take him a few more minutes but he figured he would be there on time. Delta's departure from Tampa was only twenty minutes late which for Delta could be considered an on time departure. The flight north was uneventful other than they arrived in Minneapolis on time. There he made the easy connection to Delta's commuter flight to Jamestown. The plane was a bedraggled old Shorts-Fairchild 360 series propeller jet. It had seen its better days. Because of its small size and the rather large size of the propeller driven engines on each wing, riding in a SF3 was not the least bit quiet.

Just before 1:30 the noise level from the jet engines dropped and the plane began its approach to the Jamestown airport. A light layer of clouds enveloped the countryside and when the plane popped out of them just 2,000 feet above the ground it was directly over the Research Center where Chris had spent so many productive years of his life. The hillside prairie was ablaze with flowering plants. The patches of buck brush that used to litter the hillside were still there, each of them no doubt with a singing male clay-colored sparrow buzzing away in the afternoon warmth. Although Chris had traveled throughout the world and visited every continent, this scene of returning home really made him feel a little melancholy.

A government car was waiting for him outside the tiny terminal building. Unlocking it, he departed the airport for his old office along the James River. It had been ages since Chris last entered the main building of the center. Little had changed except for the names of colleagues who used to occupy the offices. Only three people were still there from the days of Chris' tenure. One, an administrative assistant named Deb still looked like she was twenty years old. Another old colleague still scurried around acting like if his research papers weren't typed to perfection the entire world was going to end. Doug's office was downstairs.

Exchanging their greetings and getting caught up on local gossip Chris presented Doug with the datasets. He explained in greater detail what he was hoping to find from the data and why it was so important to know. Doug thought about it a bit and said, "Well, what I'll do is use several tests to see what sort of results we obtain from each of them. I will start off with analysis of variance, and some simple chi-square tests for goodness of fit. I'll also try log-linear modeling because that is quite popular right now. If push comes to shove we'll try multiple regression analysis. If two or more of those statistical tests are in agreement I would say you might be on to something. If everything is just helter skelter, then at least you got a trip back to the prairie out of the deal."

"Doug, how soon do you think this will take to complete?"

"One advantage you have is that I'm acting center director right now so I can have the computer and statistics folks zero in on it this afternoon. It's good that you mentioned the FBI and Department of Justice connection in case anyone asks why we're using wildlife computers to analyze baseball data."

"But how long do you think it will take?"

"Today is Wednesday. My guess is that at the latest you'll know a week from today if you have anything to work with."

The Dakota Inn used to be the Holiday Inn when Chris lived in Jamestown. In those heady days after his divorce, the bar in the Holiday Inn was the principal place to pick up someone if that was your intent for the night. Chris checked into the Dakota Inn and then went out to explore old haunts. He drove north on US 281 to Buchanan and then drove west on one of the dirt roads that crosses the prairie. At the top of the hill he turned north and followed a grassed prairie trail along a section line and parked at a sweeping overlook of the prairie. Scanning the grassland he had a flashback to a day thirty years earlier when he and his children, with their dog, were crossing this prairie hunting sharp-tailed grouse. Chris could still remember his oldest daughter screaming with excitement as a sharp-tailed grouse exploded from cover at their feet.

He drove a mile further and found another patch of prairie where he and Renee regularly hunted deer and from there he drove to a research station near Woodworth nestled on one of the most beautiful areas of prairie remaining in North Dakota. There he hiked across prairie that still supports nesting Baird's sparrows on the same territories where he and Doug found them thirty years earlier. He flushed a Wilson's phalarope from its nest and watched the male go into a frenzied distraction display and then scared a bull snake that ultimately scared him when he found it raiding the nest of a blue-winged teal.

Sitting on an ancient patch of prairie that he will never likely see again, Chris took out his iPhone and called Michelle. She was in Detroit for her super-secret meeting with Tigers management. The night before she was concerned about what lay ahead for her and Chris was concerned for her. She picked up on the second ring. "Hey cowboy, what are you doing?"

Michelle sounded like she may have had more than her normal limit of two glasses of wine. The sound of a bar or nightclub was obvious in the background. "Sorry to call so late. I'm in Woodworth, North Dakota sitting on a patch of ancient prairie looking at a plot of ground I used to use for bird research."

"You're where doing what?"

"I'm back in North Dakota at my old research center. I got that data on pitches and outs from the Paradise League and brought it up here for the statisticians to work on."

"You're in North Dakota? Hell that's not doing me any good with you in North Dakota and me in wherever the hell I am right now."

"Are you drunk?"

"Drunk? No I passed drunk an hour ago."

"I hope it's a happy drunk."

"You know what Tigers management did Chris? Do you know who they selected to be the next regional manager for the whole southeast United States, the Caribbean and Latin America? Do you know who they picked?"

Chris had a feeling it wasn't her. "No, I don't have a clue. The only logical choice was you."

"Well, Mr. Spock, you and your logic are...."

Then the call was lost.

28

Chris' phone died because his battery died and his charger was an hour away in the Dakota Inn in Jamestown. It had nothing to do with the ineptness of Verizon, though they are always a suspect. Michelle sounded rather distressed when she was explaining what happened at the meeting. Rather than wait he returned to Jamestown by the fastest route possible. In his room, he plugged in the phone and waited for it to take on some charge then dialed Michelle again. By now it was way past midnight in Detroit. As buzzed as she sounded he wondered if she was still functional let alone could she talk. She answered on the fifth ring.

"Hello there, cowboy. You called again. I was afraid you met some buffalo out there on the prairie and forgot about me." The sound of a nightclub was still in the background.

"No it wasn't that easy. My phone battery died and I was more than an hour from the charger back in my hotel room. Sorry about that."

"I'll bet you tell that to all your girls."

"So, what was the news? What did Tigers management decide?"

"Well, are you sitting down? You are now talking to the first female regional manager of a baseball team anywhere in the major leagues. Can you believe that? I'm in charge of everything related to the team in the whole southeast United States, the Caribbean and Latin America!"

"I don't know what to say."

"Thanks, that means an awful lot coming from you Chris."

"Does this mean you have to move to some place like Atlanta or Charlotte or something?"

"Actually no, to get me to take the job, management said I could live anywhere in the southeastern United States, the Caribbean or Latin America. The only stipulation was that I had to be near a large airport so I could fly out as needed, and preferably an airport that has nonstop flights to Detroit."

"So what did you decide?"

"I could have kept my office in Lakeland but you know how much I love the beach and love the water. I could have moved to Tampa or St. Petersburg because those are logical places to live with the big airports there. I could have moved to the east coast of Florida but there are too many retired New Yorkers over there and the east coast is all the time getting hit with hurricanes."

"So, stop the suspense. Where are you moving?"

"I thought it all over after they offered me the option, and I'm moving to Sarasota. I hear there are nice people there, it's cheap, clean, and safe, and it has an airport that has nonstops to Detroit. What do you think of that?"

Chris paused to think about this a bit and then said, honestly, "I'm glad you'll be there. It might give us a chance to spend some time together again."

"So, cowboy, when we talked at the Rays game last night you said you wanted to do something this weekend. What do you want to do?"

"At the time I was thinking of taking you camping for the weekend at Myakka River State Park. I remember how much you liked camping and I thought...."

"Wait just a minute cowboy. Let's take a time out here. I will not camp in Florida because there are way too many snakes in Florida."

"So I take it from this conversation that camping is out of the question?"

"Unless it's in a Hilton, then it's a possibility."

"In that case I have a suggestion."

"This should be good."

"Do you remember the Hilton Resort on North Ocean Drive in West Palm Beach?"

"Of course I do, you clown."

"I suggest we spend the weekend camped in that hotel on the beach away from everyone."

"That's a good idea but my car is in the Tampa airport and it's a hell of a long drive from Tampa to Palm Beach."

"My car is in Tampa also. Let's both meet in Palm Beach tomorrow afternoon. On Sunday we can rent a car and drive it back to Tampa and pick up our vehicles and go home from there." There was a long pause on her end as she contemplated what had just been suggested.

"Ok, let me get this straight. You want both of us to fly to Palm Beach to spend the weekend together. We haven't been intimate with each other in 35 years, and except for a couple of brief encounters we haven't even seen each other in 35 years and now you want me to spend the weekend in a suite at the Hilton where we stayed 35 years ago. Is that what you're saying?

"That's exactly what I'm saying. I am going to call Delta and change my return flight. I have a 6:00 a.m. flight out of Jamestown and I'll take the first flight they have from Minneapolis to Palm Beach."

"I'll do the same here. My flight wasn't originally planned until noon. I'll see if I can get there sooner. Please text me with your plans."

Chris quickly called Delta and changed his return for tomorrow to West Palm Beach. He didn't even want to know what the change penalty was going to cost. He would arrive in Palm Beach at 1:15 p.m. on a nonstop from Minneapolis.

He sent this text message to Michelle.

I am arriving PBI at 1:15 p.m. on Delta 835 from MSP. Suite reserved at the Hilton. Let me know your plans. C.

It was 1:00 a.m. and he had to check in for his flight in four hours. Jazzed by the chance to spend the weekend with Michelle he decided to stay up all night rather than risk missing a wakeup call. He could sleep on the plane. Her text message reached him between planes in Minneapolis. She was arriving Palm Beach at noon on a Delta nonstop from Detroit and would simply wait for him at his arrival gate.

With space available in first class, Chris used some frequent flier miles to upgrade to a roomier seat for the three hour fifteen minute dash back to warm weather. He barely remembered the flight attendant welcoming him onboard.

29

Chris and Michelle survived the weekend on the Gold Coast and then drove back to Tampa to retrieve their cars. Later Chris arrived in Sarasota where he checked the Reds website and looked at the results from games they played during the six days he was gone. They had completed a sweep of the Dunedin Blue Jays and demolished the Tampa Yankees in all four games played against the best team in the league. He checked the box score section and saw that both Hastert and Reed called each of the games. The same thing had happened with the Lakeland Tigers in their home stand against the St. Lucie Mets. They played four games against the Mets and won three of them Roger Schultz was behind the plate for the three Tigers wins. A different umpire, one whose name Chris had never heard, called balls and strikes for the one game the Tigers lost.

These results were through Sunday night. This evening, Monday, the Reds were playing the Port Charlotte Stone Crabs in their beautiful new stadium in Charlotte County. Derek Cunningham, a recent demotion from the Class AA Carolina Mudcats, was scheduled to pitch for the Reds. The Stone Crabs starting pitcher was a 19-year old Dominican kid named Jesus Miranda. Miranda was new to the Crabs after having been signed a week ago. On his arrival at the stadium in Port Charlotte, Jesus started talking to the player whose locker was next to his. Jesus told him and other players around him about the great deal he received for signing with the Rays.

"They pay my salary and they give me a huge bonus, almost $100,000, just to sign with the Rays. Is that fantastic or something, huh?"

Kevin Butler, the Crabs second baseman asked, "What do you mean almost $100,000? Did they give you that money or not?"

"I have an agent in the Dominican Republic. He's a great man. He helped the Rays find me, he took care of my visa problems, he made up the contract for me and he did all the talking for me. He helped me get the signing bonus for me. He said he would take only 10 percent of the bonus but he took 50 percent instead."

"That sounds rather suspect, Jesus," Butler said.

"No, no, man it's not suspect. He told me there was a mistake in the way he wrote the contract. He was sorry but 'a contract is a contract' he said."

Larry Corcoran, a left fielder in his second year with the Rays organization overheard Jesus and then remembered a kid last year who had the same story. Larry had written it down in his diary because he thought it was so bizarre that someone would take 50 percent of a signing bonus. Larry made a note to himself to check his diary when he got home that night.

Chris was standing in line at 5:30 that afternoon so he could be the first one to purchase a ticket. It always pays to get there early if you want the choice seats behind home plate. Unfortunately for Chris, the Port Charlotte Stone Crabs have a large contingent of very rabid fans, many of whom have season tickets. Most of those season tickets went to other rabid fans who love sitting behind home plate. In fact all of the good seats on either side of the catcher and 10 rows back from the backstop were sold to season ticket holders.

Instead of the prime real estate Chris was relegated to a seat 21 rows back from home plate and slightly down the third base line. This was not what he had hoped for but the Crabs fans were there first.

Finding his seat, Chris left to explore the spacious Charlotte Sports Park. With the right field and left field foul poles at 343 feet from home plate and the center field fence at 414 feet, this was one of the largest playing fields in the Paradise League. In left center field there was a tiki bar that had not only Landshark Lager on tap but also Presidente, the national beer of the Dominican Republic. He stopped there first as he circumnavigated the baseball field.

Next to the tiki bar was an open stage-like area that had been filled with tables and chairs. Any group willing to shell out the extra money to be able sit there could sit there with a commanding view of the ball field, the visitor bull pen and the tiki bar. Behind the bar and the boardwalk leading to it was a large artificial wetland, no doubt created as mitigation for the destruction of real wetlands somewhere else.

Charlie Edwards, the lead bartender in the tiki bar was just pulling off a draught Presidente when he looked across the boardwalk and saw an alligator, at least eight feet long, sauntering across the wooden planks. It had apparently crawled up from the wetland and through a break in the fence and was now determined to watch the baseball game while scaring the hell out of the fans. Several people seated in the table area by the bar screamed as the reptile sauntered toward them. Edna McGinnis, a 68 year old retiree from Toledo saw it first and screamed at her husband Jim, "Jim there's an alligator right THERE and it's going to attack us!! Jim go kill it will you!"

Jim, ever the pacifist, was anything but excited about the alligator, "For god's sake Edna it's an alligator. It's not like the grizzly bears we saw in Alaska last year. Or was that the year before? I'm starting to forget."

Anne and Matt Sullivan, recent imports from Brooklyn were sitting at the tiki bar with their ankle-biter dog, Fluffy. A Yorkshire terrier with no concept of keeping its mouth shut, Fluffy was tethered to a leash and was prancing around on the floor. Anne saw the gator first and tapped Matt on the shoulder telling him, "Ah, honey, there's a gator over there and it's walking right toward us."

Matt, once a Boy Scout and now a linoleum installer told Anne to stop worrying. "Fluffy will bark a few times and the gator will go away. I've seen it on Animal Planet. Happens like that all the time.

Charlie Edwards, behind the bar, saw the alligator also and called stadium security. "Guys, this is Charlie in the tiki bar. We have an alligator at least 10 feet long walking across the boardwalk toward the tiki bar. I need you over here now to get rid of this damned thing."

There was a long pause on the other end of the phone as the security team decided what to do. Being basically rent-a-cops like those who sit inside the door of Federal buildings, none of the security guards had a firearm or had any of them been trained by the Fish and Wildlife Commission on how to deal with a renegade gator. Pat Eggleston, the chief of stadium security called 911 and asked for someone to please help.

"We are about to have a calamity here and nobody knows what to do. Send someone right away will you."

Fluffy's persistent barking caught the attention of the deepest part of the alligator's reptilian brain. The last time it ate, which was four days ago, he was attracted to his dinner by a similar aggravating sound coming from a slightly bigger pooch. The alligator was unable to tell the difference between a large dog and a small one by its bark. All it remembered was the last time it heard that sound dinner tasted like chicken. Chicken mixed with dog treats.

Except for the patrons at the far end of the bar whose view of the boardwalk was obstructed by the closer side of the bar, everyone started to pay attention to the situation as the shrieking increased. Fluffy's barking also increased. Not weighing more than eight pounds soaking wet, Fluffy had no idea what he was up against. His genetics told him that if he barked endlessly whatever he was barking at would get annoyed and walk away. His genetics hadn't factored in an alligator.

Jumping up and down at the end of his leash, Fluffy made a perfect target for the gator who was now no more than six feet away. Anne yelled at Matt saying "that gator is way too close Matt. We need to get out of here now."

Anne barely had the word "now" out of her mouth when the gator lunged toward her feet scooping up Fluffy in its mouth and then quickly racing back toward the pond from where it came but dragging Matt along because he'd forgotten to let go of Fluffy's leash. Matt screamed at the gator to let go of Fluffy and when he did the leash went limp. The last anyone heard from Fluffy was a muffled whimper. Fluffy was now somewhere in the gators esophagus.

Charlotte County Fire Rescue and a Fish and Wildlife Commission conservation officer arrived just minutes after the alligator made a snack out of Fluffy. "I'm sorry we got here so late, ma'am," the FWC officer said. "I was chasing an anhinga with a rubber ball impaled in its bill and couldn't come here until I took care of the bird."

"What," Anne screamed. "You put a bird's life ahead of the life of a Yorkshire terrier and all these people at the tiki bar? I'm writing to the Governor about this. Your ass is going to be mine."

"I'm sorry you feel that way, ma'am, but we have a prioritized list of animals we are supposed to protect first. The anhinga is protected by Federal and state law. There is no protection for Yorkshire terriers. I had to go with what my boss calls a priority. I'm sorry."

"You miserable duck cops have not heard the last of me," she threatened.

The clock in center field read 6:55 p.m. and it was time for the National Anthem. As the Reds and the Stone Crabs lined up on the bases for the playing of the anthem, Curt Patterson the long time Crabs announcer informed the fans of the unfortunate incident involving Fluffy at the tiki bar in left center field and asked for a moment of silence in the dog's honor.

Dave Apfel was the leadoff hitter for the Reds. Despite the lousy season the Reds were experiencing Apfel was having a relatively good year. Jesus Miranda looked in for the sign, shook off the first two suggestions from his catcher and then began his wind up. When the pitch was delivered it left Miranda's hand and had no intention of crossing home plate or anywhere near home plate. It was aimed at Apfel's head. Lunging backward Apfel knew that he had come within an inch or two of being hit in the head. Never having batted in front of Miranda before he assumed the kid was just having control problems but when the next pitch mimicked the first one it was obvious this was not a random occurrence. Apfel went down and the umpire warned Jesus that one more pitch like that and he was out of the game and he didn't care if it was Miranda's first game with the Crabs.

Chris, unable to control himself, yelled from 21 rows back "Jesus, I've seen better pitching in t-ball." None of the Crabs fans laughed.

Miranda went into his wind up after shaking off only one sign from the catcher. The ball left his hand and was clocked at 98 miles per hour. Its trajectory was true and straight and again it was pointed at Apfel's head. He fell back to the ground as the ball whizzed by just over his chin. Standing up and dusting himself off, Apfel looked at the umpire and asked, "It's obvious to everyone what this idiot is doing. Are you going to throw him out or not?"

The umpire, Mark Leggett, recently signed by the Paradise League and in his professional debut quickly decided that the wise move was to throw Miranda out of the game. After all he had warned him after the second ball and now he did it again a third time. Leggett raced out to the mound and yelled "Pitcher, you're out of here," and then gave the sign like an umpire would do if someone is out at a base.

Miranda yelled "Chinga tu madre," at Leggett, then kicked dirt in his face and left the mound. Once back in the dugout he threw his glove against the wall and sat down. Crabs pitching coach Terry Webb walked to Miranda and asked him to explain himself.

"It's easy coach. My agent told me the first time I pitched against the Sarasota Reds I was supposed to tear their heads off."

Webb said, "I don't think he meant it literally." He then asked, "Who is your agent anyway?"

"My agent is Eduardo Sanchez."

30

Statistical analyses are only as good as the data being analyzed. A common adage among statisticians regarding data is "garbage in, garbage out." In other words if the data suck so will the results of their analysis. A basic purpose of statistics is to determine if what a set of numbers means is "real" or not and the more real they are the greater the chances of them being reliable. For instance, if the probability of two sets of numbers being statistically different is 0.05 that means that only five times in a hundred is the number "wrong." If the probability is 0.01 then only one time in a hundred is it wrong and if it's 0.001 then there is only one chance in a thousand that the data are wrong. It simply doesn't get any more reliable than that. Chris had a reminder of this when his phone rang at nine o'clock on Wednesday morning. It was Doug Stauffer calling from North Dakota.

"Chris, its Doug Stauffer. Are you awake yet?"

Chris looked out his bedroom window and saw that the sun was obviously up. He had no idea what the time was. He unplugged his alarm clock after the trip to North Dakota last week and had no intention of using it again until he traveled somewhere else. "I'm barely awake. Someone better be dead somewhere. What time is it anyway?"

"It's eight in the morning here in North Dakota. Must be nine there."

"Nine o'clock? I remember nine o'clock when I was still working. Now nine o'clock means that sleeping is one of the great advantages of being retired."

"I wouldn't have a clue about being retired. I wouldn't know what to do with myself either. I'll probably just die in my office chair someday."

"So, what's up? I know you didn't call to talk about dying."

"Good point, Chris. I called about the data of yours that we analyzed."

"Good stuff, I hope?"

"Good isn't a strong enough descriptor, Chris. You have some great data there and it points out a couple very obvious trends." Statisticians, it seems, can never talk about anything without mentioning a trend.

"We did the four analyses that we talked about when you were up here last week. We started out with a simple chi-square analysis and then did an analysis of variance test. The results were looking good so we did a log-linear model and ended with regression analysis"

"Those are all good tests. So what did you find?"

"We did the four tests I mentioned and the results were pretty convincing. Then to add more weight to the results we did some more tests. We did things like Mann-Whitney, factor analysis, mean square weighted deviation, Spearman's rank correlation coefficient, and time series analysis. Hell we even threw in a simple student's t-test just because I hadn't done one in ages."

"And what did you find?"

"Chi-square, analysis of variance, the log-linear model and regression analysis all came up with the same results and probabilities. When I saw that and realized how uncommon it is to have four tests in such agreement, I decided to do the rest of the tests. Each one of them came back the same."

"Well, enough with the suspense, Doug. What did the statistics suggest?"

"Every one of those tests shows that no matter who is pitching, the Reds have more called strikes against them than any other team but only if Justin Reed or Dennis Hastert Jr. are umpiring."

"It's only for those two?"

"It gets more convincing, Chris."

"What is more convincing than this?"

"Our analysis shows that Reed and Hastert are the main culprits but only if it involves the Sarasota Reds. If it's, say, the Dunedin Blue Jays playing the Brevard County Manatees then the called balls and strikes are no different than what you would normally expect. Same thing holds if it's the Daytona Cubs and the Clearwater Thresher Sharks. Everything is as you would expect it to be in a normal distribution."

Chris then asked about the called outs on runners at the bases and at home plate. "Those data are a bit more ambiguous but still they show an interesting trend. When Hastert is working the bases there is a 50:50 chance that a Reds runner sliding into a base is going to be safe. If a Reed is on the bases then it's more like an 80:20 chance the Reds will be out. It's the same for plays at the plate."

"And what about with other teams when they are running the bases?"

"It's the same there Chris. It doesn't matter who is playing whom or what person is working the bases. If it's not the Sarasota Reds then the results are no different than what you would expect in a normal distribution of data."

"All the tests show the same results?"

"Every one every time. I actually want to know if we could use these data for a paper I'd like to write on how close all of these results were when looked at over a range of data."

"Maybe some time in the future Doug that will be fine. Right now, however, I think we need to keep the data close to our chests until the FBI and DOJ have a chance to figure out what laws may or may not have been broken."

Chris paused for a second and then added, "You never told me the probabilities on these data."

"That's the thing that really got our attention. On every test the probability was 0.001 – one chance in a thousand that the numbers were wrong. In statistics it simply doesn't get more convincing than that."

Chris thought about the implications of the data being this dramatic and then thought of one last question.

"Doug, when you did the analysis did you happen to pick out about when things started to look fishy and when the games started to be thrown?

"Actually yes we did. The dataset was so complete and so robust that I can say with certainty that umpires calls involving the Sarasota Reds began to take a turn for the worst during the third week of July last year. If I had to put a date on it I'd say it was on July 16 to be exact."

"I wonder what happened on July 16 last year."

"I don't have a clue but something changed somewhere."

"Did you look at if the frequency of called strikes against the Reds has changed with time? I mean are there more called strikes now than there were last month or even last July?"

"That is another good observation Chris. It appears that once July 16 came around the frequency of occurrence of suspect calls against the Reds increased in a normal progression. However starting with the first day of the season the increase has been almost exponential."

31

Ending his call and putting away his iPhone, Chris pondered the importance of what he had just learned from his colleague. To a scientist, statistically solid data are difficult to overlook and it would be impossible to do that with the analysis of the data the Paradise League provided.

At a minimum, fraud was being committed by the two umpires and there were likely several other laws that were at least being bent if not outright broken. Chris' guess also was that none of these extra dollars that Reed and Hastert were taking under the table were being reported to the Internal Revenue Service. Gangster Al Capone was sent to prison for tax evasion but who would ever think that a minor league umpire would experience a similar fate? Because baseball is a form of interstate commerce, the crimes being committed were most likely Federal offenses not just state crimes. That meant the Federal Bureau of Investigation could likely be involved.

Chris now faced the task of discovering why Reed and Hastert and maybe Schultz were throwing games, who was paying them to do so, and what was their motivation. Thinking back to one of his most favorite movies of all time, "*Animal House*" Chris remembered that famous line spoken by John Belushi that went "My advice to you is to start drinking heavily."

Chris changed into his bicycle clothing and got ready for his daily 21 mile bike ride. Dressed in tight bicycle shorts, light green biker t shirt, his riding gloves and his helmet that everyone said looked dorky on him Chris pedaled south on Honore Avenue. He turned right onto 17th Avenue at the 7-11 and followed that road west to Beneva then south to Fruitville Road. Having had remarkable success in navigating and surviving the armada of blue hairs and snowbirds that converge on the Beneva-Fruitville intersection, he turned right on Fruitville and followed it to Tuttle. Pedaling north on Tuttle he passed Ed Smith Stadium where the Sarasota Reds were on one of the fields hitting batting practice. He was tempted to stop and discuss his findings with manager Jeremy Bergman but decided that being discreet now might be a better strategy.

After passing the stadium, Chris rode north to 17th Avenue where he turned right and followed the road to Lockwood Ridge. Following Lockwood Ridge north for three miles he came to the mall where his health club had just opened for business. At ten dollars a month for membership it was too good a deal to pass over. Every other day, like clockwork, Chris was at the club lifting weights. His regular workout circuit took him to seventeen stations where he challenged nearly every muscle group in his body. His advancing years meant that his metabolism rate was slowing down and when that happens, fat usually takes the place of muscle.

Hot, sweaty, and exhausted after each workout, he usually toweled down and then took a Ukrainian shower that consisted of spraying deodorant under each arm and putting on a new shirt. He learned about this kind of shower as a high school jock in North Dakota and for some reason even at 60 years old, considered it extremely funny to mention to anyone. Florida, thankfully, wasn't as politically correct as a place like Washington DC and here you can get away with a good Ukrainian joke once in a while.

Walking next door to the White Horse Pub, Chris took his usual seat at the end of the bar next to the cooler. His plan now was to have a late lunch and discuss his findings with Mark Bennett the afternoon bartender at the pub. With Mark such a fanatic about anything involving sports, talking with him might shake loose some ideas on how and where to proceed next with this disturbing information.

While eating lunch Chris turned his attention to the latest updates on ESPN Sports Center. Right now, even though it was June, it looked like it was going to be another shoo-in year for the Yankees. They led the American league and the Boston Red Sox by six games. It was the same story but a different year.

In the National League it was looking more and more like the Colorado Rockies and the Pittsburgh Pirates would be taking it down to the wire. Yet this was June, even before the All-Star break. This was also baseball and anything could happen between now and October. Most pleasing to Chris was the obvious fact that the Detroit Tigers had a record of 19 wins and 58 losses. The lower down in the standings the Tigers were the happier Chris would be. For once, even the Washington Nationals weren't as bad as the Tigers.

Chris turned his attention to Mark. "Mark, old boy, I have some interesting news for you."

"Hey, Chris, what's up?"

"Remember when I made that quick trip to North Dakota last week? I went up there with all the data the Paradise League had on pitches thrown by every pitcher in the league in the last two seasons, every attempted put out at a base and every call at the plate. I had all of that information analyzed by one of the top statisticians in the Federal government and I have to say the results knocked my socks off."

"What did you find out?"

"Well, without a doubt some of the games that the Reds are playing are being thrown. It's as plain as the nose on your face."

"How can you be that certain?"

"My statistician friend in North Dakota who has published more papers in scientific journals than just about anyone, completed the analysis and has statistically firm results showing that there are two umpires in the Paradise League who are, shall we say, less than honest."

"How can you be so sure of that," Mark asked.

"Well let's look at it this way," Chris started. "First, we compared the percentage of strikes called by the suspect umpires when the Sarasota Reds were batting to the percentage when other teams are batting."

"So what does that mean in English?"

"Suppose we find a dispariity for each umpire; each calls more strikes versus balls against the Reds than against the other teams. Maybe the Reds are such weak batters that teams are comfortable throwing them easy strikes down the middle."

"Well, Chris, the Reds certainly seem to suck. How do you account for that?"

"To check on that possibility, we compared the disparities for the two suspect umps to the disparities of the other umps working the league. If the other umpires show similar disparities, it could mean one of two things. Either the entire group of umpires has a hard-on against the Reds, or the Reds simply suck. However if the two suspect umpires show greater disparities than the rest of the group, we believe they indeed are biased against our Reds."

"So, are you saying that the Reds are getting screwed or something?"

"What's happening to the Reds is that someone somewhere has convinced at least two umpires to throw games so the Reds wind up losing. And given their record so far this year there is a lot of money changing hands because the Reds are doing really poorly."

"So, Chris, what are you going to like do about this?"

"First of all I want to confirm what the statistics are telling me. If I can do that then I want to dig in further to find out who is paying these two umpires. This being Florida it's easy to figure out why they are taking the money. What I really want to know is why the people with the money are doing this and what they hope to gain from it."

32

David Addison had been an FBI agent for nearly twenty five years. Originally a Kansas City police officer he saw a brighter future with the Federal government and focused his attention on the FBI. He had no intention of being the next Elliott Ness and he certainly didn't see himself as the next J. Edgar Hoover. Addison simply viewed the Bureau as the best option available. Completing his basic and advanced training at the Quantico, Virginia training facility, David was given three choices for what would be his first station.

"We like to send our newest agents to New York as soon as they complete training," the Human Resources officer at Quantico told him. "Time and again we find that the fast paced action and the variety of crimes to be investigated there result in our new agents getting their street smarts tested and they get to meet some of the best managers in the Bureau. If you have your sights set on moving up, then Manhattan is the logical first place to be stationed."

David was more interested in catching bad guys than he was in moving up the ranks of the Bureau. Already as a Fed he was making nearly twice what he made on the Kansas City Police Department so money wasn't really that big an issue. He would talk this over with his wife but he was certain he wasn't about to become a New Yorker.

"The second option we have for you is San Diego. It's almost as fast paced as New York but the weather is better. In San Diego you'll not have as much opportunity to work on organized crime issues like we have in New York. However

San Diego is ripe with immigration issues, and there's always the chance to catch a terrorist trying to sneak into the country from Tijuana."

The Human Resources officer said his third option was one that is always thrown out as a joke. New recruits are always given the option of selecting some out of the way place that is usually reserved for moving someone who is being punished for screwing up. Places like Keene, New Hampshire or Escanaba, Michigan, or heaven forbid, Winnemucca, Nevada, are always available. Invariably they are always turned down. Today the Human Resources officer had a similar option for David. "And the last option we have for you, David, is a two-person station in Grand Island, Nebraska. The Grand Island office is under the supervision of the Special Agent in Charge in Omaha and is responsible for enforcement activities in the western two-thirds of Nebraska."

"Quite frankly," the Human Resources agent said, "we never expect any of the new agents to accept a post like Grand Island. We just throw it out there to record your reaction.

David thought about the option for maybe five minutes and said, "I'll take it."

"Which station, David, New York or San Diego?"

"Grand Island."

"What? You honestly want us to move you there first?"

"I will move there in a heartbeat."

Grand Island had many benefits for David and his family. Most importantly it was just a five hour drive from there to where his parents live in St. Joseph, Missouri, and it was less than three hours to his wife Elizabeth's parent's home in Concordia, Kansas. It was a no-brainer to accept Grand Island for his first station. "You might as well start the paperwork for our move to Nebraska," he told the Human Resources officer.

The FBI office in Grand Island was a small two-room affair on the second floor of the decrepit former post office on West Second Avenue of what passes for downtown in Grand Island. Reporting for duty his first day, David met his supervisor Steven who escorted him around the building to meet other Federal employees who worked there. The entire second floor of the building was occupied by the US Fish and Wildlife Service's Nebraska State Office and Chris Ramsey was one of the employees in that office.

Steve brought David to Chris' office and introduced him as the new agent in the office. Chris and David shook hands and were invited in. David expected the walls of a biologist's office to be covered with pictures of birds and mounted heads of mammals and mounted bodies of fish. Instead, he was surprised to see pictures of baseball players and Jimmy Buffett adorning the wall. In fact there wasn't a picture of a bird or a dead fish anywhere.

Behind Chris' desk was a large picture of Jimmy Buffett, guitar in hand, wearing a t shirt that read Only Visiting This Planet. "I took that picture at my first Buffett concert. It was in South Beach, Miami in July 1985. Someday I want him to sign it for me."

On either side of the Buffett picture were two smaller pictures. On the left was a picture of Lou Gehrig standing at a microphone in Yankee Stadium on that fateful day, July 4, 1939, when he said farewell to baseball because of his debilitating disease. No baseball fan will ever forget his words, "Yet today, I consider myself the luckiest man on the face of the earth." To the right of Buffett was a picture of Willie Mays making one of his trademark basket catches in center field of Candlestick Park in San Francisco. Chris didn't take the pictures of Gehrig or Mays but he was just as proud of them. "To me there have only been two great players in baseball history, Lou Gehrig and Willie Mays. The rest of them were just wanna be's."

David, a lifelong Kansas City Royals fan took exception saying "What about George Brett? He was the cornerstone of the Royals for more than two decades."

"Brett? Did Brett ever play 2,130 consecutive games? Did Brett consistently stand in the middle of center field and throw bullets to the plate to cut down runners trying to score? Yeah, Brett was ok and he helped the Royals win a World Series, but if you want to talk great then you only need to look at the two stars in these pictures on either side of Mr. Buffett."

A smile crossed David's face as he said "You know, I could have you arrested for defaming George Brett like that."

Chris replied saying, "And I could have your fishing license revoked too."

They developed a strong friendship during Chris' remaining years in the Grand Island office but as is common when one person moves their friendship waned with the passage of years. Chris thought about his old FBI agent friend as he contemplated what direction to take in trying to uncover the people behind the umpire issue. The more Chris thought about this the more confused he became. Picking up his iPhone, Chris dialed area code 308 information and asked for the FBI office in Grand Island. Dialing the number he received a voice message saying "Agents Edwards and McIntosh are out of the office. Please leave a message and we'll get back to you. If you need immediate assistance, please call the Special Agent in Charge in Omaha at 402-555-2578. Thank you."

From the call he knew that Steve Edwards, David's former supervisor was still in the office. It was an office he would likely die in because Steve had always enjoyed being an agent in this tiny office. "Agent McIntosh" was another story. Chris didn't know of an Agent McIntosh so he knew David was no longer in Grand Island. He dialed the Special Agent in Charge office in Omaha and asked the receptionist if David Addison was an agent in that office.

"David Addison? I like don't know any agent named David Addison. Let me put you in touch with Human Resources. Maybe they can like help you." Two "likes" in two sentences.

After identifying himself to Human Resources, Chris asked if David Addison was still an agent in Nebraska and if so where was he stationed. The Human Resources officer was rightfully suspicious of the call and was unwilling to give any information on the location of any Special Agent in the agency. "Look," Chris said, "I'm an old friend of Dave's and I would like to get in touch with him. I'm a former Fed just like you are. Isn't there some way we can work this out?"

The Human Resources officer knew that David Addison was now the Special Agent in Charge of the FBI office in Tampa, Florida but she wasn't about to give that information out to someone who could be a crazed anarchist. Instead she asked for Chris' name, address, phone number and Social Security number. She said she would contact Agent Addison's current office with his information. She would leave it up to that office and Agent Addison to contact Chris. "If you are who you say you are, I am sure Agent Addison will call you personally."

Two days later, while sitting in the stands at Ed Smith Stadium watching the Reds being beaten by the Dunedin Blue Jays, Chris heard his ring tone and saw that the call was from area code 813. Hillsborough County, Florida. Who in hell could this be? "This is Chris, can I help you?"

A strong Midwestern accent answered him saying "I still think George Brett is the greatest baseball player of all time."

"Dave Addison, you old reprobate, what in hell are you doing in Tampa?"

"Tampa. How did you know I am in Tampa?"

"You don't need to be Elliott Ness to read the caller ID on a phone."

"I am now the SAC in the Tampa Field Office. "

"You're a SAC? I thought you were the guy who didn't ever want to move up in the Bureau. What in hell are you doing being a Special Agent in Charge?"

"Elizabeth and I vacationed every year in Florida and eventually we decided that we would move here when I retired. I left Grand Island and did some time in Kansas City where I impressed some people with a couple of major organized crime busts and soon those people above me were talking about promoting me. I told them the only place I wanted to be was Florida."

Chris could identify with that sentiment. "So in other words you kissed the right asses higher than yours and you got the government to pay for your final move to where you wanted to retire in the first place. Do I understand this correctly, Dave?"

"You got it. We have been here two years now"

"So are you enjoying Florida?"

"There is way too much going on here to allow anyone to get complacent. You wouldn't believe some of the stuff we investigate here. There are a lot of really sick people in this state."

"I know, Dave, I know. All I have to do is read the *Tampa Bay Times* or the *Miami Herald* any day of the week to know there is an endless source of weird people in this state."

"And, Chris, what are you doing with an area code 941 number?"

"I retired a couple years ago and moved to Florida. I moved first to Naples but there were way too god damned many Republicans. They made my skin crawl. So a year later I moved to Sarasota. It's much nicer here plus we have baseball from spring training in late February until September here with the Sarasota Reds. With luck, baseball extends to October if the Rays don't choke."

"So you're still into baseball, I guess?"

"I'm sitting at a Sarasota Reds game right now. Dunedin is beating them senseless so it's a normal Reds game."

"You know, Chris, it's been since forever that we have seen each other I think we need to get together for a baseball game sometime soon. How about coming up to Tropicana Field for a Ray's game this weekend? It will be my treat."

"Actually, David, that's a good idea because I have a law enforcement issue that I need to discuss with you. It was this issue that made me try to track you down in Nebraska to begin with."

"What sort of law enforcement issue do you have now? Remember you're not on the Platte River tracking down people who run over least tern nests any longer."

"Dave, I have irrefutable evidence, backed up by some of the best statistical analysis in the world that some umpires in Florida are throwing games to make the Sarasota Reds consistently lose. I'm not sure what laws are being broken here but I'm sure there are. And since baseball is involved with interstate commerce I think maybe some Federal laws are being broken, and that's where the FBI comes in."

"I don't know all the facts yet, Chris, but if what you just told me is true, you could be on to something. Meet me at the Gate 6 entrance to Tropicana Field on Saturday at noon. The game starts at 1:00 p.m. so we will have an hour to drink some beer before watching the Rays beat my home town Kansas City Royals. See you then."

David and Chris met at the Gate 6 entrance to Tropicana Field exactly at noon on Saturday. After exchanging greetings they found a bar near Section 142 that served Presidente beer on tap and then found their seats along the first base line. There weren't many fans in the stadium this Saturday afternoon. The Rays season was going poorly after last year's World Series appearance. The Royals' record was even more abysmal than the Rays. It was a gorgeous sunny weekend afternoon and most Floridians were thinking about being on a boat or lying in the sun. Not many wanted to be inside The Trop with its roof blocking out the sky. For the time being David and Chris could talk freely.

"David, I have been suspecting that something was up with the Sarasota Reds for a long time. They have some excellent players. However no matter what they do or who they play, it seems that if one or both of these two umpires are calling the games the Reds lose." Chris went on to say "I have sat behind home plate heckling the opposing team more times than I care to count this year and I've seen virtually every play at the plate. I've watched every pitch and observed every ball or strike. The called balls and strikes are glaringly obvious against the Reds."

He went on. "I obtained the Paradise League's database on all pitches thrown in all games last year and so far this year. That includes all teams not just the Reds and their opponents. I had one of the best statisticians in the Federal government, a colleague of mine at in North Dakota, run several statistical analyses of the data. The report back to me is that when these two particular umpires are calling games the Reds are almost certain to lose."

"Who in hell would want that to happen, Chris? I mean it makes no sense. I could maybe see it in the major leagues but you're talking Class A ball here. You're one step ahead of the instructional league. You really think something is fishy?"

"David, now that Doug Stauffer has run the statistical analysis and we have solid data to show that something is wrong, I have no doubt there is. I just need to figure out who is doing this and why. Where is the money coming from?

More importantly, what is to be gained by throwing Class A baseball games? That is the thing that baffles me."

David thought about this and then said, "I haven't seen the data so I can't say with certainty. However if what you are saying is true then most likely there are some interstate commerce laws being broken. Maybe fraud is being committed and you've heard about RICO haven't you?"

"Sure I've heard of RICO. Anyone who has watched a detective show on television has heard of RICO. I just don't know for certain what it means."

"RICO is the acronym for Racketeer Influenced and Corrupt Organizations Act. It's a Federal law that provides for criminal penalties and a civil cause of action for acts performed as part of an ongoing criminal organization. I dealt with RICO a lot when I was in Kansas City. For some reason the wise guys liked to focus on Kansas City when things got too hot for them in New York and New Jersey."

The Tampa office of the FBI is similar to a Regional Office in Chris' old agency. David, as the Special Agent in Charge in Tampa supervised nine FBI Resident Agents under his command. One of the Resident Agent's has an office on Second Street in Sarasota. "Even though the potential crimes are being committed throughout the Paradise League, because the Sarasota Reds are involved, and because we have a Resident Agent office in Sarasota, I'm going to get in touch with her this afternoon and tell her that you'll be stopping by to chat about this issue Monday morning. We will let Brenda decide what is going on and where and how to proceed."

"Who is Brenda," Chris asked.

"Brenda Livingston is the Resident Agent in Charge of the Sarasota office. She's about 40 years old, divorced, has an ass to die for especially when she has it wrapped in white slacks, and she's a baseball fan. Just don't tell her I said that about her ass or I'll have Human Resources all over mine. I have only two more years to go until I follow you into retirement and I don't want to screw it up."

David realized that he had inhaled his 20 ounce glass of Presidente while talking with Chris about the potential investigation. He twirled his empty glass in his hand and said to Chris "you know I said this game was on me, but since you're getting free legal advice from the US government, and the US government right now is incredibly thirsty, I think it's your duty to your former employer to keep this current employee well hydrated."

Chris heard the message loud and clear and left for the bar to get two more beers. On Monday he would have a chat with Brenda Livingston and learn what would be his own next move.

33

There were no baseball games in Sarasota on Sunday. The Reds were playing the Palm Beach Cardinals in Palm Beach and Chris decided that he would rather spend the day mapping out strategy than driving six hours round trip to watch another Reds loss. He knew from a source in the Paradise League that Justin Reed and Dennis Hastert Jr. were not the umpires for today's game. That meant there was at least a fifty percent chance that the Reds could win. Still there were better things to do with his time than drive over to Palm Beach for the day.

Since he first moved to Florida as a student, Chris had made a ritual out of reading the *Miami Herald* each Sunday. To him there was simply no better newspaper anywhere in the country. Many were the times he was in Lima, Peru or Santiago, Chile, or Guatemala City, and he would find a few days old copy of the *Herald* in a news stand. It always made him feel a little connected to home when he could find the *Herald* in some third world city. Now with the Internet and the ease of finding information it was simple to be able to not leave home on a Sunday morning and still be able to read the *Herald.* Just a few key strokes and laid out in front of him was the entire weird world of south Florida.

The headline story this Sunday morning was about the latest attempt by the Republic Party to derail the legislative agenda of the new Democratic President. This story had been told and re told so many times Chris felt like he had the entire story line memorized. Scanning the rest of the front page he noticed a small headline about a plane crash in Detroit. Opening the story he discovered that the National Transportation Safety Board had concluded their investigation of the crash of a private plane that was departing the Detroit Metro airport in late April that killed Stu Masterson the former Regional Manager for the Detroit Tigers. At the time of the accident the immediate suspicion was that icing of the wings had brought down the jet. The findings of the National Transportation Safety Board had a different spin on the story.

DETROIT (AP) - Investigators for the National Transportation Safety Board in Washington, DC, have concluded that the April crash of a private jet at Detroit Metro airport was the result of sabotage and not icing as had been originally speculated.

The crew of three was flying three Detroit Tigers managers aboard the Lear Jet model 25 owned by the Detroit Tigers, including their Southeast Regional Manager Stu Masterson of Charlotte, North Carolina. Everyone onboard was killed in the incident.

The NTSB investigation found a hydraulic line that regulated movement of the forward slats on both wings of the plane had been tampered with. NTSB speculates that the cold weather and perhaps bumpy conditions on the runway caused the hydraulics line to break on departure from the runway.

This was the first crash of a Lear 25 since the plane was released by the manufacturer. NTSB has now concluded their investigation of this incident and has provided three suggested changes in the design of the hydraulic system of Lear Jets.

Why would anyone anywhere want to sabotage a Lear Jet owned by the Detroit Tigers? Certainly the Detroit area was being watched heavily by the US Department of Homeland Surveillance because of the number of Muslim people living there. That was a fact everyone knew. But why would a Muslim have a hard on for the Tigers?

The more Chris thought about the crash the more it simply did not make sense that any terrorist would want to harm the Detroit Tigers. There had to be another explanation. But who would do this and why? His only connection to the Detroit Tigers organization was Michelle Coburn with whom he had spent a rather enjoyable weekend recently and with whom he had not spoken since he dropped her off at her house in Lakeland after their return from West Palm Beach. He punched in her number and she answered on the second ring.

"Hey cowboy, what's up?

"Hello Michelle. Have you seen the front page of today's *Miami Herald*? There is a story on it about the Detroit Tigers plane that went down last April, the one that Stu Masterson was on. The story includes a report from the National Transportation Safety Board who concluded that the plane was brought down by sabotage, not by icing as many had originally thought. Do you know anything more about this?"

"What are you telling me Chris? Someone intentionally brought down a Tigers plane? Who would do such a despicable act?"

"That's what I've been asking myself since I read the story. It makes no sense at all. Do you know any people higher up in the organization who might have a better idea?

"Well, Chris, Jim Biehl is my direct supervisor. He's the vice-president of the Tigers for all field operations. He's the person I go to with anything that I can't handle. Let me call Jim and see what he knows and I will get back with you. OK?"

"Good idea. I'll wait for your call."

34

Things were strange enough with the apparent manipulation of baseball games. Now added to the mystery was the likely sabotaging of a Lear Jet owned and operated by the Detroit Tigers, the parent team of the Lakeland minor league team. Was there a relationship between the two or was it just random chance? Recent events suggested strongly that more than the flip of a coin was in play.

Michelle called early that morning to let Chris know she had heard from Jim Biehl in the Tigers front office. He knew nothing more about the details of the plane crash than anyone else reading the paper. Something about that finding didn't sit well with Chris. Either Biehl was withholding information or upper management in private businesses is just as far out of touch with the goings on of their organization as is upper management in the Federal government. Armed with no more information than he possessed when he watched the baseball game with David Addison on Saturday, Chris stopped by the FBI office in downtown Sarasota. There he asked the front desk person if he could speak with Brenda Livingston, the Senior Resident Agent. He waited a few minutes and was finally escorted back to Livingston's office. It was a typical U.S. Government office with too little space, too many files and no windows. A feeling of déjà vu swept over Chris as he took a seat in her office.

"Mr. Ramsey, what is it the FBI can do for you today," Brenda began.

"Thanks for seeing me on such short notice. I really appreciate it."

"SAC Addison called me at home Saturday night and told me you would be stopping by this morning so I kept my schedule as clear as possible until you arrived." Chris noted that skid greasing was still an important way of getting things accomplished in government.

"Agent Livingston, I think I may have stumbled on to some nefarious activities involving the Sarasota Reds minor league baseball team, and I would like to alert the agency to what I've found out and also see if this is something you would be interested in pursuing."

"First of all, Chris, it's Brenda. Any friend of SAC Addison's is instantly a friend of mine. Now what is it that you've discovered about the Reds that makes you so curious?"

Chris explained his observations of lousy calls at the plate, balls being called strikes and vice versa and his other suspicions. He then explained in layman's terms what the statistical analysis performed by Doug Stauffer had turned up. "Brenda, far more than random chance is going on here and the statistics bear that out. For whatever reason someone is causing the Reds to lose way more games than a normal distribution would allow."

"That sounds intriguing, Chris. However I can't really see at this point where any laws have been broken. Who is to say that the Reds are just a poor baseball team that can't win no matter what is presented to them? I am afraid the Bureau might come out looking like a pack of fools if we started looking into something that wasn't really there when so many higher priority issues are pulling at us daily."

"Brenda, I was a minor league baseball catcher before I went back to graduate school to get my Ph.D. I have been around baseball since I was old enough to hold one. If there is anything I know more about than birds its baseball, and I can say unequivocally that the Sarasota Reds have some exceptional talent. What's wrong is that someone is jerking them around."

"Come to think of it Chris, I am a staunch baseball fan myself. I'm originally from Queens on Long Island so you know who my favorite team is. I attended several of the Reds' games last year and so far this year and I have to agree with you, they are a solid team. However, despite your statistical analysis we really have nothing to go on as far as an investigation."

"What would you need to have an investigation started?"

"A confession, of course, would make my job much easier. Only a fool would confess to something that may not even exist. What we would need is hard evidence. Maybe there is a witness or two willing to talk. Maybe there are copies of bank deposits that correlate with Reds losses. If we knew who was involved we could get records of phone calls made between the people. Tapes of conversations between the allegedly tainted umpires and their money sources would be tremendously helpful. Those are the sorts of things we would need before we would expend much human resource power on the problem."

"So Brenda it sounds like this is an impossible task. I know something is wrong and can't prove it. You are the resource needed to prove it but you don't have the evidence to warrant it."

"I wish I could be more positive on this but I can't be."

Chris thought about his options and then asked one final question. "Brenda, I'm retired and have unlimited time that I could devote to uncovering something. Would there be any issues involved if I did the snooping around myself? I know I can't get phone records, but if I can get some of the other things you mentioned would you be willing to take a look at this again?"

"The FBI never told you this, and if I am ever asked I will deny it vigorously. However if you can come up with some evidence that we would need to jump start an investigation I think we could divert some resources in that direction."

Chris left the FBI office and drove across town the White Horse Pub hoping to have an early lunch and at least one early pint of Landshark Lager. As he drove up Washington Boulevard he called Michelle to fill her in on what he had just learned.

"Michelle this is Chris. I just left the FBI office in Sarasota."

"What did you find out from the super sleuths?"

"Well, it seems that they are interested but not interested."

"What exactly does that mean?"

"The Senior Resident Agent was interested in the statistical analysis but for her law enforcement purposes there is not enough there to begin an investigation."

"That doesn't sound right, cowboy."

"The FBI told me that if I could come up with some better evidence than what I have to go on now, they might take the issue more seriously."

"Does this mean you're going to put out a shingle with the word 'investigations' on it"

"No, it just means that I'm going to do some snooping around to see what I can find out. I'd like you to help do some of the snooping with me if you're up for it."

"When does this start?"

"It will start as soon as I have a clear plan for what I want to do and how I want to do it. It's only an hour from Lakeland down here. Why don't you meet me for lunch at the Pub. We can plot out a strategy. And besides you need to spend some time down here looking for a house since you're planning to make the move here anyway."

"Great minds think alike. I was planning to come down there without telling you. I'm at exit 39 from the I-4 freeway right now. I'll be at the pub in an hour. See you there."

When Chris walked into the Pub, Mark Bennett was behind the bar assuming his usual afternoon status as master of ceremonies and the chief source of baseball information on Florida's Sun Coast. Ian Duxbury had arrived for an early lunch today. He had recently received his pilot's license and was always itching for a reason to get behind the yoke and build up his "pilot-in-charge" hours. Ian had wanted Chris to go flying with him on several occasions but until now their schedules had not meshed.

"Hey Ian, how many pilot in charge hours have you built up since I saw you last?"

"Hi Chris, it's been tough you know. I have this new job and I'm training for that double marathon in South Africa next year and my wife and daughter need my attention. I guess I haven't been doing as much flying as I want to. For a pilot that's a common complaint."

Chris was on his second pint of Landshark Lager when the door opened and through the brilliant Florida sunshine Michelle Coburn walked into the Pub. It was her first time there and after introductions she and Chris talked seriously about what was ahead of them.

"Chris, I think the best thing for you to do is follow those umpires around as they call games in to see if you can find out anything about their behaviors that would suggest they are up to no good."

"Do you really think I should be that devious?"

"Well, having had to deal with men all my life I have learned that the best way to get a straight answer is to be as obtuse as possible. If you come out and tell them what you know you are going to scare them into the hinterlands."

"If I scare them then they are likely going to stop throwing games though."

"That's true but if that happens they will just run for cover."

"This could take forever to figure out. Are you still interested in helping me?"

"My new job is going to be murder especially at first. I need to leave tomorrow morning for another meeting in Detroit. This time we are pulling in all the scouts and the general managers of our farm teams for a meeting. The meeting is for me to lay out my plans for what I want to see happen for the Tigers."

"I remember those sorts of meetings. They were usually good for frequent flier miles at least."

They ordered their spinach salads. Michelle's phone rang as she finished her first glass of merlot her phone rang.

"Jim Biehl. I wonder what he wants. I just talked to him before I left for Sarasota."

The conversation was mainly one-sided with Michelle listening and saying "uh huh" a lot of the time. Finally it was over and she closed her phone.

"Well I will be damned Chris. Guess what?"

"What. What happened?"

"Investigators for the NTSB did some additional snooping around in Detroit regarding the Lear Jet. The plane didn't belong to the Tigers. It was leased from a company in Romulus, Michigan, near the airport. Records show that it was supposed to be rented to an importer from Key West the day of the crash. However the person from Key West cancelled at the last minute and the leasing company switched the plane to the Tigers people."

"What is so interesting or unusual about that? It sounds like a normal way of doing business."

"The NTSB is still looking into it. They are thinking maybe the tampering of the plane was an attempt to take out this importer person and not the Tigers management folks."

35

Jennifer O'Neil was in charge of scheduling for the Paradise League. She was the person responsible for ensuring that all Paradise League games were covered by umpires and it was Jennifer who knew where the league's 16 umpires were at any given moment.

Chris called O'Neil and asked her if she knew where Dennis Hastert and Justin Reed were calling games that day. His excuse was that he was an old college friend visiting Florida for a few days and he wanted to meet them to catch up on the old days. Jennifer checked her computer and then told Chris, "Mr. Ramsey, your friends are both calling games tonight through Sunday at Brighthouse Field in Clearwater."

"Thank you, Jennifer. Can you tell me what teams they will be covering?"

"Let's see. Tonight through Thursday it will be the Clearwater Thresher Sharks and the Dunedin Blue Jays. Friday through Sunday afternoon Clearwater plays the St Lucie Mets."

"Clearwater is only an hour from where I'm visiting friends in Sarasota. I think I'll drive up there tonight to see if I can find them. Any chance you can tell me what hotel they stay in when they're in Clearwater?"

"Sorry sir, we can't give out that information for security reasons."

"Thank you, Jennifer. I think I will check in on my old buddies at Brighthouse Field."

That evening Chris pulled into the massive parking lot at Brighthouse Field. Walking from his car to the stadium in the oppressive subtropical heat his shirt was soaked with perspiration before he arrived at the ticket booth. Ducking into the men's room on the first level of the stadium, Chris planned to wash off quickly, then purchase a ticket, buy a glass of beer, and take his seat. On entering the restroom he was surprised to find Justin Reed standing at the sink splashing water on his face. All afternoon Chris had practiced how he was going to approach Reed or Hastert and how he was going to explain what he knew and how it would affect them. Seeing Reed in the rest room he simply blurted out his ideas.

"You're Justin Reed aren't you?"

"Yes sir, who wants to know?"

"I'm Chris Ramsey. I live in Sarasota but a long time ago I played two seasons of minor league baseball for a Detroit Tigers farm team"

"Back in your day was that still the Lakeland Tigers?"

"It sure was, Justin, however I didn't want to talk to you about my old days playing ball."

"What did you want to talk about?"

"Justin I'll be blunt. I've been watching how you and Dennis Hastert are calling ball games and especially Sarasota Reds ball games, and I've been doing it all season long."

"The Reds certainly have their problems don't they Mr. Ramsey."

"The Reds are a great team with a lot of talent but I don't think their problems are self-inflicted. I think their problems are caused by you and Mr. Hastert."

Visibly upset, Reed blurted out "How in hell can that lousy team be my problem?"

"Justin, I had all of the pitches thrown by every pitcher in the Paradise League analyzed for any irregularities. It was done by the finest statistician in the Federal government. His analysis shows beyond any shadow of any doubt that when you and Dennis Hastert are calling Sarasota Reds games, there is a greater than 80 percent chance that the Reds are going to lose."

"That's pure bullshit. Hastert and I call games as we see them."

"I wanted to believe that Justin but the data I have don't agree with your argument. When any other team is playing and any other umpires are calling the games there is a 50:50 chance that either team will win. There is also a 50:50 chance that either team will be called safe when running bases and there is a 50:50 chance that either team will be called safe on plays at the plate. There is no denying those facts." Chris continued, "The other thing that there is no denying is that when you and Hastert call Reds games they lose more often than when any other umpires in the Paradise League are calling games. It's that simple Justin."

"Like I said before that is pure bullshit and you know it."

"I'm sorry you think it is bullshit, Justin. So you are aware, the FBI in Sarasota, the Special Agent in Charge of the FBI in

Tampa and the US Attorney's Office in Tampa all believe that what is bullshit is the way you and Hastert are calling games."

"What the hell does the FBI have to do with this?"

"When I completed my analysis of the pitches I contacted an old friend who is an FBI agent and a baseball fan. Crazy bastard still thinks George Brett was the greatest baseball player of all time but that's another story. My FBI friend thinks there is something illegal going on but doesn't have the time to investigate right now. I have the time because I'm retired."

"Investigate what?"

"Ok Justin this seems to be a bit difficult for you to grasp. I think you are being paid by someone or some organization to throw games to make the Sarasota Reds look bad. Why you are doing that is beyond me right now but I want to find out and I will find out. If what I suspect is true then you are likely a party to the violation of a whole host of Federal laws including RICO, the law that prosecutors use to go after organized crime."

"What do you mean organized crime," Reed screamed.

"Justin, hold down your voice a little bit and don't be so damned obvious. For whatever reason you are on the take and I'm going to learn why. When I do and when you are prosecuted for what you have been doing you'll have several years to ponder the consequences while you sit in some Federal prison somewhere. I hear that Leavenworth in Kansas has a nice view of the Missouri River. You might like it there."

"Mr. Ramsey, you are talking to the wrong umpire. I am not now or any time before now been taking money from anyone to throw any ball games."

"That's fine Justin. Believe what you want to believe. I have evidence that suggests the opposite and I will get to the bottom of this.

"Well, Mr. Ramsey, I'm not hiding a god damned thing."

"Again, it's fine that you believe that so strongly Justin. Here is my business card with my email address and cell phone number on it. Why not talk this over with Hastert and if you have a change in your outlook get in touch with me."

Chris sprinkled some more water on his face and then walked out of the restroom. He purchased a bratwurst and an over-priced glass of beer. At the condiment table he lathered on the Dijon mustard, sprinkled on some sauerkraut, and turned to walk to his seat directly behind home plate.

The teams were finishing their warm ups when the public address announcer told the crowd that the game would be delayed for at least an hour. Apparently one of the umpires for the evening was suddenly taken ill and a substitute umpire had to be brought in to cover the game.

36

Justin Reed left the restroom on the first level of Brighthouse Field and entered the visiting team locker room where Dennis Hastert was preparing himself for the game.

"Dennis, we need to talk and we need to talk now." The look in Justin's eyes told Hastert that this wasn't about tonight's baseball game.

"I just talked with some guy who is convinced he knows we are throwing games."

"What are you talking about?"

"I'm talking about what I just said, Dennis. This guy knows we are on the take."

"How in hell does he know that?"

"I'm not sure, Dennis. He mentioned something about statistics showing that when you and I call a Sarasota Reds game the chances are 80 percent that Sarasota was going to lose."

"Eighty percent?"

"That's what he said and he seemed to be pretty god-damned sure of himself."

"Do you know who this guy is?"

"He said his name is Chris Ramsey that he's retired and he lives in Sarasota. He gave me his business card but there is no address on it other than Sarasota."

Dennis, having the connections he had through his father, knew it would be simple to track down Mr. Ramsey if they ever needed to talk with him.

"Look," Hastert started, "this guy can't possibly know anything about what is going on. My guess is that he's just bluffing us. Maybe he's some crazed fan who is just pissed off because Sarasota has such a lousy record and he's trying to defend them."

"I don't know, Dennis. He was really adamant about it and whenever I tried to steer him away from what he was saying he went right back to what he had just said. It was like he was part Rottweiler or something."

"What else did he tell you?"

"He said that he had talked to the FBI and the US Attorney's office in Tampa about it."

Hastert paid more attention to this part of the conversation.

"When my dad was in office he could have made a couple phone calls and the FBI and US Attorney would have lost all interest. Now that we have the other party in power it won't be so easy to influence things if we ever need to."

Reed thought about his conversation with Ramsey and with Hastert and the more the weight of the situation sank in the more upset he became. "Dennis, maybe we need to get in touch with Ozzie and tell him about this guy Ramsey. Maybe he knows how to handle this because I sure as hell don't know."

"Justin, just chill out a minute and think logically. As I said before, this guy Ramsey is likely blowing smoke up your ass.

There is no way he could have done a statistical analysis of the pitches thrown and the plays called. That information isn't kept anywhere and even if it was, how could you figure out anything from those numbers."

"Say what you will Dennis, I think the bastard has something on us and we need to do what we need to do to protect ourselves."

Justin's cell phone rang and checking his caller ID found that it was Osvaldo Castro calling from his Key West number. "Hello, Ozzie, how the hell are you?"

"Are you and Dennis in Clearwater this week?"

"Dennis and I are calling a game tonight between Clearwater and Dunedin. We're here in Clearwater for the next week." Justin couldn't help wondering why Osvaldo was calling just minutes after meeting Chris Ramsey.

"That's what I thought. I just wanted to confirm. I am in Oneco right now at the Oneco Beach Bar. I came up here for some R and R and to get away from the crazies in Key West. This place is worse than Duval Street."

The Oneco Beach Bar is famous along the west coast of Florida for its tacky surroundings its unusual clientele, and because it was built about five miles from the nearest beach. Osvaldo told Justin he wanted him and Hastert to meet him at the Oneco Beach Bar after the game tonight. "We have a few changes that we need to discuss" he told Justin.

"What sort of changes, Ozzie?"

"Let's just say that the way you have been doing things is about to change. I actually think you are going to like it."

Justin's mind was racing with thoughts of all sorts of scenarios that could or might be in store for him. "Ah, Ozzie, I have one other question. Do you know a guy named Chris Ramsey from Sarasota? He said he played minor league baseball for a couple seasons and he's about your age. I wonder if you ever played ball against him?"

"Let me think. The only Chris Ramsey I knew was this loudmouth catcher who played for the Tigers organization about the time I had to leave baseball. Why do you ask about him?"

"I ran onto him this evening in a restroom here at the stadium. He said he had some information that it might interest me knowing but he didn't want to tell me at the time."

"What kind of information?

"He wouldn't tell me."

"Well, Justin, I didn't know him well, but if he has information for you I think you should pay attention to what he has to say if you ever talk with him again."

"Why is that?'

"Again, I didn't know him well but he had a reputation back in the day."

"He had a reputation for what?"

"Everyone knew Ramsey as the ultimate straight shooter. If he said the sky was orange you could expect to look up and see an orange sky. He was honest to a fault and everyone knew it."

"Thanks Ozzie, that's good to know. The game will be over by 10:00 so we should see you about midnight."

Justin closed his cell phone and instantly felt the blood drain from his face and a wave of nausea come over him. His initial instinct was to run.

"Dennis, I'm not feeling so good all of a sudden. I think I need to pass on this game and take it easy."

37

Following Clearwater's resounding 9-1 defeat of the Dunedin Blue Jays, Justin and Dennis left Clearwater for Oneco. They took US 19 south to Interstate 275 then followed the freeway through the madness and mayhem of St. Petersburg. As usual Dennis closed his eyes when they reached the Bob Graham Sunshine Skyway Bridge over the mouth of Tampa Bay. It wasn't out of fear of the considerable height of the bridge or the volumes of water beneath him. Dennis was disgusted that he had to cross a bridge named for a Democrat. On the south side of the Sunshine Skyway they took the first exit for Highway 19 south and passed through Palmetto. They then picked up Highway 41 and wound their way through downtown Bradenton to Oneco. Parking in the lot at the Oneco Beach Bar they walked inside and found Osvaldo sitting at a table.

Despite having no connection to a beach or to the ocean, the Oneco Beach Bar had long been a favorite location for the Anna Maria Island Pirate Impersonators to hang out. It wasn't unusual here to see people dressed in pirate garb, complete with large sabers hanging from their belts, sitting at the bar drinking beer and causing trouble. Tonight was no different. Sue Paschall, president of the Impersonators sat at the end of the bar wearing a pirate hat, fluffy white shirt with an African gray parrot on her shoulder. Whenever she wanted another drink, which at this time of night was quite often, she simply bellowed out "Aargh, matey" at the bartender who knew she needed another Landshark Lager. Besides its reputation as a favored pirate hangout the Oneco Beach Bar was also reported to have more illegal weapons per customer than any other bar in the Tampa Bay region.

Osvaldo had taken a table near the back of the bar in an area away from most of the blaring speakers that accompanied the band. Tonight's group was just finishing their second set with *One Particular Harbour* when Osvaldo saw Justin and waved him over. "Take a seat, boys," Osvaldo said.

"Jesus Christ, Ozzie, do you think you can find a place a little less sleazy the next time we meet?"

"Sure, I'll keep that in mind."

Osvaldo then said, "You mentioned this Chris Ramsey earlier tonight, Justin. What can you tell me about him?"

"I met him in a restroom at Brighthouse Field. He said he had some information that I might find interesting."

"And what was the information?"

"He said he had done a statistical analysis of all the pitches thrown in the Paradise League the last two seasons and his analysis showed that when Dennis and I call Sarasota Reds games there is an 80 percent chance that the Reds will lose."

"What did you say to him after that?"

"I told him that was pure bullshit. I said that Dennis and I call all the games fairly and there was no way we were throwing games against the Reds or anyone else."

"That was a smart thing to say, Justin. Do you think he bought it?"

"I'm not sure Ozzie. He was all over me like white on rice. He kept telling me that he had the evidence and that he had talked to the FBI and US Attorney about it."

"What did he say about the FBI?"

"Apparently he has an old friend who is an FBI agent. He told his friend about this analysis and then someone called the US Attorney in Tampa and they found it interesting too."

"Justin, this is just exactly what we don't need. Do you know if this Ramsey character is going to take it further?"

"I think he will. He mentioned that he was retired and had lots of time and I think he's going to keep snooping around."

"Did he implicate anyone else in this?

"No, Ozzie, he just said that he was convinced that Dennis and I are throwing Reds games."

Osvaldo pondered this a bit and then asked, "So as far as you know Ramsey has a hunch that only you and Dennis are involved?"

"That's the way it sounds to me, Ozzie."

Osvaldo's cell phone rang and he took the call. After several head shakes and a couple of "uh huh's" he hung up the phone and turned back to Justin and Dennis.

"That was a colleague of mine who wants to have a chat with you. He's sending a car around to pick us up in a minute. I assume you have nothing else to do this evening?"

They finished their beers and walked to the back door of the bar. Someone once said that the Oneco Beach Bar wasn't hell but you could see it from there. Walking out the back door made you feel like you were going there. A black Ford Expedition sat idling near the back door. Two rather large men were in the two front seats and an equally large man was in the back seat. When Osvaldo, Justin and Dennis stepped into the dingy light of the back of the bar, the doors of the Expedition opened and two of the three men inside stepped out. They motioned for Justin and Dennis to get in with them. Unwittingly they did but Osvaldo did not. With the doors locked the three men inside introduced themselves to their passengers. They were Ivan, Jesus, and Maximo, three members of a Cuban organization that took care of issues for people in south Florida. As the doors locked from the inside Jesus took a Glock 9 mm from his shoulder holster and pointed it at Justin. Maximo was driving and he eased the Expedition onto US 41 north where he turned left on Cortez and drove west toward Anna Maria Island.

"Compadre," he began, "you need to keep your mouth shut and listen very carefully to what I'm going to tell you."

Jesus then handed Justin a pair of handcuffs and instructed him to put them on Dennis' wrists. Justin was then instructed to slowly turn around and clasp his hands behind his back as Ivan put a pair of handcuffs on him. With both men restrained, Jesus told them what was about to happen.

"There are some people who are very upset that you were so obvious doing your job for them that some retired guy figured out what was up."

"We are not that obvious," Justin pleaded. "We did things exactly like Osvaldo told us and when he told us to slack off we did."

"It was wise of you to do exactly what you were told but you became too obvious and people started snooping around. That's where us three come in." By now the Expedition was in the 4800 block of Cortez adjacent to the Oakmont Theater.

"What do you mean where you three come in," Justin asked."

"Justin we were asked to take care of this problem that has arisen and to do it swiftly. That's what we are going to do."

"What problem?"

"This Ramsey guy has figured out that you two are throwing games. He might not have much to go on now but he will snoop around and eventually it will lead back to the people with the money. "

Jesus continued, "Right now the only solid information source Ramsey has is you two idiots so it's been decided that the smartest move would be to eliminate you as a potential source of more information." As the Expedition reached the intersection with 75th Street, Jesus removed a syringe from his pocket and injected Justin with a dose of Thiopental directly into his neck. This fast-acting drug did the trick and Justin was unconscious in less than 30 seconds. Just before the lights went out for Justin he wondered why it seemed that Osvaldo knew about all the intricacies of the conversation with Ramsey even before Justin could tell him. It was the last conscious thought Justin ever generated. Ivan reached over Justin's slumped body and injected Dennis with another dose.

At the intersection with Gulf Drive on Anna Maria Island they turned south and followed this road past tacky tourist shops and restaurants that dream of being upscale until pulling into one of the large parking lots just before the bridge over Longboat Pass. There they quickly attached weights to their legs and their handcuffed arms. To add to the irony of the scene, the weights were bags of the circular baseball weights that batters use when warming up before their at bats. Two bags each weighing about 50 pounds should be sufficient to help submerge the limp bodies once they are placed in the ocean.

The time was 2:30 a.m. and there was little concern for traffic to be on the highway. With that in mind they left the parking lot and drove further south to the bridge that links Anna Maria Island with Longboat Key. Stopping in the middle of the bridge Ivan and Jesus acted quickly to remove Justin and Dennis' limp bodies. They first tossed Justin over the bridge wall and followed him quickly with Dennis. Looking down in the moonlight they could see the fast current from the ebbing tide moving them rapidly out to sea. As far as Ivan and Jesus knew the bodies would be off Cancun by sunrise. Returning to the Expedition they drove to the entrance to Beer Can Island where they turned around and drove back north, over the bridge, and turned right on Cortez and followed it to Bradenton. On the south side of Bradenton they abandoned their rental Expedition in the lot of the U-Haul office near the airport. There someone picked them up and drove them to the General Aviation area of the Sarasota-Bradenton International Airport where a Cessna Citation CJ4 waited for them.

On board the plane the hatch was secured and the pilot taxied to the end of runway 14. With little air traffic at this time of night the Citation was quickly given approval to depart and 42 minutes later the pilot taxied the plane to the general aviation hangar at Miami International Airport. As far as these three were concerned they never had to see Bradenton, the Oneco Beach Bar, or the Sarasota airport ever again.

Just after sunrise, Frank and Lola Anderson, recent retirees from the Pensacola, were out for an early morning stroll to the north end of Beer Can Island. They loved this walk because it gave them a chance to see birds and other wildlife before the hordes of other retirees had taken their Geritol and were able to navigate the beach. This morning as they walked north toward the tip of the island Frank and Lola could see two large forms on the shore. Their original thought was that they were walking up on a pair of West Indian manatees that had somehow beached themselves. However these forms were too small for most manatees. Maybe they were beached pilot whales or a pair of bottle-nosed dolphins. As they approached the forms in the growing daylight it was quickly apparent that they were mammals but not the marine type they expected.

They first reached Dennis who was lying face down in the sand. Lola nearly fainted when she realized Dennis was both human and dead. She had seen enough detective and doctor shows on television that she knew to check immediately for a pulse. She found none. Next they moved to Justin who was on his back, eyes still open, as they stared into eternal nothingness. As with Dennis, Justin also lacked a pulse. Frank checked Justin's shirt pocket to see if there was any identification in it. All he found was a note on waterproof paper that contained the words "Strike Three." The other thing he found in Justin's pocket was a water-soaked business card that containing the name, phone number, and email address for Chris Ramsey of Sarasota. Taking out his cell phone Frank dialed 911 and he and Lola waited for the Longboat Key Police Department and the Manatee County Sheriff's Department to arrive on the scene.

This was not a great way to begin a day.

38

Ted Jackson had been with the Longboat Key Police Department for nearly thirty years. He started as a traffic cop issuing citations to little old ladies from Ohio going eight miles an hour over the posted speed limit. Ted was enthusiastic about his responsibility as a traffic cop and soon the Town of Longboat Key was nearly solvent because of the number of fines paid from Ted's ticketing. This didn't sit well with the Florida Department of Tourism or the Longboat Key Chamber of Commerce, but to Ted's superiors in the police department he was rapidly becoming managerial material. With luck and a little pull Ted would be high up in the hierarchy of the Longboat PD in a few years and maybe eligible for early retirement by the time he was 50. He kept hoping.

As the sun rose over Sarasota Bay, Ted's wrist watch said it was 5:50 a.m. He had pulled a long shift beginning at four yesterday afternoon. At 49 years old Ted was getting to where these all night shifts were more of a drag than excitement. Still, the more of them he pulled and the more hours he logged the larger would be his pay check and that meant more money in his state retirement fund. With 28 years of service that was Ted's main goal.

The 911 dispatcher called Ted at 5:54 a.m. and told him that two dead bodies had washed up on the shore at the north end of Beer Can Island. Although his jurisdiction technically ended at Longboat Pass, Ted was north of there sitting in the parking lot of Matt and Dom's Pastry Café on Holmes Beach when the 911 call arrived. He figured that at sunrise nobody was going to know the difference. Plus he needed a donut. It was a cop thing.

"LBK 158 this is Manatee County 911."

"Go ahead Manatee."

"LBK 158 we have a report of two dead bodies that have washed ashore at the north tip of Beer Can Island. Advise that you can handle this situation."

Ted had been working 14 hours so far and had to be back on duty at five in the afternoon just 11 hours away. Yet this call would likely give him more much appreciated overtime and all of that added up to his eventual retirement status. Plus this was a possible murder investigation and if he pulled it off successfully maybe the Town of Longboat Key board would look favorably at Ted's record when it came time for the next promotion to Captain. Already a Lieutenant, Captains bars would look nice on his uniform.

"Roger that Manatee. I'm currently looking at a car illegally parked by the side of Gulf Drive. I'll be there in a couple of minutes." Ted failed to mention that he was actually far north but he decided that what the dispatcher didn't know wouldn't hurt him.

Turning on his red lights and siren Ted raced across Anna Maria Island and at the bridge over Longboat Pass turned right into the parking lot for Beer Can Island. As he passed over the bridge he could see several people milling around at the tip of the island. He could also see two lumps that were likely dead bodies lying on the beach. Before exiting his car Ted called 911 to ask if an ambulance was enroute. One hadn't been sent so Ted asked that everyone hold off on sending any emergency crews until he made a determination that the crime scene was secure.

Safely parked in the visitor parking lot for Beer Can Island, Ted sprinted over the boardwalk to the beach then turned right and moved swiftly north along the shore to the situation waiting for him at the tip of the island. Frank and Lola Anderson were still standing next to the bodies as they had been asked to do by the 911 dispatcher. Along with them were Steven and Catherine Emerson, recent retirees from Cameron, Wisconsin, and Steve and Rachel Ottoman who were vacationing on the island from the middle of a corn field near Kokomo, Indiana.

Ted identified himself to Frank and Lola and asked for an account of what they had found and how they found it. Lola blurted out that they had been out for their normal sunrise walk when they found what they thought were a couple of beached West Indian manatees laying on the shore. On closer inspection what they thought were manatees turned out to be humans. Lola had checked both people for a pulse and finding none they called 911. The dispatcher instructed them to stay with the bodies until authorities arrived and that's what Frank and Lola did.

"We are very patriotic. We only watch Fox News, we only listen to Rush Limbaugh on the radio, well occasionally Glenn Beck too when we can find him, and we only read the online version of the *Washington Times*. We figured the most patriotic thing we could do was exactly what we had been told to do by the authorities when we called in so we stayed here." Ted thanked them for their devotion and then asked them to step back from the bodies. At first he examined Dennis and then turned his attention to Justin. Turning to Frank he asked if they had tampered with the bodies at all since they had been found.

"All I did was look in their pockets for any identification," Frank said.

Pointing at Dennis he said that he found nothing on him but then pointing at Justin he said, "This guy had two things in his shirt pocket. I never checked their wallets. Anyway, this guy had a piece of paper in his pocket with the words "Strike Three" written on it. He also had a business card of some guy from Sarasota."

"Mr. Anderson, I need to see both of those things. Do you still have them?"

"Officer I put them both back in their pockets just like I saw done on CSI: Miami once."

Lieutenant Jackson examined Justin's shirt pockets and found the two pieces of paper just as Frank Anderson had described them. He then further surveyed the scene. It was obvious that both corpses had found their way against their will into the waters off Beer Can Island. Ted looked closely and noticed that there had been no insect or scavenger activity on either corpse so their deaths were likely fairly recent. Reaching under Justin's right arm he could still feel some warmth that was greater than the water temperature so he surmised that the deaths were in fact recent. He would wait for the medical examiner to tell him any different.

Looking more closely at the handcuffs Ted discovered that they were ASP Rigid handcuffs that could easily be obtained online from the handcuff warehouse and any number of other sources. The chances of having any major clue from the kind of cuffs quickly vanished. By 6:30, units of the Manatee County Sheriff's Department marine patrol and a Florida Fish and Wildlife Conservation Commission officer were in their boats approaching Beer Can Island. Given the distance from the point of the island to the nearest location where cars could access the site it was decided by the Sheriff's office that the corpses would be removed by boat.

At 6:50 a.m. the crime scene unit of the sheriff's department began documenting the scene and constructing what happened. A major question early in the investigation was whether the bodies had been placed in the ocean from the ocean side or had they been placed there from the bridge over Longboat Pass. Logic dictated that it was the latter but to make sure the investigators needed to examine every angle.

Ted Jackson placed the two pieces of paper found in Justin Reed's pocket into a zip-lock bag and gave each bag an evidence number. He placed the bag in the possession of the evidence technician but only after making a note of what was said on each piece of paper. "Strike Three" had only one meaning and that was "you're out." The business card was of considerable interest. Certainly the person who killed these two people didn't put his business card in their pockets but stranger things have happened in Florida. Still, why would a retired guy want to kill two people? Mr. Ramsey would receive a visit from the Longboat Police Department sometime later today.

Jackson removed the wallets from the hip pockets of each decedent and examined the contents. In Hastert's he found $78 in cash, a Florida driver's license, a AAA card, several pictures of himself and a woman, a card identifying him as an employee of the state baseball league, and two VISA cards.

From Reed's wallet Jackson removed $89 in cash, a Florida driver's license, a card identifying him as a member of the You Fit Health Club in Daytona Beach, one generic Master Card, and another card identifying him as an employee of the state baseball league. Inside one of the pockets he also found a small white piece of paper with the word "Oz" and some other letters on it. There was also what appeared to be an area code 305 phone number scribbled on the paper but the sea water had obliterated everything after the 305. That wasn't much of a clue. There could be a million options for the word "Oz" when it came to any place in South Florida's area code 305. At least he knew there was some sort of a connection with someone in that part of Florida. The clue might turn out to be helpful.

After interviewing Frank and Lola a second time, Ted gave permission to the Medical Examiner to remove the bodies. One would be loaded in the Fish and Wildlife Conservation Commission boat and the other in the Sheriff's Department boat and transported to a nearby boat ramp where an ambulance would carry them to the Medical Examiner's office for an autopsy. It was obvious that the cause of death was drowning but perhaps the autopsy would provide more clues.

By 9:00 the crime scene had been scrubbed free of any residual evidence from the death of Reed and Hastert. Jackson had now been on duty for 17 hours and was, at best, a walking zombie. Reporters and photographers from the *Bradenton Herald* and the *Sarasota Herald-Tribune* were present as was staff of the local SNN all-news network in Sarasota and the ABC, NBC, and CBS affiliates in Tampa.

Before leaving the scene, Jackson called Elizabeth Yearnings, a relatively new officer on the Longboat Key Police

Department to take over for him because he was desperate for sleep. Elizabeth was a 5'1" attractive redhead with a degree in criminal justice from the University of South Florida and a law degree from Stetson University in St Petersburg. After completing her law degree she realized she could make more of an impact, but much less money, as a police officer so she chose that career path. At 31 years old Elizabeth had been married and divorced twice and had two children both of whom were well taken care of by the child support payment laws in Florida. Their father was working three jobs to be able to pay the child support and he was sleeping four hours a day at most. Elizabeth smiled at the thought. She had been on the LBKPD for a little over a year and was anxious to move up the ranks as soon as possible.

"Elizabeth," Jackson began, "I need to clock out of work before I fall over from exhaustion. I need you to track down a lead we have and I need you to report back to me as soon as you have the information."

"Certainly, lieutenant, what do you need done?"

He handed her Chris Ramsey's card and said, "I need you to contact this Ramsey person to find out what he knows about these two people and to find out what he was up to last night. Right now he's our main suspect and I don't want the trail on him to get cold."

"Right away Lieutenant," Elizabeth said in her best ladder climbing voice. "I will let you know what I find out the moment I find it out." She began the walk back to her squad car once the boats carrying the corpses left the beach. Before she arrived at her car she took out Chris' business card and punched in the number. He answered on the third ring.

"Chris Ramsey."

"Mr. Ramsey, this is Elizabeth Yearnings, I'm an officer with the Longboat Key Police Department and I wonder if I could have a word with you?"

"It's Dr. Ramsey, and certainly you can. What is this about?

"Let's just say your name came up in a conversation and I need to verify a few facts."

"Certainly, that won't be a problem. Where is it I could meet you this morning?"

"I have been on duty since six this morning and haven't had time for breakfast yet. Do you know a restaurant called the Honey Tree Café in the Albertson's mall on Lockwood Ridge?"

39

The Honey Tree Café was one of the most popular breakfast restaurants in Sarasota. Its location in the Albertson's mall left something to be desired but the food served there more than made up for the lack of ambiance. Chris sat at a table in the outside dining area. He purposefully chose a table away from most of the crowd and had asked the hostess to try to keep the adjacent tables clear because of the conversation he was going to have with a police officer. He was halfway through his omelet when the Longboat Key police cruiser pulled into the lot and parked near the entrance.

Elizabeth Yearnings extracted herself from the cruiser and before moving toward the restaurant reinserted her flashlight, night stick and other accoutrements of her belt. She hitched up her side arm and walked through the oppressive heat toward the entrance. She greeted Chris who was standing to meet her as she took her seat.

"Mr. Ramsey, it's a pleasure to meet you."

"Thank you officer and just for the record, however, it's Doctor Ramsey but I would prefer that you called me Chris."

"What kind of doctor are you?"

"I have a PhD in ornithology, the study of birds. I'm not the kind of doctor who makes zillions of dollars curing the common cold."

"And it's Elizabeth, not officer. I would have arrested my parents if they had named me officer!" Chris noted a bit of flirt in her voice as they finished their introductions.

Swallowing a bite of his omelet Chris asked her if she wanted to order breakfast. "Right now I'll just have a bagel and some coffee. Intravenous coffee if that is possible."

"Did you have a long night?"

"Well Chris it wasn't long for me because I came on duty at six his morning but it was long for the Longboat PD." She elaborated a bit more. "At about the time I came on duty, a couple on Longboat Key found two dead bodies washed up on Beer Can Island. The bodies had weights attached to their legs and to their handcuffed arms."

"That's incredible Elizabeth. That sounds like something you'd see in New York City or maybe Miami but how could that happen on Longboat?"

"Our investigation will tell us more about the how. At this point we are more interested in who and why."

"This is all very intriguing to me Elizabeth, but how does this affect me?"

"The two men who were found dead on the beach this morning were Justin Reed and Dennis Hastert. Mr. Reed carried your business card in his shirt pocket." Chris was about to take a bite of his omelet and let it hang in mid-air. "That can't possibly be true, Elizabeth, I saw Justin Reed about 7:00 p.m. last night at a baseball game in Clearwater. That's when I gave him my business card."

"We checked the identification of both corpses and those names are on their drivers licenses so we have no doubt as to their identity. To be certain we will have the corpses fingerprinted and checked against that database but it seems they are who their licenses say they are. They each also had identification from the Paradise League office in Daytona Beach. Apparently they both worked for minor league baseball. Furthermore, Reed had a piece of paper in his pocket that read 'Strike Three.'"

"I know that they both worked for minor league baseball. They were umpires. I talked with Reed one time but never spoke with Hastert."

"Do you have any idea why anyone would want them killed?"

Chris thought about this for a minute before answering. He then said, "I'm not sure if anyone would want them killed but I have a hunch they might have been involved with some people who might want other people dead."

"What do you mean by that?"

Chris explained his theory of thrown games.

"How can you be so sure of that?"

Chris explained the database of balls and strikes maintained by the Paradise League. "When a statistician as world-renowned as Doug Stauffer says there is something fishy going on, you simply have to believe it."

Chris told her about his visit with the FBI Special Agent in Charge in Tampa, the Sarasota Resident Agent and the US Attorney's office in Tampa. All of them were interested in what might be happening but without solid evidence they were not going to take steps to investigate.

"When I started out with this I was going to follow Reed and Hastert and maybe Roger Schultz to see if I could catch them in some lies. However last night, just 15 hours ago, I ran into Reed in the rest room of Brighthouse Field. I told him I was convinced he was dirty and that I was going to find the way to expose him and Hastert."

Elizabeth's cell phone rang just as Chris was completing his sentence. She took the call. "That was my chief. He said the medical examiner's office in Sarasota had completed a preliminary analysis of the blood chemistry of both decedents and they found high concentrations of a drug called Thiopental in both of their bodies."

Chris took out his iPhone and did a Google search on the drug. He learned that Thiopental is a wicked barbiturate otherwise known as sodium pentothal. It was deadly in even small doses. "Do they know how much of that drug was in them?"

"The chief said was they had enough to kill a horse."

"Did he say anything else?"

"The medical examiner was also able to place the approximate time of death at between midnight and 3:00 a.m."

Chris offered Elizabeth a time line of his activities the night before and could back that up with time-stamped receipts. He said he purchased his ticket for the game at 7:00 p.m. just after he met Reed in the rest room. "I have the VISA receipt for that purchase right here." He took it from his wallet and handed it to her. He also had a receipt for gas purchased at a

7-11 on Honore Avenue in Sarasota at 12:00 midnight, and, luckily, he kept the receipt for his bar tab paid at the White Horse Pub at 1:30 a.m. Elizabeth was convinced he was not involved.

"Chris, do you have any idea who it is that may have wanted to harm these two men?"

"I really honestly don't. They are obviously being paid by someone but that is as far as I have been able to figure this out. Why they would want to buy off minor league baseball games is beyond me and especially Class A games. It just makes no sense whatsoever."

"Because you are a person of science have you seen an autopsy performed?"

"I've done more than my share of necropsies on dead birds and I took comparative anatomy as an undergraduate but I've never seen the inside of a human body."

"It just dawned on me that maybe if you watched the rest of the autopsy you might get some ideas on what happened and why. I'm not sure this will work but it can't hurt."

"Sure, I'd love to do that. How do I make this happen?"

"Let me make a call to clear it with those higher up the chain from me. If it's ok with them then just follow me to the medical examiner's office after breakfast."

40

In an effort to cut down on costs, Sarasota and Manatee Counties had agreed to share a Medical Examiner. Each County paid half the salary and expenses for the individual and the facility where autopsies are performed. Presently the Medical Examiner's office was in Sarasota.

After leaving the Honey Tree Café, Chris followed Elizabeth down heavily traveled University Parkway to Washington Boulevard where they turned south and wound their way through more traffic to the County Administration Building. The medical examiner office was on the first floor of the County Building. Elizabeth and Chris entered and signed in at the front desk. They were greeted by Dr. Benjamin Taylor a recent graduate of the University of Florida medical school who had been hired by both counties to serve as medical examiner. Dr. Taylor welcomed them to his office and then escorted them to the autopsy room.

Justin Reed lay on the table with his chest opened and the top of his skull removed. Dr Taylor said all indications were that the heavy dose of Thiopental left both Reed and Hastert unconscious, but drowning was the probable cause of death. "You see this tiny puncture wound on the decedent's neck? This is where I think the chemical was injected into his system. Whoever did this knew what they were doing because the place where the needle entered both bodies was exactly where they needed to inject the chemical in their carotid artery and instantly get the chemical in their blood stream."

Taylor continued the autopsy and noted that Reed had some spots on his liver indicating that he may have been drinking more alcohol than is healthy to consume. The factor that killed them both however was ingestion of water in their lungs. In layman's terms they both drowned. "It's pretty simple to me," Taylor said. "Both men died by drowning after they had been given huge doses of Thiopental to sedate them. They were no doubt sedated somewhere enroute to the Longboat Pass bridge. Once on the bridge they were thrown into the water."

Chris knew from past visits to Beer Can Island that the Longboat Pass was quite deep. He checked his iPhone and learned that maximum low tide this morning was at 4:15 a.m. so if they were killed before 3:00 a.m. as the medical examiner suggested they were thrown into the ocean at a period when the outgoing tide was strongest. It was likely because the current was so strong that the bodies didn't sink as deeply as someone hoped they would and they wound up on Beer Can Island where the Anderson's found them.

Taylor told Elizabeth that he would likely have his full report prepared and on the County Attorney's office in three days. In the interim it was fine with him if the Longboat PD gave out his preliminary findings to the press or anyone else who requested information

Having spent 31 years of his life as a Federal employee, Chris had some knowledge of how to get things done. An important thing to know is who is next in line in the food chain than the person with whom you are dealing. If you can't get the person at one level to do what you need done simply call his or her boss and things usually begin happening. As much as he would have preferred dealing directly with Brenda Livingston, the Senior Resident Agent in the Sarasota FBI office, he knew that to get things moving it was wiser to go to her supervisor. Chris punched in the personal cell phone number for FBI supervisor David Addison in Tampa. Addison answered on the second ring.

"George Brett is still the greatest baseball player of all time."

"Addison, you're so full of shit it's pathetic!"

"What can I do for you this fine morning, Chris?"

"Dave, it's not such a fine morning. I'm in the medical examiner's office in Sarasota where I just finished watching autopsies of the two now-former Paradise League umpires I told you were throwing baseball games."

There was a long pause on Addison's end of the phone. "You're where watching what?"

"Yes, Dave. The preliminary medical examiner's report says both died from asphyxiation due to drowning and that both had very high levels of Thiopental in their systems. If that's not interesting enough, their weighted down bodies were found washed ashore on the north end of Longboat Key. The popular thinking is that they were both drugged to knock them out, then weights were attached to their bodies and they were tossed from the Longboat Pass bridge on an outgoing tide in the hopes that they would be washed out to sea and not found."

"Chris that sounds like something the wise guys in Kansas City would do when they were killing off their rivals."

"But you're not in Kansas anymore Dave."

"Well, Chris, I think this more than qualifies as an important enough development for us to get involved. Have you called Brenda Livingston in Sarasota yet?"

"No I haven't Dave. I thought it would be best to call you first instead of going to her since she likely wouldn't do anything about this without clearing it with you."

"You remember how it works don't you?"

"Yes I do, Dave. Now how do you think we should proceed?"

"Who is this 'we' you're talking about?"

"We is the FBI, me, and the Longboat Key PD since they are the agency of record on Reed and Hastert's deaths."

Addison thought for a few minutes and then spoke. "You know, Chris, the more I think about what you've told me the more this does seem like some organized crime element is involved. Not necessarily the kind of organized crime we know from the *Godfather* but something similar. The first time we talked I told you that one possible law being violated could be RICO, the organized crime statute. The manner in which Reed and Hastert were killed makes that seem like more of a possibility."

"So, what do we do?"

"Where are you right now?"

"I'm still at the Medical Examiner's office in downtown Sarasota."

"Ok, this is what we are going to do. I'm calling Brenda Livingston right now to inform her that her new highest priority is your issue. You meet her there in twenty minutes. Once you are there I'll have Brenda call me and we'll discuss how to proceed in a conference call."

On his first day as a Federal employee, Chris' boss Chuck Madsen told him that "when everything is a priority nothing is a priority." Chris hoped that wasn't the case now.

"Dave, I think we need to include the Longboat Key PD also. They initiated the investigation of the murders and it would be bad politics to have the Feds exclude them."

"That's very true. OK. Have the Longboat Key PD in on the call as well. What is the name of the investigating officer?"

"Officer Elizabeth Yearnings."

"Let me guess. About 5 feet tall, red hair, great body, and no diamond ring."

"You got it right the first time."

"You're so predictable, Ramsey."

41

Osvaldo Castro sat in his Key West office and watched the craziness of Duval Street unfold beneath him. It was the July 4th holiday and despite the oppressive heat and humidity that invariably smothers Key West in mid-summer, the streets were jammed with tourists each trying to cram lost years into a weekend of debauchery.

He picked up his copy of the *Miami Herald* and noticed in the Florida section a small piece written by reporter Steven Danielson about two minor league umpires that had been found dead on a Bradenton beach the day before. Danielson quoted Lieutenant Ted Jackson of the Longboat Key Police Department who gave the standard line about not wanting to comment on an on-going investigation. Jackson confirmed that two bodies had been found washed up on the shore of Beer Can Island. He also confirmed that the deceased were both umpires for the Paradise League and they hadn't been dead long when they were discovered.

This was all good news because it was apparent the police hadn't uncovered much in their investigation. Being a well-established thief, Osvaldo knew that the longer the trail ran cold the more likely it was that the crime would not be solved. One paragraph after Jackson's quote, Osvaldo's positive outlook took a sudden gloomy turn with a quote by a Senior Resident Agent with the Federal Bureau of Investigation. The story said:

"FBI Senior Resident Agent Brenda Livingston said that the Federal government was entering the investigation as an

aid to both Manatee County and the Longboat Key Police Department."

What? Why are the Feds involved?

Livingston went on to say, *"The Federal Bureau of Investigation is taking a serious look at this crime because the potential exists that Federal laws have been violated in addition to state and county laws."*

This was not good news. He took out his cell phone and called his cousin Arturo in Miami.

"Art, my man, do you have a few minutes for your cousin?"

"Osvaldo, how many god-damned times do I have to tell you my name is Arturo not Art? How often do I have to remind you?"

"Ok, ok. Arturo, do you have a few minutes for your cousin?"

"I'm about to head out the door to the airport. I have an afternoon flight to Santo Domingo and I hate being late for the security lines. What's up?"

"This morning's *Miami Herald* has a story about the death of two people that you and I know."

"What are you talking about Osvaldo? Who do I know that died?"

"The *Herald* is reporting that two minor league umpires Justin Reed and Dennis Hastert were found dead yesterday morning. They washed up on a beach off of Longboat Key near Sarasota."

"And how does this affect me, Osvaldo?"

"Arturo, if you remember, those two guys are the umpires we are paying to throw games in Sarasota. Remember that?"

"Osvaldo, I don't have a clue what you're saying. How would I know anything about any umpires and especially way the hell north in Sarasota? You obviously have me mistaken with someone else."

Michelle Coburn sat in a chair on her lanai in Lakeland reading the *Miami Herald*. She feigned indignation when reading about the dead umpires and their demise on the beach in Bradenton. "I wonder if that idiot ex-husband of mine knows what just happened on his favorite island" she thought as she read the story. Her attitude changed with the repeated mention of the FBI throughout the story. The last thing anyone needed was for all those J. Edgar Hoover clones to start snooping around. She thought that her smartest action would be to take several Xanax and some red wine and wait. As the Xanax kicked in she picked up her phone and called a number in area code 313. The recipient picked up on the third ring.

"Tim, it's me. Have you read this morning's *Herald* yet?

"No, sweetie, I haven't even climbed out of bed yet. What's in the *Herald* that makes you need to call me at this god-awful hour?"

"There's a small story about the death of two Paradise League umpires yesterday. Their bodies were found washed up on the beach near Bradenton. Because of the way the men were killed the authorities suspect something other than just local thugs were involved so they have called in the god-damned FBI. Can you believe this?

"What are the Feds doing in this? I thought you said this would all be under the horizon and nobody would ever figure it out."

"Well I was wrong. What can I say? We can't dwell on the past and right now we need to be focused on the future."

"You know, Michelle, I don't like the tenor of this at all. Somehow a monkey wrench seems to have been thrown into things by the FBI being on the scene. I'm not sure what to make of this."

"Let's not start worrying just yet. A lot of things have to fall in place before people start to figure this out and right now we don't need to worry about that."

"OK. You seem to always know how to handle these situations. I'll just keep my mouth shut and wait to hear from you. What are your plans for the next couple weeks?"

"I'm leaving this afternoon for a couple days in Venezuela. There is a right handed pitcher in Maracaibo that I want to scout and I also want to spend some time on Isla Margarita soaking up rays and forgetting about things back here. On my return from Venezuela I'm going to stop off for a few days in Santo Domingo. There is a kid in San Pedro de Macoris, Juan Fernandez, who seems to be tearing the cover off baseballs. I want to check him out before someone else gets him."

"Maybe I should come down to meet you on Isla Margarita. It's been too long since we had sex on a beach."

"Good idea. And it has been." She lied and said, "It's been too long since I had sex. I'll email you my itinerary." They hung up the phone and both went back to their morning routines.

Finishing her second cup of coffee Michelle was struck by a premonition. It involved her last conversation with Chris Ramsey when they talked about electronic surveillance and how every phone call made on a cell phone can be traced almost to the exact location where the call was made. She had made some interesting calls in recent months and now not only was the content of the calls a concern to her but so was her location when she made them.

She made a note to herself to check with AT&T to see if that could be altered.

42

Chris drove from the County Administration Building to Second Street where he parked in the lot near the Hollywood 20 movie theater. Exiting his car he walked through the lot toward the brown brick edifice where the FBI has its Resident Agent office. In the parking lot with him was a van that sported Ohio license plates owned by Ed and Shirley Colbert. Several days earlier Chris followed an Ohio van down Gulf of Mexico Drive on Longboat Key. Traveling in a 45 mile per hour zone the Ohioan behind the wheel would reach the speed limit and then suddenly drop to 25 miles per hour. Once there he would speed up to 50 and then back off to 39. As the Ohioan traveled down Gulf of Mexico Drive a long line of vehicles formed behind him each wanting to pass the other.

The Colbert's were busily talking to each other, oblivious to the line of vehicles behind them. Suddenly, with no warning to anyone, Ed slammed on the brakes and stopped in the middle of the road. He then picked up a highway map and began reading it. Chris laid on his horn as he passed by, flashing a middle finger at the clown behind the wheel. He noticed that the driver had probably eaten a few too many cheeseburgers in his day. His hair was graying and he had a full bushy beard. Drivers of the next several cars responded the same as Chris. Ed remained in the middle of the road, oblivious to the world around him as he read the highway map.

The van with Ohio license plates in the parking lot looked eerily similar to the one that caused the chaos on Longboat Key several days earlier. Chris' suspicions were confirmed when he walked by the driver's side of the van and saw a rather portly man with graying hair and a bushy beard holding a highway map. He was involved in a vigorous debate with the woman seated next to him. "God damn it Shirley, I know that we have to turn right here on 3rd Street to get to the Tamiami Trail. Then we turn left and go to the bridge to St. Armand's Circle."

"Ed, if you turn right you will be going back toward the east and St. Armand's is west of here. You turn left on 3rd Street and that will take you to the Tamiami Trail."

"Shirley, we are turning right. That's west and that's the way we need to go."

"Ed, the sun rises in the east and sets in the west. Which direction did the sun come up in this morning?"

"It came up in the east of course."

"Then you need to turn left to go west."

Once he was convinced this pair was the same people who halted traffic on Longboat Key and nearly caused a multi-car accident, Chris decided it was time for some revenge. Ever the Boy Scout, Chris decided to offer some help to these visitors to Florida's west coast.

"Hi," Chris began, "Do you folks need some help?" Ed explained that they wanted to get to St. Armand's Circle and to do so they needed to turn right on 3rd Street and take that to Tamiami Trail. His wife said he needed to turn left. Knowing his help would cause them to get even more bewildered and probably make Shirley threaten to cut off Ed for not listening, Chris gave Ed and Shirley directions.

"You're right sir. Go out of this parking lot and turn right. Third Street is also Fruitville Road. Take Fruitville Road for about one mile and turn left at the stop light for Lockwood Ridge. Once you are on Lockwood Ridge stay straight ahead until you get to the Tamiami Trail. When you pass over University Parkway you know you are on the right road."

Ed thanked Chris for his help and then turned to Shirley. "You see, smart ass, I was right. We could be there by now if we had gone the way I said we should go." With the van in park, Ed started the engine, put it in gear and drove to the stop sign at Fruitville Road. He then dutifully turned right and was soon lost in the maze of traffic.

Chris turned to his left and walked toward the office building where the FBI maintained their offices. He broke into laughter as he tried to imagine in a few minutes the screaming that would be going on in the van when Ed and Shirley figure out that they had been sent east and then north instead of west and south as they needed to be. Chris figured they would make it to Bradenton in about fifteen minutes and there it might sink in that they had been given the wrong directions. It seemed like a fitting payback for the map reading incident three days ago.

Brenda Livingston was waiting for Chris when he entered the FBI office on the ninth floor of the building. "Dave Addison tells me you have some hot news about your umpire issue."

Chris gave her a quick rundown of what he knew from his conversations with the Longboat Key Police Department and after watching Dr. Taylor perform the autopsies on Reed and Hastert. Finishing his briefing, Chris said he called Dave

Addison from the medical examiner's office to tell him that it looked like his hunch had become more of a reality than a theory.

"Agent Addison was quite into this when he called this morning. He told me that working with you was my new highest priority."

Livingston took the chair behind her desk and motioned for Chris to sit on the couch against her office wall. She called Special Agent Addison in the Tampa office. Brenda put him on speakerphone once he answered. "So, Chris, it sounds like you've had an exciting morning."

"Exciting is putting it mildly."

"Yes I can imagine. I'm going to ask Brenda to begin working with you today on trying to figure out how this crime occurred."

Addison continued, "I called some people on our organized crime task force based in Miami and none of them had any inkling of why the decedents would have been killed in the manner they were killed. Our people don't think this was a mob hit in the sense of Elliott Ness."

"I guess it's reassuring to know that no Corleone's were involved."

"Chris, you have been following this more than anyone else. What do you think is happening?"

"Someone for whatever warped reason wanted them gone no doubt to hide the fact that someone is paying someone to do it."

Addison turned his next question to Agent Livingston. "Brenda, this is obviously a murder case for which I don't see a Federal nexus. We should not have anything to do with the investigation unless we are asked. I see us having a role in finding out who was buying off the umpires and why they were doing it."

"I agree Dave. And I think this is what we need to do to start. We might be on a cold trail but I've seen colder. First of all we need to subpoena the cell phone records of Reed and Hastert. I want to know every person they were in contact with for the last year. That might give us some clues."

Chris added, "A year might not be enough. Doug Stauffer said that the first date on which there was a noticeable change in the statistics was July 16 last year. You might want to look back to May or even April last year."

"Good point, Chris. April first last year it shall be. I also want to get their bank deposit records and look for any large deposits or those that come in patterns. I would imagine the Paradise League in Daytona Beach would have their banking information. I'll start with them and see where that leads."

Addison added, "We also need to check their credit card records. Both of them were married so we need to talk with their wives to find out if they noticed anything unusual in the last year or so. We should talk to the batboys in each of the parks where they called games. People hate umpires so much that only the batboys want to talk to most of them."

Chris added, "And we need to get hold of their computers and the computer hard drives. It would be interesting to see what sort of stuff they have been viewing on the net. Maybe they have social networking pages like Facebook or Twitter.

They might have been in chat rooms also. There are a lot of things on their computers that could help."

"Brenda, can you check with the local PD to see if there were any stolen cars that might have evidence in them. And, just on a wild hunch, we need to check with the airports in Tampa, St. Petersburg and Sarasota to see if there were any unusual flight departures or flight plans filed. I doubt the murderers flew out of here but you never know."

Brenda said that the Longboat Key Police Department was doing the forensic work on their clothing. She would ask them about cars and she would personally visit the airport in Sarasota to ask about flight plans. Addison said "We have a new agent who just arrived yesterday. I'll send her over to the Tampa and St. Pete airports to ask around about flights. She is just out of Quantico so she needs to feel like she's doing something important."

Brenda asked Addison about sending the note containing the words "Strike Three" to their handwriting analysts in the main FBI building in Washington D.C. Dave Addison completed the conference call saying. "There are other things we need to look at and we will sort those out as they come up. Right now we have a lot on our plate so let's get busy."

At the conclusion of the conference call, Chris asked what he could do to help things along. He had no official power to get bank records or obtain phone call records or any of the other things they discussed. "Chris," Dave Addison began, "you have done more than your share already. The statistical analysis of the data was a brilliant idea, and cooperating with the Longboat Key Police Department will be more than helpful."

Brenda said, "You could help me by going along to Daytona Beach. I need to talk with the Paradise League officials about the bank records. I could call them but there is a fugitive warrant out for someone we think is hiding in Daytona. I want to be there when they take him down so I might as well talk to the baseball people at the same time."

Brenda continued, "Didn't you say there was a third umpire involved, or at least partially involved?"

"Yes, his name is Roger Schultz. He seems to be the umpire associated with Lakeland Tigers losses."

"Maybe we need to stop by and talk with him if we can find him. And because you like to sit in baseball stadiums so much, why don't you figure out where Hastert and Reed called most of their games and go talk to the batboys in those stadiums."

"Certainly, that sounds good to me. My ex-wife is now a honcho with the Detroit Tigers. Her office is in Lakeland. We could stop in to chat with her also. She's aware of this issue but only peripherally."

"You said ex-wife didn't you, Chris?"

"Yes I said ex-wife. We were married for about a year nearly 35 years ago when I was in the minor leagues."

"You are still on speaking terms with her 35 years after the fact?"

"You could say so. I ran onto her at a ball game this spring and then a few more times this year. We still have a passionate interest in baseball."

43

Concluding the conference call Chris noticed that it was getting late in the afternoon. He wanted to travel to Longboat Key to see where the bodies had been found. Because it was getting to be about the time that most restaurants had their "early bird" special dinner prices Chris considered asking Brenda if she wanted to try a great new seafood restaurant on the island. Chris wasn't at the stage of showing up for early bird specials at Denny's but the early bird specials at the Lazy Lobster were something you didn't soon forget.

"Brenda I'm going to go out to Longboat Pass to see where the bodies were found. On the way out there I will be passing the Lazy Lobster restaurant. It has, by far, the best seafood anywhere in coastal Florida. I was going to stop in for an early dinner. Would you like to join me?"

"Sure, why not. We are going to spend some time together on this case any way we might as well get to know each other. Let me call my kids and tell them I'll be late again getting home."

They drove away from the FBI office in Chris' Ford Focus and traveled west on Fruitville Road to the Tamiami Trail where they turned south for a couple blocks to the Ringling Causeway leading to St. Armand's Circle and Longboat Key. As they drove Chris told Brenda the story of giving the wrong directions to the Ohioan. He wondered if they had enough sense to stop in Bradenton or were they still driving north. "They could be up in Pasco County by now. I wonder if they noticed driving through Tampa on their way north."

"That's the funniest tourist story I have heard in ages, Chris. It's absolutely priceless. I'm going to have to do that during season next year."

A thunderstorm was rolling in as they passed over the Ringling Bridge. It was a typical late afternoon Florida thunderstorm with intense rain, frequent lightning and gusty winds. Once the torment was over the skies cleared and humidity hung heavily in the air. It was the type of storm that kept the tourists away in summer. Most Floridians wished that it was always the rainy season solely for that reason.

The Lazy Lobster sits in a strip mall called the Centre Shops about halfway up the island. On entering the restaurant they took seats at the bar because despite the early time, the restaurant was packed. Chris ordered a Leffe beer for himself and Brenda ordered a Leg Spreader.

"You ordered a what?"

"Haven't you ever heard of a Leg Spreader?'

"Yes, but not one that you drink. What is it made from?"

"A Leg Spreader is 2 ounces of Captain Morgan rum, 2 ounces of coconut rum, 2 ounces of peach schnapps, and 6 ounces of pineapple juice. Sometimes they put in an ounce of grain alcohol just for excitement. You shake it up and pour it over ice and enjoy."

"That is about as tropical a drink as you could want to find. Does it do what its name implies?"

"It has been known to in the past."

Brenda said that her most favorite food was shrimp and Chris recommended that she try the Shrimp Norma. It's made from shrimp stuffed with blue crab, spinach and feta, wrapped in a croissant-like crust. The meal comes with rice and a vegetable. Chris ordered his all-time favorite dish, almond tilapia made with tilapia lightly fried in an almond breading. It comes with melted amaretto butter, rice and a vegetable.

Over dinner and after her second Leg Spreader, Brenda told Chris a bit about herself. She was divorced as almost everyone is. She has two children, both daughters. One girl was 13 going on 30 and the other is 14 going on 35. They were honor students at Sarasota High School but still she worried about them. "I remember what a pain I was for my parents and I don't want to receive it from my girls. I'm afraid that I might. Both of them are drop dead gorgeous and seem to have every high school boy in town in hot pursuit."

Brenda had wanted to be an FBI agent for as long as she could remember. Growing up in Miami she had experienced her fair share of illegal activity from an early age. "I earned a degree in Criminal Justice from Florida State and then stayed there to get my law degree. I thought with that as a background I would be high on the FBI's list of people they wanted on their team."

Knowing about the intense rivalry bordering on hatred that exists between Florida State University (the Seminoles) and the University of Florida (the Gators) Chris couldn't resist asking her, "Aren't Florida State teams called the Gators?" Losing the smile that had been on her face for most of the meal, Brenda calmly said, "Remember, Chris, I am hormonal and I have a loaded Glock. Now would you care to restate that question?"

Chris could tell by the slurring of her speech that the two Leg Spreaders she drank were having an effect. He wondered what a third one would do to her.

"So, Brenda, would you care for another Leg Spreader?"

"Are you trying to get drunk so you can take advantage of me, Doctor?"

"The thought has crossed my mind. Yes."

Brenda had been an agent for 20 years, starting in New York City and then doing time in Los Angeles, Houston and Washington DC. All of the travel took a toll on her marriage and she and her husband split three years ago. It was then that the Senior Resident Agent position in Sarasota became available. She applied for the job, was accepted, and she and her daughters moved to the Sunshine State. Since her arrival she had not dated much, focusing instead on raising her daughters and establishing herself as a first rate agent. As she finished the third Leg Spreader it was obvious to everyone that she had consumed a bit more alcohol than is usually recommended for a 5'2" woman weighing 110 pounds.

Chris paid their bill and they left the Lazy Lobster. Driving north up the island they passed a Longboat Key Police cruiser idling along the side of the road with its radar pointed at southbound traffic. Looking at the cruiser as they passed by Chris noticed that Officer Elizabeth Yearnings was behind the wheel. The Longboat Key Police Department made a big deal out of the murder and was mildly upset when the FBI was brought into the investigation. If they were so upset why did they assign the officer who was leading their investigation to sit on the side of the road picking up little old ladies with blue hair going eight miles over the speed limit?

Chris and Brenda parked in the public lot at the north end of Longboat Key and followed the boardwalk to the beach and then walked the shore to the tip of Beer Can Island. There they could see where Reed and Hastert's bodies were found and get a feel for how the bridge was juxtaposed with the island. At the time of their arrival the tide was ebbing and it showed how strong the outgoing current likely was at the time of the murders.

Agent Livingston made a gallant attempt at staying lucid during their stroll on the beach but her third Leg Spreader with dinner was more than her small body could absorb. "Chris, do you have any idea how horny I get when I drink Leg Spreaders?"

"No Brenda, I don't have a clue."

"Well I get really crazy horny. I'm talking major league horny and it's been so long since I have had sex I'm afraid I will go blind or something if I don't get laid really soon."

"Brenda we barely know each other."

"Can you think of a better way to get to know someone really well?"

She had a point. By now the sun had set and everyone who had come to the beach to watch the sunset had gone back to their condominiums. "Come on Chris. What's a little sex among friends? I'm just so damned horny right now"

"But Brenda, we're on a beach out in the open and you are still technically on duty."

"Look, I have handcuffs and a loaded Glock. Are you sure you want to keep arguing with a sworn law enforcement officer of the United States government?" He made a mental note to start putting a beach blanket in his day pack whenever he was with Brenda Livingston.

Their coupling was interrupted twenty minutes later when a strong beam of light from a powerful flashlight shown on them. As the beam of light came closer Chris was certain he could see a reflection off something about a foot above the light source. Then a stern female voice said "Folks, stay right there. You are both in violation of several Manatee County laws that prohibit sex in public and at least one Florida state law that bans it also. Now would you please stand up, put on your clothes, and show me some identification."

The officer was Elizabeth Yearnings, the Longboat Key Police Officer who attended the autopsies with Chris and who was heading up the investigation of the double homicide involving Justin Reed and Dennis Hastert, Jr. At least she was heading it up when she wasn't riding a radar gun in her car or finding people having sex on the beach.

When they were fully clothed Brenda pulled out her FBI badge and her credentials and Chris gave Elizabeth his business card. She didn't recognize Chris with his clothes off. Surprised by what she had found and who she found doing it, Elizabeth asked what the two of them were doing on the beach. "We were screwing like a couple of rabbits, officer," Brenda said in her not so subtle drunkenness.

"I saw that Agent Livingston. Now why else were you out on the beach?"

Chris said, "I brought Agent Livingston out here to show her where the bodies washed up. She is heading up the FBI investigation on the murders."

"And you just decided to have sex while you were here?"

"Well, Elizabeth, we stopped and had dinner and Brenda drank three Leg Spreaders and was a little out of it."

"Were they the ones at the Lazy Lobster? "

"They were one and the same."

"Now I understand. They have the same effect on me. My boyfriend is the bartender there. He really knows what he's doing doesn't he?"

44

Brenda and Chris left Sarasota for Daytona Beach just minutes after sunrise the next morning. It was their plan to be in Daytona by noon where they would visit the Paradise League offices and begin the investigation into the dealings of two former Paradise League umpires. The Sarasota Reds were playing the Daytona Cubs that evening in Jackie Robinson Ball Park.   Chris hadn't done any recreational heckling in several weeks and felt he was overdue.

They followed Interstate 75 north from exit 213 and connected with Interstate 4 toward Orlando. It seemed to Chris that no matter what time of day or night this route was followed, the freeway was filled with traffic. All of it leaving Tampa headed for Orlando and beyond and this morning was no different. Slightly past the menagerie that is Orlando they took State Road 44 east toward New Smyrna Beach. Chris suggested this diversion so he could look for birds at Ponce Inlet, one of the premier birding locations on the east coast of Florida.

Not long after making the turn onto State Road 44, they discovered a man kneeling along the side of the eastbound lane. Brenda stopped to investigate because she was concerned that he had been hit by a car. By now the man was bent over with his face near the asphalt and his hands were cupped in front of him. Walking toward him from behind Chris called out, "Hey partner, are you ok?"

Paul Corcoran, a part time resident of the Volusia County jail turned and looked at Chris and said in a voice that was laced with drunkenness, "I'm fine man. What's it to you?"

"We saw you bent over by the side of the road and wondered if you needed any help."

"I'm fine. It's this armadillo that needs help," Paul slurred.

"What armadillo?"

"This armadillo," he said pointing down at a crumpled form that was once filled with a living armadillo. "I was walking on the side of the road and found this armadillo, man. It wasn't moving and I couldn't find a pulse so I started giving it mouth to mouth resuscitation."

"You're giving mouth to mouth to an armadillo? What in hell is wrong with you?"

"I'm fine man. It's this armadillo that I am worried about."

Overhearing the conversation, Brenda used her car radio to contact the Volusia County Sheriff. As a Federal law enforcement officer she also had authority to enforce state and county laws but she knew that this case of the drunken armadillo savior was going to take more time than she wanted to admit so she called the Sheriff to dump it on them.

Chris kept talking to Paul as he kept trying to bring the road-killed armadillo back to life. "Ah, partner, don't you think you should stop this with the armadillo? I mean after all its pretty obviously dead."

"It's one of God's creatures man and God told me to revive it."

John Morris, a Volusia County Deputy Sherriff arrived on the scene six minutes after Brenda called in her report. Morris, a 13-year veteran of the Sheriff's Office was flummoxed when he saw Paul with his hands cupped around the armadillo's mouth. He kept chanting "come on little guy, come on little guy" but the obviously dead armadillo was not responding.

Morris spoke first saying, "Sir I need you to step back from that armadillo."

"I'm trying to save its life officer. If I stop now it is going to die."

"Sir, by the looks and smell of that armadillo it's been dead for days."

"Fuck you officer. I'm going to save this armadillo. It's God's will. "

Deputy Morris, himself having been subjected to the Baptist church all of his life understood about God's will. But he didn't appreciate Paul telling him fuck you. "Sir, you are under arrest for disorderly conduct right now. I'm going to give you a breathalyzer and if you fail that you'll be charged with public drunkenness. I only wish there was a county ordinance against cruelty to dead animals because I would charge you with that too."

Paul Corcoran failed the breathalyzer test without having to study. His blood alcohol content was 0.24, or three times the limit to be considered impaired in Florida. Simply watching him give mouth to mouth to a dead armadillo should have been evidence enough that he was impaired, but Deputy Morris always wanted to have numbers to back up his statements. Morris had called for backup when he arrived on the scene and when the second Volusia County Sheriff's Deputy showed up, Paul Corcoran was handcuffed and placed in the back of the Sheriff's cruiser. Corcoran was last heard yelling from the back seat of the cruiser, "but I'm not done with that armadillo yet officer."

Brenda and Chris left when they saw Corcoran being handcuffed.

"You know Brenda, just when I thought I had seen the craziest things possible in Florida someone comes along and beats the last crazy thing I saw. What is it with this state?"

"Florida is the end of the road and a whole host of weird bastards turn up here. You have no idea how many wackos we deal with daily."

Chris said he was starting to get the idea and then added, "I also have an idea for what I think you and I should be doing in about twelve hours when we get done investigating."

"Down boy, down. We aren't even in Daytona yet. I may just cut you off because you touched that god damned armadillo. Who knows where its hands have been?"

The Paradise League offices were in a small office park on International Speedway Boulevard. Jennifer O'Neil sat behind the receptionists desk on which were two computers, a telephone, pictures of three children, and an iPod. The cord for the iPod was inserted in her ear. Brenda showed her FBI badge and credentials to Jennifer and asked to speak to the President of the league. Jennifer buzzed the President's office and told him in a stuttering voice that the FBI was there to see him.

Chuck Hunter, the President and CEO of the league exited his office, straightened his tie, and introduced himself to Brenda. "I'm Chuck Hunter, the President of the Paradise League. What is it I can do for the FBI?"

"Mr. Hunter, I am Special Agent Brenda Livingston, the Senior Resident Agent of the FBI in Sarasota." Turning to Chris she introduced him. "And this is my colleague, Dr. Chris Ramsey. Dr. Ramsey is retired from the Federal government and now spends his summers mainly heckling baseball teams in the Paradise League."

Taking Chris' hand Hunter said, "Dr. Ramsey, your reputation precedes you. We have actually had a couple of complaints from our umpires about the things you have said to them."

"Really," Chris asked, "that's quite an accomplishment for a heckler to get umpires upset with him. What was the complaint?"

"Our umpire Roger Schultz filed a complaint about you saying he was really upset when you were behind the plate in Lakeland yelling at him "Hey umpire, your strike zone has the consistency of diarrhea."

"I remember that night. Schultz was lucky that's all I said to him!"

"Yes, I know, Roger has his way of doing things doesn't he?"

Interrupting them, Brenda informed Hunter about the purpose of her meeting. "Mr. Hunter, I'm sure by now you know about the untimely deaths of two Paradise League umpires, one Justin Reed and Dennis Hastert, Jr.?"

"Yes, I certainly do. It was shocking, just shocking, what happened to those boys."

"It certainly was Mr. Hunter. The FBI is working with local authorities in Manatee and Sarasota Counties to find the people responsible for their deaths and that is part of the reason Dr. Ramsey and I are in your office today." Brenda then provided Hunter with a detailed description of the murder scene, the results of the autopsies and as much other information as she could provide without compromising their fledgling investigation.

"This is shocking information, Agent Livingston. How on earth did you get started in the investigation anyway?"

"Dr. Ramsey had a huge amount of pitching data analyzed by one of the finest statisticians in the Federal government. His analysis revealed that there was little doubt that Hastert and Reed were both throwing games."

"You could tell that from pitching data? How did you do that?"

Chris added, "I will be happy to fill you in on that later but right now we have some bigger fish to fry."

Brenda explained that the FBI had few clues in the deaths of Reed and Hastert but they wanted to start digging into their backgrounds to look for irregularities. The first thing they wanted to look at was their bank accounts and their cell phone records. "We have already subpoenaed their cell phone carriers to provide us with records of their incoming and outgoing phone calls. What we need is to get their bank records to check on their deposits and withdrawals. With the

Paradise League being their employer we assumed you would naturally be the people to talk with about bank accounts."

"Certainly Agent Livingston, the Paradise League will be most happy to work with you on that. I'll ask Jennifer to pull up their payment records right now. All Paradise League umpires have their salaries electronically deposited in their banks so at least we can provide you with that information. We don't know if they have any other banks."

Jennifer dug out the bank account numbers for Reed and Hastert and handed them to Brenda. Reed's account was with Bank of America, a well-known and widespread bank throughout the United States. Hastert had half of his salary check deposited in an account maintained by Wells Fargo Bank. The other half was deposited in the Royal Bank of Canada branch in Georgetown, Grand Cayman. Brenda found this to be curious and asked Jennifer if she would see when Hastert made the switch to having his check deposited in two banks. Jennifer pulled a file from her desk and rifled through it finally getting to the form that Brenda needed. "This shows that Dennis had us make the switch on April 17 this year. Before that all of his money had been deposited in Wells Fargo."

Did Dennis Hastert have other irons in the fire or was he simply stupid? Why else would he have been so boldly obvious and especially having a salary check deposited directly into a Cayman bank account?

"Thank you Jennifer, you just made our day a lot easier. And thank you President Hunter. I assume we can get back in touch with you if we need any further assistance on this investigation?"

Chuck Hunter said, "Of course you can." He then added, "What is your next step in the investigation?"

"President Hunter I can't get into too many specifics but I will say that Dr. Ramsey and I will be checking bank records this afternoon. "

45

Michelle Coburn caught an early afternoon American Airlines flight from Orlando to Miami. There she waited in the Admiral's Club for American flight 723 to depart for Maracaibo at 4:15 p.m. While sipping on a glass of merlot she sent an email to Arturo Kirkconnel.

The email read:

A – Nice work last week, but only one problem. Check out the story in the Herald if you haven't seen it. It suggests we have an issue that needs to be dealt with before we move forward. I'm going to Venezuela for a few days and then to Santo Domingo. Meet me at the Embassy Suites near San Pedro a week from tonight. – M.

Knowing that Chris was on to the umpires she wondered if he had any information on their murders. Anything she could gather that would keep her ahead of the investigation was valuable information. She sent an email to Chris.

Hey Cowboy. How are you? I still think of that great weekend we had in Palm Beach and can't wait to see you again. I'm off to Maracaibo then to Isla Margarita and finally Santo Domingo. Have a hot prospect in San Pedro de Macoris that I have to check out. He throws bullets from center field to the plate. Did you hear about the horrible murders of the umpires? Do you know if they have any clues about who did this to those boys? Flight is boarding. I'll write from Venezuela. M.

American flight 723 left Miami on time and four hours later Michelle walked from the air conditioned comfort of the Maracaibo airport into the sultry heat of the Venezuelan lowlands. There she took a taxi to the Maracaibo Hilton and checked in. Chris noticed the LED indicator on his iPhone flashing at about the time Michelle's plane left Miami. He checked the message and found a cheery note from his ex-wife. He was in the car with Brenda when he opened the message. He read the message, put away his iPhone and turned to Brenda. "That was a message from Michelle. She's not in Lakeland so we can't stop and talk with her. Right now she's on a plane headed to Venezuela. I guess we have to wait until she gets back before we can learn anything from her."

"I find it so curious that you and your ex-wife of 35 years are still in contact. How does that work," Brenda asked.

"It was a strange relationship with sex and baseball as its foundation. And I think the foundation was in that order. I divorced her when I caught her in bed with someone else. Then 35 years later she showed up at a baseball game in Sarasota and was seated next to me. We have talked a few times since then and I have told her about umpires on the take."

Brenda then said, "She might be a good source of information given her connections to the game. It would be wise not to piss her off at least until after the investigation is over."

They pulled into the parking lot of the Bank of America on International Speedway Boulevard and parked. Gathering their belongings they went inside where Brenda flashed her FBI badge and asked to speak to the bank manager. Gil Netter, manager of this branch of the Bank of America dynasty leaped up from his desk and darted out to the customer receiving area where he introduced himself to Chris saying "Special Agent, it's nice to meet you."

Brenda removed her badge from her pocket and showed it to Gil. "Mr. Netter, I am the Special Agent here. My colleague Dr. Ramsey is a consultant to the FBI." After exchanging niceties, they retired to Gil's office where Brenda explained her purpose in being there.

"Mr. Netter, we…"

"Call me Gil."

"Mr. Netter, we are investigating the murder of two Paradise League umpires. Part of that investigation requires that we look at the banking records of both men. One of them was a patron of Bank of America. I am here to ask for your cooperation in reviewing the bank deposit and withdrawal records of Mr. Justin Reed. His account number of record is 4350-3809-2211."

"Certainly, Ms. Livingston, we'll be more than happy to help you. In fact I can pull that information up on my computer right here. How far back do you need records?"

"We think something fishy began in July last year so let's go back to April last year and look up everything including today."

Gil Netter hit a few key strokes and he soon said, "Well, here it is. His account has been very active since July last year through last week Monday. Since then there has been no activity other than what looks like an automatic transfer that same day. Right now his balance is $1,300.58 but it looks like much more has moved through his account."

"Mr. Netter, would you please print out each monthly statement so I can look at the information more closely."

Netter hit the print icon and soon his printer was humming with page after page of bank summaries extending back to April of the previous year. He handed the print outs to Brenda who asked Gil, "Mr. Netter do you have a quiet work area where Dr. Ramsey and I can go over these statements? I would appreciate it if we could look at them here in your bank so we would have access to you if there are any questions."

Netter picked up his office phone and punched in the extension for Rhonda Ambrose his personal assistant. "Rhonda, would you please clear out the conference room. I have an FBI agent here who needs to spread out some paperwork and examine some transactions." Netter nodded his head saying "uh huh" three times, then hung up.

"Agent Livingston, if you will follow me I'll escort you to our conference room where you can begin your work."

In the conference room she divided the 64 pages of paper almost equally and handed Chris one stack. She instructed him to start with the first statement and look at each transaction to see if there were any apparent patterns. "Something seems to not be right if he has only $1,300 and some change in his account."

Chris skimmed the transactions for the previous April, May, and June. It appeared that at two week intervals a check for $1,400 was deposited in his account. After the deposits there were regular withdrawals such as $46.05 and $600, and $38.00. These were all likely things such as rent or cell phones or Internet access. That pattern remained constant until last July when suddenly in addition to the bi-monthly $1,400 deposits there were $900 deposits at odd intervals. Some were on back-to-back days while others were more infrequent. All of them, however, were for $900. The same pattern continued through August and September. In October the deposits went back to just $1,400 every two weeks. Almost all of the $900 deposits were followed the next day by a $900 withdrawal. Like clockwork the money came in one day and left for somewhere else the next day. There were exceptions where there were $400 withdrawals from an ATM somewhere, but for the most part there was a consistent movement of funds in and out of the account at seemingly regular intervals.

"Brenda, starting on July 18 last year the deposits in Reed's account increased from two $1,400 deposits a month to include numerous $900 deposits."

"Is there any pattern to the $900 deposits?"

"They seem to come and go. Sometimes they are almost daily and then others they are more scattered. There is one stretch of five straight days when $900 deposits were made. In almost every case the $900 deposits are followed the next day by $900 withdrawals."

"I'm finding the same thing here Chris. From November through March there were just the same $1,400 deposits every two weeks. Then in April I see him with $900 deposits one day and $900 withdrawals the next day. Each of the $900 withdrawals has a code that reads 69RBCCI in the transaction information."

"Come to think of it I saw that same code on the $900 withdrawals last year. I wonder what it means."

"I don't have a clue but I'll bet Mr. Netter does."

Brenda stood up and walked to the door where she got Rhonda Ambrose's attention.

"Ms. Ambrose, we need to speak with Mr. Netter. Is he still in the bank?"

"Yes, Ms. Livingston. I'll buzz him and ask him to come in right away."

"Thank you for that, Ms. Ambrose."

Two minutes later Gil Netter appeared at the conference room door.

"Mr. Netter we have discovered something interesting in the pattern of deposits and withdrawals and we need your help interpreting something."

"Certainly; anything you need. What is it that you don't understand?"

Brenda then explained about the RBCCI code after each $900 withdrawal. Netter briefly looked at the transactions and turned to Brenda. "These are all electronic bank transfers. Do you see that code "69" in front of the RBCCI? That is the code that Bank of America uses to indicate an electronic bank transfer. So, these withdrawals were all sent somewhere else."

"Can you find out for us what RBCCI means?"

Netter pulled out his Blackberry and made a couple of key strokes and then waited.

"Our database says that RBCCI stands for the Royal Bank of Canada branch office in the Cayman Islands. Last time I was down there that was not far from Seven Mile Beach. I wish I was there right now actually."

"Thank you very much Mr. Netter. I think we could all use some time in the Cayman Islands."

After Netter departed the room Brenda turned to Chris and stated the obvious. "It seems that our boy had some sort of gravy train going on and he didn't want the gravy to stay in the United States. By my calculation there were about 50 deposits last year and there have been about 25 so far this year. That's about $67,500 dollars in and out of an account that consistently ends the month with about $1,300 in it. "

Chris added, "I have a hunch those $900 deposits came into his account when the Reds or the Lakeland Tigers lost games that Reed was umpiring. And I'll bet once we get over to Wells Fargo Bank we are going to find the same pattern in Hastert's account."

Brenda asked Chris to check the Reds record for last year and the first half of this year. "I need you to figure out what days the Reds played last year and so far this year. Then I need you to figure out what the final scores were on all those games. My guess is that every time there is a Reds loss the next day Mr. Reed became $900 richer."

"That shouldn't be too difficult. All of the scores for the last two years are stored on the Paradise League website. It will just take some digging but I can certainly find out the answer."

"Good. Let's leave here and go to a Wells Fargo Bank branch and see if we can access Hastert's account information."

Chris checked Wells Fargo's website and learned that the nearest branch was on Seabreeze Boulevard in Daytona Beach about one mile from the Bank of America.

Exiting the conference room Brenda and Chris said good bye to Gil Netter and thanked him for his time. Netter quipped that he wanted to be invited along if Brenda had to travel to the Cayman Islands. Brenda smiled politely and didn't answer.

In the car and driving east on International Speedway Boulevard she asked Chris, "What is it with you men?"

"What do you mean 'you men'"?

"I mean just exactly what I said. I made the mistake of smiling at Netter back there at the bank and immediately got the impression he wanted to jump my bones."

"Well, Brenda, having recently jumped your bones I can see why he wanted to. However, I think it gets down to an issue of testosterone."

"Is sex pretty much the only thing men think about?"

"That and baseball, yes." They rode in silence to the Wells Fargo Bank branch on Seabreeze.

At Wells Fargo they repeated the same scenario as at the Bank of America branch and were given access to Hastert's bank account records. However Hastert's records showed no evidence of any $900 deposits or withdrawals. His account showed only the regular $700.00 deposits twice each month from the Paradise League. Brenda spoke first, "It appears that if our friend Mr. Hastert was dirty also, he wasn't running his money through Wells Fargo first. My guess is that the money went directly to the Cayman Islands from the start."

"You're probably right, Brenda. Remember the Paradise League said that his checks were split with half of them going to Wells Fargo and half to the Royal Bank of Canada on Grand Cayman."

"I wonder when Mr. Hastert learned to become so sneaky?"

"Brenda, don't you recognize his last name? He was the son of Dennis Hastert Sr., the former Speaker of the House of Representatives."

"Oh, that's why it's familiar. And being sneaky and subverting laws was something his father was a professional at accomplishing. Must be a case of like father like son?"

Brenda then said, "It looks like one of us is going to have to go down to Grand Cayman to see if we can access the bank accounts there. My guess is Mr. Hastert was receiving $900 deposits on the same day that Reed was transferring funds from Bank of America to the Caymans. "

Chris volunteered to make the trip. "You have so much on your plate Brenda I think it would be only fair for me to go down so you don't have to be pulled off the investigation for this case."

"Ramsey, there is no way I'm not going to go to the Cayman Islands. And there is no way you're not coming along. I should be able to get the Bureau to cover your airfare. We'll call you an investigative consultant. And if I get in trouble for it I'll just tell Dave Addison it was your idea."

Chris looked at the clock on his iPhone. "It's almost 5 o'clock. We have a baseball game at 7:00 and neither of us has eaten anything since breakfast. Let's get out of here and find our way over to Jackie Robinson Ball Park. There are restaurants near there or we can just eat ball park food. What do you prefer?"

"I suggest we go directly to the ball park. There are a couple of good seafood restaurants near it. Let's have dinner and then walk over to the ball game."

"Sounds like a plan to me."

"While you're planning and I'm driving I want you to check flight schedules to Grand Cayman. I would like to fly out of Tampa tomorrow if possible. See what's available will you please?"

"I assume we are flying in Business Class?"

"You were a Fed, Ramsey. You know we can't fly anything but coach on any flight less than 14 hours long."

"But I'm a consultant, Brenda. Don't consultants always fly in Business Class?"

"You will be swimming rather than flying to Grand Cayman if this keeps up.'

"OK. Coach it is. Let me check."

American Airlines flight 903 left Tampa the following day at 2:00 p.m. and connected with American flight 1011 in Miami at 6:20 p.m. With the time zone change, the flight arrived in Grand Cayman at 6:50 p.m. local time.

"With tomorrow being Friday, I suggest we fly down on that flight then lounge around on the island for the weekend and hit the bank on Monday morning."

"What do the returns look like?"

"We can fly out on American at 7:30 a.m. or 12:40 p.m. and connect in Miami or come back on the Cayman nonstop at 11:20 a.m."

"There is no way we can get into and out of a bank in Grand Cayman in time to catch either an 11:20 a.m. or a 12:40 flight on Monday. It simply won't work out that way."

"So what do you suggest?"

"I'm calling my secretary right now. I want to go out tomorrow afternoon on American and back Tuesday on the Cayman flight. She will book two rooms for us and set up a rental car. She also needs to contact our international division and let them know about the trip. International will contact the State Department and we'll have someone in the embassy grease the skids for us to get to the right people in the right bank to get some answers."

"Why are we getting two rooms?"

"Stop whining you big baby. They think you are a consultant. I can't have a consultant sleeping in the same room with me. You'll not sleep in your room one second. I promise you that."

Brenda made the call and thirty minutes later her iPhone chimed with an incoming email as they sat in a seafood restaurant having dinner. "Samantha is so good. She works late and never complains. She has us booked out of Tampa on American tomorrow at 2:30 pm and returning on Tuesday on Cayman Airways at 11:20 a.m. She has us booked in the Marriott Grand Cayman Resort and we have a rental car with Alamo."

"We're staying at the Marriott? Marriott is owned by the Mormon Church for Christ's sake. I don't want to give one penny to a cult."

"Care to sleep on the street in the Cayman Islands, Dr. Ramsey?"

"I'll shut up."

"Samantha said that confirmation of our contact in the embassy will arrive by email tomorrow. She also said we have a window and middle seat together on all flights."

"Any chance the seats are near the rear of the plane?"

"Why? So we are near the galley and you can get a snack more easily?"

"No, so we can sneak into the restroom and join the Mile High Club."

"Is sex all you think about?"

46

American Airlines flight 1011 was over central Cuba beginning its initial approach to the Grand Cayman airport when Chris remembered something important from their visit to the Bank of America yesterday. "Brenda. Did you bring along those bank statements from Reed's account we looked at yesterday?"

"Sure I did. I made one copy in the Admiral's Club in Miami and mailed it to my office from there. I brought along the other copy in case we need to reference something while we are on Grand Cayman. Why did you ask?"

"Something just dawned on me. We got all excited about the transfer of funds from the Bank of America to Grand Cayman, but neither of us thought to ask if they could tell where the funds originated."

"What do you mean?"

"Reed was receiving $900 dollars on a more or less regular basis. The money came into the Bank of America system and sat there for one day before it was transferred to an account in the Cayman Islands. What I want to know where was the money the day before it came to Bank of America?"

"That's a very good question. I'm ashamed of myself for not thinking to ask that of Gil Netter yesterday. Now I'm kicking myself."

"Let me check those statements. I want to see if there is anything that looks like a code on the incoming money that might help us."

Brenda removed the statements from her briefcase and handed them to Chris who commented, dryly, "You know, if we were in Business Class there would be a lot more room to work on these things."

"Do you want some cheese with that whine?"

Chris took the bundle of bank statements and surveyed each $900 deposit carefully. After looking at five of them he noticed that the same code was present on each of the deposits. He then looked three months forward and the same code was there. "Brenda, every one of these deposits, no matter which day they are made, are preceded with the same code. It is just like the departure codes when the money leaves the country for the Caymans only this code is all numbers."

"Tell me the code."

"Each incoming transaction is accompanied with the code USB3485867-001. Every one of them has that code."

"I know that USB means that little plug in thing on a computer. You know the boy part that slides into the girl part."

"Stop talking dirty to me."

"USB could also stand for U.S. Bank. I think they are based in Fargo or Grand Forks or some god-awful cold place like Billings or something."

"Hey, I'm a native North Dakotan. We are proud of the cold. We even have bumper stickers that read 'Minus 40 keeps the riff raff out' so be gentle with my home state."

"Ramsey, I knew there was something strange about you. Now you've confirmed it. But let's go back to USB. When we get to Grand Cayman I'm going to call my office and have someone see if they can track down this code and what it means or where it's from."

American flight 1011 touched down on Grand Cayman a few minutes ahead of schedule but at the correct time to see a spectacular sunset over the Caribbean. It was one of those classic sunsets with more reds than purple and more greens than orange and all of them coalesced into a kaleidoscope of color better than any acid trip either Chris or Brenda had ever been on. Heather McCutcheon, a cultural attaché at the United States embassy in Kingston, Jamaica, was in the arrivals lounge in the Grand Cayman airport to meet Chris and Brenda. The Caymans are too small to have their own embassy, so diplomatic issues are handled by the embassy in Kingston just a 45 minute plane ride away. "Agent Livingston welcome to the Cayman Islands. And the same to you Dr. Ramsey," Heather began.

"Thank you for meeting us on such short notice, Heather. The Bureau appreciates your efforts."

"Do you two want to go to your hotel first and freshen up?"

Chris said, "You know Heather, neither of us has really eaten since breakfast. We munched on some pretzels in the Admiral's Club in Miami and that was it. I absolutely refuse to pay "$7.00 for a beer and $5.00 for a bag of peanuts on American Airlines so both of us are parched on top of being hungry."

"In that case I suggest we go to dinner first and then take you back to your hotel. Do you have any place in mind you would like to try for dinner?"

"Heather, there is a Margaritaville Café over by the cruise ship dock. I have a personal need to go there for a beer and a Cuban sandwich. I suggest that we spend our first night in that café. If we make it to our hotel later that's fine. If not, that's fine also."

Six hours and too many pints of Landshark later, Chris and Brenda poured themselves into Brenda's room at the Marriott. Heather, who worked for a different branch of government, was not allowed to stay at a hotel as expensive as the Marriott and she retired to the Comfort Suites for the night. Plans were to meet for a mimosa breakfast at Margaritaville at ten the next morning.

Chris and Brenda awoke at 8:30 the next morning each fully clothed and splayed across each other and the bed at odd angles. Both awoke to the roar of their hair growing. "Good God, Ramsey, if we had sex last night it was by osmosis. I can't believe I didn't get undressed."

"I can't believe we found the bed to fall onto."

"I think it was the turtle races they had last night that got to me. I got so excited cheering on my turtle that I forgot all about the time," Brenda said.

"Sure, and eight gallons of margaritas didn't contribute at all?"

"Shut up."

"You're starting to sound like a wife."

"Is that an insult or a compliment?"

"Can I get back to you on that?"

Monday morning at 9:00 a.m. Chris, Brenda and Heather were at the front door of the Royal Bank of Canada office waiting for it to be unlocked so patrons could enter. Once inside Brenda showed her FBI credentials to the customer service representative and Heather presented her diplomatic passport. They then asked to speak with Wellington Pinder, manager of the bank. After a twenty minute wait they were ushered into Mr. Pinder's office where Heather explained the purpose of the meeting and the urgency with which they needed Mr. Pinder to cooperate.

"You see, Ms. Livingston, we have very stringent bank secrecy laws here in the Cayman Islands, and I just can't allow you to have access to any information about any of our clients."

"I understand that Mr. Pinder, but as you know things are changing in the world of bank secrecy. Switzerland and Bermuda have both agreed recently to no longer have secret accounts in their banks. No longer will they have numbered bank accounts. I know that the Cayman's haven't adopted this policy yet. However I believe that soon there will be enough international pressure brought to bear on your government that you will have to cooperate."

"We have heard many of the same things but so far there are no requirements to cooperate with any officials of any government. Our priority is to our clients and their anonymity."

Brenda continued, "Mr. Pinder I respect your position and I am trying to understand it. Right now, however, we need only to check two accounts in your bank. I don't want to copy anything. I don't want to take anything. All I want to do is see if both accounts have received funds in a certain amount on a regular basis. I also want to see if the routing codes for the deposits are the same as they are for similar accounts in the United States."

Chris scanned Pinder's office as he and Brenda talked. On one wall away from the entrance door he spotted a print of the front of the DVD for the hilarious John Candy movie "*Cool Runnings*" the true story of the 1988 Jamaican bobsled team.

As Pinder thought about Brenda's request, Chris chimed in with his observation. "Mr. Pinder, I see that you're a fan of *Cool Runnings*?

"Yah, mon, it is about my most favorite movie of all time."

"Mine too Mr. Pinder. I think I've watched it at least 60 times. I simply can't get enough of it."

"Yah, mon. The Jamaicans they almost pulled it off you know."

"I know. Each time I watch the movie I fantasize that the bolt holding the front blade to the sled doesn't come loose and they win the race."

"One of these days Jamaica is going to win the race. I wish we had a Cayman bobsled team. I'd try out for it."

Everyone laughed as they tried to imagine a bobsled team finding a hill to train on in the Cayman Islands.

"You know," Pinder said, "there probably won't be anything wrong with you looking at those accounts. Just don't make any copies of anything. Ok, mon?"

"Certainly Mr. Pinder we won't copy a thing."

Pinder called his assistant and asked her to bring in copies of the bank transactions for both Reed's account and for Hastert's. Left alone in the room to examine the transactions Chris remembered that he promised not to copy anything but he failed to say that he wouldn't photograph anything. Removing his iPhone from his carryon bag, Chris took a digital image of every sheet of paper provided by the bank.

Examining the transactions they were able to confirm that the transfers from Reed's account matched the amount and time of their deposit in the Royal Bank of Canada. Hastert's transactions were similar except that he had twice monthly deposits of $700 each on top of the regular $900 deposits, each of them on the same day as Reed's deposits of similar value.

Closing out the transactions, Brenda spoke first. "Well, it appears we have confirmation of what we found in Daytona Beach at both Bank of America and Wells Fargo. We also now know that the code USB3485867-001 was attached to every transaction into Hastert's account here. To me this is very convincing evidence that they were taking money from elsewhere and putting it in their accounts."

"So we know they were dirty?"

"No Chris. We know that they received money from a source or sources and that the amount of money was always the same. There is no way I could take anything right now to the United States Attorney. He would laugh me out of the office."

"Well then what does this mean?"

"It means that if these transfers can be attributed to the deaths of Reed and Hastert we have the proverbial Federal case because of wire transfers and the use of international banks. It looks like you are going to be stuck with me until we get this solved."

It was just past noon when they emerged from the bank into the blinding tropical sunshine. Their flight back to Tampa left in about 22 hours which gave them some time to play but before they did Brenda felt the need to contact her office. She asked Heather if there were any secure phones anywhere on the island that she could use.

Chris remembered an experience he had in the Caribbean long ago when he needed to contact Special Agents at Kennedy Airport in New York while he was on a small island in the Lesser Antilles. He was able to do so by befriending an airline pilot who took him into their corporate headquarters on the island and he made calls from there. It might work the same here on Grand Cayman.

The three of them took a taxi from the Royal Bank of Canada to the airport where Brenda showed her badge and Heather showed her diplomatic credentials to the American Airlines station manager Neville Brothers. Mr. Brothers was more than willing to give them access to his office phone and the security his office could provide.

Brenda called her office in Sarasota and her assistant Samantha picked up on the first ring. "Hi. This is Brenda. Did you have any luck tracking down that bank code I called you about the other day?"

"Hi. It was easy to track down. USB stands for U.S. Bank, and the account number was traced back to a bank in Detroit, Michigan."

"Detroit? What does Detroit have to do with this?"

"I'm not sure, Brenda, but that's where the account number originated."

"Thank you. Thank you a lot for that. You just made my day much easier. Do you have any news on what any of the other teams are digging up with this case?"

"I know that Hastert's wife and Reed's wife have been interrogated. Neither of them was really aware of anything although Reed's wife said she was surprised at times to call her husband when he was on the road and find him eating meals at places like the restaurant at the Ritz-Carlton in Sarasota."

"Why did she find that surprising?"

"His salary is typical of most of them in Florida. It sucks. And her salary was not much better. They barely made ends meet but she would call her husband and find him eating at the Ritz. That just did not compute."

"What else has anyone found?"

"That's it for right now, Brenda. There are leads out there and we keep following them but nothing is for certain yet."

"Well, keep up the good work. I'll be back in Sarasota tomorrow afternoon around five or so."

Cayman Airways flight 201 landed in Tampa a little ahead of schedule at 2:10 p.m. on Tuesday afternoon. Once through immigration and customs Chris turned on his iPhone to check for messages and emails. He had 32 phone messages, 11 missed calls, and 101 email messages. Most were spam messages trying to get him to take an ointment that would make his penis larger. 'Ha," he thought, "as if I need that."

Scrolling through the messages, the forty-fifth one was from his ex-wife Michelle.

"I'm in the wilds of Venezuela here. I think they call this the llanos or something. There are lots of birds around and I wish you were here to identify them for me among other things. Have you found out any more about who killed the two umpires? Has the FBI has developed any more leads since we last talked? I am going to Isla Margarita tomorrow to unwind then to Santo Domingo for a couple days to check out a player. I'd love to get together with you when I get home. Think of me. M."

Chris thought it strange that she had such an intense interest in this case, in the FBI and how the case is proceeding. He also wondered if he was doing the right thing telling her any information. Oh, well, too late now.

47

Michelle Coburn connected in Caracas and then flew to Porlamar airport on Isla Margarita. She had spent only a day in Maracaibo where she completed her required visit to watch Miguel Mante play baseball. She was not impressed. Michelle decided the night before that she needed to fire the scout who convinced her to fly down here. That would happen upon her return to Lakeland.

She checked into the Hotel Macanao at Calle los Uveros in the Costa Azul district because it was reputed to be the best hotel on the island. With the salary she earned from the Detroit Tigers and the money she and Tim had from his salary and their investments, a $400 a night hotel on a Caribbean beach was a cheap luxury. There had to be a way to deduct a trip like this from her taxes. She'd have to consult with her tax advisor when she returned to Florida.

Dressed in a flower-covered sarong and little else, Michelle took her 5'2" body to the beach where she selected a beach chair and then staked out her place in the sand. A waiter making the rounds of the sun worshipers arrived and asked her if she wanted a drink. "I'll have sex on the beach. In fact I'll have two of them." She then thought that if all worked out she'd be having her drink for real before sunset. One of the many young studs on the beach would work just fine.

Despite portraying her relationship with Tim was a disaster, it was anything but. While on the road she told men that she was divorced and when Tim called she said that she had been out with girlfriends. There was some strain on their marriage with Tim in Michigan and Michelle in Florida but it wasn't anything that frequent conjugal visits and a lot of phone sex couldn't cure.

Given her background Michelle was enjoying what she called her "double life." Tim thought she was the quintessential devoted wife. Michelle knew differently. She had long ago discovered his multiple indiscretions but being vain she decided she would put up with them to keep the gravy train of Tim's executive salary and their investments available to her.

Two years earlier, on a return flight from Asia where they spent several hundred thousand dollars on pieces of Asian art, she and Tim discussed plans for their future. Between his 401(k), their diversified investment portfolio, stocks, bonds, and a $3.5 million home in Grosse Pointe near Detroit their financial health was exceptional. Still there was something missing.

Their Delta flight from Tokyo to Detroit was approaching Attu in the Aleutian Islands when their discussion changed to baseball. Having been a fan almost since birth, Michelle had long fantasized about owning a baseball team even before she met Tim. It might have been the second container of heated sake that came with their Japanese dinner in Business Class but something made her talk about owning a team.

"Tim, before I die I want to own at least one major league baseball team somewhere in the country. I'd love it to be the Tigers or maybe the Cubs. I'm not sure but I want to own one."

Considering her suggestion Tim knew that between them they did not have enough fluidity in their cash flow to allow them to start buying Major League teams. The same wasn't true for minor league teams. "You know, owning a minor league team would be a good way for us to break into baseball ownership. We could start off small and work our way up after we've learned the ropes. By doing that we could eventually own a big league team. Can you imagine our friends faces when we actually owned the Detroit Tigers?"

Michelle liked the idea and agreed that they should begin looking at options. There are minor league teams in almost all of the lower 48 states but the only places there are concentrations of multiple teams are in California, Florida, Virginia, Montana, Pennsylvania and New York. Perhaps the best strategy was to focus on one "state" league. Perhaps with time they could eventually own an entire league. Teams in Montana are in the Instructional League. These are kids who have virtually no chance of ever making it to the show yet local towns enjoyed having their teams. The California League had a storied history dating back to its debut in 1941. A Class A advanced league the Cal League had produced its fair share of major league players. Classic among them were Mark McGwire, Ken Griffey Jr., and Evan Longoria. The Paradise League in Florida was likewise an Advanced Class A team and it had its own historic past. Some of the real greats in baseball had played there. People like Stan Musial, Johnny Bench and Cal Ripken Jr. among others could all say they had experience in the Paradise League.

"Honey, I think we should start with the Paradise League. We already own property in Florida, we will probably retire there and besides it's a hell of a lot closer to Grosse Pointe than California ever wanted to be. I'd like to see if we can purchase a team there and then if that works we expand our little empire to more teams," Michelle said. She then added,

"If we do this right, in a few years we'll be major league owners. Just watch."

Tim thought about her comments for a minute and then, when their plane was directly overhead Dutch Harbor, Alaska, decided that being a baseball owner was going to be a wise investment. Weeks later they received a report from an investment banker associate who informed them of the considerable cost involved in purchasing a baseball team, even at the Class A minor league level. The cost was prohibitive unless they followed one of two courses of action. First they could (and probably should, the report said) seek out loans from any number of banks to fund the purchase. This option was viable but with interest payments the final price was considerably more than they would want to pay over time. The other option, given their cash reserves, was to find a team or teams that were at very low value and purchase them outright with their own funds. Once they owned the team or teams they could change management and bring in better players and let them mature. Over time both the team and the players should increase in value.

Scanning the list of teams in the Paradise League, Michelle focused on two of them for immediate attention. The Lakeland Tigers were her team away from home because of their affiliation with the Detroit Tigers. They consistently had a poor record despite having very good talent on the field and at the mound. A change in management would likely fix that discrepancy. The other team that caught her eye was the Sarasota Reds. Their potential was great but they never came together as a team. Their record was the poorest in the Paradise League almost every year and there was considerable talk of them actually leaving Florida for greener pastures.

Attendance was abysmal with an average of only 180 fans per game in the stands. They were, as some say, ripe for the picking.

Still the Reds were controlled by a crotchety old woman from Bakersfield, California, who had been a baseball owner or in the family of baseball owners since the days of FDR. Only a hugely unpopular team and horrible attendance would help make the Reds owner more likely to cut her losses and move on.

Through her connections in organized baseball, Michelle knew just the people to talk to about making baseball teams less valuable. Some calls were made and some trips to Montego Bay were completed, and soon Tim and Michelle were on their way to owning the first parts of their baseball dynasty. Her Montego Bay connection knew exactly how to make the teams even more unpopular at the same time making their value plummet. "Just leave it to me Ms. Coburn."

After two days on Isla Margarita soaking up the sun and drinking sex on the beach, she flew north to Santo Domingo in the Dominican Republic. Arturo Kirkconnell met her at Las Americas airport and drove her to the Embassy Suites near San Pedro. "Didn't I tell you to meet me at the Embassy Suites," she barked.

"Sorry. I only wanted to be helpful," Arturo said.

Enroute from the airport she asked Arturo about the deaths of Reed and Hastert. "I'm glad Osvaldo got the job done for us, Arturo, but the blithering fool knows way too much for his own good and for ours. I think we need to get rid of him for our own protection," Michelle said.

Arturo became noticeably upset and replied, "Reed and Hastert were killed because they knew too much. Now you want Ozzie killed because he knows too much. How do I know that I won't be next?"

"Arturo you are the key to our success in this effort. When this is over and Tim and I control minor league baseball in Florida you are one of the people we want to have managing Florida operations. I predict that you will be making well over $200,000 annually in less than five years if you stick with us."

Suspecting that he wasn't being told the entire truth, Arturo agreed with Michelle and said that he looked forward to being a major player in the future of minor league baseball in Florida. Michelle failed to tell Arturo that she had earned a Ph. D in lying and that she continued to practice on her former husband Chris Ramsey and on her current husband.

They stayed up until after 4:00 a.m., dancing and drinking rum drinks in the disco at the hotel until they were almost the only people left there. Returning to her room after leaving the disco Michelle felt the urge to contact her husband. She turned on her computer and let it boot up. Her email read:

Tim – Contacted A this evening and everything is cool. Need to make arrangements for his departure. Calling E tomorrow to tell him his services are no longer needed. We need to start making inquiries with the teams about acquisitions. The records of the two teams we want are good evidence that new management is needed. Wish you were here making me misbehave. Love you, Michelle.

Fifteen minutes after sending the email, Arturo Kirkconnell knocked on Michelle's hotel room door. He left about 9:30 that morning.

Tim Coburn read his wife's email the following morning and then called his attorney. He wanted advice on how to proceed with becoming the next owner of a Paradise League team.

Michelle opened the shades on her hotel room windows and looked out over the Caribbean. It had the greenest greens and the bluest blues she had seen anywhere in the islands. She had always thought that owning property in the Dominican Republic would be a wise move some time in her future if for no other reason than having a place to run to. Her preference was to watch her fortunes grow through ownership of the Paradise League and several of the teams in it. She was on the verge of making that happen now.

They lay in bed and had one more round before going downstairs for the breakfast buffet. Michelle had always fantasized about having Latin lovers. Arturo was her first Cuban. She decided she would like to have more. Before leaving the room, Michelle pulled out her lap top and wrote another email. This time it was to Eduardo Sanchez:

Ed – Things are progressing well and we have decided that we no longer need your expert assistance on this issue. I am, therefore, releasing you from any further involvement with our venture. Our final payment for your services will be forwarded to your Montego Bay account. Let us know if we can ever assist you again. Good luck, Michelle Coburn.

Eduardo Sanchez never liked being told no and no uppity gringa was going to start now. He knew people who could and would handle these situations and do so like a ghost. Michelle had not heard the last of Eduardo Sanchez.

48

Richard Slicer was the manager of the U-Haul office on North Tamiami Trail in Sarasota. His office was directly across the highway from the Sarasota- Bradenton International airport. Several days ago he noticed a black Ford Expedition with a Florida license plate sitting in his lot. Not one to create waves, Richard decided to wait for the owner to return and claim his vehicle rather than call the police or have the Expedition towed which was his right. After all, if he understood someone else's plight they might rent vehicles regularly from U-Haul. If nothing else they might at least buy some storage boxes from his office. The more sales he made the more likely it was that Richard would move up in the U-Haul management hierarchy. Richard was set on moving up.

Slicer was willing to put up with almost anything if it meant getting ahead. However he had his limits and after a week of looking at the same Ford Expedition parked in the same space in his parking lot, Richard knew it was time to take some action. Fed up with the vehicle he called Hauling Assets, a local vehicle towing company that was nearest to his office and asked them to immediately remove the Expedition.

Cooter McKenzie, the principal driver for Hauling Assets arrived at the U-Haul office ready to remove the Expedition. As he attached the cable to the chassis, he noticed a sticker with a bar code placed on the driver side of the windshield. He examined it and saw that the code was for the Avis Rental Car Company. Rather than transport the vehicle to their impound lot, he called Andrew MacLaren, manager of the Avis outlet at the Sarasota airport and told him about the Expedition.

"Andy, this is Cooter from Hauling Assets. I think I have one of your Expeditions here. I am about to move it but before I do I wanted to check to see if this is actually an Avis vehicle. Would you mind checking this inventory number and letting me know if it's one of yours?"

"Sure, Cooter, what is the license plate number?"

"It's Florida 837J969. The bar code is A83939575792920-12." Cooter could hear Andrew typing on his keyboard and after a minute or two Andrew replied.

"Well, Cooter, I'll be god-damned. That Expedition was a one-day rental at Tampa International Airport a week ago. It was reported missing three days later and nobody has seen it since. Where did you say you found it?"

"It's at the U-Haul office on North Tamiami Trail. What should I do with it?"

Andrew said to return the U-Haul to the Avis lot at the Sarasota-Bradenton Airport. Avis would pay for the towing and Andrew would take care of the internal paperwork himself.

Sasha Brewer, a recent graduate of the FBI Academy in Quantico, Virginia, was hoping to rise quickly in the Bureau organization. At 5'3" and 110 pounds with long black hair and a hyper active sex drive, Sasha was certain to move quickly. Dave Addison, the Special Agent in Charge of the Tampa office had personally picked Sasha to determine if any flights had departed nearby airports at unusual times on the night of the murders. She checked at Tampa International and at St. Petersburg – Clearwater airports and found no small plane departures that were at unusual times or to unusual destinations. She was in the office of Sean Reid, manager of the Sarasota airport, inquiring about unusual flights when Reid's phone rang. Listening to the caller, he wrote down the information about the Ford Expedition that was being transported to the airport for impoundment.

Sasha began her inquiry saying, "Mr. Reid, the Bureau is working with the Longboat Key Police Department on a double homicide. As part of the investigation, we are asking local airports to determine if any of them had logged flights by non-commercial airlines or charter flights that left at unusual times. Specifically we want to know about any last Monday after 1:00 a.m. It would be very helpful to us if you would check your flight records to see."

Reid, a retired Marine, was always willing to help the authorities. He felt it was his civic duty.

"Certainly I will Agent Brewer."

Reid checked the flight logs and noticed that at 3:10 a.m. on the previous Tuesday a Cessna Citation with tail number N1193F departed Sarasota with two crew and three passengers. The plane landed at Miami International airport forty-two minutes later. "We are such a small airport that any unusual departures or arrivals are something we pay attention to. A middle-of-the-night flight like this on a Citation should have raised a few eyebrows," Reid said.

Agent Brewer thanked Reid for his assistance. As she rose to leave, Reid casually mentioned that a Ford Expedition that had been rented in Tampa the day before the unusual flight was being transported to the airport at that time. "Mr. Reid,

I'm not sure if the Expedition and the flight are related but I would like to have the vehicle examined when it arrives."

"That won't be a problem. Hauling Assets, a local towing company, is bringing the Expedition in right now.

Brewer accompanied Reid to the Avis rental car area. The Expedition had been parked in space 108 on the west side of the airport. Sasha flashed her badge at the Avis lot attendant and said she needed to make a cursory examination of the vehicle before anyone else touched it. When Sasha opened the driver side front door of the expedition she noticed only that there were some small grains of sand on the floor beneath the accelerator and the brake. Looking to the passenger side she noticed one rather obvious foot print outlined in sand. She was also confronted immediately with an unforgettable odor that was more of a stench than a smell. Stepping back from the vehicle she told Reid, Cooter, and MacLaren that she needed each of them to stand clear of the vehicle, to not touch anything and to generally make themselves scarce. Her next move was to take out her Blackberry and speed dial a number in Area 813 for the FBI crime lab technicians.

"This is Agent Sasha Brewer. I'm in the parking lot of the Sarasota airport and I need your assistance immediately. We have found a vehicle that may have been used in the commission of a crime the Bureau is working on and I need you to go over it with a fine toothed comb. Right now I can see the outline of someone's foot print and there is that inescapable stench that we all know from investigating bodies that have long been dead."

She paused to listen to Brewster McAfee speak to her and then continued, "No, I have not opened up the back of the vehicle but I have looked in from the windows. I cannot see a corpse anywhere but that doesn't mean there isn't one." She gave Brewster directions to the airport and hung up.

"Gentlemen," Sasha began, "through considerable luck you have uncovered what might be an important clue in a case that the FBI is investigating. Right now I can't say how valuable this clue is but regardless we wouldn't have this if it wasn't for your interest and diligence."

Despite heavy traffic on Crosstown Expressway, the FBI technicians were able to get out of Tampa and wind their way through outbound commuters and find their way to Sarasota in only 75 minutes. William Pullman, the lead evidence technician opened the passenger side rear door of the Expedition and immediately smelled the odor that Brewer had mentioned. His experienced eyes directed him to the floor covering and the rear seat where he detected what was likely a urine stain or maybe two. There was also the distinct odor of human feces that had been allowed to bake in the heat and humidity of south Florida. The strong smell was coming from it.

Technicians spent the remainder of the day scouring the seats and flooring of the Expedition. They took digital images of what turned out to be three distinct foot prints outlined in sand and also found several strands of hair. Pulliam looked at the hairs and based on his experience conjectured that they were from a Hispanic man or from Hispanic men. Samples of the sand were extracted from the foot prints and preserved for later analysis.

After four hours of painstaking analysis the technician team completed their investigation and turned the vehicle back to Agent Brewer. Sasha called Brenda Livingston to tell her about her discovery. Mid-way through the examination Livingston showed up at the airport to oversee the technicians. She brought along Chris Ramsey in his unofficial capacity as a consultant on the investigation.

Chris looked at the sand that was in the foot prints and thought it looked decidedly white and powdery quite unlike sand in many other parts of Florida. On a hunch, he left the airport and drove to Beer Can Island to gather sand for analysis. He took samples from the Beer Can Island parking lot and then passed over Longboat Pass to the public beach parking lot where he obtained another sample and crossed the road to the Coquina Baywalk parking lot for a third sample. Finally he stopped at the parking lot of the Beachhouse Restaurant and grabbed some sand from in front of the Beachhouse. Maybe some of this will match the samples from the car. If so, then there is a strong possibility that it was in one of these areas that Reed and Hastert had been drugged and weights placed on their bodies before they were thrown over the bridge at Longboat Pass.

Two additional FBI agents were conducting other aspects of the investigation. Carl Benz, an information technology specialist with the Bureau in Tampa examined the hard drives of lap top computers owned by the decedents. Hastert's Hotmail account contained fairly bland things like updates from the MLB network and occasional messages from a woman in St. Augustine who was definitely not his wife. Reed's hard drive was more interesting. He regularly received emails from a Yahoo account named "Super Ump" regarding meetings and compliments on how well Reed was handling directions and "making things happen for the people above us."

The Bureau subpoenaed Yahoo and was able to track down the IP address of "Green Flash." Apparently the address was owned by Osvaldo Castro in Key West, Florida. Benz told his supervisor who contacted the Special Agent in Charge in Miami who directed two agents stationed in Key West to interview the account holder.

Credit card records were analyzed by others in the Bureau. Again, none of Hastert's credit card transactions generated much interest. Reed, on the other hand, maintained four cards, one each for VISA and Master Card plus an American Express and a Discover card. He made payments every month to cover his costs and owed none of the card companies a penny.

Being short-staffed, the Longboat Key Police Department didn't have the human resources for intensive investigations. Instead they asked detectives from the Manatee County Sheriff's Office to assist with reviewing cell phone records that the FBI had obtained from their phone carriers. Over 17 months Reed made or received nearly 3,000 calls. In the same time he sent nearly 5,000 text messages. Investigators made copies of the text messages and learned that Reed was occasionally bedding someone who wasn't his wife. His wife would never find this out. There was no point in telling her now.

One thing revealed by the analysis was a pattern of calls to and from an area code 305 number registered to an Osvaldo Castro. Other calls to 305 were made to a company called "Square Grouper Imports" in Key West. The President and CEO of Square Grouper Imports was Osvaldo Castro. The agents assigned to work in Key West were told to interview Mr. Castro.

Later in Key West, two FBI agents visited the offices of Square Grouper Imports. The receptionist said that Mr. Castro had not been in the office all day yesterday or today and he had not called in to talk with her either. She found this quite unusual behavior for her boss.

As the agents in Key West were learning about Osvaldo Castro, Agent Sasha Brewer received a report from the FBI forensics lab in Tampa confirming that the sand taken from the passenger front seat floor of the Expedition was an exact match with sand in the sample Dr. Ramsey had collected in the public parking lot at Bradenton Beach on Anna Maria Island. The other thing in the report is that DNA from samples of feces found on back seat of the Ford Expedition and urine extracted from the back seat carpeting matched the DNA of Dennis Hastert.

There was little doubt now that Hastert had been in the Expedition and that it had likely stopped in the Bradenton Beach parking lot. If Agent Brewer's training was correct this probably meant that the weights attached to the bodies of both the decedents had been placed there when the Expedition was parked in the parking lot. At least it was a pleasant beach to be on for your last few minutes on earth.

49

Arturo Kirkconnell caught American Airlines flight 778 at 3:50 p.m. from Santo Domingo's Las Americas airport, and was back in Miami about 6:30. Before leaving the airport he called Miguel Vasquez, one of the three men who recently took care of a problem for him in Sarasota. Speaking in English so only 10 percent of the population of Miami could understand him, Arturo explained to Miguel that his services were needed one more time and this was for someone closer to home.

"Miguel, mi amigo," Arturo began. "We have an issue in Key West that needs your immediate attention. If you can handle it like you did that issue a couple weeks ago we would all be very appreciative."

Arturo gave Miguel the office address for Osvaldo Castro and sent him an email with Osvaldo's picture attached. Miguel assured Arturo that the issue would be resolved quickly and quietly. Miguel, Jesus, and Ivan left the city in a rented Ford Expedition shortly after 8:00 p.m. that same evening. Miguel had this thing for Expeditions and he preferred driving them at all times. They exited the city and followed State Road 836 west to the Palmetto Expressway where they turned south. Despite it being late the Palmetto was jammed with traffic in both directions.

Eventually merging onto Florida's Turnpike they followed it south to its terminus in Florida City where they connected with U.S. Highway 1, itself jammed with traffic headed for the Keys. The new bridge over Jewfish Creek made for a brief scenic interlude, but the 18 miles from Florida City to it were still a death trap. Even if the road was widened to four lanes there were still enough idiots out there to cause endless traffic accidents.

A few minutes before passing the Boca Chica Naval Air Station, Ivan, Jesus and Miguel discussed their plan. They knew from things that Osvaldo told them in Bradenton that he preferred to hang out at Captain Tony's Saloon on Greene Street. Osvaldo liked this bar because it was mentioned in a couple of Jimmy Buffett songs and also because when he was alive, Captain Tony himself was some of the best entertainment in the Keys. Nearly 90 years old when he died Captain Tony probably hit on more women per night in his bar, using some of the lamest lines ever invented, than most men ever use in their life time. Captain Tony was worth the cost of admission even when there was no cost of admission.

Despite having been paid immediately for the work in Bradenton, their plan was to find Osvaldo and tell him that they had not received payment for the last job. They would convince him to go with them to his office and make Ozzie take cash out of his safe to pay them. Once in their car, however, they would drug Ozzie like they did Hastert and Reed and then ensure that he was not heard from again. If Ozzie wasn't in Captain Tony's tonight they would pay a visit to his office in the tomorrow morning and chat with him there. If that was the case Ozzie would simply be shot as would his receptionist and anyone else in the office at the time.

Walking down Greene Street from Duval they could hear music pulsing from Captain Tony's. It was nearly 1:00 a.m. and the place was hopping. Almost like clockwork there were two drunken tourists from Vermont standing under the giant grouper that hangs over the front entrance and were trying to throw quarters into its gaping mouth. Like watching for the Green Flash at Mallory Square, tossing quarters into the mouth of Captain Tony's concrete grouper was also a Key West tradition.

Osvaldo was sitting at the end of the bar nearest to the men's restroom where he had one arm around Tabitha McConnell a busty redhead from Massachusetts. She had recently left her husband and came to Key West to see if all the things she'd heard about sex with strange men was what it was cracked up to be. Osvaldo was her first pick of the trip. Miguel approached Osvaldo first and told him that they needed to talk. Having had a few too many Landshark Lagers that evening Osvaldo began to protest. "What do you need to talk about, Mickey? Can't you see I'm up to my eyebrows in pussy right now?"

"Ozzie, we never got paid for that consulting work we did for you and we need the money."

"Never got paid? You're so full of shit Mickey. Of course you got paid. I wrote the check myself."

"Ozzie, we only work for cash. It's in the contract like that. There is no way you could have written us a check."

"Are you sure I didn't give you a check?"

"Ozzie, what did I just say to you?"

"Ok, Ok, I get the message. Let's go over to my office and get you the money. I need to tell Tabitha here that I'll be right back unless she wants to come along with us."

"No Ozzie, we don't want her coming along. You will be gone from here maybe 10 minutes if you're not too drunk to open your safe and then you'll be right back here."

Turning to Tabitha, Ozzie said, "Well sweetie, I need to go to my office to take care of some business for these friends of mine. Stay right here and I'll be back in 10 minutes." Fearing that she was about to be dumped and left sitting at the bar, Tabitha insisted that she come along with Ozzie to his office. "Ozzie, I want to see where you work anyway. Let's go do this and then come back later if you want."

Miguel, on the other hand, was put off. They had not planned on killing two people this evening, just Osvaldo. Because Tabitha had seen Miguel and heard his voice she could be a witness against him some time in the future so it was necessary for them to get rid of her also. Plus, if he put up much resistance it was likely that Osvaldo would sense that something was wrong and protest leaving. Instead, Miguel just bit his tongue and made quick calculations on how to get rid of Tabitha and Ozzie when they only had the equipment to do the job on one.

Exiting Captain Tony's they walked slowly south on Greene Street to its intersection with Fitzpatrick Street where Ivan was standing on the street corner and Jesus was in the Ford Expedition waiting for instructions. They realized while driving down the Keys that as soon as Ozzie saw the Ford Expedition he would likely figure out what was about to happen so they decided to keep the vehicle out of his sight as long as possible. Ivan stepped from behind a large gumbo limbo tree growing on the corner and greeted Ozzie. "Ozzie my man it's so nice to see you." Ozzie's eyes became as big as saucers as he figured out who greeted him and what was about to happen.

Ivan punched Ozzie in the solar plexus and he immediately bent over in pain. As his upper torso bent over to greet his knees, Ivan smashed Ozzie across the neck with the side of his hand. Ozzie let out a loud "ummmmpf" and lay sprawled on the sidewalk. The last thing a conscious Osvaldo Castro ever experienced on dry land was the sight of Tabitha McConnell's left breast. He wished then that he could have at least touched it once before he died.

Tabitha, having had a few too many rum runners at Captain Tony's was slow to react, let alone think about running away. Tabitha's last conscious experience was seeing Miguel's right fist as it smashed into her nose breaking it's bridge and sending bone chards into her brain's frontal lobe. Rather than take Tabitha and the copious amount of blood pouring from her into the Expedition, Miguel dragged her behind the gumbo limbo tree and left her lying there. Someone would find her in the morning and try to figure things out. It wasn't Miguel's issue any longer.

Loading Ozzie's limp body in the back of the Expedition they drove slowly but deliberately through some of the back streets of Key West to Atlantic Avenue where they turned left and followed this road along the ocean. They passed Key West International Airport and the Best Western then turned north and at the second set of stop lights turned right onto US Highway 1 where they left Key West. Once over Cow Key Pass they continued straight on to Stock Island. Despite all the glitz and glamour used by the Keys Tourist Promotion Board to lure tourists, they always fail to mention Stock Island. If the Keys had an anus it would be there.

At the end of Maloney Avenue, Jesus turned right on to the last road on the island and followed it to a 27 foot Shearwater boat moored at the end of the dock. Through prior arrangements with the boat's owner the keys were in the ignition and several tarps lay on the floor. Parking the car to block the view of the Monroe County Sheriff's Deputy if one made a patrol pass through the island they removed Ozzie from the Expedition and carried him to the Shearwater. Before moving him further Ivan applied handcuffs to his wrists and larger restraints to his ankles. Ozzie looked like he was in a reverse fetal position. Ivan, Jesus and Miguel boarded the boat and slowly motored out of the small harbor. Intersecting Hawk Channel about five miles off shore they steered the Shearwater on a southwesterly course toward the Sand Key Light. Less than a mile from the light they encountered a navigation buoy that was used to help mariners find the channel leading to the west entrance to Key West.

Miguel brought the boat to rest next to the buoy as he let the outboard engine idle. Ivan tied a line to one of the cleats on the base of the buoy and secured the boat. Using tricks from the past, Ozzie's hands were tied off to the cable that connects the buoy to its anchor at the bottom of the Hawk Channel. When sufficient weight was added to Ozzie's legs and ankles, his body was eased over the transom. On hitting the water it sank quickly.

The shock of feeling water on his body caused Ozzie to wake momentarily. On opening his eyes he could sense that he was under water. Struggling to move his arms and legs he learned quickly that they were tied behind him. There was no way he could escape or swim. As the inevitable consumed him, Ozzie prayed for a hammerhead shark to swim by and grab him before he made that last futile attempt to inhale air.

Ozzie's disappearance remained a mystery until five days later when six intrepid birders from the Wisconsin Society for Ornithology were on a trip to look for seabirds off shore from

Key West. The navigation buoys near Sand Key Light were well known as places to find brown booby or masked booby resting and at times a sooty tern or maybe even a bridled tern could be found on the buoy.

Randy Rogstad, long time birder and former president of the Wisconsin Society for Ornithology was driving the boat as they approached the buoy. Having been here several times before Randy expected to see several birds on the buoy but was surprised to see several dozen birds including some Audubon's shearwaters that appeared to be attracted to a large oil slick directly starboard of the buoy. As the birders enjoyed the sight of all the seabirds, Rogstad noticed that the oil slick was coming to the surface from below the buoy.

Motoring up to the edge of the buoy to investigate, one of the birders in the front of the boat, Nancy Olson, screamed as she looked down in the water at the base of the buoy. There, maybe five feet below the surface of the water was the bloated face of Osvaldo Castro staring back into the nothingness of the water as little droplets of his body fat, now quickly being converted to oil by the salt water and warm temperature, bubbled to the surface.

When Ozzie was tossed over the transom nobody could see that the navigation buoy was tethered to an anchor only 20 feet below the surface of the water. It had been placed there to serve as a warning to cruise ships that shallow water was nearby. Ozzie had been attached to only 10 feet of cable when he was put overboard. His body went down ten of the twenty feet on the buoy anchor cable and became lodged there rotting in the subtropical heat.

Nancy Olson was excited about the new birds she could find on the ocean's surface. She just never expected what was beneath the surface. When the image finally settled into her brain she lost everything she had eaten during her $30 breakfast at the Hyatt Key West Spa and Resort.

50

Thursday's Florida Keys edition of the *Miami Herald* contained a story by reporter Rosie Bottoms detailing the gruesome murder of Osvaldo Castro, an otherwise respected Duval Street business person. The story focused on the investigation being conducted by the Monroe County Sheriff's Department and because they maintain the navigation buoys, the United States Coast Guard. Jason Severson, Commanding Officer of Coast Guard Station Key West, told Bottoms that the Coast Guard would cooperate in every way possible with the investigation. Severson added that he had learned the FBI was also interested in Mr. Castro's untimely death. He wasn't sure why the FBI was interested but the Coast Guard would cooperate with them as well.

Nancy Olson, the visiting Wisconsin birder who first saw Castro's body beneath the buoy was quoted saying "I've never seen anything this gross in my entire life. I lost my breakfast when I saw the holes that used to have eyes in them staring back at me from under the water. I haven't slept a moment since seeing him."

Bottoms' story concluded by saying that authorities would continue to search for clues and that if anyone had any idea who could have been involved in this heinous crime they should contact the Monroe County Sheriff's tips line at 1-800-ALL-TIPS. The story was accompanied by a picture of Osvaldo Castro before he was tethered to the buoy cable several days earlier.

Chuck Ford, a thirty something UPS driver from Altoona, Pennsylvania, was inhaling coffee at the Green Parrot bar as he tried to recover from last night's debauchery on Duval Street. The highlight of last night's entertainment was watching two gay men orally pleasure each other on the grass near a bar called "The Bull." Chuck strummed through the *Miami Herald* as he inhaled his fourth cup of coffee and on reaching the front page of the Keys section stopped when he noticed Osvaldo Castro's picture.

He read the story of Ozzie's gruesome death and then saw the request for tips if anyone had any information. Unless Chuck was totally wrong, on top of being totally drunk, he remembered seeing that guy in Captain Tony's a couple nights earlier. He remembered the man solely because he was sitting with a busty redhead who had promised Chuck a blow job the next night. She wanted to try out her date, Ozzie, but she would contact Chuck the next day. She never contacted him.

Chuck dialed the tip line and gave the information to the desk officer on duty. Chuck was staying in room 215 of the Hotel La Concha in case anyone from the police department needed to talk with him. Unfortunately he would be leaving the island for home in two days. The police immediately sent an officer to Chuck's location. Other than confirming that he was in the bar and that he saw Osvaldo Castro attached to a busty redhead, Chuck mentioned a man who walked into Captain Tony's about 1:00 a.m. and he seemed like a friend. Chuck Ford remembered Osvaldo calling him "Mickey," but that was about all he remembered.

Mention of the busty redhead caused the police officer to remember that a redheaded woman about 35 years old had been found with no identification on her. The body was found behind a gumbo limbo tree just off Greene Street about two blocks from Captain Tony's. The officer asked Chuck Ford to accompany him to the morgue to see if he could identify the body.

Chuck looked at the body of the redhead lying on a stainless steel slab in the morgue and immediately recognized the red hair and her breasts. "That could be the girl who was with the guy in the paper. I'm not sure. I remember her hair and who could forget those tits. In fact I looked more at her tits than I did her face. Wish I could be of more help, but, hey, I am on vacation and I'm male and trying to get laid." Chuck was still wishing he could have collected on the blow job.

Michelle Coburn traveled east a few miles from her hotel to San Pedro de Macoris to visit with a very hot prospect named Francisco Cardenas. Several other major league teams were interested in Francisco because of the incredible breaking balls he was capable of throwing. He had speed when it was needed but Francisco's forte was the breaking ball. Tiger management knew that they needed someone like Francisco to bolster their starting pitcher lineup. Michelle wanted to sign him if she could. A funny feeling crept over her as she sat in the new baseball stadium in San Pedro de Macoris. Something told her to call her ex-husband.

Michelle removed her phone with the international calling plan and dialed Chris' number. He was having dinner with Brenda Livingston at her home on Siesta Key. He answered on the third ring. "Hello, this is Chris Ramsey."

"You don't have to be so formal cowboy, it's just your ex-wife."

"Michelle. What on earth are you doing?"

"I'm watching a baseball game in San Pedro de Macoris and I had a couple questions for you."

"Sure, fire away."

"Well, first of all cowboy I wondered if you knew any more about how the FBI is doing with that investigation of the death of those two umpires we talked about. It is just freaking me out that once you knew about them they wound up dead."

Remembering her ability to lie, and knowing that a leopard rarely changes its spots, Chris had decided several days ago to give Michelle information about the investigation only by giving her bits and pieces. "Sorry but I can't really help you there. I know that the FBI is involved and I know they have been tracking some leads but that's about it." He then added, "You certainly seem to have an intense interest in this case especially since you're calling from the DR."

"Oh, cowboy, you know me. Once I want to learn about something I don't stop until I learn it all."

Chris paused a moment and then asked, "So, Michelle, what was the other question you wanted to ask me? All we've talked about is the dead umpires."

"Well, cowboy, I have been missing you badly. I have not had sex since the last time I saw you and I have this incurable itch that can only be scratched a certain way. And as I recall you have the best scratcher east of the Mississippi." The compliments got Chris' attention. He's male after all.

Michelle continued, "I woke up in my hotel room a couple days ago and looked out at the Caribbean and all I could think about was you and how much you love the Caribbean. And

I also thought about how much I would dearly love to make love with you on a Caribbean beach."

She had Chris' complete attention now. "Cowboy, I was thinking that since you love the Caribbean and I love making love with you that maybe you could come down here for a few days of R and R with me."

Thinking quickly he told Michelle that he had some serious things in the works right now and really couldn't take time away from them.

"You're retired for Christ's sake. What could be serious for an old retired guy?"

"Michelle, I really can't get into it right now but this investigation into the umpires is getting very deep. I think we are into a few things but I can't divulge them." He could tell by the loud sigh on the other end of the phone that Michelle didn't like hearing what she was just told.

"Well that's just fine cowboy, just fine. I think what you really mean is that you're screwing someone there and don't want to take your time away from her. My guess is she's probably 40 with a tight body and big tits."

"That's not it at all," he lied, "I just feel my time would be better spent here."

Michelle hung up without saying good bye.

Brenda Livingston heard the entire story. Her FBI side found the conversation interesting while her female side found it threatening. "Your ex-wife sure seems to have a lot of interest in you. Are you certain you've been divorced from her 35 years?"

"Yes I have been. And she has been divorced from her last husband for at least five years."

"Are you sure she is divorced," Brenda wondered.

"Of course she's divorced. She told me she was."

"Chris, she also told you that she was not having an affair with anyone when she was sleeping with that duck guy before you got divorced."

Chris considered this a minute and said, "You know what, you're right. She told me she was divorced and I just believed her. She spends a lot of time up in Michigan where she said she lived before getting divorced. I wonder now if she is."

51

The following morning Brenda Livingston received a call from the FBI field office in Detroit informing her that through the assistance of US Bank officials their account USB3485867-001 was assigned to an alleged non-profit organization called "T and M Associates." The company address was listed as Grosse Pointe, Michigan. Further investigation with the Michigan Department of Revenue showed that T and M Associates was owned by T. Coburn .

An earlier call to another contact in Michigan revealed that there were eleven divorces involving "Coburn v Coburn" in the last eight years in the counties of the Lower Peninsula. Three of the Coburn v Coburn divorces were in Wayne County but none of them involved any Coburn's whose initials were "M" or "T." In fact there were no "M" or "T" Coburn's involved in a divorce in Michigan since 1989, the year before Tim and Michelle were married. When Brenda told Chris this information, his initial response was "she's been lying all along."

Brenda decided that her next move should be informing her supervisor, Dave Addison, the Special Agent in Charge of the Tampa office. Addison found these latest bits of information to be more than curious. "Tell Chris that his ex-wife is an accomplished liar," Addison said to Brenda. He wasn't telling Chris anything that he had not already figured out.

Because Brenda was now the lead Federal agent investigating this case, Addison authorized her to immediately travel to Detroit to interview Mr. Coburn. "And, yes," Addison said, "You can take that disreputable bastard Chris Ramsey with you and we'll pay his airfare." Addison then added, "Tell that son-of-a-bitch he is flying Business Class only if he pays for it." Brenda and Chris caught an early afternoon Delta nonstop to Detroit. Both flew in cattle class.

Chris knew from earlier conversations with his ex-wife that her supposed former husband was an executive with Yupper International Investments. "I'll bet that son-of-a-bitch votes a straight Republican ticket too," Chris added. After picking up their Bureau car from a low-level FBI agent who was assigned to meet them at Delta arrivals, Chris and Brenda drove first to the Yupper Investments corporate headquarters not far from downtown Detroit.

Brenda flashed her FBI badge and credentials at the rent-a-cop at the security checkpoint in the main lobby of the Yupper Building. "Alert Mr. Coburn that we are here and your nuts are in a vice and that vice looks exactly like my right hand," she told the guard.

Once on the executive floor they asked the receptionist if they could speak with Tim Coburn.

"What does this concern," snapped the prissy blonde at the front desk.

Flashing her badge in the receptionist's face Brenda replied, "It involves the FBI and your future as an employee of the Yupper Investments. Now can we see Mr. Coburn?"

The receptionist escorted Brenda and Chris down the hall to the fifth door on the left. Knocking on the door panel she said, "Mr. Coburn, you have visitors." Thanking the receptionist, Tim Coburn stood and walked to greet them.

"Hello, I'm Tim Coburn, Vice President for International Strategies. What is it that I can do for you?"

Brenda again flashed her badge and credentials and identified herself as the Senior Resident Agent in Sarasota, Florida. She then turned to Chris and introduced him. Coburn thought about Chris' name for a minute and then said, "My wife was married to a Chris Ramsey at one time. What a coincidence that you have the same name."

Chris smiled and said, "First of all Tim thanks for confirming that you and Michelle are not divorced as she tells everyone including me. Secondly it's not a coincidence that I have the same name as her ex-husband because I am her ex-husband." Coburn's face suddenly became ghostly white.

"Mr. Coburn," Brenda began. "As I said earlier I am the Senior Resident Agent for the FBI in Sarasota, Florida. We have been investigating what began as a double homicide involving two minor league umpires in Florida but the case has now become much more." Continuing, Brenda said, "Our investigation has led us down several paths and one of those paths leads to you, Mr. Coburn."

"Me? How in hell could it possibly lead to me?"

"Mr. Coburn, we have looked at the cell phone records and the banking transactions of those two umpires. The cell phone has taken us down several avenues. However the banking records are unequivocal because they lead us to you."

"How does this lead you to me," Coburn screamed.

"Mr. Coburn, the two murdered umpires were named Justin Reed and Dennis Hastert, Jr. They were employees of the Paradise League in Florida. Dr. Ramsey has attended many games of the Sarasota Reds and thought the results of the games were suspicious especially when the decedents were calling balls and strikes."

"Again, how does this involve me?"

Chris jumped in and said, "Tim, I can call you Tim can't I?"

"It's Mr. Coburn to you."

"Ok, Tim. I analyzed the pitching records of every ball and strike thrown in the Paradise League over the last two years. When those two umpires were calling games there was a greater than 80 percent chance that the Sarasota Reds would lose the game played." Chris went on to say, "I had the best statistician in the Federal government analyze the data and he says the results are unequivocal. That means the numbers are not lying."

Brenda continued, "The two umpires Dr. Ramsey mentions are now both dead. They died when their bodies were thrown in the ocean off Bradenton, Florida. Subsequent investigation of their banking records showed that since July 16 last year every time the Sarasota Reds lost a game the following day a $900 deposit was made in their bank accounts. The money for one umpire went through the Bank of America system and then into an account in the Cayman Islands. Money for the other umpire went directly to the same bank, the Royal Bank of Canada branch in Georgetown, Grand Cayman. Dr. Ramsey and I know this because we were in Grand Cayman earlier this week to confirm the information."

Brenda then added, "Mr. Coburn, we also know through tracking bank records that the money that went to both accounts originated in a US Bank account that was opened in Grosse Pointe, Michigan. Further investigation shows that the account is in the name of "T and M Associates" in Grosse Pointe, Michigan. Finally the Michigan Department of Revenue has confirmed that you and your wife Michelle live in the house that is the home address of the company."

Rather foolishly, Tim Coburn then asked, "So what are you saying, Agent?" Before Brenda could say anything, Chris blurted out, "She's saying that you are fucked Timmy."

"Never mind Dr. Ramsey's outburst, Mr. Coburn. What all of this means is that you are under arrest for money laundering and for violating three subsections of RICO, the law that prohibits various organized crime actions."

"Organized crime," Coburn screamed. "I'm no Corleone."

"Mr. Coburn, we are also trying to determine how, at this point, we can charge you as an accessory to the murders of the two umpires, Mr. Reed and Mr. Hastert."

Tim Coburn then blurted out, "This is pure bullshit. I've never done a god-damned thing wrong in my entire life. It's that calculating little bitch I'm married to at the moment. It's always been about her."

As Brenda read Coburn his Miranda rights, he stood up and said that he needed to use the restroom. "I will be right back."

"Mr. Coburn, I can't let you do that. You are under arrest and you are a risk to flight. Now turn around and extend your hands behind you."

Doing as he was told, Tim Coburn, investment executive, felt the cold steel of handcuffs on his wrists. When he heard and then felt the cuffs collapse around his wrists the room was suddenly filled with an odor that told everyone he no longer needed to use the executive restroom.

52

Tim Coburn's arrest cast an entirely different light on the investigation. For one he confirmed that he was still married to Michelle despite her protestations to the contrary. Secondly, his actions and statements made later in the presence of his now-perplexed attorney confirmed beyond even the most unreasonable doubt that he and his wife had conspired to cause baseball games to be thrown in an attempt to drive down the value of the Sarasota Reds and the Lakeland Tigers. Coburn eventually admitted that their ultimate goal was to acquire those teams at rock bottom prices so they could begin their own baseball dynasty.

The FBI and local authorities had collected sufficient evidence to show even a skeptical jury that Tim and Michelle had orchestrated and paid for the murders of Reed and Hastert. Furthermore, while under interrogation by the FBI, Coburn made statements suggesting his involvement in the sabotaging of a charter jet. That sabotaging resulted in the deaths of three members of the Detroit Tigers management team including former Regional Manager Stuart Masterson. Curiously his wife was selected to replace Masterson after his untimely death.

Simply put, the more Tim Coburn opened his mouth the deeper the hole became that he was digging for himself and his wife. And the more he talked the longer he and Michelle were likely going to remain in a Federal prison. The FBI wanted him to not stop talking. His attorney finally convinced him otherwise. The FBI said that Leavenworth in Kansas was a pretty place to be in spring time. Coburn was flown by the

United States Marshalls Service from Detroit that afternoon to the Federal Detention Center in Miami where he would wait for this trial.

Unaware that her husband had been arrested and detained by the Feds, Michelle left the Embassy Suites by Hilton Los Marlins Hotel and Golf Resort between Santo Domingo and San Pedro de Macoris and traveled east to La Romana. Michelle always stayed at this Embassy Suites hotel when she visited San Pedro de Macoris. After all it was a Hilton property. In La Romana she checked into the Casa de Campo all-inclusive resort where she planned to stay for three nights before returning home. The Casa de Campo was not a Hilton property but it was the most expensive property in La Romana and the only true 5-star so it was marginally acceptable. At $700 a night including all her food and all the sex on the beach she could drink, Casa de Campo was a bargain at twice the price. Besides, she needed time to think about what to do next now that the FBI was all over this case.

Concerned that the Feds were getting a little too close she needed to talk with someone. Chris was obviously out because she couldn't get him to travel to the Dominican Republic to be with her and he knew too much.. Instead she called her husband. He would be jealous that she was at Casa de Campo without him. Tim didn't answer his cell phone after five rings so she left a message.

Honey, this is Michelle. I'm at Casa de Campo in the DR for a couple of days. I wanted you here with me but that isn't going to happen. I talked with my ex Chris and it seems the authorities know a bit more than we wish they knew. I'm getting scared. Call me. Love you.

Upon his incarceration, Tim Coburn relinquished control of his cell phone and it was put in the custody of the FBI. The Bureau in this instance was Brenda Livingston, the lead FBI investigator on the case. Brenda intercepted the call from Michelle and recorded its contents.

"Your ex-wife is now at the Casa de Campo resort in the Dominican Republic. She just called her husband and told him her location. She also said that her ex-husband, that would be you, told her more than she wanted to know about the investigation. Just what in hell did you tell her Chris?"

"Brenda you were sitting next to me when she called me and you heard everything I said to her."

"Was that the only time you've talked to her?"

"You sound jealous not like an investigator."

"God damn it Chris, answer me. Remember I have a loaded Glock and handcuffs!"

Trying to put some levity in the situation Chris replied, "The handcuffs could be fun. I'm not so sure about the Glock though."

"Chris, unless it is your desire to be cut off immediately you will begin answering my questions and I don't want any bullshit from you."

"Ok, I'll stop. The only time I have talked with her on the phone was when you were present. You know everything that was said. I have shown you every email message that I have received from her and I have forwarded to you every text message she has sent me since the day we started this investigation. The only person who knows more than you about my communications is me."

"In that case, Dr. Birds, I think that tomorrow you and I are traveling to the Dominican Republic. I believe it is time we had a face to face conversation or confrontation with your ex-wife."

"That's great news. Are we flying in Business Class?"

"I'm not going to give that question a second thought. Will you please get online and see when American Airlines can get us to Santo Domingo?"

Chris removed his iPhone from its holster and pulled up the American Airlines app. Once it finally loaded he checked flights and times from Tampa to Santo Domingo. "Well, Brenda the only flight that has any seats available tomorrow is American 903 at 2:30 p.m. It connects with American flight 1901 in Miami at 5:00 p.m. and gets us to Santo Domingo about 7:10."

"Can you book us two seats? The Bureau will reimburse you."

"Sure, I'd love to book two seats, but there is just a slight problem."

"And that problem is?"

"American has seats to Santo Domingo tomorrow but only in Business Class. There are no cattle class seats available on any airline tomorrow. If you want to go there tomorrow we are going to have to buy Business Class seats. Swimming is our only other option."

Brenda mulled this over and before she could give Chris an answer, Chris was on the phone to her supervisor Dave Addison. He explained the situation and Addison approved the purchase of Business Class seats. Hanging up the phone and explaining what had just happened, Brenda asked, "So do you always get your way?"

"Am I required to answer that?"

American Airlines flight 1901 left Miami on time at 5:00 p.m. The Boeing 767 was only half-full in cattle class and there were only two passengers in Business Class. One of them sat in the port window at the bulkhead,. The other, Chris, sat beside her.

"Ramsey you are going to get me fired for this. You know we can't fly Business Class unless it's an emergency and authorized."

"Brenda, didn't your supervisor give verbal authorization for you to purchase Business Class tickets?"

"No, actually, he gave you verbal authorization to buy Business Class tickets."

"Ok. You're picking nits now. The fact remains that we were authorized by your supervisor to buy the tickets. Now will you relax, put down the *Miami Herald*, have another rum drink, and kiss me."

"I will put down the paper and I'll have another rum drink but there is no way in hell I'm going to relax or kiss you at the moment."

"I sense that despite going to a romantic tropical island with you I'm going to be cut off for the duration?"

"Keep it up and you will be."

53

Eduardo Sanchez was seeing red after receiving the email severing any further involvement with Michelle Coburn. "I have never once in my life let a gringa jerk me around and I'll be god-damned if I am going to start now." Eduardo Sanchez and Arturo Kirkconnell were not only business associates but they were also relatives. They were first cousins to be exact. Eduardo's father and Arturo's mother were brother and sister. Both of their parents had escaped Cuba in 1959 just before Fidel Castro made his triumphant entrance into Havana and changed the entire make-up of the island nation. As pandemonium engulfed Havana, Eduardo and Arturo's parents were playing with their cousins in Miami.

In 2001, just before the September 11 attacks, Eduardo came under the intense scrutiny of the US Attorney in Miami because of his now-sloppy dealings with some Colombian drug dealers. He knew that the cocaine trade was big business and wanted to be a part of it. Once, while in Cali on business he met Rosa the daughter of the man in charge of the Cali Cartel, one of the most ruthless drug organizations in South America. They were married three months later and now Eduardo was in the driver's seat to become a major player in the drug cartel.

The Cali Cartel, given their power and influence, had a snitch on the inside of the Drug Enforcement Administration. The snitch found out about the impending arrival of a massive quantity of cocaine that was leaving Cartagena in a personal submarine and headed for the Florida Keys. Before its arrival, the DEA and the US Attorney in Miami had agreed that it was time to cut Eduardo off at the knees and they set up a sting operation designed to capture Eduardo. However his inside information saved him from the clutches of the US government.

While DEA agents waited to meet Eduardo under the guise of acquiring drugs from him, Eduardo was on a Caribbean Airways flight to Kingston, Jamaica. He remembered waving out the window of his First Class seat as the plane passed over Key Biscayne where the meeting was supposed to take place. Arriving in Kingston, Eduardo bought a ticket to Havana and when he was back in the capital, he renounced his American citizenship much to the happy surprise of Fidel and his brother Raul. The Castro government made certain that the American press learned that a Cuban had given up his American citizenship and was returning to his roots. They made a big deal of it in *Gramma Internacional*, the official media voice of the Castro government.

Carlos Alvarez, the station chief in the US Interests Section on the malecon in Havana was livid when he read the *Gramma Internacional* story. He alerted his superiors in Langley who, in a rare case of sharing information, passed on the story to the DEA and the Department of Justice. Having been snookered by Eduardo, the Department of Justice issued a warrant for his arrest. Should Eduardo Sanchez ever step foot back in the United States or any of its Trust Territories he was to be arrested immediately. Furthermore, should any authorized United States law enforcement officer have contact with Eduardo in any country that has extradition treaties with the United States, that law enforcement officer was authorized to use all necessary force to bring Sanchez to justice. In more simple terms, Eduardo's ass was grass if any law enforcement official from the United States ever caught him however he had no intention of being caught. Because of his desire to remain free he made a vow to never step foot again on any land that was under the jurisdiction of the United States government. That included Puerto Rico, the US Virgin Islands and even Navassa Island off the coast of Haiti that was a National Wildlife Refuge inhabited only by anoles and birds

Arturo was leaving the hotel in Santo Domingo when Eduardo's phone rang. At the time Eduardo was sitting in Jimmy Buffett's Margaritaville Café in Montego Bay nursing a Red Stripe and contemplating the Jamaican woman who was his server.

"Ed this is Art. I'm in Santo Domingo and I have some great news for you."

"Let me guess. Dick Cheney suffered a massive stroke and he's now a vegetable."

"Not that good but close. I know that Michelle Coburn severed her financial relationship with you and that means also with me. I know you're not happy about it. I also have a hunch that she is going to make sure that the same thing that happened to those two umpires and to Osvaldo Castro happens to me. I want to make damned sure that never happens."

"I don't want that to happen. I just want to get my hands around her neck for about one minute."

"Well, Ed, that opportunity may be presenting itself now."

"What do you mean?"

"She just left this hotel where I have been in bed with her for two days and is headed to Casa de Campo for three nights. She thinks I'm flying back to Miami this afternoon but I'm not. I want to make sure she is eliminated before she can eliminate me. That is where you come in." On hanging up the phone Eduardo took a taxi from the Café to the Montego Bay airport and purchased a ticket to Santo Domingo. Eduardo developed his plan while flying east.

Chris and Brenda were waiting to clear immigration and customs in Santo Domingo as Eduardo lifted off from Montego Bay. He would be there in about an hour. Picking up their rental car from Avis, Chris made certain to check that it had a full tank of gas. The Dominican Republic has a tendency to have their gas station owners go out on strike for almost no reason at all. Leaving Santo Domingo with a full tank of gas was one way to ensure that any unexpected gasoline strikes would not interfere with their plans. On entering San Pedro de Macoris, Chris read a sign announcing a baseball game tomorrow afternoon between the Dominican Summer League Marlins and the DSL Rays.

"Maybe if we get this work done soon we can catch a baseball game? I've not heckled anyone in Spanish since that kid threw the bat at me a year ago."

"First we need to find your ex-wife and have a chat with her before we do anything. With luck she will be in handcuffs and leg irons by this time tomorrow so I doubt we'll be able to watch a game."

"But it's the Dominican Summer League, Brenda. Some of these kids are going to be in the major leagues in a couple of years and I would love to watch them before they make it."

"Chris. Let us put it this way. We can stop and watch a baseball game played by 50 unknowns, or we can affect the arrest of your former wife and you can see her sitting in jail tomorrow. Which of those two options do you prefer?"

"Since you put it that way, Brenda, it's a no-brainer. Can I at least have the satisfaction of putting the handcuffs on her?"

"Let me guess. This would not be the first time you have ever put handcuffs on Mrs. Coburn?"

"Look Brenda, there's an ashy-faced owl sitting on that fence post."

They drove the rest of the way in silence.

Arriving at Casa de Campo they received keys to separate suites on the ninth floor and went immediately to Brenda's where they planned to spend as much time as possible. Should Michelle show up that would be an extra but the current plan was to not leave the room except for oxygen.

"Damn it, Ramsey. You make me so uncontrollably horny just being near you," Brenda said as she separated herself from her clothes and fell onto her king sized bed. "Why is it that you have so much control over me?"

"Maybe it's because you give me the control."

"Why are you so god-damned smart, Dr. Ramsey?"

"Maybe it's because I have my doctorate?"

"Shut up and kiss me."

"That is my most favorite Mary Chapin Carpenter song. How did you know that?"

"You listen to something other than Jimmy Buffett?"

"There is that possibility."

Brenda was recovering from her fourth orgasm when there was a knock on the door. Chris opened it and was greeted by a bellman delivering a fruit basket and two bottles of Bermudez rum. "This is complementary for all guests when they check in," the bellman said.

While Chris made love with his newest lover, his ex-wife was sitting in her suite next door to them trying to contact her current husband by phone and email.

"Honey, this is Michelle. I have been trying to reach you for a day and you haven't answered and I am starting to get scared. I called your office and Tiffany said you hadn't called in sick today. So where are you? Call me when you get this."

Arturo met Eduardo outside the customs arrival area at Las Americas airport. "Hola, Eduardo, como estas. Bienvinedos a la Republica Dominicana."

"Speak English for Christ's sake Art."

"Sorry Ed."

"So, what's the plan here?"

"I want to get in there, take care of business, and then get the hell out of here. Do you know how we can draw her outside to take care of it?"

"I have contacts on the island who provided me with a 30-06 rifle sighted in for 300 yards. I also have a Glock 9mm pistol if you want to take care of her up close."

"Actually, Art, I would like to do this with no bloodshed if possible."

"That might be possible, Ed. I know from staying at this hotel in the past that every new guest gets a complimentary fruit basket and a bottle of rum delivered to them after they check in. We can assume that she has received hers already. We will just show up at her door, tell her we are bringing her a second complimentary welcome basket. Once we are inside the door you can do anything you want to with her."

After Chris and Brenda had a half bottle of Bermudez rum and after Brenda had her fifth orgasm they each got dressed and went down to the pool tiki bar where they planned to stay for the rest of the evening.

Arturo and Eduardo arrived at Casa de Campo about 9:00 p.m. They asked at the front desk which room Michelle was occupying and were surprised how easily the reception desk clerk gave up that information.

"Senor, she is in room 917." Pointing to his left the front desk person said, "You can take that elevator behind you."

Arturo and Eduardo were the only people on the elevator as it opened on the ninth floor. The sign outside the elevator said that room 917 was to the left. They walked quickly to the room and Arturo knocked.

They heard Michelle ask, "Who is it?"

Eduardo answered, "Its room service, ma'am."

"I didn't order room service."

"This is our second complimentary bottle of rum and fruit basket. It's our new policy." Having consumed most of the first bottle of Bermudez rum, her defenses were low. She opened the door. Arturo burst through the door and grabbed Michelle covering her mouth with one hand. He pushed her back through the foyer and onto her bed. Eduardo walked in behind him and stood over her.

Looking down at her as fear covered Michelle's face, Eduardo said, "Now, Ms. Coburn, are you sure you want to terminate our agreement? Remember I was supposed to assist you until you owned a minor league team. Remember that you bitch?" Michelle nodded her head in agreement and tried to respond. No words came out of her mouth.

Arturo saw the remainder of Michelle's unconsumed bottle of Bermudez rum sitting on the night stand and poured what little rum remained in the bottle over her body. It couldn't hurt to make her smell drunker than she already was.

Eduardo opened her guest services portfolio and took out a piece of Casa de Campo stationary. On it he wrote this note, "I am sorry for all the pain I have caused people with my lies and deceptions. Taking my life is the only way I know to stop the hurt I have caused. I pray for God's forgiveness, Michelle Coburn."

Arturo kept his hand over her mouth as he pushed her toward the sliding glass door leading to her balcony. Eduardo opened it and they walked onto the landing. Michelle wet herself when it was obvious what was about to happen. The last thing that Michelle Coburn ever heard when her feet were on something solid, was Eduardo saying, "You should have never fucked with me, gringa."

Arturo kept his hand over her mouth until they were at the rail of the balcony. He kept it there as Eduardo lifted her body over the rail and then let gravity take over. As Michelle tumbled toward the hard surface of the Casa de Campo's courtyard directly in front of the night time bar she could hear meringue music pulsing from the stage below. Arturo and Eduardo left the ninth floor through an emergency stairway. On reaching the sixth floor they entered the elevator and rode it to the lobby. There they sauntered out the front door and got in their car.

Brenda and Chris sat in the tiki bar drinking rum and listening to meringue when they heard a woman screaming. Turning toward the sound they saw a human body plummeting toward the ground at 32 feet per second each second. The speed of gravity had taken over. They both raced toward the human projectile plummeting toward earth. As they did they heard the sickening crunch of bone and flesh as it coalesced with cement. For Michelle it was permanent lights out. Chris hoped that whoever collided with the cement was dead before hitting the ground. A large pool of blood formed at the head of the person who landed on the concrete in front of the meringue band. Band members screamed as did most of the people dancing in front of the band. Some of the others seated nearby were splattered with blood, brains, and other body fluids.

Chris reached the body first. Despite considerable disfigurement caused by the impact with the cement he was able to immediately identify the dead body. "Oh my god this is Michelle," he said. "Jesus Christ why did you do this?"

Local authorities were called and they began their investigation. Brenda presented her FBI credentials and said in broken Spanish that she wanted to assist. On entering room 917, the Dominican police found an empty bottle of Bermudez rum lying beside her bed. On the night stand they found an apparent suicide note. Its contents were convincing and the police concluded that Michelle had committed suicide.

Later, in the 24-hour tiki bar, Chris said that when he read the suicide note he knew it wasn't Michelle's handwriting. "I was married to that woman. I received hand written notes from her after we divorced. I have been with her in recent months and seen her hand writing on various documents. The hand writing on that note was not the hand writing of Michelle Coburn."

At 8:00 the next morning Eduardo Sanchez boarded a Caribbean Airways flight that touched down first in Kingston and an hour later landed in Montego Bay. He was drinking a Red Stripe in the Montego Bay Margaritaville Café by 11:15 that morning. Arturo caught American Airlines flight 882 at 8:30 a.m. and arrived at Miami International at 11:00 a.m. By1:00 p.m. he was sitting in his office overlooking Miami Beach.

Chris and Brenda had sought out the help of the United States embassy so they could have Michelle's body removed from the country and returned to Florida. Given what they saw in her room and interviews with others at the Casa de Campo resort, Brenda was convinced that Michelle had committed suicide. As far as she was concerned the case against Michelle Coburn was closed and the government's attention should be focused on ensuring that her husband became a permanent resident of a Federal prison.

54

Passing over the Sunshine Skyway Bridge in the south bound lane, Chris pulled out his iPhone and checked on the scores of recent Sarasota Reds games that had been played while he and Brenda were in the Dominican Republic. Actually he had to check back further than that because so much had happened so quickly since their quick trip to the Cayman Islands. Chris was completely out of touch with the team and its record.

Only ten games remained in the Sarasota Reds regular season on the day that Brenda and Chris returned from the Dominican Republic. Their record at this point was 62 wins and 68 losses. They weren't quite at .500 for the season but more importantly they were no longer had the worst record in the Paradise League, or even the second worst. That distinction now rested with the St Lucie Mets and the Palm Beach Cardinals each with a record of 50 wins and 80 losses. Even if the Sarasota Reds tried their hardest at this point it was mathematically impossible for them to come in last. It had been quite a comeback season for them.

At the top of the Division was the Charlotte Stone Crabs, the Class A affiliate of the Tampa Bay Rays. The Rays themselves were tearing up the American League Eastern Division leading the Red Sox by one game and the New York Yankees by six with only a little over a month remaining in the season. Rays management hoped they could hang on to that slim lead. Management also was hoping that each of the

Rays affiliates in the minor leagues could produce remarkable records the same year.

Taking the first southbound exit after the south toll booths for the Skyway, Brenda and Chris followed US Highway 19 south to its intersection with US 41. Passing over Terra Ceia Bay Chris was livid when he saw more mangrove wetlands being destroyed. "Just what Florida needs is another god-damned condo development to house more snowbirds who don't have a clue how to drive," he mused. "I thought mangroves were protected in this state and that developers weren't allowed to fill them in."

"Chris, remember, this is Florida and no matter what the local law says, if someone pays off enough County Commissioners or city officials those who enforce the laws have a tendency to look the other way," Brenda told him.

"It still pisses me off Brenda. These bastards have no respect for what remains of the wetlands in this state. I think I'm going to do something about that."

"And what are you going to do?"

"I'm not sure. When I do you'll be the second person to know."

On a lighter note, as they drove into Bradenton and turned west on Manatee Avenue, Chris told Brenda that the Sarasota Reds were in town for a ten game home stand. They would end their season in Ed Smith Stadium and there was a chance no matter how remote that the Reds could earn the chance to get in the playoff's of the South Division if they could win every game remaining that season. Over lunch at the Beachhouse Restaurant on Anna Maria Island, Chris told Brenda that he had to go to every game for the rest of the season. "I feel it's my civic duty to be there to cheer them on."

"It's your civic duty my ass Chris. You just want an excuse to eat bratwursts, drink beer, and heckle whoever the Reds are playing."

"Well, yes, that aspect entered my mind also."

"I'm sorry but I'm not going to be able to attend every game with you. Remember I have a family and a job and I have been away from both of them way too long. There is a ton of paperwork I need to finish before we take Mr. Coburn to trial and I'm sure a few other disasters have happened since we got into this case."

Brenda's two children were 14 year old Cassidy and 13 year old Sarah. Both were mildly amused with the "old guy" that their mom was seeing and both were a bit more than mildly interested in baseball. Sarah had attended one game and despite finding Chris' heckling embarrassing at first she also found it highly amusing. "Mom, one day someone is going to come off the field and shove a baseball bat down Chris' throat," she told Brenda after the game.

"Honey, someone almost did that already. You aren't the first to think of it."

Chris took Cassidy or Sarah or both to the next nine games and watched the Reds win eight of them. Their record was 70 wins and 69 losses with one game to go. The Charlotte Stone Crabs had clinched first place in the Division with a record of 75 wins and 64 losses. Fort Myers and the Reds were tied for second place and the last game of the season for the Reds was against the Miracle. It had the potential to be the best game of the season. If nothing else, even if they lost, the Reds would have at least a .500 season, something unheard of at the beginning of the season.

Chris, Brenda, Cassidy and Sarah were all sitting behind home plate for the last game of the Reds season. They were about to watch the make or break game all die-hard Reds fans had been hoping to witness. They had arrived early, purchased their much-needed beers, cola, and bratwurst and took their seats. Chris told them that because this was the last game of the season and the stakes were so high he was probably going into overdrive this evening heckling the Miracle. "It's my religion to do this. Just don't be too embarrassed if I get out of control." Brenda reminded Chris that she was carrying a loaded Glock 9mm and would use it as necessary to keep him in line.

Adding to the pre-game excitement was the announcement that Ed Johnson, owner of Big Johnson Concrete Company in Sarasota was not only throwing out the ceremonial first pitch of the game but also singing the national anthem. "Nobody in the history of the Reds has ever held down both responsibilities for a single game," Don Prince, Reds substitute announcer said into the public address system. "Let's all give Ed a huge round of applause!"

"Good God," Chris whispered, "couldn't they find anyone better than this clown? My neighbors gold fish can sing better than Ed Johnson."

Drew Begley, the Miracle left fielder led off the top of the first inning. He had barely stepped up to the plate when Chris let fly with his first invective of the night. "You call yourself a hitter, Begley? You couldn't hit water if you fell out of a boat." Begley swung and missed the first pitch.

"Hey loser, that was a Louisiana pitch. It went bayou!" Begley promptly stuck out swinging on next two pitches, both of them obviously balls.

Paul Grossman the Miracle second baseman batted second. He met with Chris' taunts as he walked to the plate. "Here comes the human strike out!" Chris yelled that for each pitch and Grossman went down swinging.

Batting third was Tim McClure the designated hitter. Tim took three practice swings, spit some chew on the ground, scratched his crotch a couple times and settled in for the first pitch. From behind him he heard "You're the designated hitter? It's more like you're the designated out, you loser."

The first pitch was a fast ball inside at the letters. McClure swung and missed. "Wow, feel that breeze. It's like winter back here." The second pitch was a ball and so was the third.

With the count two balls and one strike McClure dug in and waited for the next pitch. It was a curve ball that broke over the edge of the plate. McClure swung late and sent the ball careening off an empty seat in section 101 behind the Reds dugout. "Do your parents know you are this big an embarrassment?"

McClure was visibly upset. He dug in and waited for the next pitch. Before it arrived, he heard Chris taunt him from behind, "Do you think you can get the next one past the mound you loser?"

The next pitch was a change up at the belt. McClure had anticipated this pitch. He began his swing just as the ball left the pitchers hand and he made perfect contact. It was one of those balls that when it is hit, it produces a resounding "thwack" in the ears of everyone nearby. McClure's towering hit did just that. The ball left his bat like the space shuttle leaving Cape Canaveral. It flew over the pitcher's mound and was last seen as it cleared the top of the batter's eye in center field at least 408 feet from home plate.

Chris made a note to himself, "Never again heckle a hitter by asking if he can hit the ball past the pitcher's mound. Never"

With the score Fort Myers 1 and Sarasota 0, Miracle cleanup hitter Carlos Santana (no relation to the singer) took the plate. As he walked to the plate the Reds announcer played a clip of "Black Magic Woman" under the uninformed assumption that the batter and the singer were the same.

Rattled by the massive home run McClure just hit despite some of his best taunts, Chris continued his heckling. "I've seen better hitters at a drug bust." Swing and a miss, strike one.

Santana went down swinging after four pitches. Chris felt like he had his groove back.

As the Reds took their first at bat, Chris' attention turned to the Miracle's pitcher and to the umpires. With Brad Hunter on the mound for the Miracle, Dave Apfel led off for the Reds in the bottom of the first inning. The first pitch he saw was supposed to be a fast ball high and outside but it missed the batter's box and went past the catcher.

"You call that a pitch? Dick Cheney has a better aim than you do!"

The second pitch was low and outside and should have been a ball, but the umpire called it a strike. "Hey ump, I thought only horses slept standing up?"

Hunter's next pitch was a fastball that must have had "hit me here and hit me hard" written all over it because that is what Apfel did. As gravity finally brought the ball back to earth it hit the Fort Myers team bus parked 100 feet beyond the left field fence. The score was tied 1-1 and it stayed that way through the first six innings.

Brenda's cell FBI cell phone rang in the top of the seventh inning. Looking at the caller ID she could see that Dave Addison, her boss in Tampa, was calling. Opening up the phone she greeted Dave. The one-sided conversation that Chris, Cassidy and Sarah heard was mainly "uh, huh" or "ok" or "Jesus that had to hurt." Eventually she ended the call saying "Yes, Dave, I'll be sure to tell Chris."

"What on earth just happened?"

"That was Dave Addison. He just received a call from the US Marshall's Service in Miami informing him that Tim Coburn died about an hour ago in the Federal Detention Center."

"Wow. That sure brings the case to a screeching halt doesn't it? Do they have any idea how it happened?"

"Normally when an obviously white collar inmate comes into the facility they segregate that person from the general population for their own safety if nothing else. Unfortunately for rich guy Coburn a couple weeks ago as he was being processed into the facility he made a comment about wanting special provisions made for his clothing and bedding. He made a general ass of himself. The admissions clerk decided to even the playing field a little and put him in with the general population."

"Ouch."

"Ouch is right. Apparently after a couple weeks of detention, our friend Mr. Coburn hadn't learned that the best policy is to keep his mouth shut. Earlier this evening, while in the mess hall, Mr. Coburn uttered a racial slur to a member of the race he slurred. The inmate slowly stood up from his table and punched Coburn directly in the Adam's apple. The force of the blow sent him flying backward into the edge of the table behind him. Coburn hit the table at the base of his skull and he hit it with enough force to break his neck. He died instantly."

"Jesus. That couldn't have happened to a nicer guy. What does this do to your case?"

"Right now there is no case. Tim Coburn was the only perpetrator we had in custody and he is no longer with us so I guess the case is closed. It was over before it began is how I think that comment goes."

"So let's watch some baseball. I have a feeling the Reds are going to win this one and make it to the playoffs."

With the score still tied at 1-1, the Fort Myers Miracle came to bat in the top of the ninth inning. Catcher Jerry Anderson led off the inning and walked on four pitches.

Next up was Nick Romero who watched the first pitch thrown at him called a strike. From behind him Nick heard Chris yell "hit it like you have a pair." Romero struck out swinging.

Tim Williams, the Miracle right fielder followed Romero. With one out in the top of the ninth inning Jerry Anderson stunned even himself by stealing second base. The Miracle now had the go-ahead run in scoring position.

"Betty Crocker makes a better batter than you, Williams!"

Strike one.

The next pitch was a slider low and inside that was just too tempting for Williams to pass up.

Strike two.

"You want some pepperoni with that slice?"

With the count 0 balls and 2 strikes the Reds pitcher had some wiggle room to play with so he decided to throw a split finger fastball he had been working on. Checking the runner on second base he went into the stretch and delivered the ball.

It broke like crazy and had Williams confused. He started his swing just as the ball hit the catcher's mitt for strike three.

"Next time call ahead when you know you're going to be late."

With two outs in the top of the ninth Fort Myers' ninth batter in the lineup, 6' 11" Mitchell Spinks came to bat. He took his position and made a couple of practice swings. Reds pitcher Justin Webb looked in for the sign. Checking the runner at second base he whirled around and faked a throw to the shortstop in an attempt to hold the runner close to the base. Looking in again for the sign he shook off the first two suggestions and settled on a fastball high and outside. Jason Webb hadn't listened to the scouting reports that said Mitchell Spinks prefers fastballs high and outside. Tonight Spinks chose to turn the high and outside fastball into a double. When he did the runner scored from second base. Fort Myers took the lead 2-1.

First baseman Kelly Thompson was next at bat but posed little threat. He hit the first pitch thrown to him off the handle of the bat. It dribbled out to Webb who threw to first base ending Fort Myers chances to score another run.

Still the damage was done. The score was Fort Myers 2 and Sarasota 1 going into the bottom of the ninth inning. This was an all or nothing inning for the Reds. A win would put them in the Division playoffs. A loss would leave them at 70 wins and 70 losses marking the first time in franchise history that they had a .500 or better season.

Dennis Philomena led off for the Reds and promptly struck out. It was his tradition and one that he was apparently content in continuing. David Morgan was next. He swung at a fastball and missed. It was clocked at 92 miles an hour.

"Hey pitcher, one finger means fast ball not one mile an hour."

David looked at the second pitch and took it for a ball.

"Call out the search party. This pitcher can't find the plate."

The third pitch was a sinking slider that seemed to slide exactly where David wanted it to be and he sent the ball on a high arching ride toward the left field fence. Unfortunately it didn't have enough power behind it to make it to the fence and was caught on the warning track. Two outs.

The Reds last hope was Alan Simpson, a recent addition to the roster who was brought up from the Rookie League

Gulf Coast Reds as a backup first baseman. He was making his first appearance at the plate now in what was probably the most dramatic moment in Sarasota Reds history. His batting average in the Gulf Coast League was .488 and he was known to tear the cover off the ball when the opportunity presented itself. Coach Jeremy Bergman decided to give Simpson the chance to show himself in a clutch situation.

Alan looked at the first two balls thrown to him. Both of them were called strikes. He wondered if he was really cut out for this clutch hitting idea. The Miracle pitcher looked in for the sign then began his wind up. He had decided to throw a fast ball thinking that Simpson was expecting a breaking ball with a 0-2 count. Simpson assumed that, given the situation, the pitcher was expecting him to be anticipating a breaking ball so he dug in and waited for a fastball.

Completing his wind up the pitcher let loose a tremendous fast ball. It was clocked at 99 miles per hour. It caught Simpson looking. He had barely lifted the bat from his shoulder. Umpire Eric Putnam went into gyrations with his hands and arms and yelled "strike three!" The game was over. The Reds lost again.

Rather than leave the field and head for the dugout, the Reds remained nearby to sign autographs and talk to their fans. Chris was massively dejected by the Reds loss. "They came so close, so aggravatingly close."

As he sat in his favorite seat, Reds manager Jeremy Bergman walked off the field, into the stands and over to Chris where he introduced himself. He asked Chris, "so who are you, anyway?"

Chris asked what he meant and Jeremy said, "All season long, it didn't matter where we were playing or who we were playing you always sat in the same seat behind home plate. You started heckling whomever we played before the first pitch was thrown and you didn't let up until the last out. You were relentless. I asked my players if you were a father of one of the kids on the team and nobody knew you. So who are you?"

Chris told him that he was a retired wildlife biologist who moved to Sarasota and discovered the Reds. He then said "When I watched you guys play you took me back to the days in high school and college when I was a baseball player. Watching you made me feel like a kid again, and I knew that I had to do something to help you win."

Jeremy asked, "So did you make it to the minors or just play in college?"

Chris told him that he'd played in the Tigers organization for two years after college but didn't make it beyond that level.

Jeremy then said, "So what position did you play?"

Chris said, "I was a catcher from the fourth grade on."

That explained everything.

Epilogue

Friends and relatives searching through Osvaldo Castro's belongings found several references to his cousin Arturo Kirkconnell. Those references related to baseball umpires, two of whom had met an untimely death in Manatee County. State and County investigators looked into the matter and found enough probable cause to hold Arturo as an accessory to the murders of umpires Justin Reed and Dennis Hastert Jr. At last report Arturo was in Florida State Prison sleeping with one eye open each night in his cell shared with a 400 pound redneck rapist from Walton County whom everyone referred to simply as Bud.

Eduardo Sanchez learned of the apprehension and trial of his first cousin Arturo Kirkconnel and decided that it might be a wise move to get out of Jamaica. Boxing up his essential belongings he bought a one-way ticket from Montego Bay to Havana and returned to his homeland. It was better for society having him sequestered in Cuba at least until the United States policy against the country is lifted. If that happened any time soon, Yemen was beginning to look very inviting.

The estates of Tim and Michelle Coburn were worth a little over $23 million. Their children were the rightful heirs but both of them were embarrassed by how their parents had lived and the crimes they committed. Each child took $1.5 million themselves and then authorized the court to donate the remaining $20 million to the Paradise League to use as it saw fit.

Brenda Livingston was afforded accolades from the FBI for her dogged pursuit of the perpetrators in this crime. Principal among her awards was the Meritorious Service plaque given to her by the Director of the FBI at the Justice Department building in Washington DC. The President of the United States was there that day and when he learned that Brenda had worked on an issue related to baseball, the President asked her for some tips on how to improve his throwing saying "when I threw out the first pitch at the Nationals game I really sucked." Brenda was offered a promotion to Special Agent in Charge of the Jacksonville FBI Office. She declined the promotion saying her children loved Sarasota. Brenda said she had other fish to fry or, as she put it "other bird eggs to collect." Nobody was quite sure what that meant but she remains in Sarasota as the Senior Resident Agent. Brenda was also able to keep everyone from finding out that the FBI paid for Chris and her to fly to Santo Domingo in Business Class when cattle class was available. The Bureau had trained her well in keeping secrets.

Chris Ramsey was so excited after the Sarasota Reds season ended that he took Brenda on a two-week birding trip to Ushuaia, Argentina. There they drank lots of red wine and listened to Jimmy Buffett's song "Party at the End of the World" every day. On his return to Sarasota, Chris opened his own environmental consulting firm whose purpose was to investigate crimes like illegal phosphate mining, the filling in of mangrove wetlands, and the continual building of condominiums on Florida beaches. Unfortunately being Florida Chris will have no shortage of illegal things to investigate. He keeps praying for a Category 6 hurricane to come along some September and cleanse the entire coast of Florida of all the condos. Brenda accepted the fact that she had fallen in love with a renegade baseball loving bird nut who was old enough to be her father. A trained investigator she agreed to occasionally help Chris with his fledgling business. Her motto was "I'll bring the Glock, if you bring the handcuffs." Nobody but Chris and Brenda knew for certain what that meant.

Would you like to see your manuscript become a book?

If you are interested in becoming a PublishAmerica author, please submit your manuscript for possible publication to us at:

acquisitions@publishamerica.com

You may also mail in your manuscript to:

**PublishAmerica
PO Box 151
Frederick, MD 21705**

We also offer free graphics for Children's Picture Books!

---

www.publishamerica.com

PUBLISHAMERICA

CPSIA information can be obtained at www.ICGtesting.com
Printed in the USA
BVOW08s2048040915

416623BV00001B/190/P